the

consolation

duet

CORINNE MICHAELS

The Consolation Duet
Copyright © 2015 Corinne Michaels
All rights reserved.

ISBN 978-1-942834-10-6

No part of this publication may be reproduced, distributed or transmitted in any form or by any means including electronic, mechanical, photocopying, recording or otherwise, without the prior written consent of the author.

This book is a work of fiction. Names, characters, places and incidents either are products of the author's imagination or are used fictitiously. Any resemblance to actual events or locales or persons, living or dead, is entirely coincidental and beyond the intent of the author or publisher.

Editor:
Lisa Christman, Adept Edits

Proofreading:
Ashley Williams, AW Editing

Interior Design and Formatting:
Christine Borgford, Perfectly Publishable

Cover Design: Okay Creations
Cover photo © Perrywinkle Photography

consolation

CORINNE MICHAELS

To Crystal, there are few women who can endure the life you do. You're strong, beautiful, and no one's consolation prize. I hope you never lose your sparkle.

prologue

natalie

"OH, CHLOE, IF you'd like to come out, please wait until your Daddy gets back," I insist, holding my belly as another Braxton Hicks contraction hits. I grip the dresser and try to breathe through it. It seems like they're coming more frequently.

Once it passes, I try to finish what I came in here for. Aaron is away, but I want the nursery done so we can enjoy the next few weeks once he returns. I walk around what will be her room, putting a few more of the pretty pink dresses in the drawers. Aaron and I have fought about the vast array of pink things that are now strewn around the house—he hates it, I love it.

He insisted we paint her room in camouflage. Brown, green, and black camouflage for a girl? No. I almost sent myself into labor with that argument. I got home and he and Mark were drawing it out on the walls. I launched various household items at Mark while throwing him out of the house. My husband found out shortly after how much he could suffer by my hands. I may not be a SEAL, but you don't mess with me either. In the end, I won with purple walls and the sheer netting around her white crib.

"Daddy's going to love this room, Chloe. I can't wait to see his face when he sees the pretty butterflies." Needing to take another break, I sit in the rocking chair and rub my stomach. It soothes me knowing she's in there.

I can protect her—it's my job. I love being pregnant and it's a miracle we were able to conceive her. I've already told Aaron I want to try for another one as soon as she's born. I close my eyes and sink, allowing the world to fade away.

I imagine holding her in my arms, sitting here in this chair, soothing and kissing her. I picture Aaron with her asleep on his chest as she gets to hear his heartbeat. She'll own his world and have him wrapped around her finger.

Knock, knock, knock.

I hear the door, but it takes me a few seconds to get out of the chair.

KNOCK, KNOCK, KNOCK.

They bang louder this time.

"Coming!" I yell at the door. Jeez, give me a second.

Waddling to the door takes me a minute since I'm the size of a whale.

I open the door and see Mark Dixon, Aaron's boss and close friend. He works at Cole Security Forces with Aaron and served with him for years. His head is hanging low and when he looks up, his eyes are full of sorrow.

"What's wrong?"

"Lee," he chokes on the one syllable of my name. The one Aaron uses. Something is definitely not right.

"What happened?" I ask again as I begin to shake.

Tears fill his eyes and I know. I know my life is never going to be the same. I know everything I've ever feared is about to come true because Mark doesn't cry. Mark wouldn't be at my door if something weren't really, really wrong. "It's Aaron."

My heart stops beating and the world I live in ceases to exist. "Don't," I beg with tears blurring my vision and my breath accelerating.

This can't be happening.

"Please, don't, Mark. Please," I beg him again, because once he says it . . . but I know it's futile. It doesn't matter because he can't stop it. It's already happened.

"Natalie, I'm so sorry."

The dreaded words that every military wife fears. Only I wasn't supposed to have to worry about this anymore. We were done. We got out. I wasn't supposed to ever fear this again.

Please, God, don't take him from me. Please!

"But, I'm p-pregnant. I'm having a baby," I stammer as if that will somehow make none of this real. "He said he'd be back. He said he . . ." I trail off as it becomes difficult to breathe. My hand flies to my mouth to stifle the scream about to escape. Everything goes colorless.

"It was an IED. I'm sorry," Mark says as his eyes glimmer with unshed tears.

I fall.

But he's there, cradling me in his arms. "I'm so fucking sorry."

"No. No. No." Mark holds me as I sob clutching my stomach. "You're lying," I hiss, tearing myself out of his embrace.

"I wish I were," he says as I struggle to get up.

"It was a mistake. He's having a baby. He said it was a simple in and out!" I scream and throw my hands against his chest. "You're lying!" I scream, even knowing it's not a lie.

"I'm sorry."

"Stop saying you're sorry!" My sorrow turns to hatred. I hate him. I hate everyone in this moment. I hate Aaron and everyone who was there. I hate this house and everything in it. I hate the air that he no longer breathes. Hate consumes me. Hate smothers me. "Get out!" I yell and push against his chest. "Get the fuck out of my house! Aaron will be back in a few days and then we're going to get ready for our daughter to be born."

"Please," Mark beseeches and I refuse to look at him.

This isn't happening because Aaron's alive.

He's not dead. How dare Mark lie to me.

"He'll be back. He wouldn't leave me. He promised." Aaron wouldn't lie to me. He never does. When he left for missions, he would always say goodbye like it could be our last. But this time he kissed the tip of my nose and said, "Now don't have that baby until I get back."

"Can I call someone? Your mom?"

"No, you can't call anyone because he's not dead! Go get him, Mark! Go get my husband and bring him home." I step back pointing my finger at him. "You all promised. He promised." I clutch my stomach as a sharp pain radiates, but it's nothing compared to the agony sitting on my chest. Tears flow relentlessly as I struggle against his hold. "He promised."

"I know he did," Mark says as he holds my head against his chest.

"He lied."

My life is gone.

My heart is dead.

I'm a widow at twenty-seven.

chapter one

~ three months later ~

"AARON GILCHER WAS a man who left this Earth too soon. He was a loving husband, father to his unborn child, and friend," the priest speaks softly. "We are gathered today to say goodbye but not farewell. He will live in our hearts as long as we hold on to him." A sob escapes my chest. I can't hold it in. My stomach drops with the realization that he's gone. He's really gone and this solidifies it. The final piece of a puzzle that I was desperate to not put together.

I feel hands grasp my shoulders and squeeze. I don't need to look to know who they belong to. Jackson and Mark are at my back on either side. Protecting me when my husband no longer can. My mother grips my hand while my father holds Aarabelle. After she was born, I wanted to honor her father. I battled with the name we'd chosen versus something special. In the end, when I saw her, I knew. I wanted her to have part of her father for the rest of her life.

"Lord, please lift the hearts around us and grant them peace during this time. Help us to remember Aaron and give us a sense of calm knowing he's in your arms." He finishes the prayer and the part I've dreaded most is next.

"Lee, I'm right here," Mark whispers from behind me.

I nod because if I allow myself to speak, I know I won't be able to control the emotions threatening to escape. *Be strong, this will all be over soon.* I look down at my black dress and try to focus on anything but this. I tuck the long, blonde strands of hair that fall around my face back behind my ear. I begin to tremble and Mark's hand tightens.

The honor guard that had been standing off to the side rounds in front of me. I know the four of them. They were his friends, his brothers, and now they have to give me the last thing any wife wants to ever hold in her hands.

The emotions are shoved down deep, but I can see in his best friend's eyes how much pain he's in. Liam flew in from California to be here. He was Aaron's closest friend for the last eight years. They graduated SEAL training together. The bond forged from risking their lives was unbreakable. The news of Aaron's death rocked him and he'd vowed to be here.

Liam and Jeff pull the flag taut as I try to keep my eyes open, but I can't. I hear the slapping of the fabric being snapped tight. I inhale and focus on exhaling. The pain that emanates from my chest is unbearable. I'm being torn apart from the inside out.

I feel my mother squeeze my hand. I look up to see Aaron's former chief kneel before me. "Natalie, on behalf of the President of the United States and the Chief of Naval Operations, please accept this flag as a symbol of our appreciation for your loved one's service to this Country and a grateful Navy."

Tears fall uncontrollably as my heart falters. His hand extends and I know I need to take it. I have to . . . but I can't move my hands. I lift the one and it trembles as I nod. When he places the flag on my hand resting on my lap, I sob again. *This can't really be happening.* I mean, I've known for three months he was dead, but this . . . this flag is it. It's the finale I don't want to happen, proving this isn't a lie.

My hand drops. I look in his eyes as another tear splatters on my skin.

"I'm sorry, Natalie. Aaron was a great man."

"Thank you," I somehow manage to say.

I close my eyes and drop my head.

How is this my life? Why did this happen? How do I go on? All of these questions jolt through me and seethe, festering in my heart.

I hear the sounds of crying all around me, but none of it matters. No one can know the extreme agony I'm living right this moment. Losing the love of my life, the father of my child, eats me alive. My life was exactly as I wanted it. It tears through my body taking anything good and swallowing it whole.

Fuck life.

Fuck love and fuck everyone who told me they were sorry.

I look over at my baby sleeping in her grandfather's arms. I have Aarabelle. I have a beautiful girl who needs her mother.

The SEALs begin their ritual. I've watched and pitied wives who had to sit through it. I wasn't the one having to suffer during those moments, nevertheless here I am.

Senior Chief Wolfel moves forward and removes the trident from his chest. He steps toward the urn, where a wooden chest sits beside it. The wooden chest takes the place of a casket. There's no body to bury, just a piece of him. He was blown apart, just like me. Wolfel stands there for a moment before pressing it into the box and pounds it with his fist. The sound of the metal piercing the wood travels through my soul. It's as if it were penetrating me.

He turns to the urn and salutes.

One down, twenty more to go.

"I'm sorry for your loss, Aaron was a great man," another member of his former team says to me. I nod, unable to speak, knowing the imminent sound of another pin being pounded will breach the air in a moment. Over and over, the men approach me, offer their condolences, and then continue their ritual with their tridents.

I can't do this.

I start to shift, but Mark's hands hold tight. Before I can think, Liam steps forward. His crystal blue eyes are bloodshot as he tries to hold it together. It's obvious he's shaken. The bond between Aaron and Liam was unbreakable. "Lee, I . . ." He stops and swallows. I place my hand on his giving him a sign that I don't need his words. I know what he's feeling. The loss is evident in his eyes.

"I know," I say softly. His head bows forward and touches my hand. I place my other hand on the back of his head and I feel him shake.

"He was my brother," Liam says as another tear falls from my cheek.

"I-I . . ." The stuttering of my words are all I can get out while he looks at me.

He takes a second and draws a deep breath, stands, and walks over to the box. Initially, Liam refused to accept Aaron's death, since there was very little to identify him. He wanted to believe he was alive somewhere, but I knew. I felt it once I came to accept it.

I glance at my daughter once more. She lies cooing in her grandfather's arms, completely unaware that she'll never have the comfort of a father. I'm fortunate to have the man who rocked me and held me when I was in pain hold her now. If I could go back in time and ask my daddy to hold me as his little girl and tell me it'll be okay, I would. She's safe and secure, while I feel open and exposed.

Gazing at the sailor who stands before the memorial, I close my eyes and try to dispel the thoughts that assault me. I've lost him after all this time. The years of worry and dread while he was active duty I'd endured. Only to have a false sense of security descend once he left the Navy. Now look where all that comfort landed me.

Finally the last pin enters the box and I look up to see Jackson with his head hanging. The guilt he carries for sending Aaron to his death is insurmountable, but I know Aaron wouldn't have had it any other way. He wanted to die with valor and honor. If it were Jackson or Mark who'd died, he would've wished it were him. But now my daughter and I pay the price for his choices.

Glancing around, I acknowledge the others who grieve the loss of this amazing man. I look at the crowd and see the faces of his friends and family. His mother who sobs uncontrollably next to his father. She's drowning in her anguish as she buries her only son. Former sailors who served beside him and friends from Cole Security Forces sit grief-stricken over his loss.

There are a few faces I don't recognize. A pretty blonde stands to the side, wiping her eyes. A brunette, who I assume is Catherine, mourns in Jackson's arms. There are so many people, so many uniforms. It's a black sea of mourning. Aaron was a loved man, so I'm not surprised, but no one loved him more than me.

Today is the last day I will allow myself to feel sorrow, the last day I will shed tears, because tears don't change anything. I need to harvest whatever strength I have and hold it tight. I'm a mother who has an infant that needs me to be both mom and dad.

One day, they say. One day this will stop hurting.
Lies.
This will never be okay or stop hurting.
I'll never be the same. The woman I was before died the minute the knock on the door came. I'm a shell of the

woman I was. The woman who was loving, open, and full of hope is gone. Hope is a weak bitch who couldn't give two fucks about what you want. So I rely on faith. Faith that I'll make it through this and find my heart again.

chapter two

*T*IME PASSES. HOURS become days, days turn to weeks, months pass in a blur, and I continue to live. But am I living? I breathe, I get up and get dressed, but I'm numb. Sure I smile and throw on a happy face, but it's all an illusion. Inside I'm lost in the abyss of grief.

It's been three months since Aaron's funeral. Same shit different day. My daughter is growing and I have no one to share it with. Thankfully she's sleeping through the night, so I'm not a complete mess. Those first few months were enough to put me over the edge, but at the same time, she kept me going.

Loneliness consumes me, but I don't let anyone know.

"No, Mom. I'm fine," I huff and put the phone to my shoulder, trying to assure her for the millionth time. If it's not her, it's Mark calling to check on me.

"Lee, you're not fine. You're barely functioning. I'm getting on a plane," she chides.

That's the last thing I want. She stayed with me for a month after Aarabelle was born, and I thought I was going to lose my mind. Her nagging and forcing me out of the house was enough to make me question my decision to let her come at all.

"Jesus, I'm fine. I'm living and Dad needs you at home. Aarabelle and I are doing great even," I lie. I stopped letting anyone know what my life is like six months ago. Apparently there's a time limit on grieving before people start talking. My friends are still concerned that I haven't really done anything. I don't go out, and I refused to go back to my old job as a reporter. I don't want to be on the air and talking to families going through tragedy. I'm going through it now.

She gives a short laugh, "Liar."

"I'm not lying." I grab the baby monitor and head out on the deck. Which is the best thing about this house. When Aaron and I found this place, I fell in love. It backs to the Chesapeake Bay and the deck is where I spend most of my day. I feel close to him here. I can feel him in the wind—which is crazy, but when I close my eyes, it's like his hands are touching me. His breath glides across my neck, pushing the hair off my face. The sun warms me and I can pretend. I can allow myself the illusion that he's here. He's just out on a mission and will be home soon. I hold on to the feeling as long as I can because it's so much better to pretend than face the fact that my husband is dead.

"Right. You're always *fine*. You're a damn zombie," she scolds.

"I got a job," I blurt, hoping it'll throw her off.

"Doing what?" she asks skeptically.

"I'm going to work for Cole Security." I can almost hear the disapproval through the phone. Too bad I don't care what she thinks.

"Oh, that sounds like a great idea and a wonderful way to start moving on."

"Glad you agree," I reply, knowing damn well she's being sarcastic.

She doesn't understand. She and my father are still happily married. I lost my happily ever after. I want to be close to him, to feel something, to still have something to share with him. Cole Security Forces is the last place

Aaron was alive. It's the place he spent his days in working for Jackson. He's in that office. He's in this house. I can't move on. I can barely breathe . . . but I do. For Aarabelle. Every day I get my ass out of bed, I get dressed, and I live in what small way I can. And all I want is a tiny piece of what I once had, so I'm going where I can feel him more strongly. It's starting to fade here. I can no longer see him in the bathroom shaving, or remember what he sounded like when he laughed. I try so hard to hold on to it. I want it, but each day I lose another part of my life with him. The pain remains, but my memory of Aaron is slipping away.

"Natalie?" she questions as I wait in silence. "I think you should come for a visit. Maybe if you get away for a little, it'll help you move on."

"I am moving on!" I yell and then draw a deep breath.

"How? Have you met with the insurance people? Have you taken care of any of the paperwork you needed to?" she pesters me.

I swear she's picking a fight just to get me to lose my temper. "I am. I'm done talking." I don't have an answer for her because the reality is . . . I'm stuck. I'm living in an endless cycle. Nothing changes. Nothing happens. I refuse to clear out his drawers or closets because then he's really not coming home. Of course, I can't tell anyone this. I need him. I want him so badly, but he left me that day. He kissed my nose and then my belly and told us he'd be home in a few days. He lied.

My eyes close and I can see his face. At least I still have that. His deep, brown eyes with tiny flecks of gold flash through my mind. The way his hair was always kept in a buzz cut. Aaron. My world.

"Natalie . . ." My mother's soft voice breaks my daydream. "Please, let your father and I come get you and Aarabelle. We'd love to spend some time with you both."

"No. I love you, Mom, but I'm doing good." I see the

monitor light up and Aara's voice breaks through. "The baby is waking, I gotta go. I love you."

"When you decide you're not fine, call me. I love you, baby girl."

I press the end key and put the phone away. Sitting here for a few minutes, trying to get a grip before I get my daughter. I love her so much, but she's a clone of her father. Every time I look at her, it takes every ounce of strength I have not to cry. She gazes at me with those innocent eyes so full of love and it breaks a piece of my heart apart. Why won't she ever get the chance to hold her father's hand? Make him a cake. Tell him how much she loves him or to just know the love of a father. She deserves that. She should have both of her parents to guide her, but instead she only has me . . . a broken woman.

Each time her "uncles" come around, I hate them a little more. I hate that they can see her, hold her, touch her, but the one man who created her never will. The anger boils in my soul like a black cloud. It covers the light I'm desperate to see. Making the hope die out before it has a chance—because he's dead. He took it away when he left this Earth. I want him back and not only in my dreams. I want to roll over and feel him next to me—instead I get cold sheets and an empty bed.

"Aaaaaa." I hear my beautiful, little girl call out and I struggle to pull myself together. She makes random sounds while lying in her crib as I sit here in misery.

Stifling the emotions that burn, I gather the strength I rely on from my paltry reserves and go get my daughter. "Hi, peanut," I coo as I enter her room. Just looking at her puts my life in focus. It's amazing to me how children can completely alter your world.

Aarabelle is on her back looking at me with the love I'm desperate to hold on to. To her, the world is perfect. She doesn't know pain, and in some ways she's lucky. At least Aara didn't fall in love with her father to have him stripped from her life. The things I worry about she'll never fear because she'll never have known it.

"Aaaaa!" she squeals as I look down at her. Her dark brown hair sticks out haphazardly and her brown eyes shine with adoration. She makes me want to get through this.

"Hi, baby." She kicks her legs and her arms flail uncontrollably as I bend to scoop her up.

I hear a knock on the door as I cradle Aara in my arms. Every single time it happens, my heart clenches and my stomach turns. It's been six months since that knock happened, and it still feels like the first time. For a while, I prayed it was Aaron going to show up and tell me this was all a giant misunderstanding. I place Aarabelle in her swing and draw a deep breath.

Unhurriedly, I move to the front door trying to quell the desires I conjure without permission. It'll be Mark again . . . I tell myself and focus on breathing. It's like having a mini panic attack each time.

I answer the door and a man is there with his back to me. His arms are thick and his shoulders broad. The tight shirt clings to every ridge on his body. I take in the walnut-colored hair that's short and trimmed. He seems familiar, yet it couldn't be because he's in California. "Liam?"

Slowly he turns, easing into a wide grin. His tall, hulking body blocks the sun behind him. My face falls as seeing him brings it all back. Liam Dempsey. If having Mark and Jackson around is what I consider difficult, then Liam is going to be agony.

He removes his aviators and there's a gleam in his eyes. "Hey, Lee. I was in the neighborhood. Wanted to come say hi." His crystal blue eyes shimmer in the sun and I secure my mask firmly in place. If we're going to talk about Aaron at all, I need it. I don't feel . . . I don't hurt.

"I didn't realize California and Virginia are now neighboring states. Last I heard you were still out west?" Even I can hear the monotone in my voice. There's no way these guys don't see it. I'm not fooling anyone, but I really don't care. I pull my long, blonde hair to the side and grip the door.

I take a second to look at him. He looks bigger, taller, or maybe I haven't been around enough people. But everything about Liam looks . . . different. His frame takes up more space than I remember and he's let the scruff grow out on his face. Yet it only helps define his strong jawline. I may be grieving, but there's no way to ignore how good-looking he is.

"Can I come in?" he asks sweetly.

He's Aaron's best friend, his swim buddy, his brother through and through. Liam has been a part of our life for a long time and seeing him makes me feel Aaron's loss even more. I nudge the door open and allow him to enter. *Just focus on breathing, Natalie . . . he'll leave soon.*

"I tried to call," he says while looking around.

"Oh, I never saw it." The lie slips out. He's taken this oath to Aaron far beyond my patience. I've started ignoring his calls because he wants to talk about the past. The stories of them in the field, or worse when he wants to reminisce about my wedding. Liam also has this uncanny way of seeing too much. He knows how to read people, but especially me.

He walks over and grins, his blue eyes shimmering with amusement. "Sure you didn't. We haven't really talked much since I went back to Cali."

Because I don't want to. I bite the words back and go for a softer response. "Not much has changed." Yet everything has.

"Aarabelle has gotten big and you look great," he says as he tosses his phone and keys on the table.

"Thanks."

Liam smiles and pulls me into a hug. "I'm not worried about you dodging my calls anymore," he says, letting me go.

"Why's that?"

"I'm living here now."

What?

Crap.

chapter three

"DON'T LOOK SO happy. I was in the area and wanted to come check on you since you were missing my calls." Liam's eyes divert to the flag encased on the mantel. It sits there, reminding me daily how that'll be the only thing I have of him. I want to throw it against the wall. Smash it until there's nothing left and burn it. I hate that flag because I'd rather have *him*. I want Aaron, not some token for his service.

"I *am* happy. I just didn't know you were up for orders," I say as I grab Aarabelle and pull her into my arms.

His eyes stay on the mantel. "Is it really that bad?" he asks.

"No, of course not," I say, wishing I had some way to pull his attention away from the awkward conversation we're having.

Liam turns and his eyes stay fixed on Aarabelle. "She's beautiful, Lee." His hand grazes the top of her head. "I have something for her."

I draw a deep breath and cradle Aarabelle close. "Really?"

He chuckles and removes a necklace out of his pocket, "I got this for Aarabelle before you had her. When I was overseas I thought it was something a little girl should have, but . . . well, I'm never having one." His lips twitch with amusement as he lifts the gift in the air.

consolation

Stepping closer, I look at the hangs on the end of the chain. It's yet breathtaking, surrounded by dia. is too much."

"Nah, like I said, not like I'll ever h. to find a girl who actually might like me. hoarsely and looks out the window.

"Yeah, I could see where that could b you," I joke and relax a little. "Thank you beautiful."

He smiles and places his hand on Aarabe she."

She is. She's tiny and a handful, but to me sh fect. Everything I've ever dreamed of is wrapped my arms. I hold her close and nuzzle her. "Yeah, I so too."

Liam clears his throat, bringing my attention back him, "I saw his car is still in the drive. Have you met wit the Veterans' Affairs people yet?"

I nod and try not to look at him. I've put off doing the things I know I need to do. Closing out all of Aaron's accounts, his will, selling his car, maybe even this house, but I don't want to. "I've been busy."

He steps closer and his hand grips my shoulder gently. "I can help if you need me to."

Everyone always offers to help. That's the thing I've learned the most about death. People come out of the woodwork offering a hand. They cook for you, clean your home, fix the broken shutter, but it's all superficial. No one knows what to say, so they try to *do,* but after a week or a few months, the help no longer comes. You have no choice but to face life head-on and learn that people forget—they move on. But I haven't. I live the hell that was forced upon me day in and day out.

"I'm fine." I give a fake smile. "I have Mark and Jackson if I need them, plus I'm sure you have plenty of other you need to worry about. You just moved and I checking in takes a lot of time."

took leave, plus I like bugging you anyway."

Really, I can handle it."

No one is saying you can't. I'm saying you don't have lean on the people around you. He was my friend and are too, so don't be too proud." His eyes pierce mine he locks his gaze.

What is with these men and their inability to let me ?

"Okay, fine," I concede.

"Good. Not like you had much of a choice. I'm kinda relentless."

I snort, "I remember."

An awkward silence falls between us. Thankfully, Aarabelle stirs, bringing my attention to her.

"Have you heard from Patti?" Liam asks.

"No, she's pretty much disappeared since Aaron's death." My mother-in-law understandably didn't take the news well. She's cut off contact with all of us. She refuses to see Aarabelle and wants absolutely no part in my life. She claims if I loved him, I wouldn't have let him go. I would've demanded he stay. If she knew her son at all, she'd know that wouldn't have worked.

Liam takes a step toward the mantel and his hand reaches out to the flag. He stands there staring at my mini memorial. Aaron's photos line the shelf. His boot camp photo, our wedding, and one of the two of them all sit next to the flag. His trident sits in front. Liam's hands brace the stone wall and his head falls. I watch him as his fingers tighten and turn white from clutching the ledge. It's as if he's forgotten I'm here. Tears threaten to fill my eyes as I watch his closest friend silently mourn. It's a moment where I can almost feel the pain radiating off of him. I turn my back and give him some privacy.

"People handle shit differently I guess," Liam mutters

quietly.

I turn back around as he grips his neck. "How are you handling it?" I question.

He turns and shakes his head. "I've called his number a few times. I was drunk, and I don't know, it was just instinct to call and tell him something stupid. The first time it went to his voicemail and . . ." Liam's eyes snap back to mine as he catches himself. "What about you?"

My façade shifts into place as I repeat the speech I've given so many times. "I'm living. It's hard, but I'm handling it."

Liam knows me. He's also an interrogator for the SEALs. He's one of the best, and for some reason I forgot who I was lying to. "Really?" he asks unbelieving.

His large frame moves forward as he assesses my reactions. I try to remember all the things Aaron practiced on me. How he would make me stand my ground, not shift or move my eyes, but Liam is a different ball game. "Yes," I say confidently.

"You know who I am, right?" His calloused hand grazes my wrist and my heart rate accelerates. I'm not afraid of him, but he's the first man to touch me intimately since Aaron's death. Even though we're just friends, my chest tightens. "You're lying to me," Liam says in his deep voice.

I suppress a shiver and try not to look into his eyes. I don't want him to see what I'm hiding deep inside. He can read me, he's trained to see through my layers of bullshit, and I need to keep myself shielded from him.

"Natalie." He lifts my chin, but I keep my eyes closed. "You can tell me. I can't imagine if it were *you* that *he* lost that he'd be fine. He'd be a fucking mess, a lunatic with broken furniture all over the house. So you don't have to be okay. You can be angry or whatever else."

His words seep through my soul and I open my eyes. "I don't get to be whatever else. I have Aarabelle," I say as I look at the baby in my arms. "I have to be fine." The steel wall I hide behind is strong and solid. I'm safe there.

"That's not true. You're going to keep bottling this shit up and then explode."

I grit my teeth and let out a deep breath through my nose. "What's your deployment schedule look like? Will you be around?" There's no doubt in my mind he knows I'm diverting. I want out of this conversation.

"You know I can't tell you that, but I'm here for you. I'm going to do a few things and then we can figure out what else has to be done."

"I really don't need the help," I say even though I don't know what I need anymore. Aarabelle stirs and I rock her gently.

"Okay, well, I need to do something for the next month I'm on leave, so you're helping me."

"Now who's the liar?" I ask.

Liam rolls his sleeves and winks. "I never lie."

I laugh an honest laugh for the first time. He's lying about lying. Aarabelle begins to fuss, and as much as I want to argue with him, she needs to eat.

"Which SEAL team are you with?"

Please don't say four.

I don't know why it matters. The way he lets out a hesitant sigh, I brace for it. "Four," he steps closer and puts his hand on my shoulder. "He should be with me."

"No, he should be with *me*."

"Yeah, he should," Liam says and the sadness is apparent in his eyes.

This hurts us both. Liam and Aaron were brothers. If one died, they both died. Aaron once spoke of the brotherhood they shared in comparison with that of Jackson and Mark. While they were all close, he and Liam were almost blood thick. They carried each other through BUDs training, and when Liam's sister died, Aaron was by his side the entire time.

"I'm sorry, Demps," I say as I shift Aarabelle in my arms.

"Why the fuck are you sorry?" he asks, sounding affronted.

"You two were close. I know this isn't easy for you."

Liam pinches the bridge of his nose. "Is this what you do?"

My jaw falls slack as I try to figure out what he's asking me.

"You pretend." Liam's eyes soften as he studies me.

"I don't know what you all want," I say, exasperated. He smiles and I want to slap him. What the hell is he smiling about?

"Finally some emotion. I'll see you soon. I've got work to do around here."

"You're an ass."

"Yup. Go take care of Aarabelle. I've got the other shit." Liam kisses my cheek and then the top of Aara's head and leaves.

I stand here knowing I'm not going to get rid of him. He's noble, honest, and when Liam made a vow to Aaron, he meant it. He will be here for me in whatever way I need.

Liam Dempsey is going to be my demise.

chapter four

"HELLO?" I HEAR my best friend, Reanell, call out from the kitchen.

"In here, Rea."

"There you are. I brought over a few meals the wives made this week. I put them in the freezer." Her generous heart causes a warm glow to flow through me. She's been my rock these last few months. Stopping over, bringing food, watching Aarabelle so I can nap.

"Thanks, but I'm doing good. I promise."

This used to be me. I was the one who headed the relief groups. Made sure that the wives of fallen SEALs had food, help, and friends. Funny how life works—now I'm the wife I used to pity.

"Never said you weren't. Now gimme that baby," she says with her hands extended as she takes Aara from me. "Hello, princess," Reanell coos and snuggles Aarabelle. She's impossible not to love. "So?" she questions me.

"So?"

"Who was the guy outside messing with Aaron's car?"

My eyes widen and I rush over to the window. "What?" I ask, pulling back the blinds. "Who the hell would be messing with the car? There's no one there. Why didn't you call the cops?" I look down the driveway, but I don't see anyone.

"He smiled and waved at me, so I didn't think much of it. Plus, he had the telltale signs, so I assumed maybe you were finally accepting some help," she remarks.

"What signs?"

She sighs and lifts Aara up and down, "G-shock watch, tribal tats, and the whole I'm-so-amazing-just-ask-me vibe. Typical SEAL."

"I'm going to check it out. Can you watch her?"

"Stupid question."

I open the door and stop short.

"Hey," Liam is standing there covered in grease.

"Hey, yourself." I clutch my chest and try to slow my racing heart.

He wipes his hand on the rag he's holding. "Sorry, I didn't mean to scare you. I knocked earlier but you didn't answer."

"I must've been with Aara. What are you doing?" I question.

Looking down at his clothes then back up, he raises his brow. "I've got his car running again."

"I see that. I mean, why are you working on his car?"

"I'm helping."

Letting out a deep breath, I count backwards from ten. I can do this. I need to sell his things and start putting my life in order. "Okay, I thought maybe I'd have a few days, but . . ."

"My leave is up in four weeks, I figured I'd get started right away."

Makes sense, but there's no part of me that's ready for this. In my head I know this is the right thing to do, get it over with. Start to move on, but it makes my new reality so final. But death is final, so why am I trying to fight it all?

"You're right. It's fine."

Liam takes a step closer and the look in his eyes sends a shiver down my spine. "One day that word is going to leave your vocabulary and you're going to realize lying to me is pointless."

Now I know why he's so damn good at his job.

"Yeah, okay." Trying to brush him off, I smile and tuck my hair behind my ear. He turns without another word and heads back to the driveway.

"Well, that was intense." I jump at the sound of Reanell behind me. I forgot she was here and always lurking.

I turn and see her with Aarabelle asleep in her arms. "He was Aaron's friend. He's stationed with SEAL Team Four and is helping around the house—apparently."

"He can help me when he's done here," she says as she looks out the window.

"I doubt your husband would approve," I chide and flop on the couch.

She laughs and sits in the rocking chair. "Mason isn't the jealous type," she jokes. Her husband is the commander of Team Four. Reanell might joke, but she would never do anything. However, she loves to irritate him and rile him up. "What team did you say he was with?"

I pull my legs up and giggle, "Four."

"Fuck."

"Dumbass," I reply laughing. Huh. I laughed again.

"Well, well. It seems someone is helping in more ways than one," Reanell marvels and then looks away.

"Why?"

"Because you're laughing."

"I laughed before," I retort.

"No, you fake laughed. This is the first laugh that didn't look like it physically hurt you. Sure, you've put on a great show. But I think this Liam guy is a miracle worker," she murmurs and walks out the room.

Maybe he is. Or maybe he's the first person to not put up with my shit.

chapter five

"DO YOU HAVE any questions, Mrs. Gilcher?" Mr. Popa asks. He's the liaison sent by our insurance company who plans to guide me through the paperwork.

"I'm not sure," I mumble. In all honesty, I haven't heard a word that he's said.

"If she has any questions is there a number where she can reach you?" Liam asks from beside me.

He's been here almost every day, making sure I go through one more thing on my list. Hell, he even made the list. I don't look at it though. I get up and make sure everyone is fed. I can't worry about all this other crap because it doesn't matter. Well, I guess this part does. I'm not working yet and have no income coming in. I need to take care of everything, but I keep worrying about functioning. Then Liam comes in and makes me handle it all.

"Sure, here's my card. Mrs. Gilcher, once we get the forms signed, the sooner we can get the money moved over. It's imperative we get this process started. A lot of time has already lapsed." He hands me the card.

"Thank you, Mr. Popa. We'll be in touch." Liam shakes his hand and walks him to the door.

I feel him sit beside me and he pulls me against him. I take the comfort he offers and lean into him. "This will get easier, right?" I ask.

Of course no one knows. Even the wives who lost

their husbands tell me it does and yet it doesn't. Amy lost her husband last year in a firefight and she said every day she wonders how she gets up and breathes. Jillian said the only way she finally felt human again was when she got rid of almost anything Parker touched, but I can't do that. Making it like he never existed wouldn't make my pain go away. But handling all the death paperwork and dealing with putting him to rest . . . this is what hurts.

"I'm not sure," Liam replies honestly. Thank God for that. He never lies to me or tells me what I want to hear. He gives it to me straight and yet is never hurtful. These last two weeks I've come to rely on him more than I ever thought possible. His friendship means the world to me.

"Yeah, me either."

"Why don't we get Aarabelle and go do something?" he suggests.

I gaze into his blue eyes and see the excitement. He's been here every day for the last two weeks and has done nothing but care for me in some form or another. Here is this single, very good-looking man who has put his life on hold for his best friend's widow.

"You don't have to babysit me. I'll be fine."

His mouth falls slightly slack. "Am I bothering you?"

"No!" I exclaim. "You're a single guy. You don't need to be spending your time with me."

"Shut up. You're loads of fun. I mean, where else could I get to meet a woman who's not trying to get in my pants?"

I burst out giggling. "Happens often, huh?"

Liam tilts in conspiratorially, "Well, I don't mean to brag, but I've been known to break a few hearts . . . and beds."

"Breaking beds because you're a fat ass doesn't count."

His face falls and he looks genuinely affronted. Next thing I know, he tears his shirt off and every ridge and ripple in his skin is on display. I've known him for years, seen him in a bathing suit more times than I can count, but there's something different in this moment, but I'll never let him know.

"Fat? Show me!" he challenges me.

I stand and poke his side. "What, you don't giggle like the doughboy when I poke you?"

Liam laughs, "I don't think you should joke about poking, Lee." He smiles and grabs his shirt.

"Why do you make everything dirty?"

"Because I'm a guy," Liam says like it should be obvious. "I'm going to go for a run and a couple hundred push-ups since you think I'm fat."

"Ohhh, don't cry . . . it happens to everyone when they hit that age," I joke and it feels foreign. I've forgotten this part of myself. I find myself laughing more and more, reminding me of the person I used to be.

Liam turns and eyes me cautiously. "Let's pretend you didn't call me old and fat in the same minute."

"Pretend away . . ." I trail off and saunter into the kitchen. Before I reach the door, I glance over my shoulder to see his reaction. He stands there stunned with his mouth agape. I grin and proceed forward, leaving him there.

"I'll show you fat," I hear him say under his breath as the door swings closed.

I stare at the countertops across the kitchen. The trace of a smile lingers on my lips when a part of me starts to hurt. The part that thinks it's too early to feel okay again. Shouldn't I hurt and be sad? It's only been six months. Then there's the other side of me that says *It's been six months already . . . live.* Aaron wouldn't want me to be alone. He wouldn't want me to be sad all the time.

"You got any coffee?" Liam asks as he yawns, walking into the kitchen.

"Do you know who you're asking?" I say laughing. I get the things out and pour him a cup. "I'm a single mom. Coffee is my drug of choice."

"Thanks." He lifts the cup and practically chugs it. "I'm gonna head out and work on the car again. There are still a few things I need to fix before it'll sell."

Liam inclines back, not breaking his gaze. I look at him, really take a second to look. His eyes always have a gleam to them . . . a little sexy and a little mischief brew behind them. The three-day-old beard he always wears makes him appear rugged and tough. Of course his body screams danger, but he's not overly in your face about it. He knows he's sexy, but he's relaxed.

"Okay, I'm gonna take a walk down to the beach while she's still asleep." I walk over and place my hand on his shoulder and grab the baby monitor. "Thank you, Liam. I appreciate everything."

His hand covers mine. "Anything you need, I'm here." He pats my hand and I walk away with a soft smile, thinking about how it feels having him around.

I put away the coffee mug sitting on the counter. Opening the cabinet, I see Aaron's favorite cup. The one I gave him on our last anniversary, it says: No one loves you like me. The past hits me full force.

"Aaron, stop!" I giggle as he grabs my waist and throws me down in the sand in front of our house.

"Say 'uncle'." He tickles me as I squirm beneath him.

I giggle and try to get out from under him, even though I know it'll never happen. "If you love me, you'll stop."

Immediately his hands leave my sides and he places them beside my head. "No one will ever love you as much as I do."

My hand glides up his arm and I press it against his cheek. "No woman will ever love you as much as I do."

"No woman will ever get close."

"Better not."

He rolls to the side and pulls me against his chest. I rest here and relax into his embrace. "Do you ever think about what you'd do if I was gone?"

His question startles me. "Sometimes." It's been three years of him being in the teams and I'd be lying if I told him I didn't think about it. He's deployed almost every six months, and each time, they get harder and harder. I want my husband, but I understand his duty. It's difficult to love someone and know they might not come home, but the idea of not loving him is unimaginable. I was built for this life—not every woman can be a military wife, but even fewer can handle being a SEAL wife. You have to love deeper, stand stronger, but know that at any moment bonds can break. We fight like everyone else, but Aaron and I want this. We've seen so many friends go through infidelity and divorce, but we keep our love on course. He leaves in three days and I'm soaking up as much time with him as I can.

"I'd want you to love again, Lee," Aaron says as he kisses the top of my head. "Promise me that if something happens to me you'll find someone else."

I don't want to promise. I don't even want to think of the possibility, so I stay quiet.

Aaron bristles and forces me to sit up. Turning to look at him I see his eyes harden. He's not going to back down. "Promise me."

"Nothing's going to happen, so my promise isn't needed. Besides would you really want someone else sleeping in our bed? I don't."

"I need to know you'll be loved. I need to know if I'm gone, you'll have someone to protect you."

His words both warm me and infuriate me. "I don't need protection."

"Natalie," he says tenderly. "I know you're strong, babe. I know you don't need to be protected, but I need this. I need to know you'll find someone to be there."

"I really don't want to talk about this."

He pulls me back across his chest. "I know, but I don't want to leave without it."

"Then don't leave."

The laugh escapes his chest as we both know it's funny because it's not his choice and he surely would never skip out.

"Fine," I say reluctantly. "I promise." Hoping it's the one promise I can break.

A tear falls and the need to leave this house makes it impossible to breathe. I rush out of my chair and head out onto the deck. I wish I could forget it all. He would talk about valor and courage, he would tell me how he always hoped when he died it would be for something. It feels like it was all for nothing.

I start to walk down the beach as the water rushes up and covers my toes. The wind blows and I close my eyes and feel it wash over me. I stand in the wake of the waves and try to feel him.

"Aaron, I miss you," I whisper into the wind. "I hate that you left me. I wish you could see what each day is like for me. Our daughter is growing so big. I need you. She needs you." More tears fall upon my cheek as I pray to my husband. "You made me make these promises. Promises I can't keep."

"Hey," a deep, thick voice calls gently from behind me. "Lee . . . you okay?"

I turn and Liam steps closer. "Yeah, I'm fine," I reply as I wipe under my eyes.

He walks closer, blocking the sun behind him. "I saw you run out and then you didn't answer me when I called out to you."

My guard is down and I'm vulnerable. I know he can see it all. "I'm fi—"

"Don't say 'fine.' You're not fine. You're crying and

you've never been a liar so don't be one now. Come here," he says as he steps forward with arms open.

I walk toward him and slam into his chest as his arms wrap around me like a vise. The mix of emotions comes crashing around me and I sob in his arms. "Why did he have to go? Why couldn't he just stay home? I hate this. I'm so alone. I want him home," I cry out as my fingers grip his shirt and hold on. "I need him so much! I miss him so much it hurts to breathe!" I pull Liam close as I lose it. "God! It's not fair!"

"No, it's not," he says as he rubs his hand up and down my back.

"But he left and now I live every day wishing he didn't get on that damn plane. He was out! He wasn't supposed to die!" My legs start to crumble but Liam keeps me up.

"You're so strong, Lee." I look up and his eyes say so much. "Don't downplay how hard this is."

His words envelope me and I know it's true. I'm strong, but there are parts of me that aren't. I never want to know pain like this again. I've built a fortress around myself because I have to protect my daughter and myself. I realize where I am, in his arms, crying in the ocean. "I'm a mess. I'm so sorry."

"Natalie, goddammit, stop saying you're fucking sorry. Have you cried at all since he died? Have you let yourself grieve at all?"

I step back and he grabs my wrist. My eyes stay downcast as I try to muster any strength I have left. "Yes, I grieved." I glance at him and draw in a deep cleansing breath. "What good does crying do? He's dead. He won't ever come home. I have a daughter, a house, a mortgage, and a shit ton of other things to worry about." The words rush out uncontrollably. "You get to go on your missions and escape the hell that slaps me in the face every day. I'm alone, Liam. He left and all I have is a folded up flag and a lifetime of heartache. So, yeah, I grieve."

Liam releases my arms and steps out of the waves. "You think missions are an escape? We all remember the men we've lost when we go out there. We look around and know the plane could be one body less. That it actually *is* a body less. I know the chances and I live for this. I hate that you have a flag on your mantel and would give anything to trade places with him. What the fuck do I leave behind?"

I take a step toward him and close my eyes. I know how they all feel about each other. They trust each other more than a husband and wife. To Aaron, his teammates were whether he lived or died. So many nights we spent talking about how he would take a bullet for any of them. I remember being so angry and yelling about how stupid he was. How he was willing to die for one of them and how that would affect me. He would kiss me and tell me it was the way it was.

"I think Aaron would've wanted it this way."

Liam looks up and our eyes lock. I see the man he is. The man who would've taken his place but can't, so he's here—for me. Every day, Liam is here. He helps me, makes me laugh and smile. Cares for us.

"He would've what?" he asks confused. His hands clench, and I step forward and give him some of the comfort he's given me.

"Wanted to die like this. To feel like it was for something or someone. If Mark or Jackson would've gone on that mission, he would've hated himself. Wishing he could've taken their place. He always wanted to go down in a blaze of glory. To die for a reason. I don't know what the damn reason is though."

"Me either. I would've gladly changed places with him. He had you and Aarabelle to live for." Liam's hand grabs mine and he pulls me close. "Are you gonna be okay?"

I do have Aarabelle and I have my entire life ahead

of me. I deserve to be happy and it's time I started to live like it.

I look up and give a tiny nod, "I think I will be."

"I think you will too."

chapter six

"KNOCK, KNOCK," I hear Reanell call as she opens my door.

"What's up, my love?" I ask, my voice radiating with delight.

"You're awful perky this morning," she looks at me skeptically.

I'm starting a new outlook from this day forward. I can continue to be sad and mopey or I can remember Aaron as the man he was. The husband, sailor, and hero, not the martyr I've made him. I go back to work in a few weeks, I have a great support system. It's time to start taking baby steps.

"Well, who wouldn't smile at your beautiful face?" I ask sweetly.

"Could it be the sex-on-a-stick outside shirtless fixing the shed?" She looks out the window as she moans. "God, men like him aren't real. They're sent to toy with us."

Looking behind her, I suppress a groan. She'll take that as something it's not. But seriously, holy shit. His back is taut and the muscles ripple as he lifts the two-by-four and then nails it into place. His arms flex and I gawk. He wipes his brow as the sweat trickles down his face and I fight the urge to keep looking. I turn my head but my eyes stay glued to him.

Reanell clears her throat and stares at me with her brow raised. "Well, well, well. What do we have here?"

"Nothing. What?" I pretend to sound confused at what she saw.

"Right. Nothing at all."

"Nope. Nothing to see here."

She looks back out the window. "There's plenty to see my friend. Plenty indeed."

I need to flip the attention. "Did anyone ever tell you you're a horny housewife who needs a job?"

"A few times. Mason appreciates that I can shop without buying."

I laugh and slap her arm. "Yeah, it's about the only thing you don't buy."

She looks away and snorts. "Accurate. I'm also not buying your diversion. I saw you eating him alive."

"No, I'm not even ready to go there. Let's change the subject, okay?"

"No, not until you admit he's hot."

"Why does it matter if I think he's hot?" I scoff.

Rea smiles and puts her hands on her hips. "Admit it."

"Fine, I won't deny it. He's hot."

"I knew you thought so," she smirks.

I roll my eyes and smother the desire to choke her.

"Besides, if you did deny it, I would be worried," she laughs. "How about while Aarabelle's sleeping, we can do some stuff around here?"

I look at the mantel and my heart falters. I can feel him everywhere and I'm not ready to lose that. Already I've lost so much. Just pulling into my drive without his car there will be one more reminder. Loss and anger are at war in me. I'm mad at everyone and everything, but then I have to go on day by day. I don't get to sulk and be sad because there's a tiny baby that we made together. I close my eyes and think of him.

"Sure," the word falls out.

We spend the next few hours cleaning papers and things around the house. I'm sweating and huffing from carrying all the boxes up and down the stairs. It's been a long day and I look like hell but feel a little lighter. We've got things organized, and as much as I want to stop, I also want to keep going. I worry the strength I've harnessed will be lost tomorrow.

Before I can tell Rea my plan to keep on, she looks over and frowns. "I need to get home. Mason wants dinner early and I want a new purse."

She's a mess. "How do those go hand in hand?"

"He likes to eat. I like Michael Kors. If I don't get a bag, he can starve," she winks and grabs her purse.

"Sounds perfectly reasonable," I reply with a huff. "I'm going to finish up. Thank you for today."

Reanell kisses my cheek. "I'm proud of you. I know this isn't easy, but it was time."

"Thanks, you know that it's been seven months today?"

"Since he died?"

"Yeah, crazy, right? Aarabelle is so small to me that I forget."

Reanell sits on the couch with her purse in her arms. "I think we all do. You were pregnant when he died and then Aara kind of shifted time. It's a good thing though. She's given you a way to keep moving."

"Maybe."

"And Liam being around making you do stuff helps too, no?"

I think about what she says and try to come up with an argument. But it's true. Liam has forced me to handle everything in the last few weeks. In a short amount of time he's taken care of months' worth of things.

"He's helped a lot."

"I better bounce, but I'm glad you're doing well. You

look better too."

"Thanks, I think."

"Don't do anything I wouldn't do," she winks.

I nod and she leaves. Aarabelle is taking her afternoon nap in her playpen. She ate and played for a little and now I have about an hour before she'll need to eat again. I decide to hang the curtains in the living room that have been sitting in the closet for months.

Getting all my tools out, I grab the ladder and mark the spots where the new rod will go. I can do this. Take that, Martha Stewart. Once everything is up, I get the screw and it won't go in. I try again and the screw falls and I fumble with the drill. "Damn it," I curse as it falls to the floor. Grabbing the drill, I hear a laugh behind me. "Am I amusing you, Dreamboat?" I ask as I try to align the screw. I know using his call sign pisses him off . . . which is why I said it. Aaron used to lose his shit when I called him Papa Smurf.

"I think you want to wound me."

"Never. I'm just . . ." I struggle with the stupid screw that refuses to go in. "Stupid damn drill is broken!"

"You have it set to reverse," Liam says chuckling and he climbs the ladder behind me.

"Get down!" I yell as his weight makes the ladder tilt a little.

"Push that button there," he says against my neck. "You're not going to fall. I'll be the one who breaks their neck."

I suppress a shiver as he lifts my hand and pushes the back of the drill. "Fine, maybe I'll elbow you," I joke to try to keep my mind off how his body is pressed against mine. The body that I stared and marveled at. *He's only helping, Natalie.*

"I'll take you with me. Now, push hard and screw."

I lose my grip on the drill. "That sounded so bad!" My head falls forward and we both laugh hysterically.

"Oh," I say as my stomach hurts.

"You made it dirty!"

"You told me to push hard and screw," and I start laughing again.

Liam rests against me and we both try to control our breathing. "Okay," he breathes again. "Now, make sure it's aligned in the hole."

"Oh, God. Get down. I can't do this." I giggle and snort.

"You snorted!" he says as he grips my hips and helps me off the ladder.

"You made me," I reply incredulously.

"Well, put it in the hole and screw."

"Stop!" I hold on to the ladder as tears fall from laughing so hard.

Liam keeps going. "If you don't know how to put it in, I can help."

We both laugh and I hear Aarabelle cry.

"Now you've done it," my voice is full of humor.

Liam grabs the drill, "You get Aara, I'll make sure you don't have to re-plaster the walls."

I clutch my chest and reply dramatically, "Oh, my hero."

He gives a mock salute with the drill and I leave him to his power tools. Maybe he really is a miracle worker.

After a little while, Liam has all the curtains hung and a few pictures I found during my cleaning. Aarabelle plays happily in her swing.

"A little to the left," I instruct Liam as he tries to align the photo.

"Here?"

"Ummm, maybe to the right? But just a smidge." I laugh to myself as his head drops, clearly frustrated.

"Lee, I'm going to nail this to the ground if you make me move it again," Liam grumbles as he moves it back to where it was originally.

I take a step back and try to keep from laughing because this is actually fun. "You know," I muse. "I think maybe I should put it in the hall." I bite my lip to keep from busting out.

He groans and puts the photo down. I hear him take a few deep breaths. When he turns, I bat my eyes innocently. "I'm going to let this sit here for a minute."

"Oh, but I want to hang it." I giggle and Liam bursts out with a loud guffaw.

"You're a giant pain in the ass."

"Yeah, but where else would you go for abuse?" I simper and shrug.

"Work."

"True. I mean, they probably won't call you fat or old . . . yeah, right, they totally will," I tease, reminding him of our previous discussion.

"Take it back."

I raise my brow. "Never."

"Do you really want to brawl?"

"You'll lose. I was trained."

He breaks out into a run straight for me and I sprint toward the kitchen laughing. He's going to kill me, but I can't back down. I lean against the door hoping I can keep him from coming in.

"Why are you running, oh trained one?" he asks from the other side of the kitchen door.

Shit. I'm trapped.

chapter seven

"LIAM, I WANT to remind you that I'm in possession of many sharp objects here in the kitchen."

I hear him snicker once. "You forget, I'm trained in knife fighting."

"Ugh. Okay, can I just say uncle?"

"Maybe," he says but then nothing else.

After a few seconds of silence, I try to ask again, "Liam? Uncle."

No response. I wonder where the hell he went. I hear Aarabelle over the baby monitor and know I can't stay here forever. "Liam?" Again, no response. I have two choices. I can try to keep myself blockaded in here or I can grow some lady balls and face him. I can do this. I've given birth naturally, buried a husband, and still manage to function. Screw him.

Slowly I creep the door open and he's not there. Well, that wasn't what I was expecting. I take a step into the hallway and look around. These guys are stealthy and Aaron used to love to scare the crap out of me when I wasn't expecting it. He'd hide behind doors and in closets then jump out so I'd scream.

"Liam?" I ask, trying to sneak toward the living room. When I turn, I see him holding Aarabelle with a sly smile.

"Saved by the baby."

"I wasn't scared," I say confidently.

"Liar. But I'll let you have it."

I laugh and extend my arms. Liam hands me Aarabelle and I pull her close.

"I like that sound," he says almost as an afterthought.

"Huh?"

Liam steps forward and brushes my hair back. "Your laugh. It took a while to get it to come back more."

My jaw falls and I stare into his eyes. He's brought me back . . . almost. Given me back my smile and I hadn't even known it. Liam's been here and managed to help the old me come out. "I . . ." I trail off unsure of what to say.

"I gotta get going, but I wanted to give you this. I found something in Aaron's glove box."

"What?"

Liam pulls an envelope out of his back pocket and his eyes tell me what it is. The *If you're reading this* letter. When I didn't receive one after he died, I assumed he shredded it when he got out of the Navy. Considering it's usually left with your closest friend, and neither Mark nor Jackson had given it to me, I presumed. Then with Liam being around, I thought for sure Aaron threw it out, not thinking we'd need it. But here it is.

I extend my hand and take it.

"Was there anything else?"

The one thing I wanted was our wedding ring. After the explosion, no personal belongings were sent back. Maybe he left it too?

Liam looks at the other letters in his hand, and I hate the pain I see. "A letter for Jackson, Mark, and one for me were in there as well."

"I don't know if I can read this," I reply honestly.

"You'll read it when you're ready. I've got some things I need to get done," Liam says and grabs his coat. He kisses the top of my head.

I nod and gaze at the letter in my hand. I want to read it, but I can't right now. Not with Aarabelle awake. I have no idea how I'm going to handle this. I place it on the table and decide I'll read it later.

The night passes and I get Aarabelle to bed. I'm exhausted and worn as I flop on the couch and turn on the fireplace. The letter sits there and the need to read his words is too much to fight. I miss him and maybe this will help me feel close again.

My throat is dry as my finger tears through the seal. My heart beats rapidly in my ears as dread begins to claw its way through my body. Can I read my husband's final message? Inhaling through my nose, I count backwards as my hands shake.

The wind blows and I know he's here with me.

Biting my lip, I think about Aaron and what he'd say to me right now. He'd tell me to "man up" and read it. I smile to myself as I hear his voice in my head. Tears blur my vision, but I wipe them away and read my husband's last words to me.

Lee,

If you're reading this, I'm no longer here. I've broken my promise to come home to you, even though it was a promise I knew I couldn't really make. Know that I didn't go willingly. I wanted a life with you—forever. There's not a single part of me that ever wanted you to read this. First, because I'm not good at this crap. Second, because I've failed you on some level. I always told you I am a SEAL—the best, elite, and untouchable. I believe that. There's a reason why we're trained like we are—we do the shit that no one else could. So, somehow I fucked up. I got in a situation and my training failed. I'm sorry.

My life was never the same after we met in Ms. Cook's class. You sat next to me and I knew I was a goner. Then I saw you before the homecoming game and you had that damn skirt on. I almost fucked up the game thinking about how to get you to go on a date with me. After weeks of telling you how awesome I am, you finally caved. I felt like I'd won the lottery. You were the best prize. Hell, you are the best prize. We went to that awful restaurant but you smiled the whole time. When I walked you to the door and you kissed me before I could have done some stupid awkward shit, I knew one day I'd marry you. I knew you'd be the woman I'd spend every night next to. Because you're my fucking world, Lee. You're the sun, the stars, and the everything in between.

Everyone says in these letters we give these great speeches about random things. I've probably rewritten this damn thing twelve times. I can only tell you this: I love you. I've always loved you and I'll love you far past my death.

I can't tell you what to do because, well, I'm gone and you wouldn't listen anyway. But, you made promises. You deserve to have the life you wanted . . . one with a man who loves you more than his own life. A man who will give you a family and the love that you need. If we have kids, I hope you give them a father. They'll need that. Someone to teach them to throw a ball, how to ask a girl out, how to keep the stupid boys who only want one thing away. If we have a girl she's never allowed to date . . . ever. Make sure that no boy puts his dipstick anywhere near my daughter. Tell them about us. Tell them about how much I would've loved them. If they ask why, tell them I was protecting them. I'm not a proud man, but I'm proud of the life we've had. You've stood by me, pushed me, and made me a better man.

I've made mistakes in my life, but you were the best thing that ever happened to me. You loved me when I probably didn't deserve it. Know that when I close my *eyes at night I always see you. And when I draw my last breath at the end, it'll be your name I say last. Without you, there would be no me.*

Love me when I'm gone.

Aaron

The tears fall and I clutch the letter to my chest. "I'll love you forever," I whisper and hope somewhere, somehow, he hears me.

CHAPTER EIGHT

LIAM

"FUCK!" I YELL out and punch the tree. My knuckles scream out in pain.

I pick up my pace and start to run again. I need to work out and be ready for the team. I can't be sitting around and then not be in peak physical condition, but every damn day I'm at her house. I can't stay away or stop myself from checking on her. It's like a drug. So I run . . . I run and try to stop my mind from drifting to her and Aarabelle. I think about the way she laughs, how her smile lights up the room, and how much I like being the one to put it there. This shit needs to stop.

The music blares in my ears as I sprint. I count and breathe, focusing only on that. I can't think about her blonde hair. I won't worry about whether she's read the letter. I refuse to worry about whether she remembered to call the mortgage company. Because I'm not her fucking anything. I'm the dickhead who won't leave her alone because of a promise. At least that's what I keep telling myself. I'm nothing to her and I can never be. I shouldn't even be thinking about this.

I run faster and stop to do some push-ups. I'll show her fat and old.

My phone rings and it's a California number.

"Hello?"

"Dreamboat, it's Jackson."

"Hey, Muffin. What's up?" I ask as I try to catch my breath. I've met Jackson Cole a bunch of times. Aaron worked for him when he left the Navy and our teams were both deployed together at the same time to Africa. We weren't really close but drank together a few times.

"Not much. Wanted to check on Natalie and see if she needs anything."

Natalie told me about how he took Aaron's death hard. He felt like he was responsible. He got himself shot when he went over to investigate and bring Aaron's remains home. Not that there were many remains left. "She's putting on a good show. She's stubborn as all hell but finally taking care of some things."

He sighs and I wonder what he was expecting. It's only been about seven months since he died. No one would be ready for much more than she is.

"She starts working for me this week. I wanted to make sure everything is okay."

I forgot about that. Shit. "Yeah, I'm sure she'll be good. My leave is over this week and who knows what the deployment schedule is like."

"Ahhh, I heard. Four, huh?"

"Yeah, man." I lean against the tree since this is going to be another few minutes. "How's Cali?"

He laughs and pauses, "I'm adjusting."

"She worth it?"

"You have no idea."

"Thank God," I say. This is no life for a woman. The home-again-then-gone-again life. How the hell any of these guys are dumb enough to marry someone I'll never know. It's unfair and I don't need anyone clouding my judgment when I'm on a mission.

Jackson laughs as if he knows something I don't. "One day. One day everything you thought, you'll forget—for her."

My mind flashes to Natalie and Aarabelle. The grin comes without any thought. Fuck. I'm not supposed to feel anything for her. Goddammit. This isn't allowed.

"Or not."

I push it down because I'm sure it's not anything.

"One day," Jackson repeats.

It's because I'm spending so much time there. Helping her hang pictures, mowing the lawn, and taking care of the things that need to be done. Yeah. That's it. Nothing more. I'll lock that shit down before it becomes anything else because she's my friend. She's my best friend's wife.

"One day. I gotta run. Literally," I say to Jackson and stretch so I can get back to running. I need to get this crap out of my head.

"Take care. I'll be back east soon and maybe we can grab a beer."

"Sounds good, Muff." I disconnect the call and blare some Jay Z hoping I can get lost in the bass.

Trying to focus on the trees passing by and how bad my muscles are going to hate me later, I end up thinking about the letter sitting in my car. Why the fuck did he write to all of us? My letter sits in my rifle case and it goes to my mom, not any of the guys. I start to think of Natalie and how she's doing. Did she read the letter? Did he tell her something that is going to cause her pain or will it put her at ease? I turn and head back on the trail, running faster than I did before.

Once I reach my car, I throw my phone on the dash. I can't go back there. I'm not her boyfriend and I never will be. I need to get laid. I grab my phone and call my buddy who's stationed here.

Quinn answers on the first ring. "What up, dirtbag?"

"Hey, fuckstick. I need to go out tonight. You game?"

"Hot Tuna? Lots of willing pussy."

Sounds perfect. I need to get balls deep in some girl and get the other one out of my head. "Meet you there around ten."

I disconnect the phone and lean back in my seat. My legs are screaming after the run I just did. Every time I would start to zone out, I'd start thinking about Lee and Aarabelle, wondering what they are doing. You can't not love that kid. She looks like Aaron, only cuter. What the fuck have I gotten myself into? And where in the last few weeks did this shift at all? She's Lee for Chrissake. She's the messy hair, sweat pants, and no bra girl I've known for eight years. I've seen her practically naked and even though any man would have to be blind not to look twice at her, I've never had anything more than friendship towards her. So what the hell is different?

Enough thinking.

Time to get wasted and laid.

"HEY, FUCKER! WASN'T sure you were going to show." Quinn sits back with a beer in his hand.

"Passed out after my run," I state.

Quinn and I have been friends for a few years. We both went to the same training site in Nevada and kept in touch. When I found out I was heading to SEAL Team Four, I was glad I at least knew a few guys.

"Been a while since you worked out, huh?"

"I've been busy," I say and signal for a beer to the bartender.

He looks at me and smirks. "Busy . . . right."

"That's what I said."

Quinn nods and looks at the game on TV as I look around the bar. He's right. This place is crawling with women looking for some attention. They're not even subtle. Fine by me.

"So, what's been going on? I haven't heard from you."

"I've been helping Natalie get stuff done. Since Aaron wasn't active, the Navy is no help."

"Yeah, I heard about that. Aaron was a good guy. Sucks about how he died." Quinn taps my beer and we both take a gulp.

"It's fucking weird. The whole thing."

"What do you mean? The IED in Afghanistan?" He looks at me as if I sprouted another head. "Tell me where the weird part is."

My training tells me there's more to that explosion. "Why the fuck was he there? Why was his caravan hit? I know these assholes don't give a shit, but Jackson's company isn't stupid. They know that region. Then the fact that Cole was shot when he went to the site doesn't add up. Why and who is targeting Cole's company?"

The thing about Quinn is he's an easy read. Which is why he's a sniper on our team and not intelligence. "Don't start trying to look for shit that's not there. He was killed by an IED and you said it yourself—they don't care. So they killed him because they could. Plain and simple. As to why Jackson was shot, again they're American—enough said."

"Sure," I reply to placate him. I don't think it's plain and simple, but Quinn is too stupid or self-absorbed to give a shit. He's simple and follows orders, never thinking about it again. I, on the hand, don't do either well.

"Hi there," I hear from behind me. Quinn's eyes widen as he takes in the company we have.

I shift and see the two women. One has black hair cut right above her clearly fake tits. The other has blonde hair pulled to one side. She's fucking hot.

"Hi, ladies."

"Is that seat taken?" the blonde asks, biting her lip. I'm fucked . . . and hopefully she will be soon too.

"What's your poison?"

She smiles and sits on the stool next to me and crouches down, showing me her rack. Her fingertip traces the wood right by my arm and my cock stirs. "What's your name?"

"Liam," I reply and lean closer.

"Well, Liam . . . I'm Brit. How about you buy me a shot of whiskey and we'll find out what else is my poison?"

On a normal day, this type of shit would piss me off, but today, Brit seems to be just what I need.

The hours pass and we drink and spend the evening with Brit and her friend, Claire. They're both practically begging to go home with us. I'll never understand what these bitches think. Why would any man want to take you home to Mom if I was able to fuck you the first night we met? That's not the kind of girl I want to have a life with. That's the girl I'm going to fuck and forget.

"I'm probably too drunk to drive," Brit whispers in my ear.

"Want me to give you a ride?" I ask, and her lip is back between her teeth.

She nods and her tongue darts out and licks the red marks. I'm going to lose my shit.

"Let's go then," I sweep my arm forward and Brit stumbles into my arms.

"Yes. Let's."

chapter nine

natalie

"SHHH, IT'S OKAY, Aarabelle." I'm starting to get nervous. It's been almost two hours straight of her screaming. Tears fall and nothing is soothing her. It's almost two o'clock in the morning and I don't know what's wrong. I gave her medicine when she felt warm before, but she's still not calming.

She wails over and over and I can't get her to take a break. She still feels hot to me, so I grab the thermometer, and my heart races when I see her temperature.

Throwing things in the diaper bag, I need to get her to the hospital. She's running a 105.2-degree fever. I grab my phone and toss it in the bag. When I turn to get her, I see her eyes roll back and she begins twitching on the floor.

"Oh my God!" I scream and run over to her.

Her body convulses and I turn her to her side. Aarabelle's limbs flail and panic grips me. I hold her as she shakes and tears stream down my face. It only lasts a minute, but my heart is in my throat.

"Aarabelle!" I burst out as she starts to cry again and I rummage through my bag for my phone. I dial 9–1-1. I lift her in my arms and hold her tight.

The dispatcher's calm voice comes through, "9–1–1, state your emergency."

"My daughter. She's had a seizure I think. I don't know. Her fever . . . it's high . . . and I don't know what to do!" I blurt trying to gather my wits. I'm frazzled and frayed. Aarabelle cries loudly as I rock her back and forth in my arms.

"Is she conscious, ma'am?"

"Yes, she's crying and has a high fever. I put her down to get ready to go to the hospital and then she began shaking," I cry and every part of me feels weak. My heart is racing as I watch her, hoping it doesn't happen again.

"Okay, what's your address? I'm sending an ambulance."

I give the dispatcher the information and she stays on the line as we wait for help to arrive. In minutes, the EMTs arrive and they instruct me to grab her car seat as they take her vitals. I throw my phone back in my bag, grab my stuff, and climb in the ambulance.

"Okay, Aara. Mommy's got you," I say soothingly as I buckle her in her seat. "We'll be at the hospital in a few minutes."

She cries and I fight the tears threatening to come again. I've never been this scared in my life. Watching her shake uncontrollably was terrifying. I couldn't survive if something happened to my baby.

The lights and sirens blaze as we rush to the emergency room at the children's hospital.

"Her fever is still high, but we should be at Children's Hospital of Kings' Daughters in a few minutes, ma'am," the young EMT says.

I'm not sure if I even acknowledge him because I'm so focused on Aarabelle. She's finally stopped crying, but I'm not sure if it's a good thing or not.

Once the ambulance stops, they rush us into a room where the nurses are waiting.

"Hi, Mrs. Gilcher. I'm Dr. Hewat," she walks in quickly and heads over to Aara. "What's going on with Aarabelle?"

I explain what she's been like during the night and how she's been extremely fussy. She examines her and explains the course they're going to take to get her fever down immediately. They need to get an IV started and then they're going to run some tests.

The nurse comes in and gets the IV hooked up. She makes sure Aarabelle's monitors and fluids are working and lets me know how to call for help. Once Aara settles a little, the nurse takes her temperature and vitals again. She's finally fallen asleep from exhaustion and I have a second to think.

"Any changes?" I ask hesitantly.

"Not yet, but the medicine can take a bit," she says and heads out of the room with a sympathetic smile.

I grab my phone to send a text to Reanell, letting her know where we are and to call me when she wakes. No point in worrying her.

"Sir," I hear outside the curtain before it flies open.

"There you are!" Liam exclaims and looks panicked.

"Liam?" I stand and he looks at Aarabelle.

"I heard you talking about the hospital. Why didn't you call me?"

I look at him, his face is ashen and his eyes are wide.

The nurse pushes him back, "Ma'am, do you want me to call security?"

"No, he's fine." I step forward and Liam looks at Aara again. "What are you doing here?"

"I heard my phone ring and I saw you calling. You never call me, so I figured something was wrong. I heard you talking about a hospital, but you wouldn't answer me. I had to drop someone off and then I came running. I didn't know if she was okay." Liam barely gets the words out and my heart falters. He looks so concerned.

"I'm sorry. I didn't realize I called you."

"Why the hell didn't you?"

My jaw falls and I see how hurt he is. "Why would I? I can take care of myself and my daughter."

He closes his eyes and lets out a deep breath, "I never said you couldn't, but why the hell should you do this alone? I'm your friend, aren't I? I told you I want to be here for you. I thought . . ." He trails off.

"Thought what?"

I see it in his eyes. He's holding something back.

"I thought you would've called."

"I'm sorry, I didn't want to bother you." I don't know what else to say. I honestly never thought of calling him. Liam's been so much help, but I don't want to rely on him.

"What's wrong with her?" he questions.

I look at Aarabelle sleeping and I brush her hair back. "I don't know. She started running a high fever and then she had convulsions. I called emergency services and they rushed us here. They're running some blood tests and they're waiting to see what comes back."

Liam comes around the side of her bed and puts his hand on mine as I begin to cry silently. I pray it's nothing serious. I can't handle anything more. Between Aaron's letter the other day and now Aarabelle, I'm going to lose my mind.

Dr. Hewat enters and looks over the papers. "Hi, Mr. Gilcher, I presume?"

My eyes shift to Liam.

"No, just a friend," he says with an easy grin.

"Sorry, my mistake."

"Is she okay?" I ask, needing answers.

She looks to me and then her eyes move to Aarabelle. "Right now I'm ruling out a few things but I need to run an additional scan. With her fever still not coming back to normal, I need to be sure. Her counts are elevated indicating an infection. They'll be here in a few minutes to take her for the test."

"What are you testing for?"

"Let's rule out a few things and then we'll know the best course of action," Dr. Hewat replies and walks out.

Liam is by my side in a heartbeat. "It'll be fine."

"Right. Like Aaron would be right back."

"Lee," he chides and then stops.

I wish I had the confidence he does. It must be nice to be the one who doesn't have to sit around and worry. They go and do. They fight and live off the high while the families sit around and wonder. We don't know if they're okay. We just suffer through it. Now, I sit here months after my last tragedy and wonder if my daughter is going to be okay.

He sits beside me and I lean on his shoulder. I'm exhausted both physically and emotionally. What the fuck else is life going to throw at me? Once again, I have to be strong though.

Aarabelle rests and I close my eyes. Liam's strong arm wraps around me and I take the comfort he offers. I inhale his sandalwood and musk scent, and it calms me. I love the smell of a man. I miss the smell of a man. Especially this kind of man—one that exudes strength, confidence, and dominance. They command the space around them.

I focus on how secure I feel in this moment. The way I used to feel when Aaron would hold me. I think of the letter he wrote urging me to love again. Could I give another man a chance to hold me like this? Right now . . . I don't know. But being in Liam's embrace makes me want to be open to the idea.

Something shakes me gently and I open my eyes. The hospital smell hits me first and I realize I must've drifted off to sleep. Rubbing my eyes, I sit up and Liam stretches. His shirt lifts and I see the ripples of his abdomen. *Look away, Natalie.*

"Mrs. Gilcher?"

I nod and head over toward the nurse. "Yes."

"We're going to take Aarabelle for her scan. She'll be about forty minutes. You can wait here or you can come up and wait outside. It's totally up to you."

"I'll come with," I say matter-of-factly. There's no way in hell you're keeping me away from her.

Liam places his hand on my shoulder. "I'm going to run and get some coffee. Need anything?"

My heart swells at his concern. "No, I'm good. Thank you for being here."

"I'll always be here for you, Lee."

"I know. You promised him."

His thumb grips my chin and he forces me to look at him. Blue eyes shimmer with some unnamed emotion. I want to look away, break the connection, because I feel it. I feel something and I don't want to. I'm not ready. It's way too soon, but it's there, starting to make its way through me, and I'm terrified he'll see it. The need to close my eyes becomes intense, but I can't, or maybe I really don't want to. Maybe I want him to see it, but God, if I'm not scared. "Go with Aarabelle," he says as his hand drops.

My cheeks paint red and I close my eyes finally. Shit. I was wrong. Maybe he doesn't feel anything for me.

"Ma'am?" The nurse calls to me as she unlocks the wheels on Aarabelle's crib.

"Ready," I say, knowing I feel anything but. This is all too much and my feelings couldn't have come at a worse time. I need to focus on my baby and then I can worry about myself and my stupid feelings.

chapter ten

WAITING IS AGONY. Waiting sucks. Waiting is all we seem to be doing.

"You should head home," I grumble as I snuggle into Liam's chest. I want him to want to leave. Which is stupid because he's my pillow right now, but if he wants to go, this nagging, festering feeling inside might leave me alone.

Liam sags in the chair so I have a more comfortable position, and the rumble of his laughter vibrates through his chest. It's now 5 A.M. and no one but Aarabelle is sleeping. "I'll leave right now if that's what you really want."

Butterflies stir in my belly. What do I want? I wish I knew.

"Nah," my reluctant reply falls out. "I need my pillow. I'm going to keep using you for now."

"You can use me anytime, Lee."

I can reply or choose to pretend. I'm going with pretending. The nursing staff has the world's worst or best timing, depending on how I want to look at this, because she strides in to check on Aara. My head rises and I head over to be close to her.

"We're just checking her fever again," she explains and begins to assess her vitals.

Standing next to my daughter while they check her again, the fear gnaws its way up. Wondering whether the fever has come down any lower, and if not, what's the next step? She looks at the thermometer and shakes her head no. She's still running around 101, but at least we're out of the danger zone.

"Are the test results back from her scan?" I ask.

"I'll check on it, but the doctor will be in as soon as we know anything." She smiles and grips my hand. "It's a good thing the fever isn't rising."

I close my eyes and nod. I guess it's good. I wish she wasn't sick at all, but I'm happy Liam is here. The waiting has been agony and I can't imagine not having his support. I look over at him as he rests in the recliner and fight the urge to giggle. This six-foot, bulky man is spilling over this tiny chair. His legs almost touch the crib Aarabelle is asleep in and his arms practically touch the ground. It's comical. His hair is a mess and his three-day-old beard only makes him look more adorable. He was always handsome, but the more I look at him, I see the small things. The crinkle around his eyes and the scar on his forearm that add to his appeal. He's going to make some woman very happy.

"Are you done staring?" he grumbles with one eye open.

Shit.

"I wasn't staring. I was trying to figure out if you were dead since you weren't moving," I lie and turn so he doesn't see my cheeks redden.

"Sure you were . . ." He gives a low chuckle.

"Whatever, you're old and fat." I wave my hand at him.

Liam's large frame rises and casts a shadow over me. He takes a step toward me with a smirk on his face. My eyes stay locked with his. He's out of his mind if he thinks I'm going to back down.

With a measured step he comes closer. Neither of us breaks our gaze.

consolation

I read the hesitation behind his eyes. He's as unsure as I am, but we're both too stubborn to give in.

"Aaaaaa," Aarabelle cries out, and I break and look at her.

"Hi, baby girl," I say softly and lift her carefully so I don't disconnect anything. She still feels warm and begins to fuss. Why isn't the fever breaking?

Liam's firm hand squeezes my shoulder as if he can read my distress. "I'll call the nurse," he declares and goes to press the button.

Before he can, Dr. Hewat walks in, lifting papers in the chart. "Okay, we got the results back from the scan and her blood screen." She looks at us both with empathy swimming in her eyes. "She has a urinary tract infection that spread to her kidneys, which is what caused the fever. We need to treat her with antibiotics and make sure her kidneys are functioning properly. Also, I want to watch the fever since she did have the convulsions. But she should be fine. I'm going to order the medicine now."

I release a breath with relief. She's going to be okay. Thank God.

"Will the fever come down?" I question.

"It should. Can you place her on the bed for me?"

I lay her down and the doctor comes around the other side. She begins to listen to her heart and abdomen. "She's doing well, and I think once we get the antibiotics working, the fever will break and she'll be back to normal," Dr. Hewat explains and pats my hand. "In the meantime, we need to keep her hydrated and watch her closely."

"Okay," I nod and Aarabelle lifts her arms for me to pick her up.

Scooping my baby in my arms, I pull her close and say a silent prayer of thanks that this was not anything serious. She's my world and I don't think I could survive burying my husband and my child in the same year. I can't even allow my mind to drift there.

Liam's eyes gleam as he rubs the side of her face with adoration in his eyes. He's a good man and he cares about Aarabelle and me. He could've been at a bar or doing whatever else he wants, but he came to us. I'm grateful that he's here. I place my hand over his and a charge runs from my fingers to my shoulder. We both look at each other and my body locks. I see the catch in his breath as he feels it too.

Moving my hand away quickly, I take a few seconds to calm my racing heart and walk to the other side of Aarabelle's crib. Distance . . . I need to keep my distance. I don't understand what's happening. Liam is my friend, he's Aaron's friend . . . it's wrong to even think about him.

"Lee?" Liam breaks me out of my thoughts. He begins to step around, but I put my hand up to stop him.

"I'm fine. I think I'm overwhelmed, but I'll be fine."

"Back to 'fine' again. Got it."

Screw him. I am fine. "What does that mean?"

"I'm tired. You're tired. Tomorrow if you're feeling up to a sparring match, I'm game." Liam yawns and flops in the chair behind him. He pulls his beanie over his eyes and smirks.

Bastard.

chapter eleven

"OKAY, MISS AARABELLE, ready to head home?" the nurse coos as I buckle Aarabelle into her seat. The IV of antibiotics finally got the infection under control, which brought her fever down. After two sleepless days and nights, I'm more than excited to be heading home.

"I'd say we are, right, baby girl?" I ask rhetorically as I nestle the blanket around her. I can't wait for the day when she'll talk. Then I won't feel so silly having full-blown one-sided conversations.

"Well, good thing that hunk of a man came here, huh?" she asks me, looking around the corner.

I try to hide my amusement and giggle silently. "Yeah, he's a good friend."

"Oh, you're not dating?" her eyes grow and she bites her lip.

"No," I say slowly and I realize she's fishing. A pang of jealousy stirs in my chest. He's not mine by any stretch, but he sure as hell isn't hers. "Well, not officially," I add on and mentally slap myself for it.

There's no reason I should be cockblocking him, but something inside of me doesn't want her to have him. Or have a chance at him. I'm going to hell.

"Hang on tight to that one, because that beanie and that smile . . ." She slaps her hand over her mouth, clearly embarrassed at what she's said. "I'm sorry. I don't know what got into me."

Placing my hand on her arm, I giggle. "It's okay. He's easy on the eyes."

She gives a short laugh. "Yeah, you could say that."

Before I can respond, Liam walks in and gives a knowing look. He heard us. Great, this should be fun.

"You girls ready to hit the road?" he asks with an underhanded chuckle.

I shake my head and bite my tongue.

"I could leave the room, if you want to keep talking about my hotness," Liam offers and flops in the chair he slept in two nights in a row. He refused to leave Aarabelle's side.

I walk over and rip the beanie off. "Arrogance doesn't suit you, Dempsey." The giggle escapes me at the way his hair sticks out in various directions. "No one thinks you're hot right now, buddy."

He stands and walks toward me slowly. His warm breath bathes my neck as he leans in so only I can hear, "I think we both know that's not true." Liam's finger glides against my arm and I shiver. "We can pretend though." Slowly his finger reaches my hand and my heart is racing. I enjoy the feel of his hands on me more than I should. I can't explain what's happening between us because it's never been like this. It's always been friendship. He shifts back and snatches his hat from my hand.

I look over and try to get my breathing under control. Liam tries to pretend, but I see the desire pooled in his eyes. He's not as unaffected as he's feigning, but Liam is trained to restrain his emotions. Fine, I can play the game too.

I pull my hair over my shoulder and lean down a little, giving him a tiny glimpse of skin. "It's not pretending when one of us doesn't feel that way." I grab the diaper bag . . . *real sexy, Natalie* . . . and try to maintain my alluring look.

Liam isn't buying it and he lets out a deep, loud laugh. "Nice try, babe. Let's go." He grabs the diaper bag off my shoulder and heads out of the room.

"Looks like Mommy's lost her touch," I say to Aarabelle as I grab the car seat and head out.

"YOU MEAN HE stayed the whole time you were in the hospital?" Reanell asks suspiciously.

"Yes, he wouldn't leave." I grab my coffee mug and curl up on the sofa. We've been home for a few days and Liam hasn't stopped by. He texted me yesterday to wish me luck on my first day of work, but I haven't replied.

"Hmmm," Rea says as she taps her lip. We've been trying to analyze everything, because there's a part of me that wonders if I'm making this all up. "I mean, he was Aaron's best friend."

"I know. I think it's just his duty to him. It would explain why he kinda disappeared after he dropped us off."

She looks at me trying to see through me. "Do you want him to stop by?"

"Reanell, please. It's not even been a year. There's no way in hell I want another man. I love my husband."

Grabbing her drink, she comes over to the couch and sits next to me. "I know you do, but you're a woman. Liam is a good man. A man who seems to care about you and Aara very much. Would it be such a bad thing?"

I think I've entered into another dimension. My friend who told me if her husband died she'd join the convent because it would be too hard is urging me to entertain this. "Yes, it would be bad. First off, Liam has never had a serious girlfriend, let alone taking on a widow and a baby. Second, he's a SEAL!" I yell out and then recover. "Fuck . . . he's a SEAL. Deployments, possible death. I couldn't." I start to panic.

"Hey," Reanell grips my hand. "I'm not saying it's good or bad. I'm just saying sometimes the heart wants what the head says no to. I don't know if your heart or head want anything."

"Sleep. They want sleep."

She laughs and releases my hand. "That's why I'm here. Go take a nap. No more talk of boys. I'm glad he came to the hospital and took care of you. You needed someone and he was there."

"Yeah, he was. Okay, I'm going to rest. Thank you for coming over and watching her for me. I can't keep my eyes open." Reanell is a godsend. She called and I filled her in on everything, and without saying another word, I heard her car start to head to my house. It's a sisterhood, being a military spouse. Even though Aaron wasn't active anymore, we're still family. When one needs us, we're there, especially in the special ops community.

"Any time, my friend. Now go get some beauty sleep."

I kiss her cheek and head to bed. Once I'm stripped down to my shorts and tank, I lie on my back and stare at the ceiling.

Rolling over, I grab Aaron's letter and read it again. His words give me hope for the future and yet at the same time break me further apart. All I wanted was a life with him. I read about how he felt when we met. If only he knew. "You didn't have to work so hard to get me," I say aloud, relying on my faith that he can hear me. "I loved you from the moment I met you. I was yours before you even spoke a word. God, you were so handsome," I sigh and close my eyes.

"I remember the first time I saw you . . . you had that stupid hat on backwards and were wearing your football jersey. You nodded your head to me like I should fawn at your feet. Idiot," I laugh softly. He was so cocky and full of himself. There was no way I was going to let him know how much I already wanted him. "Now I'm here without you." Tears stream down my face. He's gone and I'm in pain.

"Why, Aaron?" I roll and face where he would be if he were in our bed. My hand grazes his pillow and another tear falls. "You say to move on, but how? You didn't tell me how to do that. I can't love anyone else. I don't know how. You were my first love, my only love, the first man in my heart and in my body. Hell, you are my heart and I don't know how to let go of that. If I let someone else in, then I'll lose you forever." I continue to speak to myself, praying for an answer, because I don't know how to give him up. "You have to show me, or give me a sign." I clutch his pillow and sob relentlessly until I fall asleep, wishing I were in his arms. Safe and happy in the arms of my husband.

chapter twelve

"HER FOOD IS labeled and I wrote down all the times she needs to eat," I instruct the nanny I hired. She's a friend of Reanell's and came highly recommended.

"We'll be just fine." Paige bounces Aarabelle on her lap as she giggles.

"Okay, I'm sure I'll call only around a hundred times."

Paige smiles reassuringly. "I expect no less. First days are scary, but Aarabelle and I have a busy day of fun planned."

I secretly love that she's paying more attention to Aarabelle than me and my neurotic-ness. First day of working at Cole Security and I no longer think this is a good idea. Leaving Aarabelle and then stepping foot into the building where Aaron worked is daunting. I thought maybe I could feel closer to him, now I'm not so sure if this is the right move.

"I'll have my phone on me and the number to the office is on the paper by the fridge." I'm clearly stalling. I don't know how to spend the entire day away from Aarabelle.

Paige brings Aara over to me. "It'll be fine. If we need you, I'll call. I promise."

Nodding and drawing a deep breath, I kiss my daughter and turn to head to work.

I can do this.

Once I reach my car, I notice the note and flower on the windshield. I open the note and my lip turns up.

Hey Lee,

Sorry I've been MIA but I'm back at work and my schedule is jacked up. Have a good first day. Be sure to give the guys hell.

Liam

Sitting in the car, I try to wipe the smile off my face but I can't help it. It's the sweetest, most thoughtful thing anyone's done for me in months.

Starting the car, the phone connects to the bluetooth and I decide to call him.

"Hey," he answers on the first ring.

"Hi," I say, still smiling. "I got your card and flower. Thank you."

"I was jogging and wanted to let you know I didn't forget about you. I've been busy getting checked in and caught up to speed." Liam's voice is thick and restrained. There's a part of me that doesn't fully believe him.

"Right. No, it's fine. I've been busy too," I lie.

Liam chuckles, "I got a call on Aaron's quad if you're still wanting to sell it."

Another part of Aaron that I'll lose. "Sure."

"Lee?" Liam utters my name reluctantly.

"Yeah?"

He pauses and clears his throat. "How's Aara?"

That wasn't what I was expecting based on the tone of his voice. Not that I had any idea what he was going to say, but Aarabelle isn't a touchy subject. "Good, she's with the nanny and I'm freaking out," I laugh. "I'm sure she'll be fine but it's the first time I'm leaving her." I turn into the parking lot of Cole Security Forces and nerves begin to stir.

It's Mark and Jackson, but still. I'm worried that being in there will make his loss even more prominent . . . not that it can be any more apparent. He's dead. I'm alone and a single mother.

"You okay?" Liam asks, and I realize I've been silent.

With my eyes closed, I shake my head. Am I okay? I don't remember the last time I felt okay. "I'm fine."

You can almost feel the disapproval over the phone. He hates that word, but it's my crutch. "I figured. How about I bring a pizza over tonight? We can go over some of the papers for the sale of his car and now the quad."

"Sounds good."

"Good, see you around seven."

"Seven it is." This is awkward. I feel like there's something neither of us is saying but neither of us knows how to proceed. "Okay, I gotta get in to work."

There's some rustling in the background and Liam's hand covers the phone, "I'll see you later. Good luck today."

"Thanks, see you later," I reply and hang up the phone.

I'm going to need a lot of luck.

Exiting the car, my nerves flare again. These men have been a part of my life for years, yet it's as if I'm just meeting them. Things have changed over the course of seven months. Jackson and Mark still call and check on me, but our friendships have changed. Hell, I've changed. Mark came around a lot in the beginning, but as life happens, he's moved on or pulled away. Liam, however, has stayed constant.

Here goes nothing.

"Lee!" Mark exclaims and comes walking over. "I saw you pull in and I was coming out to get you. Thought maybe you didn't know where the door was." He angles in and drops his voice, "It'll be okay."

I nod and press my lips together. "I've missed you

guys."

"There are some papers in the conference room we need you to fill out and then I'll show you your office and go over what we need done, sound good?"

I look at my friend, the man who carried my husband for a mile when he was hurt on a mission, the one who is my daughter's godfather and also the man who destroyed my world, and see his hurt. The pain in his eyes is prevalent because it mirrors mine. As hard as this is for me, this can't be easy on them either. Mark, Jackson, and the rest of the men here were his friends. Seeing me is probably difficult for them as well.

My hand grips his arm. "I'm happy to see you."

Mark in his true fashion smirks, "I'm not a bad view, eh, Lee?"

These guys are all the same. Morons. "Sure, you're the most handsome man I've seen in weeks . . . well, besides my mailman. He's pretty dreamy."

"I think I could take him."

"Pretty sure that's a federal offense."

"He can't touch these guns," he retorts and flexes.

I roll my eyes and snort, "Oh, dear God."

I laugh as we walk to the conference room and I notice the stares, but I pretend not to.

Mark notices my unease, "I know this is going to be awkward, but give it a few days and you'll be one of the guys."

"Do I really want that?"

"I can make up a cute name for you . . . let's see," he sits in the chair and looks deep in thought.

"I'm worried you'll burn what little brain cells you have left if you keep thinking that hard," I taunt him. Being around Mark is like being around a puppy. He naturally brings out the fun and playful side. And he's caring yet strong and has this undeniable pull that makes you want to be near him.

"Keep it up and your name will be something you don't like," his brow raises and his lip curls. "You know you don't get to pick. Call signs are given. They're a rite of passage and you get no say. I mean, you think I wanted to be called Twilight?"

Leaning in my chair, I tap the pen. "I don't know, I mean, you look like you could have a thing for vampires."

He laughs and I follow. "Fill out the paperwork and then I'll be back." He walks over and places his hand on my shoulder. "I'm glad you're here. We need the help with Muffin gone."

My hand rests on his. "I know it's hard having them both gone." In a matter of a few months, Mark lost his two best friends in a manner of speaking. Aaron and he were extremely close. They spent weekends rebuilding Aaron's car, barbeques on the beach, and then Jackson moved to California. I can't imagine it's been easy for him either.

"You know me," he replies and removes his hand. I look at the paper and I hear the door click closed. Aaron's death has rocked our worlds and none of us are acknowledging it.

Once I finish filling out what feels like three hundred forms, I head out to find Mark.

Not paying any attention, I open the door and hear a deep voice, "Hey."

I drop the papers and look up to see Jackson. My hand clutches my chest, "Hey, you scared the shit out of me." I give a nervous laugh.

Well, this is unexpected. Jackson called the other day to see how we were doing and make sure I was still planning to come to work for him. He towers over me with his six-foot-three frame. I'm not short by any means, but he makes me feel tiny. He crouches and picks up the papers.

"Sorry about that. Catherine says I do the same thing," he laughs and his eyes light up when he says her name.

"How's she doing?" I ask. I've spoken to her a few times since her move to California, but with the time difference, we seem to miss each other.

Jackson's joy is prevalent in his features. His eyes brighten, his lips lift, and my heart cracks. I remember being that in love. "Great, we're great."

I laugh to cover the pain that's building. "I didn't ask about you," nudging him, I say playfully.

"Yeah, yeah. Everyone cares about her and couldn't care less about me," he winks. "How are you doing?" he asks, wrapping his arm around my shoulder and pulling me in. He's carried immense guilt for all that's happened and offered me a job any time I wanted to work. The flexibility and ability to make my own hours was more than appealing. As a journalist, I had to go when the story came. There would've been way too many nights I wouldn't be able to put Aarabelle to sleep.

I let out a slow breath as he releases me. "I'm living. Liam's been around taking care of things around the house. He's helped a lot with the stupid, mundane stuff."

"Dempsey's a good guy. I spoke with him last week."

"Oh," I reply, a little surprised. I didn't know they were friends like that.

Jackson chuckles at my response. "I have to check on you somehow since you won't answer my calls."

"I answer!" I exclaim defensively. "Well, sometimes . . ." I trail off.

"It's okay. I know you're busy and Demps says you lie anyway," he gives me a knowing look. Jackson is good at reading people. They all are. Sometimes being friends with all SEALs isn't all that great. Sure, I'm always safe and protected, but it's impossible to hide anything. Aaron being gone for a while has made me a little lost as to how to act. I drew my strength from him, now I have to rely on my own. Which I think I've done a pretty good job at.

"I don't lie . . . I'm just tired of saying the same thing over and over."

"Yeah, I remember that feeling," Jackson replies.

Oh, how could I forget? Jackson knows better than anyone else. He's been exactly where I am when his wife died. I'm an idiot and insensitive. "Jackson," I place my hand on his arm, "I can't believe I've been so stupid."

He gives a short laugh and guides me into his office. "Sit," he says with authority, but still gentle.

It always amazes me how Jackson can be so hard because he has the biggest heart of anyone I know. He'd literally cut off his arm so someone else didn't have to be in pain. Aaron always admired him and said it was an honor to serve with him. I think he'd be proud that I've come to work for Jackson, even if he died because of the job he was doing for him.

Jackson sits across from me, "I'm not one to talk about Maddie and all that happened. I've been better since Catherine, but it's still something I work through. I know you say you're fine, and that's okay, but you don't have to be fine with me. Or Liam," he gives me a pointed look.

"I don't know what everyone expects, you know?" I ask. "I mean, do people expect me to be doing cartwheels down the halls? In love already? Married? Or would they prefer me drunk so I don't have to feel?"

He huffs, "No, they don't expect that. They don't know what to expect either. I refused to date after her death. I never wanted to have a fucking woman near me."

I smile, because I know where he's going.

"Yeah, yeah. Don't even say it." Jackson's grin grows again.

"You're cute in love," I lean back and smirk.

He crosses his arms and mimics my stance, "I'm always cute, but that's not the point."

I roll my eyes at his arrogance. They all need therapy. "Between you and Mark, I don't know how anyone can get any work done."

"Why?" he asks, confused where I'm going.

"Well, I mean you're both *sooo* good-looking. I'm sure everyone just stares all day," I reply sarcastically.

Jackson's laugh echoes in the room. "You'll get used to it," he winks.

"Cat deserves a medal for putting up with you. One day she'll see the truth."

"I'll marry her before that happens. I just need to convince her that I'm worth being around forever." Jackson is always honest. It's the one thing we can count on.

"How are you guys doing?" I think Catherine is good for him. She keeps him on his toes and he complements her.

"Good, she's doing her thing and I'm happy to be back in California. I'm close enough to San Diego, which worked out well. Anyway, enough about me . . . we were talking about you."

"Let's not."

Jackson puts his hands up in surrender. "I'm just saying you have to do whatever you need to in order to survive, but after a while, surviving isn't enough. Catherine showed me that. I could've been in a much better place if I hadn't lived in limbo for two years."

There's not much I can say. I know he means well, and I know he genuinely understands how I'm feeling. Even I don't understand what the hell I'm feeling or why, but still. "Thanks, Jackson."

"Enough heavy shit. How's my beautiful goddaughter?"

The smile at the thought of Aarabelle is automatic. I love that little girl more than my own life. "Thankfully, after the medicine knocked out the infection, she's been good. You should come see her."

He laughs, "I was coming whether you offered or not. I had Mark get your office put together last week. I meant what I said about being flexible . . . if you need to work from home because she's sick or whatever the case, you can do that. We want you to be happy here and if you need something, feel free to drive Mark absolutely insane until you get it."

"I'll be sure to do that just for fun."

Jackson stands and extends his arm forward. He escorts me to my office.

We enter and I stop short. It's bigger than his office. I would think this is a conference room. "Wow, Jackson, what the hell?" I question him. "This office is huge. Mark, who's basically running things from here, is in a cubicle. This is nuts." I'm blown away and it's completely unexpected. I'm a receptionist. I won't go on missions or do anything but file some paperwork and get their ridiculous filing system in order. Honestly, it's highway robbery for what he's offered as a salary.

"You may have to bring her here once in a while. We all agreed you'd need something bigger," Jackson states without batting an eye. "I left some things on your desk if you want to get started. Shoot me an email when you're ready to leave."

"Ummm, sure." I stand gaping at this room. It's crazy and completely overboard. I should've expected it though since Jackson Cole does nothing half-assed.

Time to get to work.

chapter thirteen

"HELLO?" I HEAR Liam's raspy voice call out.
"In the kitchen!"

Aarabelle sits in her highchair as I feed her dinner. She's growing so fast. Already she's eating cereal and a little baby food. Soon she'll be crawling and I have no one to celebrate with. Her father will never see these milestones and it breaks me apart.

"You should really lock the door," Liam huffs as he throws his coat over the chair.

"But then I'd have to get up to let you in," I state matter-of-factly and go back to feeding the baby, trying to put aside my worries. The fact is . . . this is reality. I have to deal with it.

"Uh huh. Hey, Pumpkin," his eyes alight as he crouches down by Aara. It's adorable hearing grown men use a baby voice. It gets a little softer and higher pitched.

The corners of her mouth lift and she throws her arms in the air when he gets close. My heart sputters seeing how happy she gets seeing him. Liam kisses her head and she giggles.

"At least someone is happy to see me," he says playfully.

"I'd be happy if you brought me a present," I joke.

He laughs and goes into the pocket of his coat. "Just so happens I did, but since that's the only way you'll be nice, I'll hold on to this until you've earned it."

Practically leaping out of my chair, I rush over. "What is it?" I try to peer around his back as he holds the mystery item.

Liam's lips curl as he sees how much I want this. I don't even know what it is. Jeez, I'm an idiot. "Nope. We eat first, then maybe you'll get it."

"Watch, it's a freaking Pez dispenser or something stupid."

"Guess you'll have to be nice to find out." He shoves the item into his back pocket and I fight the urge to reach and get it. "How was work?"

We spend the next thirty minutes going over my day and Jackson's return. Liam never mentioned that they spoke, but he's surprised to hear he's in Virginia. After we finish the pizza, Liam somehow convinces me we should watch a movie. I get Aarabelle to bed and come down to find him sprawled out on the couch.

"By all means, make yourself comfortable."

Liam pulls his beanie higher on his forehead and his eyes glimmer with amusement. He sits up and puts the TV on. "I picked the movie."

"What?" I ask with mock incredulity. "It's my house. Why do you get to pick the movie?"

"Ummm, I'm the guest." He shrugs as if this should be an obvious answer.

I groan and lean back. "What crappy, shoot-'em-up movie do I have to endure?"

"You'll see. It's a classic." Liam wraps his arm around me and pulls me to his side.

I cuddle into his chest without thinking. After practically sleeping on top of him in the hospital, I have no qualms about cuddling. I miss cuddling and if he's one of the rare men who enjoy it, I'm good with that. The selfish part of me likes him touching me. Yet I don't want to like it. It's wrong to enjoy another man's arms around me so soon.

The movie begins and I want to tear my eyes out. "No!" I yell and sit up. "No. No, no, no. I'm not watching this horrible crap," shaking my head vehemently, reaching for the remote.

"'Friday After Next' is Oscar-worthy." Liam snatches the remote and tucks it in his pants.

"Are you serious? Did you just shove my remote in your pants?"

Liam sits there daring me to go get it. Infuriating man.

"Now, are you ready to watch the best movie ever?"

"I hate you."

"I can live with that." He pulls me back down and I seriously contemplate getting the remote. "One day you'll realize how much you love me."

"Doubtful."

Maybe he'll enjoy when he has to watch 'Pitch Perfect' on our next date. Date? Wait. I called this a date. This is just two friends snuggling and watching movies after dinner. Oh my God. Between the hospital, him calling, taking care of me, and all of the other things, it starts to click. No. He's my friend and he doesn't feel that way.

I don't feel that way.

I mean, sure he's good-looking, but he's off limits. He's Liam. The best man in our wedding. The man who helped move Aaron and I into our first home. Lines can't be blurred. My body tenses and Liam notices.

"If you really hate this, we don't have to watch," he offers.

I look into his blue eyes and fear flutters in my stomach.

"No, I'm fine. Let's watch."

"Now, come get comfortable so I can school you on the top flight security of the world," he says in his best movie imitation.

"Can I have my present?" I ask.

Liam reaches in his back pocket and pulls out a pack of gum. I give him my best resting bitch face and he laughs. "I never said what it was."

"You really know how to woo a girl."

"You'll know when I'm actually trying, babe."

He pulls me against his side and starts the movie. I pray he doesn't sense the change in me. The tension rolls off me, but I try to relax and enjoy tonight.

CHAPTER FOURTEEN

LIAM

SHE FITS INTO my side like she was meant to be here. I should've left. Hell, I never should've come over, but I wanted to see Aarabelle. Well, that's the bullshit I keep telling myself. The truth is I missed Natalie.

And that makes me a douchebag.

"This movie is so dumb," she mutters next to me.

Some women should get a handbook on movies men will never hate. This would be one. "Top Gun" would be another. That movie has hot chicks and bad ass Navy shit. "It would be a lot better if you weren't complaining," I reply, thankful for the distraction.

"Asshole," she mumbles under her breath, but then wraps her arm around my stomach.

I want to give a smartass comeback, but I don't want her to move. The feel of her body against mine makes me want more. It's wrong on so many levels. I'm breaking the ultimate man-code, but I can't stop myself. I can only hope that Aaron would want her to be with someone like me. The fuck if I know why I'm even thinking about any of this . . . she doesn't want me. She wants her husband, and I'm just her asshole friend who won't go away.

Natalie's arm rubs against my stomach and I try to stop the hard-on forming.

Nuns.
Spiders.
Justin Bieber.
Grandma.

I shudder from that last one, but thankfully that did it.

I would never be able to explain my dick getting hard from this freaking movie. She'd know for sure what's up. Her fucking hand being that close to my junk causes me to have to breathe through the list again. I need to focus and stop thinking.

The movie plays on and she begins laughing at it instead of letting me know how stupid everything is.

"See, I told you. Comedic gold." I lean back a little more and smirk at her.

She looks at me and then looks away quickly. I saw it though, the way she stared at my lips a little longer than a beat.

Natalie shakes her head and when she looks back at me, she has her mask firmly in place. "When I force you to watch 'Pitch Perfect' or 'The Notebook,' we'll see how you feel about cinematic gold."

"You'll have to tie me down and gag me to make that shit happen, sweetheart. The only chick movie I'll ever watch is 'Lethal Weapon,'" I reply smugly.

"First of all, 'Lethal Weapon' is not a chick flick." She stays put, but I feel her stir. Natalie is easy to wind up. When she gets heated, I see a piece of her old self coming back. Not this fake happy bullshit.

"I have to disagree." My hand falls and rests on her back.

"You would."

"You just fail to see the epic romance."

Natalie scoffs, "You're an idiot. There's no romance at all! It's two cops trying to not get fired."

I laugh and pull her close, "Mel Gibson is trying to

get what's-her-face to be with him."

"That's a subplot. It's not even the basis of the movie."

"Total chick flick. I win." I grin knowing that I have absolutely no argument. It was just the first movie I thought of and I'm totally grasping at straws.

She lets out a deep sigh. "I give up. You can't fix stupid."

I'll let her slide on that one—this time.

My fingers start to rub her back as we both quiet down and return to watching the movie. I don't even notice I'm doing it until I feel her tense. Her breathing stops and she sits up. Which further proves my point about her not wanting me.

"Want something to drink or maybe popcorn?" she asks.

The way she tucks her hair behind her ear, her eyes looking at the floor, and her perfect lip in her teeth shows me everything. She needs to get away and gain some distance.

"Popcorn would be great."

I need some distance myself.

chapter fifteen

natalie

"WHAT THE HELL is wrong with me?" I say out loud while grabbing the popcorn in the kitchen. I just got all stupid over nothing. There's this *thing* happening to me. I don't understand it. The pull between us grows stronger and as much as I want to fight it, I feel helpless. I want to be around him. I want him to come over and be here, but then I don't, and honestly the only reason is that I'm scared.

Scared of having feelings for another man, and a man exactly like my husband. One who will lay down his life for another. It's the same fate I'm living now, and I don't know that I could endure this again. I definitely don't want my daughter to ever know the hurt of losing yet another man in her life. Only this time, it would be so much worse. She would actually *know* Liam. So I have to stop this—whatever it is.

I head back out into the living room with the bowl and sit next to Liam. His stance is ridiculously rigid as my obvious diversion must not have gone unnoticed. "Want some?" I ask, handing him the bowl.

He laughs and digs his hand in, tossing a few kernels

at me. "Smooth, Lee." Liam chuckles and I laugh despite my embarrassment. "Come here, let's finish our movie."

Taking a grounding breath, I lean back into him.

The movie drags on forever. I will never understand how I got stuck watching this. This was one of Aaron's favorite movies too. He and Mark would recite lines to each other any time they could. I miss the little things. A tear pricks and confliction overtakes me once again.

I settle in and try to let my mind stop turning. It's crazy how easy and domestic this moment is. Lying in Liam's arms, watching television after working all day. How we had dinner, put Aarabelle to bed, and now we're just spending time together. It's only felt weird because I've made it weird. It's felt . . . right. I could do this every day and be content.

I shouldn't want this.

But I do.

I shouldn't be comfortable in his arms.

But I am.

I should make him leave and put some distance between us.

But I can't.

I hear the line Aaron used to recite from the movie, *"Hold up, wait a minute, let me put some pimpin' in it."*

I burst out laughing and so does Liam. I look at him as I remember. I remember how he used to sound, how his face was after he'd say it. The way his eyes crinkled and he'd smile when I'd roll my eyes. I remember it all and I start crying. Not tears from laughing, but full out tears. It hurts to remember. The pain crashes over me like waves on the shore. They roll in one after the other and each one breaks my heart a little more. I want the pain to stop.

Liam's eyes go wide when he realizes I'm not laughing. He immediately takes me into his arms and holds me close. "Lee? What's wrong?" The panic is clear in his voice.

"Oh my God!" I cry louder and it doesn't stop. "I can't," I say in between breaths. Holy shit, I'm falling apart. "I can't breathe."

Guilt assaults me for thinking of a life with Liam while I'm still so fresh to this new life, making it hard to breathe.

Liam holds my face in his hands and wipes my tears with his thumbs. "Why are you crying? What happened?" he asks confused.

I keep crying as he stares at me like I'm a wounded animal. Which is exactly what I must look like.

He shuts the movie off and the tears continue to fall. "I can't," I say and he grips my face again.

"Tell me what to do. I don't know why you're crying," Liam's voice trembles and he's looking around frantically for . . . *something,* anything that would help. "Natalie, calm down."

"I don't know. I just . . . it hurts. I don't want to hurt anymore!" I exclaim as my breathing becomes more labored. I'm having a fucking panic attack. "Make it stop hurting," I beg.

Liam's eyes drop and he pulls my face to his slowly. He looks at me as his mouth gets closer and I snap out of whatever the hell that was. "Liam!" I say and pull back. "What are you doing?"

He leans back and grips his neck. "You were crying and I just . . ." he says quickly. "I don't know. I mean, tears and girls . . ." Liam rambles and gets up. He stands there and wipes his hand down his face. "Guys don't know what to do with tears!" he says, frustrated.

I smother my enjoyment at the situation. I really do, but he looks ridiculous and endearing.

"Lee, I'm sorry. You were begging me to make it stop." He starts to pace and speaks fast. "I mean, Jesus."

"Yeah, but why did you think you should kiss me?" I

ask, trying to not smile again. But right now, he's adorable. He's flustered and out of his element. I stand and put my hand on his arm to stop him from pacing.

"I don't know. I mean, what the hell? You were crying. Like full blown tears! I'm a guy. We don't do tears." He throws his hands up and starts to mumble to himself about women. "Fucking tears. I mean, I just thought . . . if I kissed you then you'd stop fucking crying."

I burst out laughing again and grip his face. "You're so dumb," I laugh and he relaxes. "Next time a girl is crying, just hold her."

"Don't cry anymore. Ever. I'm not equipped to deal with that shit."

"I can't promise that," I look into his eyes.

Liam's arms wrap around my back and the urge to kiss him rises. "I hated seeing it," he murmurs.

"What?"

"Watching you cry. I've never felt so helpless." Liam shakes his head and then looks down. "I'm sorry I tried to kiss you."

I pull his face back to me.

"Liam, I . . . it . . ." I want to see. I want to kiss him and ease his embarrassment, but more than that I want to kiss *him*. I may hate myself later, but I'm not sure about anything right now. Liam makes me feel safe. Aaron is gone. I look into his eyes, and battling the need to feel this man, to feel desired, to be kissed by him becomes insurmountable.

Slowly, I lean in. His eyes watch mine as I pull his head closer and he lets me. He allows me to lead this and I see the desire build behind his eyes. I watch the storm pass across his face as he processes, and I measure what I'm doing.

"Natalie . . ." he says low and reverent.

The way my name rolls from his lips makes me want him more. We breathe in each other's breaths. Taking and giving this moment, my stomach tightens as I press my lips to his. I don't think. I try not to focus on the differences. The way his lips are firm but yielding. The way he doesn't move and every part of him is stiff. I don't allow myself to compare the differences in height. How I have to lift up on my toes to reach him. My fingers glide to the back of his head and thread in his hair. I want him to kiss me, but right now he stands like a statue. Tilting my head, I try to get him to respond, but the only thing I feel are his hands tightening against my back as he grips my shirt. I break away and we both open our eyes.

Whatever he's looking for in my eyes, he finds, and Liam's resolve cracks. His hand moves to my upper back as his mouth is on mine. This kiss is his. This kiss isn't asking—it's taking. His lips press against mine, firm and strong. I sigh unconsciously and he takes that as permission. I feel his tongue brush against mine and the muscles in my stomach clench. Liam holds me against him and holds me together. I lose myself in his touch. Even in this moment, he gives to me. He pulls me closer and my fingers tangle in his hair and grip. I don't want to stop.

I want him.
I want this.
I need this.
I hate this.
Conflict stirs suddenly as realization dawns on me.
I'm kissing Liam Dempsey and I like it.

chapter sixteen

MY FINGERS LOOSEN and then his grip does. Liam releases me and we both try to catch our breath. I look at him and his eyes drift to the mantel. He stares at the flag and my insides hurt.

"Natalie," he grumbles in a low tone. He's upset. "I . . . fuck . . . I just . . ."

"Please, don't," I request hoping he won't say this was a mistake or that he's sorry. I hate the word "sorry" and I sure as hell don't want to hear it from his mouth. I'm tired of people apologizing. You're not sorry. You don't know what to say and I'm over hearing it.

"No, listen," his hand grips my arm as I try to turn. "Fucking listen. I don't know what this is. I mean, you're . . . well . . . you!" he exclaims and drops his hand. "We've been friends for a long time and you've always been his wife. I don't know if I'm making any sense."

This whole situation is confusing. There's a part of me—a big part—that's weighted and suffocating in guilt. I feel in some small way as if I cheated on my husband. I know I didn't. I know that he's gone, and hell, he wanted me to move on, but it's there. Deep in my gut, I'm tormented that this was wrong. Then there's the other side of me—the woman side—that wanted and needed to be touched. I enjoyed the way his lips felt against mine. The way Liam took me in his arms and the way my body molded to his. It was everything I needed and nothing I wanted to need. But I initiated it. I went to him and I would do it again.

"I'm not sure what to say," I reply honestly. "I wanted to kiss you. I wanted to not want to kiss you," I give a half laugh.

Liam steps forward and pulls me against him. "I wanted to not want to want you, but I do. I don't know how or when, but I have these feelings for you. I don't know if we should do this. I don't know that either of us is ready for this," Liam says quietly as we hold each other.

"I don't either. Maybe we should take all of this one day at a time. I don't know that I'm ready." I look at him as he gazes into my eyes. "I know I don't want you to stop coming around, but I don't know what I'm capable of. I mean, it's not even been a year and I just . . ." Tears pool in my eyes as I try to process what happened. I kissed my friend. I kissed Aaron's friend, and I'm not sure if it's wrong.

"You're not getting rid of me. And I don't want to push you. But I want to kiss you again. Unless you want me to stop?" He waits and my breathing increases.

The anticipation builds inside. It roils and grows, taking up every inch of my soul. I want this. I measure the parts of myself, trying to see whether it's guilt scraping its way through me or whether it's desire. The desire pools and smothers any guilt. My heart wants this and so does my body. I inhale and close my eyes, taking in each note of spice and sandalwood. The feel of strong arms wrapped around me. I shiver even though there's not one part of me that's cold.

"Do you want me to stop, Lee?" Liam's voice is husky and laced with want.

Liam's hands make their way up my spine and then back down around my hips. He lifts me off the ground and his breath warms my face. I can feel him grow closer and closer. "Now's the time, sweetheart," he says, practically touching my lips.

"No," I breathe the word.

"No, you don't want me to stop, or no, you do?" he asks, his nose brushing against mine. His lips are a millimeter from mine and one nudge and we'd be touching.

"No, I just . . ."

He pulls back the slightest bit. "Just what? What do you want?"

What do I want? I want it all. I want to not hurt anymore, and when I'm around Liam, it's not so hard. He makes me smile and laugh when I feel like I'm drowning in sorrow. But the best part of him is that he doesn't even realize he's doing it. It just happens when he's around.

"Kiss me."

He presses his lips to mine softly. There's no rush, no urgency, he kisses me like I'm delicate and breakable. Liam cherishes me as he holds me in his arms and gives a piece of himself to me. I'm open and vulnerable and this kiss shows me he knows that. He's not pushing me. He's giving me strength and understanding.

All too soon he pulls back and presses his forehead against mine. We stand embraced and his hand rubs my back. "I'm going to get going. You have to work tomorrow."

"Okay," I say and keep my eyes closed while he holds me. "Maybe you can come over again this week?" I ask awkwardly. I mean, I don't know how all this works. Do I invite him over or does he keep showing up like he has the last month and a half?

He pulls me close again and chuckles. "How about we go out on Friday night?"

I look at him and my heart rate picks up. I'm not sure I'm ready to go out.

"Lee, we don't have to go on a date. I just meant

maybe we can go out with friends as friends."

Liam's hands drop and I let out a deep breath. "I don't know if I can leave Aarabelle."

"Think about it. We can all go and celebrate you going back to work. Mark and Jackson are here, you said. I'm sure everyone would love to go out."

I nod and wring my hands. "I'll think about it."

"Okay, I'll call you soon," Liam says as he grabs his stuff.

"Okay," I mutter. This all of a sudden has become weird.

He walks to the door and pauses with his hand on the door. Slowly, Liam turns and his eyes glimmer with sincerity. "No matter what, I want you to know that your friendship means everything. I'll always be here for you and we never have to mention tonight again if you don't want to. We can pretend nothing ever happened. I want you to be happy, and if you needed to kiss me because you needed something, I won't be upset."

"Liam, I . . ."

His hand lifts to stop me and he gives a reassuring smile, "I'll let you use me if you need that. I don't know when things changed for either of us, but whatever you need—tell me. If you want to forget tonight, if you want to be friends, or if you want to see whatever this is—I'm here. I'll let you lead for now."

Before I can respond, Liam turns the doorknob and walks out. I walk to the door and place my hand on it and close my eyes.

Now I need to figure out how to lead a dance I don't know the steps to.

I head up the stairs and look at the pictures that line the walls. My wedding photo, our first date, and my maternity shoot all stare at me as I take each step. My lips tingle from our kiss and my mind reels. I kissed another man, and not just any man, but someone who was there for most of these memories.

How could I do this? Can I do this? I pause at the top of the step where Aaron's photo hangs in a dark frame. It has his shadow box with all his medals and ribbons under it. My hand touches the cool glass and a tear falls. Here I stand staring at the man I loved while my mouth still tastes of Liam.

I grab the photo of Aaron off the wall and lie in my bed with my husband in my arms and fall asleep wishing this guilt would stop.

"SPARKLES, CAN YOU bring in the new contract that was faxed over a few minutes ago and head into Jackson's office?" Mark pauses at my office door and then rushes away.

I grab the papers and head over to his office. It's been two weeks since I've been working here and so far it's been great. They realized quickly I was definitely overqualified and I'm now handling all the scheduling and mission preparation.

"Hey," I say as I walk in. Jackson and Mark are laughing at God knows what.

"Hey, come in," Jackson instructs and he slaps Mark. "I need to see how many guys we have open to send if we get the Africa mission."

I nod and hand over the papers I brought with me. The way Jackson was able to start this company and handle complex missions is seriously impressive. They've been getting more requests and aren't able to fulfill them all due to staffing. Apparently Aaron handled recruiting and they've not filled his position.

"I think you guys need to do a recruiting session or something. There have been a lot of inquiries and you're turning clients away," I suggest and they both glance at me with a pensive look.

"Lee," Jackson says with caution. "I know you just started, and let's face it, you're doing way more than what we hired you for. I need someone who's smart, who can read these guys, and get some new blood in here. I'll turn away business before I'll send anyone unprepared or understaffed."

"Are you offering me another promotion?" This is by far the fastest anyone has ever moved up in a company.

Jackson nods and Mark laughs. "I'm sure you're bored out of your fucking mind answering a phone that rings once every hour. Besides, dickface leaves in a few days and I need someone with a brain."

I look out into the office where there are others who've been here for a long time. They bust their asses and have been dedicated to the company far longer than me. "What about the others?"

Mark glances over, and for the first time, looks serious. "There's a lot you don't know regarding what they do. They aren't administrative."

"Okay," I say confused, but I let it drop. "What all does this entail? I mean, I have Aarabelle and I didn't even want to come back to work."

Jackson stands and heads over to the wall of pictures. "I would never let this take away from Aara. Mark and I will make sure of that. You just have to be honest with us and let us know." He rubs his hand down his face. "If you take it, there are going to be some background and clearance things I'll need you to do."

Mark kicks his feet up on Jackson's desk and gives a taunting look. "Don't make Muffin suffer too long. He's already starting to go grey."

"Fuck off."

"Do I get to referee you two?" I ask and slap Mark's leg.

Mark laughs and drops his legs. "I always win."

Jackson scoffs and walks behind us, slapping Mark in the back of the head. I swear these two are like children. It's some kind of genetic tic they all have.

"Okay, if you think I'm the right person, Jackson, I'll do whatever you need."

Both of their demeanors shift slightly. I can feel the tension from both of them. "Lee," Jackson says drawing my attention to him, "You'll have access to a lot of information and files. Things that are locked on your computer now because of your clearance. When we do this, you'll no longer be locked out."

"Ummm, okay?"

"I don't have any doubts you'll get the clearance, so I want to tell you about one."

Mark puts his hand on my shoulder, "It's about Aaron."

chapter seventeen

"WHAT ABOUT AARON?" I ask hesitantly. What could they possibly have in a file that I don't know about? It was an IED . . . there's not much else to have in a secret file.

Jackson sits on the edge of his desk and the serious look in his eyes scares me. "We've been investigating the attack on his vehicle. I think it was targeted."

"Targeted how? I mean, who would target him?"

He grips the bridge of his nose and exhales. "Not him. I think they wanted to attack me. I don't know. At this point, we don't have much info, but there's a file and I didn't want you to find out about it from someone or some other way."

"I don't understand," I say conflicted. I was told his death was just that—a death. It doesn't make any sense as to why they'd be looking into it.

"Natalie," Mark calls my attention to him. "No one kills a member of this team without us following up. There were issues with our supply drop. Aaron went out there to investigate and then he died. Then, we go out and Muff gets himself shot. It doesn't add up." The tone of his voice is commanding and yet still the Mark I know.

I should've known they weren't going to let this go, and honestly, I'm glad. These are good men, honorable men who won't let someone's life go without having answers. However, this isn't going to be easy for me. I've started to feel again, to live, and then this thing with Liam. Hell, I don't even know if it is a thing.

"I'm not sure what to say."

Jackson tilts forward, "I'm telling you that no member of this team gets killed and we just let it go lightly. Someone will pay for his death. Someone will pay for almost killing me. I didn't want you to be blindsided."

Every part of me wants to tell them to stop. To let it go because no matter what, it won't change a thing. The cruel hands of fate have already slapped me once. I really don't know if I can survive another round.

"Okay, I guess thanks for the heads up." I battle with myself if I should ask for more information. If there is a file, then there is something inside of it. I'm not sure I have the restraint not to look. "Jackson?" I ask hesitantly.

"You want to know?"

"Yes and no. I just need to know if there's anything in there I should know because I don't know how much I can handle," I respond honestly. My heart is pounding and my mouth goes dry as I wait.

Jackson and Mark look at each other and they both shift uncomfortably. Mark clears his throat, "All we know at this point is we think our company is being targeted. Also, we think they believed Jackson would be in that car."

My hand flies to my chest and I gasp. "Why?" I stutter. "Why would anyone want to target you?" The words fly out of my mouth and I stand. These are my friends. This was my husband and my family that were caught in the crossfire.

"We don't know, but we'll find out. This isn't something we're going to drop." Mark stands and pulls me into his arms. "He was one of us."

I nod and step back. This is a lot to process and I'm

not sure there is anything that will make this okay. Regardless, my husband was murdered, so finding out why, for me, is irrelevant. It won't bring him back.

"Okay, let's get to the meeting. I have a lot to think about and I want to be able to focus on work. I have to take tomorrow off to bring Aarabelle to the doctor for a follow-up." Her appointment is later in the day tomorrow, but I want to spend some time with her since I feel like I'm missing out being back at work. Plus, I don't want to talk about Aaron . . . not today.

We wrap up the rest of our meeting and go through some things that need to be done. I flop in my chair and spin so I'm looking out the window. What a clusterfuck this all is. My heart was starting to heal. I was finding a way to put one foot in front of the other without stumbling, but now I'm on shaky ground again.

My office phone rings, halting my inner turmoil.

"Hello, this is Natalie."

"Hello, Natalie," his gruff baritone voice causes my heart to falter.

"Hello, Liam," I say as my lips turn up on their own accord. I sink into my chair and twirl the chord. Jesus, just him saying hello has reduced me to a teenage girl.

"What are you doing?"

"Working," I reply sarcastically.

"Smart ass. I'm calling to ask you on a date."

Liam's been gone the last week. They had a training mission that required them to go to Florida. We haven't spoken much while he was gone other than a few quick text messages, but I feel better about what happened between us. Reanell and I spoke at great length and she helped me see everything clearly.

Liam cares or he wouldn't give me the space I need. He knows me after years of friendship, and also Aaron was his best friend. I don't think he's capable of tarnishing his memory. There's not a part of Liam that wants to take my love that I shared with Aaron away.

"You are? A date?" I grin and bite my lip as I toy with him a little.

He laughs, "I am. Are you available?"

"I don't have a babysitter. I kind of need a little more than a few hours' notice, but maybe tomorrow."

"Check your text messages," Liam instructs.

"Ummm, okay."

I grab my phone to check and sure enough, I have a text from Rea.

Hey, I've got Aarabelle tonight. Have fun. Have sex . . . or don't, but you know, you could.

"Well?" Liam asks already knowing the answer.

"Huh, well, what do you know? A friend is abducting my daughter."

"I'll pick you up at seven." Liam's confidence is thick through his voice. Part of me wants to slap him, the other part wants to plant my lips against his again. "Oh, Natalie?" he asks and his voice is low and gravelly.

"Hmmm?"

"Wear a dress," Liam says and then disconnects the call.

I shoot a quick text to Reanell.

It seems you've made a new friend.

It seems you've got yourself a boyfriend.

What are we, twelve? I don't even know if people call them boyfriends. I mean, we're not exclusive. Or maybe we are and I'm just stupid—which is possible. My palms start to sweat as I think about this. I'm not sure I'm ready to have a boyfriend.

No, we're friends. He's just taking me out.

Okay. Whatever you say. I'll grab Aarabelle from the sitter's on my way home. Have fun. Love you.

I love her so much. She's the closest thing I have to a sister. She was there holding my hand when I delivered Aarabelle, she slept in my bed for three days when I found out Aaron died. I don't know how I'd survive without her.

Love you more! I'll call you tonight.
Or don't. That could get awkward.

She's crazy if she thinks that's happening. Oh my God, what if that's what I'm supposed to do?

I need a drink.

CHAPTER EIGHTEEN

LIAM

"HAVE YOU LOST your fucking mind?" Quinn stands at my truck giving me shit about going out with Natalie tonight. "Natalie Gilcher? As in your best friend's *wife*?"

"Fuck off. It's not like you think."

He shakes his head and claps me on the shoulder. "You're going on a date with Aaron's wife. Let me know where I'm missing something. Because it seems crystal clear to me."

I shrug him off. He has no room to talk since he was screwing one of our buddy's wives, but apparently he has short-term memory loss. "Maybe we should talk to Bueno about missing something. You seemed to be awfully confused when you slipped your dick there."

"I was drunk." He steps back and shakes his head.

I'm not going to sit back and let him give me shit. I do that enough myself. I don't want to be that guy. The one who fucks his boy's wife. Shit, up until the last month, I never even looked at Natalie that way. It's not like I was chasing her skirt when he was alive. We're friends and it fucking happened.

"Whatever, man. I'm just saying don't give me shit. I'm not doing anything wrong. We're friends and I'm taking her out so she has a night away for once. It's been nine months since he died."

"Did you fuck her?"

I step forward and ball my fists. "Watch your fucking mouth." First of all, it's none of his damn business. Second of all, if that happens, I don't plan on telling him. "If and when we do . . . it sure as shit won't be fucking."

Some of the team guys are worse than a bunch of women. I'll have to listen to all their opinions and unsolicited advice. I don't want to hear how either they agree or don't. It's not up to them. As far as I know, I'll show up tonight and she'll tell me to fuck off—which is quite possible.

Quinn shakes his head. "Be careful, man. That's all I'm saying."

"I'm always careful."

"Yeah, well, this time you're playing with fire. It's not just some girl. It's *his* girl and *his* kid."

"I'm going to be kinda fucking obvious here, man. He's dead. I'm not doing anything to tarnish his memory or life. He was *my* best friend. I would've gladly been in that Humvee when it was hit. I would've traded places with him in a heartbeat. Natalie and I are friends and there's something there. So I'm not doing anything he would disapprove of," I explain and he nods.

"I know you're not like that, but I wouldn't want my wife to marry another SEAL."

"You'd have to find someone dumb enough to marry you first before you need to worry about that." I try to diffuse the situation. I get that Quinn thinks he's helping, but he doesn't see it. He only sees what he wants right now.

"This would be true. And I'd have to give up one-night stands. I'm good." He shakes my hand and laughs. "I'm going to the gym. I'll talk to you later."

"See you later."

Tonight is going to be the first time I've seen her since we kissed. I tried to give her the lead. Let her text me first. I swear I lost my dick and grew a pussy. I'm doing the damn three-day shit. Ridiculous. I want to slap myself or pull my own man card. But she's Natalie. She's got a kid and she's not some girl. I've known her forever. I was at her wedding for Chrissake. I can't just jump the gun and go all caveman on her. She needs to feel in control.

I get home, shower, and make sure everything is set. When I called Reanell to have her watch Aarabelle, she gave me "advice" on what to do tonight. Not that I had a brilliant plan, but apparently Reanell wasn't impressed at all. So, she provided me with the restaurant and where to take her after dinner.

Sixty seconds seem to take forever. The clock is broken because I swear it's not moving. Fuck it. I'm going over now. I'll annoy her until our reservation.

I grab my coat and head out the door.

The ten-minute drive gives me a chance to talk myself out of embarrassing myself. Even though we've been friends for years, this is definitely something else. I've seen her in dresses. I've seen her in a bikini. But this is different.

I park outside her house and open the glove box to grab the gift I got her and the letter from Aaron falls out. Fuck. I forgot about that.

Here I sit outside his house to pick up his wife for a date and I haven't even read what he wanted me to know. I'm a fucking douchebag. I stuff the letter in my console. Tonight, I want to be with her. I don't want his ghost haunting me and I already have enough guilt about this date.

I think about what Quinn said and how I'm stupid. Partially, I am. She's a widow, a single mom, and trying to put the pieces of her life back together, but there's something there. She draws me in and I don't even realize it's happening. She makes me want to be a better man.

I went from dreaming about guns to thinking of the way her blonde hair looks when she's tired and it falls in her eyes. The way Aarabelle looks when she's asleep and how much I want to have that at some point. I can't explain it. I don't know if there's even a way to put it into words. But she does something and here I sit trying to talk myself into doing something I'm not sure I should. If she'd never been Aaron's wife, I would've been at her door already. I would've had her in my bed, in my arms, and in my heart, but she comes with a warning sign. One I've chosen to ignore because I can't. I'm weak to her and I don't know why.

But I'm going to find out.

chapter nineteen

natalie

KNOCK, KNOCK, KNOCK.

The sound of the tap on the door causes the fear to stir like a snowstorm inside of me. The way your face grows cold and it hurts to breathe—which is crazy since it's summertime. I know it's not bad this time, but I'm still terrified.

It's a date.

With Liam.

I glance at my dress and press it down with my hands, smoothing the soft, satin fabric and at the same time trying to calm my nerves. I do a quick mirror check, fluff my hair, and pinch my cheeks. I wore my favorite red dress. I was worried after so long it wouldn't fit, but luckily it fits better than the last time I wore it. My breasts are fuller thanks to Aarabelle, and it clings to my curves perfectly. The soft, flowing curls hang to my mid back and I have my nude heels on. It's the first time in months I've taken any time to really look pretty. Usually I'm in sweats and a ponytail. Not much need for vanity around a baby.

"Here goes nothing," I say to myself before opening the door.

Liam stands there with his hand on the frame and my mouth goes dry. Holy shit. He's dressed in black dress pants and a dark blue shirt. His sleeves are rolled showing his forearms and the fabric clings to his muscles. *What is it about a man's forearms that are so damn sexy?* My eyes travel his body and absorb every part of him. It's not normal how good-looking he is. It's not fair. He makes it impossible for any woman to resist him. I make my way up to his face where the grin is painted. He watches me watch him, clearly enjoying himself.

I haven't really *looked* at a man like Liam. I don't usually pay attention, but with him . . . it's impossible not to. He's tall and steadfast, commanding and alluring. Every part of him screams danger, yet I see inside his heart. I see the man who cares for me and Aarabelle. The one who arranged an entire night out after not being able to see each other for a few weeks. I see the heart he wears on his sleeve with me. I want him to push me, but he knows somehow that I need to go to him.

I stand there admiring the insanely sexy man at my door as he stares at me. "Hi," his rich voice is low and seductive. One word and my heart begins to race.

"Hi," my voice cracks and I look down.

Liam steps forward and grips my chin. He pulls me so we're eye to eye. "You look breathtaking. I missed you."

"You did?" I ask already knowing he did. He sent me texts the entire time he was away letting me know he was thinking of me and Aara. That's the one thing with Liam—I can't help but let him chip at my walls. He cares for Aarabelle and loves her. When she was sick, he came running. Not out of some stupid obligation, but because he was concerned. You could see it in his eyes and it was another crack in my armor.

He laughs and steps closer so we're toe to toe. "I did. Did you miss me?" Liam's finger lightly travels down my arm, leaving goosebumps in its wake.

I shrug and reply playfully, "Eh, you know. I needed someone to hang a couple of new photos, so I guess I did..."

Liam's hand flies to his chest in mock horror. "I'm the handyman. I'm crushed."

I take a small step forward and wrap my arms around his torso and hold tight. "I missed you."

His strong, thick arms wrap around me and my body molds to his. "We're going to be late," he says and presses his lips to the top of my head.

I look into his blue eyes that glimmer in the moonlight. "Where are we going?"

"That's a surprise."

"Wow, you're really going for the kill."

"I don't know how many of these I may get, so I'm going to make it count." Liam's lip rises and he wraps his arm around my waist and guides me to the car.

"Keep this up and you may get a few more dates," I joke and nudge him.

"We'll see. I'm not the only one on probation," Liam simpers and I slap him in his chest.

"Yeah, okay. You wish, buddy."

He laughs and I follow as we walk arm in arm down the driveway.

"God, I love your car," I say aloud as I climb in. He has a 1968 Dodge Charger that he restored with his dad. It's candy apple red with tan interior. Every part of this car screams Liam. It's sexy, mysterious, loud, and yet it fits him in some odd way.

"You match," he muses as I settle into the seat. "Robin's been good to me. She never lets me down," he says as he grips the wheel. "We have an understanding."

"You named your car?"

"And this surprises you? She's my baby. You wouldn't not name your child, would you?" Liam asks completely serious.

"That's stupid."

"No, it's not."

I laugh and buckle my seatbelt, "Yeah, it totally is, and why a girl? Why not name the car after a guy?"

Liam smiles and backs out of the driveway. His hand glides over the dashboard as he speaks of his car. "Same reasons ships are named after women. Ships have personality and character. They protect us on the seas and bring us home. They mirror what is beautiful about every woman. Willful, strong, protective, and faithful, and Robin is no different."

"I think I've heard it all."

"Well, I could say it's because it's not the initial expense but the upkeep that will kill you." His mouth curves as I roll my eyes. "But that might be considered sexist."

"Might?" I retort.

I try to fight laughing or smiling. I try but fail.

"See, I can always make you smile."

"And at the same time make me want to punch you."

Liam chuckles and pulls into the parking lot at the Lynnhaven Fish House. Which is one of my absolute favorite restaurants in Virginia Beach. "It's a gift—at least that's what my mother says."

"She's biased."

"Natalie?" Liam asks slightly apprehensively. I look over and he sits with his hand on the door. "I'm glad you agreed to come out tonight."

Not that I had much of a choice, but of course I did. I could've told him no and gone home to Aarabelle. There were a hundred other things I could have chosen, but instead, I put on a dress and went blindly with him. "Me too."

"Stay here," Liam requests and exits the car quickly.

My lips widen in approval as he opens my car door a few seconds later. He extends his hand and I place my palm to his. I don't know that I've ever had a date be so chivalrous. No. I will not compare. I need to be here in the moment.

"Thank you," I say and kiss his cheek. "By the way, how did you know I love the Fish House?"

"Lucky guess," he says but I sense there's something more to that.

We enter the restaurant and are seated at the window overlooking the bay. It doesn't matter that my house backs up to this view, I'll never tire of it. The way each wave brings new water to the sand, washing away the footprints we leave and giving everything a new chance. It's ... hopeful.

Once we order and get our wine, Liam grabs my hand that's resting on the table. "You okay?"

"I'm great. Why?" I ask, perplexed.

"You've just been quiet." He looks out to the ocean and then back to me.

I smile tentatively and flip my hand over so we're palm to palm. "Is this weird for you? I mean, it's *us*."

Liam sighs and his finger whispers over the skin on my wrist. "Weird? No. Unexpected? Yes."

That's a good word to describe what all of this is. Neither of us thought we'd be sitting here on a date, yet that's exactly what we're doing. "It's a good unexpected though, right?"

"Natalie, I wouldn't want to be sitting here with anyone else," he answers and the truth shines through his eyes.

I want to reply *me either*. I want to say the words, but they die on my tongue. Aaron's face flashes in my mind and my stomach drops. The guilt begins to grow heavy and sits on my chest. It weighs on my heart and begins to crush it. I'm on a date with another man at the restaurant my husband took me to on our anniversary every year.

"Lee?" Liam asks as tears pool in my eyes. "What's wrong?"

"This . . . this place," I say and try to get myself under control.

"Did I fuck up?" he asks and comes around the table, crouching in front of me.

"No," I say and dab my eyes. "It's just . . . Aaron." I look away because I hate even saying this. "He . . ."

"He took you here?" Liam asks, not sounding upset, but concerned.

"Yeah," I look back at him as a tear falls. "I'm so sorry."

"You don't have to apologize. You don't have to pretend with me." Liam grabs my hand and turns my chair so I have to look at him. "Listen to me. He was your husband, the father of your child, and my best friend. You don't have to pretend he isn't here between us. If you think he's not in my mind every time I look at you, you're wrong. I'm struggling with thinking of you the way I do. Imagining doing things with you that he'd beat my fucking ass for."

Again, a part of my heart breaks, but this time for Liam. This thing between us isn't easy for me, but I never thought about how it would be for him. I wonder if we're doomed from the start. I don't know if it's even possible for the two of us to have a chance at this. There aren't simply two scarred hearts trying to find a way. There's also a ghost between us.

"I don't know how to do this," I reply honestly.

"Me either. That's why I said we take this slow. You can talk to me though. If you're missing him or if you want to talk about him. He's not an off-limit topic. You never mention him with me. Why?" Liam grabs my hands as we sit in this beautiful restaurant and people look at us. He doesn't waver from me. Instead, he kneels on the ground, holding my hand, while I have a mini breakdown.

I pull my hands from his and rest them upon his face. The short beard he keeps is trimmed and it tickles my hand. I brush my thumb back and forth and stifle the emotions that were stirring. I lean forward and kiss his lips gently. "Thank you."

His brows set into a straight line and looks away. "I don't know what for. I made you cry again . . . which I begged you never to do again. Although," he stops and gives a quick laugh, "You tend to kiss me when you cry, so maybe I should rethink this. But you didn't answer my question."

"I don't know. I feel like it's wrong to talk about him with you. I loved him so much and now I have these feelings for you and . . ." I trail off unsure of what to say.

Liam's eyes never falter. He stays trained on me, waiting for me to finish. "You need to tell me because I promise I can't read your mind. I can try. I can read your body. I can tell right now you're nervous. Your heart is racing, your eyes are shifting, and the way you're stuttering tells me everything I need to know. But I don't know what is going on in your mind or your heart."

"I just wish he was here, and then when I'm with you, I don't think about him so much. It makes me feel like I'm a horrible wife."

"You're not horrible. I don't think what we're doing is horrible. Neither of us thought we'd be here. I think with my good looks and charm you were doomed." Liam winks and his mood shifts to playful.

I laugh and wipe my face with the napkin. "You're a mess. Now please get off the floor and let's have dinner."

Liam returns to his seat and I place my hand out asking for his in return. He wants me to lead this and right now his touch soothes me. I'm not going to think about why that is, I'm just going to enjoy it. This is our time tonight and I want to be in the moment for the remainder of it.

"Okay, let's just enjoy our date," Liam says as the waitress walks over.

Liam orders practically everything off the menu. I swear he's feeding someone under the table. No human can consume this much food. By the time dinner is served, I'm totally full but he's still going.

I joke with him about his appetite and laugh as he tells me the stories from their training mission. Some of the guys Aaron was close with are still in the teams. I know their wives and families and it takes me back a little. I've missed these stories.

"How's work going?" Liam asks.

"Good. I got promoted again. I swear it's the fastest anyone's ever gone from entry-level to management in history," I say and take a bite of my lobster.

"Muffin's a smart guy. I'm sure you were never hired with the expectation of staying entry-level," Liam says as he sits back. "What do they have you doing now?"

I put my fork down and take a deep breath. I know Liam said Aaron isn't off limits, but I still feel uncomfortable. On the other hand, Liam deserves to know in some way too. "I'm doing all their mission prep. I'll handle all the logistics and make sure everything is properly staffed and they have all their supplies. Which apparently was the issue that sent Aaron to Afghanistan to begin with. But today I learned some other stuff . . ." I trail off.

"Like?" Liam's hand covers mine. It's as if he knows I need the extra support.

"They're investigating Aaron's death. I mean . . . I don't know what they're going to find. It was pretty clear-cut to me. It was an IED . . . what is there to investigate?" I ask and Liam's eyes move a tiny bit to the left. I wouldn't normally care, but I know that's his tell. "Liam?"

"Look, I thought all along something wasn't right. I mean, not the IED . . . that stuff is common, but then when Jackson got shot over there, it was a red flag for me. That region wasn't on our radar, but then two Cole Security guys were injured or killed? I don't know. It's the skeptical part of me that questions it," Liam says and links our fingers.

"Should I be worried?"

Liam squeezes my hand. "I wouldn't be okay with you working there if I didn't think it was safe. I'd make up some bullshit and sabotage it. There's no way I'd let you be in danger, and neither would Jackson or Mark."

I take a deep breath and release it. He's right. No one would ever put me in harm's way, but the questions nag at me.

chapter twenty

"OKAY, YOU READY?" Liam asks as he has me blindfolded for our next part of the date. I focus on everything around me. I can smell hay or maybe it's just that clean, open air . . . I think. I can't place it, but there's no noise at all. It's completely quiet. I breathe in again, and grass and flowers register.

"Where are we?"

I feel him behind me. He stands there not touching me, but I can feel the heat of his body. It sheaths me and the anticipation builds. I lean back so I feel him and he chuckles.

His hands graze my bare arms as the tips of his fingers glide across my skin. My head falls back on his shoulder and my breathing accelerates. "When I was stationed here the first time, I found this place. It's where I came after we kissed. I come here when I need to remember how small I am in this world." Liam breathes against my neck. "Sometimes our problems feel so big that we forget how to be grounded and humble." His hands move to my shoulders. The touch is tender and sensual.

He unties the blindfold and my eyes adjust. It's pitch black except for the stars and moon above us. It illuminates the beauty that I'm surrounded by. Trees line the field and tall grass encompasses the entire area. It's untouched except for the small circular patch we stand in.

Liam's arms wrap around me from behind and I take it in. "Wow," I breathe. "It's so beautiful and yet so desolate."

"You're not alone," he says, and I sag into him. My head rests against his chest as he holds me tight. "No matter what happens, you'll have me. As a friend or whatever this becomes or doesn't."

"It scares me. I feel like it's so soon. I miss him still, Liam." I turn in his arms so I can see his profile. "I loved him my whole life and the idea of moving on terrifies me. I don't know that I won't get gun shy and pull away."

His hands cradle my face. "I'll never push you. I know he was your world. I saw the love you two shared and I would be full of shit if I said it doesn't scare me. You're supposed to be untouchable, and yet here you are in my arms. I don't know if I'm lucky or a fucking idiot. I just know that when we're together, it feels right. It feels like we're supposed to be."

Even in the dark, Liam's eyes shine bright. He won't hurt me. He won't betray me. He'll be patient and kind because that's who he is. My hands tangle in his hair as we stand together. Our foreheads touch and he holds my face as I hold on to this moment. I'm at peace in this very second. No hurt consumes me, no fear, just Liam. I close my eyes and allow myself to feel and pray.

Please, Aaron, be okay with this. Please understand I'll always love you, but Liam makes it a little bit better. He'll be good to me. So please, forgive me.

I lift my head and press my lips against his. His hand cradles my cheek and he holds me as we kiss. I grab his neck and feel the weightlessness from letting a little part of myself go. He kisses me adoringly and cautiously, allowing me to lead but still commanding me. I lose myself a little more as I moan when his hand presses against the small of my back.

"Let go," he says against my mouth. "Let me take it

for you."

Before I can say anything, his mouth is on mine again. Our tongues thrash against each other as the kiss becomes hungry. He pulls me close so there's no space between us. The low sound resonates through his chest, sending shivers down my spine. It's sexy, and before I know it, my hands are traveling to his chest. I pull his shirt out and my fingers trail up his chest. I want to feel his skin.

Liam breaks the kiss. "Natalie," my name is both a plea and a request.

"Shhh," I instruct him as I unbutton his shirt. "I want to feel your heart."

My hands glide up and he trembles beneath my touch. We stand here with my fingers resting on his chest, feeling his heart beat beneath me. He's alive and here with me. His hands stay at his sides as he once again lets me decide where I'm going with this.

"I want to touch you so bad," he admits and his hand lifts then drops. "I'm fighting every muscle in my body right now."

"Stop fighting," I say without thinking.

Liam grips my arm and pulls my hand down as his lips find mine again. He kisses me roughly. Taking from me whatever I'm willing to give. I don't know how far I can go, but right now I'm lost to him. I don't see, feel, or want anything but him. My mind shuts off completely and for once I'm living in this moment. In the field with him, I'm not drowning. Liam breathes the air into my lungs for me. The life that left my soul months ago, when it was ripped from me, starts to find its way back. I'm alive in his arms. His touch elicits the part of me I closed off to come back and ignite.

"Liam," I sigh when his lips leave mine and he kisses my neck.

"Tell me to stop."

"Liam," I breathe his name again as I feel his tongue glide against my collarbone.

"Tell me this isn't wrong," he says in between kisses.

I grab his face and force him to look at me. I need him to see it in my eyes. I want him to know I'm here with him and only him. "This isn't wrong."

He closes his eyes and pulls me against his chest. We hold each other as our breathing comes back to normal. It's crazy how much he frees me from myself.

"I could stay here forever," Liam says, breaking the quiet.

"I'd love to see it during the day."

"One day, sweetheart. Let's head back to the car before I do something stupid." Liam releases me and takes my hand and we start to walk back up the path. "I've come once during the day, but at night you feel the peace. You can see the light through the black. The stars and the moon remind me that life is short and I need to live each day. My job demands I respect death."

"Respect death? How can you say that?" I ask with doubt dripping from my voice.

He stops and stands before me. "Without death there is no life." Liam pauses as if weighing his next words. "When one of us dies, it's not in vain. We don't go lightly and if I don't respect the sacrifice someone made in honor, then what?" Liam asks.

"There's no respect in death for me. It takes from you. It makes things go dark and gray because there is no solace for the remaining. I'm left here, picking up the pieces of my destroyed life because of death." I choke on the words as he shifts uncomfortably.

Liam steps forward and I instantly regret my words. "Your life isn't ruined. It's altered. Things didn't go the way you thought, but you have Aarabelle, you have friends who love you, and hopefully you'll have me. I can never replace him and I never want to. He was my best friend and I'd give anything to have taken his place so you didn't have to hurt."

"Liam," I try to stop him, but he puts his finger to my lips.

"No, I would. I hate seeing you hurt. I hate knowing Aarabelle will grow up not knowing him. I feel guilty getting to touch you, kiss you, and hold you in my arms. But I respect that Aaron saved more lives than we'll ever know. He gave his life because he was going over there to make sure his team had what they needed. He's a hero to the men he helped. A patriot. And for that, I respect death." Liam's hand presses against my shoulder and he opens the car door.

I don't speak because I don't trust myself. I climb in the car and let the weight of his words come down around me.

He was my hero too, and I lost him.

The drive home is quiet as we both feel the emotions settle. There's a lot to be said, but not tonight. Tonight was our first date, and it doesn't slip past me that I spent a good majority in memories or tears. I know that if I were with anyone other than Liam, it would've been the date from hell.

The car stops in my drive and we sit awkwardly.

"Liam? I know it might not seem like it, but tonight was sincerely special to me."

He leans over and grins. "You're special and deserve a night out."

"I just need time to get there. I want us to keep seeing each other. I want to be . . . well, whatever we are." I laugh and wring my hands nervously. This is so uncomfortable it's a little ridiculous.

"We're friends, Lee. Friends who kiss a lot."

I smile and let out a shaky breath. "I like kissing you."

"I'm glad. Now come here and show me just how much." Liam's voice is husky with desire.

I shift slightly and give him exactly what he asks for.

"HEY, BABE!" REANELL screams as she runs over. "You look amazing."

"I look like crap," I reply as I look down at my sweats.

"Yeah, I was being nice. You look like shit."

Leave it to Reanell to be so sweet.

"You ready for the gym?"

Reanell and I decided we needed to get off our butts since it's summer, and if I have to get in a bikini, I'd like to not jiggle so much. Even though there's not an ounce of fat on her five-foot-three frame. She's the kind of woman people hate to be friends with, naturally skinny even though she eats a bag of chips in one sitting. Has long, dark brown hair that always looks as if she spent hours doing it when she just woke up. But her eyes are most coveted—she has hazel eyes framed with the longest black eyelashes. I want to hate her, but then she opens her mouth and is the kindest person I know, so hating her is impossible.

"Can we go out to lunch after?" she asks as she sits on the couch.

I slap her leg and scoff. "Get up or we'll never go, and no, we can't go out to lunch."

"Ugh," she groans. "Such a damn killjoy. Okay, let's go stare at hot men while they work out."

"You're impossible," I laugh and lock the door.

Paige has Aarabelle at the park while I go work out for an hour. I don't know how I ever survived without her. She's sweet, nurturing, and Aarabelle loves her. Plus, she's available every time I call her. I've been working from home a little more frequently since that's a perk Jackson said I have. Being around Aarabelle for the first eight months of her life and then feeling like I never see her anymore has been extremely difficult for me.

"So," Reanell says as we get in the car.

"So?"

"Are you seriously not going to tell me about what's going on with you and Liam?" she asks with raised brows.

I laugh and try to deflect. There's no way to explain because we're not defining anything. Since our date, he's been busy gearing up for another short training mission, so we haven't seen each other. I miss him though, so that's something.

"Not much to say. I mean, we're just taking it one day at time."

She shifts in her seat and faces me. "Is he a good kisser? Did he touch your boobs?"

"I swear." I roll my eyes and focus on the road.

"Oh, give it up," she huffs dramatically.

"Fine," I reluctantly agree. "He took me to dinner and then to this open field. We kissed and then he was a gentleman and took me home."

We kissed a lot, but I'm not about to give her any ammunition. Reanell was half asleep when I went to pick up Aarabelle, so she wasn't pestering me for details. It seems like today is going to be a different story.

"That's it?" she sounds unimpressed. "I mean . . . it sounds adorable and all, but I was hoping for something juicy."

"Sorry to disappoint you." I clench the wheel as we pull in to the gym. When we park, I turn and look at her. I'm tired of how she thinks I should so quickly dismiss my husband and move on. It's not that easy and I'd bet my ass that if it were her, she'd never talk to another man. "I'm pissed at you."

Reanell turns in her seat and her jaw falls slack, "Me? Why?"

"Because you make it seem so fucking easy, Rea. It's not easy."

"I never said it was easy. I just watch you and it's hard. But . . ." She places her hand on my arm and her voice softens. "I hate seeing you like that. You're my best friend and if it were me and Mason died, you'd push too. I think you're so strong. You've handled this all with grace even while you were dead inside."

I look away and she shakes my arm. I wanted to yell at her and now she's making my heart physically ache.

"Look at me," her voice is pleading. "Liam came around and I thought maybe he'd help you take care of things around the house and introduce you to someone. I never thought he'd be the one to open you up. You smile now." Tears pool in her eyes and they mirror mine. "You smile and laugh. I couldn't get you to laugh. I would try and try, but you were just void."

"Rea . . ."

"No, it's just that he did. If Aarabelle had gotten sick before, you would've called me right away and begged me to come running. But you didn't, because Liam was there. Don't you see? It's happening and you're not even trying. I don't want to see you push him away."

"I'm scared," I admit quietly. That's the bottom line. I'm absolutely terrified. He's everything that I shouldn't want. He's a replica of my husband. Honorable, courageous, and willing to die for the greater good. If I let him in my heart, there's no way I can handle losing another man. If I let him into my daughter's world and he leaves too soon, I'll never forgive myself.

Reanell pulls me into her arms and rubs my back. "I know you are. You can't keep this all in, Lee. Talk to me."

Everyone wants me to talk, but when I let even a tiny bit out, I feel like the flood is going to overtake me. I'll wash up on the shore alone and unable to breathe. There are times it feels like the tide is going to wash me away. So much hurt. So much pain. But then Liam comes around and it's a little bit easier.

"When I found out Aaron died, the idea of touching anyone else was beyond my thought process. I'd forgotten how to laugh because it was easier to stay behind the wall." I look at her and the empathy swims in her hazel eyes. "I don't want to hurt anymore."

Her lips turn as a sad smile forms. "I know you don't, but life is having it all. You can't know real love unless you've had true pain. You're life isn't going to fit in some box. We're all bigger than that box. You, me, Aaron, Mason, and even Liam . . . we don't get to define the box. But you," she clenches my arm, "You're loving even through your pain. You're beautiful even when you tried not to be. When Aaron died and you had Aarabelle, you lived because you're better than the box you've put yourself in."

I listen and let her words comfort me. I take each syllable and savor it, really take it in, because she's right. I know this, but sometimes I forget. The pain and sorrow are easy to get lost in. For some reason, it's almost easier to be unhappy, but I don't want to live a life full of misery. I have a beautiful daughter, a fantastic support group, and I have Liam.

"I don't want to live in a box," I admit with tears streaming.

"I won't let you, but it's not me who opened the lid and for that reason I think he's good for you." Reanell pulls me into a hug then pushes back. "Now, do you still want to go in there or should we go get ice cream?"

I laugh despite the tears and hug her again. "Let's go get our gym on."

She groans and her head falls back against the seat. "You're so damn evil."

"No, I'm just stepping out of the box."

"Fucking box."

"Yup, fucking box."

chapter twenty-one

I'M DYING. THERE'S no other way to describe the immense pain and discomfort I'm in. I blame the gym. Plus, Aarabelle was sick the last few days and, of course, now I have it. Aches and shivers plague my body and I want to crawl in a hole.

"Aara, please stay in one place," I plead as she starts to head toward the other end of the room. She's crawling, which makes this illness a hundred times worse. And she doesn't nap as often, so I get no time to rest.

Three days of her awake all night was bad enough. Now that I'm thoroughly run down, I get whatever bug she had . . . awesome. Liam is due home today from another work up. I forgot how much I hated the stupid training missions. Gone all the time and then they leave for the deployment. I used to beg Aaron just to go for an extra month so it wasn't one week here and one week gone. Maddening is how I'd describe it.

When they're gone, you have your routine. You know what your day will entail. These small training missions screw up your rhythm. Even though Liam and I don't actually have a rhythm—yet. We speak every night on the phone. He's trying to let me decide the pace, but for right now, I'm happy with how things are. There's no real definition. We enjoy each other's company, he makes me laugh, he's attentive, and caring. Most of all, he's good to

Aarabelle, which matters more than anything to me.

"Lee? You in there?" I hear a knock on the door, but I must be hallucinating now. Fantastic, the fever has gotten so bad I now hear voices.

I hear the banging again and Aarabelle squeals. "Okay, okay. Shhh," I beg the door and Aara, since my headache is now full out throbbing.

"Natalie . . . I'm going to use the spare key if you don't open," Liam's voice is warning as I drag my body to the door.

I open it and lean against it. My eyes squint from the bright sun and I moan.

"What the . . . ?" he trails off as he looks at me.

Glancing down at myself I realize what has him mystified. I'm in my grey Navy Wife sweatshirt and orange sweatpants. I lift my hands up to smooth my hair, only to feel that it's half in a ponytail and half out. Well, no going back now.

"If you're going to judge, you can leave." I cough at the end and he steps in the house. "Enter at your own risk. I'm dying."

Liam chuckles and shuts the door. "You're not dying." He steps in and kisses my forehead. "I think you need to take more medicine and go lie down. You're burning up."

Sleep.

Sleep sounds good.

Sleep and drugs.

"Okay . . ." I trail off as I drag my feet. "Wait!" I exclaim and then cough.

"What?" he asks, picking up one of the burp clothes with a pencil.

"Aarabelle. I have to watch Aarabelle," I remind him and start to shuffle back toward the couch.

Liam grabs my shoulders, laughing. "I've got her."

Well, that wakes me up. "Huh?" My eyes are wide as

I look at him.

He shrugs and smiles. "I've got Aarabelle, you go to bed. Maybe a shower too," he nags while laughing. *Dick.*

"Bed. Okay. Are you sure?" I question him one more time. This is his last out. Otherwise, I'm going to bed and taking some heavy medication. I need to kick this virus and fast.

"I've fought in wars, survived BUDs, dragged bloody bodies out of firefights, and much worse than a few hours with a kid." Liam cocks his head and the confidence he has rolls off him in waves.

I half laugh and half cough again at his self-assuredness. He has no idea what watching a mobile child is like. But okay, I'm sick as a dog, and honestly, I'm afraid I'll fall asleep with her awake, so at this point he's better than I am. "She just ate, she'll probably be hungry around five. She woke up from her nap a little while ago, so you'll have to entertain her," I say as he scoops her into his arms and she giggles. They grin at each other and Aarabelle slaps her wet hand she had in her mouth on his face.

"Baby slobber," he says and wipes his cheek. "We'll be fine. Go." Liam juts his chin out instructing me to head to bed. "We've got this, right, Aarabelle? Uncle Liam and you are going to watch football while Mommy sleeps." I stand there for a moment and watch the scene before me. The man who I've known for years, the one I never could've imagined feeling anything for in a romantic sense . . . standing here as my heart swells. Each time I wonder if this is right, he does something that smothers my doubt.

Liam owes me nothing. He's here, again, because he cares about us. Last we spoke, he wasn't due home until tomorrow, but he got back and came right here. I lean against the wall as he talks to her and I could cry. Only this time, they're tears of joy and love.

"Okay, the Packers are on and we want them to annihilate the Bears. Say 'Go, Pack, Go!'" Liam plays with Aarabelle and lifts her arm toward the sky.

I tiptoe to my room, take the strongest flu medication I have, and pass out in my bed.

Hours pass and I wake feeling rested and slightly disoriented. It's dark, which means I've slept way past the two-hour nap I'd planned. I climb out of bed and clean up, brush my teeth, and try to fix my face. My hair is unsalvageable, so I do the best I can. I look a little better, but the bags under my eyes are not normal.

I check Aarabelle's room to see if she's in there, but it's empty. Afraid of what I might find, I head to the living room where nothing could've prepared me for what I see.

Lying on the couch is Liam with Aarabelle fast asleep on his chest. Her tiny hand is wrapped around his and they're both holding on to each other. His huge body shields her as his arm holds her tight. It breaks my heart and mends it at the same time. Two parts of me are pulled apart. The one side that's sad it's not her father. The other part which is grateful it's Liam. Aarabelle shifts a little, and even in his sleep, he moves to accommodate and protect her.

"Feeling better?" Liam's rich voice cuts through the silence and I jump.

"Hi," I whisper and kneel so we're face to face. "I didn't mean to wake you."

His eyes crinkle and he nods. "I don't think I ever sleep fully. I could feel you watching me. Plus," he yawns and shifts Aara, "She moves every five seconds."

"I can take her."

"No, she's fine."

The television is muted but it illuminates the room. Liam's eyes are tired and yet he still won't let me take her. He lies here and lets my daughter listen to his heart.

I place my hand on her back and Liam places his over it.

"Thank you," I smile softly.

"I wouldn't thank me yet . . . I made a mess."

I grin and look around the room. He's not kidding. There are bottles, food jars, and about ten diapers strewn around the room. For the first time, I really notice that Aarabelle doesn't have clothes on and I burst out laughing.

"Oh my God," I whisper and try to calm my laughing. "Why does she have two diapers on? And is that rope?"

Liam shifts and cradles Aara into his arms so he holds her like a football. "Who made these stupid things? Those tabs rip off for no reason, then who the hell can figure out which way the thing goes? So I tied it on."

"With rope?"

"I had some in my bag," he whispers and kisses the top of her head. "It works."

"I don't even know what to say to you," I giggle and cough a little.

"How about . . . 'Oh, Liam, you're so amazing, sexy, funny, and I owe you a lifetime of favors which you can collect at any time,'" he quirks his brow.

"Not likely, dumbass." I stifle my laugh and kiss his cheek. "Give her to me, I'll put her to bed."

He hands Aarabelle over and I grab a diaper as he stands there with his arms crossed.

"You know how long it took me to put that on?"

I look down and there are at least three knots and the rope is looped around her waist and under her legs. I can't believe she even fell asleep with this thing on.

"Watch how long it takes me to put it on the right way," I laugh and look at the knots. "What the hell kind of knots are these anyway?" I ask while he stands there looking proud of his work.

"Need help?"

"I need a knife to get her out of this!" I whisper-yell.

He's insane. I start at the one knot and it lets out. I glare at Liam in mock anger. "I swear if she wakes up, I'm going to tie you up."

He huffs, "I might like that."

"You wish." I sneeze and cough wishing I were back in bed. Liam crouches down and unties the other two knots on the makeshift diaper. I look over at him, "I'm surprised you didn't use duct tape."

"I would've if I knew where it was," Liam scoffs jokingly.

The emotions swirl through me. He could've woken me but he handled it. Yes, he tied a diaper on her, but it's sweet and shows, once again, how lucky I am. We both have fears about going into this, but right now, I don't want to fight it anymore. There are things we have to figure out, but Liam has given me a part of myself I'd forgotten about. He sees me as a woman, not a widow.

"Look," I say as he sits beside me. "It's easy." It takes me literally ten seconds to have the diaper on her.

"I swear I had defective ones."

"Sure you did," I say as I pick up Aarabelle. Liam follows behind me to her room. He kisses her head and says goodnight then I place her in her crib. Every night when I put her to bed, I say a prayer for her and ask her daddy to watch over her. Then we thank him for allowing Liam in our lives and ask for him to help us heal.

When I turn, Liam is standing at her door, leaning against it. I stand across from him and we gaze at each other. Both of us are saying so much right now even though nothing is being spoken. My heart and my eyes tell him everything.

Liam leans forward and brushes the hair from my eyes and lingers a little longer. His thumb brushes across my lip and I sigh.

"Liam," my voice is a breathy whisper.

"I should probably leave," he says as his finger rubs

back and forth.

My eyes close and I breathe him in. "You probably should."

I want him to stay, but I need him to go. My defenses are down and I'm not ready.

"Okay," his voice is low and rough. "I should. Plus, you're sick and need to rest."

"Yeah, probably . . ." I grip his shirt and hold on. "Or . . . we could snuggle on the couch?" I say, reluctant to let him go. I want him to stay and this is my safe way of having him close. I know men don't want to freaking snuggle, but I just want to lay with him, and there's no way I'm ready to have him in my bed.

Liam laughs quietly and pulls me in his arms. "Yeah, I could go for that."

chapter twenty-two

"OKAY, SPARKLES, DO you have the applications for the new team?" Mark requests, walking in my office.

We've taken over for a company that failed at two contracts for support in Africa, and now that Cole Security Forces won them, we need to staff them. I've become extremely passionate about my new role. I feel like I'm ensuring everyone comes home safe. The issues the company had previously were due to poor planning. I now make sure the teams we send over there have all the equipment they need. It's also given me a chance to see that Jackson spares no cost for it. Any time I've asked for more funding for supplies, he grants it with no questions. He'd rather cut funding on our end than on the front lines.

"Yeah, they're right here." I lift a stack of papers and keep writing. "I hate that you somehow have given me the call sign I could kill you for." My middle name is Star thanks to my father's hippie days. Mark found out on my application and said I sparkled like a star.

"It's a gift. You should've seen Catherine the first time I called her 'Kitty.'" He stands there and laughs.

"I hope she punched you."

"Nah, she loves me."

"How is it you manage to drive people insane but

they still keep you around?" I ask, still keeping my eyes on the paper I'm trying to fix. The wording is wrong and I want to get it right.

"You know you can take a break *and* we have killer coffee," Mark's New York accent is thick and I can't help but want to mock him. It was the one thing they've always made fun of him for.

"Cawfee?" I smile and mimic him, putting the pen on the desk.

"I see we got jokes."

"Only with you, Twilight."

"See?" Mark says as he sprawls out on the loveseat I have in my office. "We make a good team. You're Sparkles and I'm Twilight. It's like a match made in heaven."

I laugh, "I think you're hitting on me, Mr. Dixon." I know he's not, but it's fun to rile him up.

"No, I'm just kidding." He lifts his hands in mock defense. "I wouldn't disrespect you, Natalie."

"Calm down," I shake my head. "I know you're not. Aaron would kick your ass," I reply jokingly and my hand flies to my mouth. "I meant . . . I . . ."

Mark stands and heads over toward my desk. "He would, and so would Liam. It's okay."

"Did someone say my name?" I hear Liam's voice and my eyes snap up. Oh, great.

"Hey," I greet him and walk over.

"Hey, Dreamboat!" Mark smiles and they shake hands and hug.

"What's up, man? Long time no see."

Liam and Mark finish saying hello and catching up briefly before Mark heads out. I don't know if Liam heard, and if he did, whether it would bother him. Regardless, I'm surprised to see him here.

"I wasn't expecting you." My voice is wary.

He enters and closes my door. "I know. I sent you a text but you didn't answer. I figured I'd just stop by."

"Well, I'm happy to see you." He steps closer and I take a step back. Why am I retreating from this man?

"You look beautiful."

"You look incredibly sexy in uniform." I appraise him as he approaches. He's wearing his woodland camo. His sleeves rolled up make his already large biceps look huge. The way the top clings to his chest is hot, and I can only image how amazing his ass looks. Something about the uniforms always makes their asses look fantastic. *Maybe I'll have him spin so I can see.*

Liam's lip slowly rises as if he's reading my mind. "What are you thinking about?" he asks as he approaches.

I trail his body with my eyes and then back to his face with a grin. "Your ass."

He laughs and then his eyes darken.

I love the game we play. Playful but seductive. I keep pushing him and soon enough he's not going to be so patient.

"I'd be happy to let you see my ass . . ."

"I bet you would, but I'm at work and that would be all sorts of inappropriate." I giggle and put my hand on his chest to stop his approach. Liam pushes me back slowly as if I'm not even there. "What can I do for you, sailor?"

"The guys are going to a bar tonight," he pauses and I nod. "I haven't gone out with them in a long time."

Another step he pushes me back.

"Okay?" I respond slightly confused where he's going with this.

Liam's eyes lock with mine. The way he's looking at me leaves me breathless. I take a deep breath but it does nothing to help, all I smell is him. His cologne mixed with a hard day's work filters through my body and makes my head spin. "I want you to come with us. With me."

"I-I . . . but . . ." I trail off and look away. "I don't

know if that's a good idea." I keep my eyes down but, of course, Liam isn't having it.

His arms cage me in as he presses me against my desk. "I don't want to go and have to push away random skanks all night. I want you by my side. I want to spend the night with you, Natalie." Liam's lips press against my neck and I shiver. He slowly trails feather-light kisses down my collar, then to my shoulder, and I groan. "I want to walk in and have every motherfucker look at me and think 'damn, how'd he get so lucky?' Then I'll take you in my arms . . ." Another kiss and he moves his way up my neck to my ear. "And I'll . . ."

"You'll . . . ?" I whimper when he bends back.

"You have to tell me if you're going to go first."

It's impossible to say no to him. His blue eyes glimmer with hope and he has me practically trapped between his arms. This date will be different. It's us going out as a couple with mutual friends. People who knew Aaron and then will see me with Liam. I have to choose whether I will let my past define my future.

"Who's going?"

"Does it matter?" he counters.

"Yes," I say looking at him. "Of course it matters. I mean, what do we say?"

Liam's eyes don't waver. "Don't go inside your head. It's just friends, going out for a beer."

"No, it's you and I going out with our friends. Friends that don't know us as us. Plus, you've already told me what you plan to do," I reply with a taunting look.

"Lee," he says cautiously, "This doesn't have to be strange. I'll keep my hands to myself the whole night."

I look at him with raised brows. "Right. After you assaulted me in my office with all your promises."

"Hey, I can keep myself in control. It's you I worry about. I'm prime meat and you may want to mark your territory. And my assault was working?"

The laugh that escapes me is loud and effortless. My head falls back and his lips find my neck again. I sigh and wrap my arms around his shoulders. "You use your sexiness against me."

"All part of the plan, sweetheart."

I squeal and smile, "Okay, you win. I need to see if Paige can watch Aarabelle tonight."

"Mmmm," he groans against my collarbone before looking at me. "Hands to myself, right?"

I lean up and kiss him chastely. "It's not tonight yet."

"No, no, it's not," Liam says before he presses his lips against mine. He reclines me against the cold desk but I only feel heat. His heat. He holds me close and cradles my head in his hands, winding my hair around his fingers. My heart thumps erratically in my chest as he kisses me relentlessly. I claw at his back and pull him closer.

I open my mouth to him and his tongue brushes against mine. And it's like a switch is turned off. He devours me and takes away all the fear I was holding on to. I'm floating from my body as his weight is on top of me. He won't let me hurt. He'll protect me even if it's from my own guilt.

I feel his joy radiate from him. Both of us have found happiness through each other. It's scary but also beautiful. I want to give him more. I want to give him what I know he wants. I'm just not sure I'm ready.

AARABELLE IS ASLEEP when Paige arrives. This girl saves my life being available on zero notice. I'm not sure what to wear since this is the first time I'm hanging out with everyone. I change over ten times, but finally settle on my favorite jeans and an off-the-shoulder purple top. Cute and comfy is my goal for tonight.

I hear Liam's car pull in the drive and I give myself a

mental pep talk.

I can do this. It's just friends, and Liam and I aren't doing anything wrong. Hell, we're not even sleeping together. Just a lot of kissing. Really, really good kissing. Amazing kissing.

Before he knocks, I open the door. Once again, this man is too good-looking for his own good. How did I never notice this before?

"Hi, sweetheart." His deep voice is velvety seduction. I melt at the way he draws out the "heart" in "sweetheart" as he appraises me.

"Hi, yourself." I smile and grab my clutch.

"You ready?"

"As I'll ever be." I close the door and reach up to kiss him but he moves away. What the? "Ummm?" I question with my eyes wide.

Liam puts his arm out in a gesture for me to loop mine through, but I stand there waiting for an answer.

"What the hell was that?" My voice is filled with indignation.

"That," he says, tapping my nose, "Was me keeping my promise. You want me to behave, so you can't go starting off the night using me for your pleasure," he informs me, putting his arm back out.

"You're joking."

Liam leans down and his lips barely touch my ear as his voice drops lower, "If I touch you now, the rules are off. I want to be able to have my hands on you tonight, but if I start I won't stop. So you choose. I want you . . . don't doubt that." He pulls away and I know this has to be my choice.

Talk about a decision.

I want him and he makes me happy. "And if I want you to kiss me now?"

"Then I get to kiss you later, when I want."

"What if I don't want you to kiss me later?"

He laughs and moves his lips so they align with mine, "I think you'll like me kissing you now, and I know you'll like me kissing you later."

"Well, since you put it that way," I grip his shirt and pull him flush against me. His lips meet mine and I lose myself in his arms. Liam's hands slide down my body and he cups my ass, lifting me off the ground. Pressed between him and the door, my hands grip his neck and I give him what he wants.

Kissing Liam is unlike anything I've felt before. He's rough, but at the same time tender. His tongue dances with mine as if we've been doing this our whole lives. There's no awkwardness. When he gives, I take, and vice versa. I could spend my entire day kissing him and be completely content.

I moan in his mouth and he grinds his hips against mine. *Oh. My. God.* My body starts to shake and he does it again. My lips break from his and I'm freaking panting.

"We should go," he grumbles against my neck.

"I'm going to need a few beers after this." I shake my head and slide down Liam's body.

"I need a cold shower." Liam grabs my hand and we walk to the car. He opens the car door for me. "Seriously, though," he pauses and waits until our eyes meet, "You're beautiful."

My arms wrap around his neck and our lips press together. "Thank you."

He kisses the top of my head and I climb into his car.

I pray I can make it through tonight without anything exploding.

CHAPTER TWENTY-THREE

LIAM

MY GOD, THIS woman is killing me. She's got me wrapped around her finger, but she doesn't see it. I can't stay away from her no matter what I do. Running is useless anymore. I wind up thinking about her during any song that comes on. The gym is a joke, every blonde that walks past me I compare to how Natalie's body is better. I'm growing a fucking vagina.

She looks at me like I'm saving her. I wish she knew how much she is saving me. I've always been reckless on missions. There hasn't been anyone waiting for me at home, so I'd take a bullet for anyone. Now, during our training, I think about how she'd feel. How it would be for her if something happened to me. Not that she loves me...yet. But I know she cares. She sure as hell wouldn't kiss me like that if she didn't.

"So, what fine establishment are you guys meeting at?" Lee asks as she shifts in her seat. Two of my favorite women are with me right now. Robin and Natalie.

"The Banque," I reply and wait for her reaction. The Banque is a country line-dancing bar. It's a little run down, but we get in free thanks to the owner, and there's never a shortage of women willing to give it up.

Natalie tilts back with a groan.

"What's the matter, sweetheart?" I ask a little condescendingly. I know she hates that place. All the wives do.

"It's almost as bad as Hot Tuna. I mean, do you guys even want to try to have some game? Or pick up women who aren't laying it all out there for you?"

She's so adorable when she's like this.

"I'll let that slide."

"Let what slide?"

"I have plenty of game," I let her know. "I've never had to work hard."

She snorts and shakes her head. "Arrogant ass."

"Don't worry, only you get to see my game," I gleam and put my arm behind her seat.

Natalie slaps my chest and smiles. "Well, maybe you should try a new playbook because you're not getting much here, sweetheart."

"That hurt."

"You'll live."

"You'll pay for it."

Natalie laughs, "I'm *sooo* sure. You don't scare me, Liam Dempsey. You're scared of me though."

"Damn fucking right I am," I say under my breath but I'm pretty sure she hears me. I'm terrified of her. She's everything I want and I have no business wanting her. She's got a kid and has already lost a husband. I live a dangerous life. I love my life and won't give it up. There's so much more to fear in this entire thing than just the fact that she's my best friend's wife. Natalie has walls and fears that are valid and I know this. And I'm a selfish prick because I really don't care. If she doesn't want me, then she can say so, but until then . . . I want it all with her.

We drive the next few minutes and she stares out the window. I don't know how to handle her sometimes. Like with the tears. Tears I don't do. When we pull up to the bar, Natalie sighs. She gets so deep in her own worries, it's hard to pull her out. I know this isn't easy and I hate it. I don't have the baggage of worrying what everyone thinks the way she seems to. Quite frankly, I don't give a shit. People will judge no matter what, and Natalie and I are grown adults.

"Lee?" I ask her and her head falls to the side as she looks at me.

"You ready to stake your claim, Dreamboat?" she smiles and my worry fades away.

"Stake my claim?"

"You know . . . let everyone know we're together."

I lean forward and she turns to look at me. "Is this what you want?"

"Liam, of course."

"No, I'm serious." I pause because I want her to actually hear me. "If you need time, if you don't want to keep going, we can just go back to friends. I'm only saying this before I get any closer to you. I've known you a long time and it feels like once we flipped the switch from friends to more, I don't want to slow down." I admit this because I know she needs to hear it. She's had a shit year and I can respect that, but my feelings for her grow each day.

"That's what scares me. I think about you all the time. I worry this isn't normal because it feels so easy." She looks out the front window and then back to me. "I care about you so much. You make me happy and . . . I just . . ."

"Just?"

"I don't want to go too fast and then screw it up. I don't want to lose you either. I have to think about Aarabelle, and I worry about when we take the next steps, how I know I won't be able to guard my heart from you." Natalie's eyes are open and she's vulnerable. I know how she struggles with letting go and it'll be next to impossible to ignore the feeling that a ghost is watching.

When we're in her house, it's strong. I see Aaron

around every corner and it freaks me the fuck out. I can't imagine what it's like for her.

"I'll never hurt you intentionally. You don't have to guard your heart."

Natalie's eyes fill with tears and I feel my body start to go into panic mode. She swipes at her eyes. "You're going to make me fall in love with you, aren't you?"

"I'm pretty sure that's a done deal."

She laughs and opens the car door, breaking the moment. "We'll have to see about that."

When she reaches me on the other side of the car, I pull her against me. "Yeah, we will."

I haven't been to this bar in years, but the place hasn't changed too much. There's a dance floor in the middle and it's surrounded by tables. There are two bars on either side and there's a huge bar in the back of the room. The pool tables are always occupied, but maybe I can convince Natalie to play a game or two. Maybe she'll need me to teach her.

I start to imagine what she'll look like with the stick, bent over the pool table. The way her hair will fall and her eyes will find mine. I'll walk behind her and feel her ass press against my dick. The way she'll wiggle . . .

Nuns.
Puppies.
AK-47s.
Diapers.

Glad I got that back under control. We find the table where a few of the guys are already sitting.

"Hey, fucker!" Quinn stands and claps me on the shoulder, already giving me his bullshit-disapproving stare.

"Hey, where's what's-her-name?" I ask knowing he cycles through women like it's nothing. I don't think he's ever fucked the same girl twice.

"I'm looking for fresh meat today." He gives me a

look and turns to Natalie. "Hey, beautiful!" Quinn walks over and gives her a hug. I swear if he upsets her, he's going home to ice his balls.

"Hi, Quinn. I haven't seen you in a long time." Natalie's voice shakes a little. She's nervous, which I try real hard to not let bother me. I'm ready to show everyone where we stand and I wish she was too. I know it's been less than a year and I know it shouldn't bug me. But the problem with knowing and letting are two different things.

We're good together. I've known her for almost nine years and never did I imagine I'd be with her like this. She brings something alive inside of me.

I say hello to the rest of the guys from the team, and when we get to the end, Natalie shrieks.

"Rea!" she runs over and hugs her best friend. "I didn't know you'd be here."

The infamous Reanell Hansen. The two of them giggle and I see Commander Hansen tip his beer to me. Fuck. How the hell did this happen?

"Commander," I say and shake his hand. It's one thing when we're all deployed, but to be drinking with your boss when you're home is another thing.

"Dempsey, today it's just 'Mason,'" he says and grumbles under his breath.

"Oh, Mason, stop being a dick," Reanell says, and she stands, walking over to me.

"I'm Reanell. It's nice to finally meet you for more than two seconds in passing."

"Nice to meet you, ma'am."

"You did not just 'ma'am' me."

I laugh and immediately like her. "No. Never."

"That's what I thought. Now, sit and let's get some alcohol going so Natalie looks like she can breathe." She smiles and makes us sit.

"Sounds like a plan."

"So, tell me, how much can you bench press?" Reanell tilts her head as she looks me up and down before shifting forward with her chin on her fist.

Natalie slaps her arm so her chin falls off. She and Mason laugh as Reanell gives her the death stare. "Stop being stupid and drink your beer."

"It was a valid question," she says and orders a round for all of us.

Natalie relaxes a bit and begins to talk about her job and Aarabelle. We laugh and enjoy small touches. She places her hand on my leg and looks at me under her long lashes with a shy smile. My hand covers hers and squeezes. The little things like this are hard for her, but I appreciate them. I lean back and put my arm around her and she sinks into my side.

The lights dim, indicating it's a slow song. "Wanna dance?" I ask her quietly for two reasons. One, if she says no, I'll never live it down with these assholes. Two, I don't want her to feel like she has to say yes.

Before she can answer me, a short blonde comes up behind me and places her hand on my shoulder. It takes a second to register.

"Hi, Liam. Would you like to dance?"

Fuck. Brittany.

The girl I almost used to fuck Natalie out of my mind.

chapter twenty-four

natalie

LIAM SHIFTS AS a really pretty woman stands behind him. They obviously know each other and I swear she looks familiar. I can't place her though.

"No, thanks though," Liam replies.

"I haven't seen you since that night," she says and looks over at me. Well, isn't this nice.

Liam stands and extends his hand to me, making his intentions clear. My palm touches his and he squeezes my hand pulling me up. "Yeah," he tries to brush her off.

"I figured you'd call."

"Listen, Brittany, I'm here with my girl and I appreciate you coming over, but I'm not interested."

Brittany turns to me and extends her hand. "Hi, I'm Brittany Monaco."

I stand and look at her hand. It's bothering me, because I know I've seen her around. "Natalie Gilcher," I reply and her eyes widen quickly but then she looks away and recovers.

Odd.

"I'm—" she begins to speak, but Liam clears his throat dragging my attention to him.

"Come on, sweetheart. We have a dance floor waiting." Liam's eyes never leave mine as he speaks, focusing all his attention on me.

"Okay." My voice wavers a tiny bit. He seems anxious to get me away from her and I wonder. My stomach flutters as we walk toward the wooden square. I want to ask him about her, but I'm not sure I have that right. We're not exclusive—well, I am—but I've never given him that definition.

The wheels spin in my mind, each spoke that passes bringing a new worry. If he did sleep with her . . . does it change anything? He's with me all the time, so I don't even know when he would've had the chance.

"Ask me, Natalie," Liam says as his hand wraps around my back and he pulls me against him. "Just ask me."

I pull back slightly and our eyes lock. I hesitate and look away.

"Ask me, because I know it's killing you."

"Why won't you just tell me?" I ask, still not able to force the words out.

"If you want to know, you're going to have to ask," Liam says, looking deep into my eyes.

Drawing on all the strength I have left, I release a deep sigh and ask, "Did you sleep with her?"

"No." The honesty is clear in his eyes and his voice. He didn't blink or pause. "I wanted to. I won't lie to you, but I never got close."

"When?"

"Before I ever touched you." He pauses and presses his forehead to mine. The music plays and he holds me close to him. We sway to the music and my heart thumps erratically in my chest. Liam sighs and rubs his nose against mine. "I was thinking about you all the time and I wanted it to stop. I wanted to get you out of my fucking mind." Liam's voice is low and sounds almost angry.

"Why didn't you?" I ask apprehensively.

There's no reason for me to feel threatened, but I do. He's single, incredibly sexy, and has no reason to stay. I have a past, a child, and fears that gnaw at me about getting close to him. He has every excuse at his disposal, nonetheless he keeps coming back.

"Because she wasn't you." I look at him, and his eyes stay closed. He looks pained and I want to ease it. I lift my chin slightly and gently touch my lips to his. Here in the middle of the bar surrounded by our friends, I kiss him. I don't care that I'm sure people are looking. I want him to know how much his words mean. How even though we weren't together, he chose me in some strange way.

He pulls back and rests his head against mine again as we slowly sway to the music. His arms encase me and he guides me through the dance. I can feel the eyes burning holes in my back. The stares of friends who now know where I stand. Where we stand.

"It was the night Aarabelle got sick. I had her in my car," Liam begins to tell me quietly. "The whole time she was sitting in the front seat, I kept thinking how all I wanted was to drop her off and go to you. Tell you how I was starting to feel. And then you called."

"Liam, you don't have to tell me," I murmur.

"I know I don't, sweetheart. But I want you to know everything. I won't keep shit from you." He kisses the tip of my nose and I melt into his embrace. "When I saw your name on my screen, I knew there was no way I wanted to touch her. I turned around before I even answered and then when I heard what was going on . . ." he trails off and I look over at Brittany. She shifts and stares at me, biting her nail. "There was no fucking way I wasn't going to be with you, and if I had touched her," he pulls my chin back toward him, "I would've been wishing it was you."

His words soothe my heart and I smile tenderly. "You

make this easy for me. You make it hard to fight because you make sense to me. How can you know exactly what I need all the time?" I ask.

"Because I know you. And this is easy for both of us because it's right. I know your heart, and I won't take that for granted."

"I know you won't," I reply as the song ends. This time it's Liam who kisses me.

We walk hand and hand off the dance floor as Reanell's eyes light up. I'm going to need more beer.

We sit and enjoy a few beers and I even get Liam to dance with me during a couple's dance. I'm not the best dancer by any means, but I do love it. I used to come here with my friends a lot when Aaron was deployed. Liam dances with me even though he has no idea of the steps. I give him an "A" for effort—he really is something special.

Throughout the night we all talk and laugh, and I can't help but look over at Brittany. There's something festering inside of me about her. She looks over a couple of times, but looks away quickly. Maybe it's nothing, but then I don't know. Maybe she did sleep with Liam and he's lying. Which doesn't make sense because he seemed so genuinely honest. Plus, he has no reason to lie to me.

I head off to the bathroom to check my face, and when I get back, Liam and Reanell are dancing. I nearly fall over laughing because while the man can do just about anything—except diapers—he has awful rhythm. Well, there's a flaw I found.

"Having fun?" Quinn plops in the chair next to me. Quinn and Aaron were close when he was active duty. They were in the same section and worked together a lot. He was the one person I was worried about disapproving of this whole situation.

"Yeah, how about you?"

"Where there's beer and boobs, I'm a happy guy."

"You haven't changed a bit." I chuckle and take a

drink. Quinn has always been this laidback country boy. He drinks a lot, sleeps around, and has more guns than any human should ever need. His dark hair is buzz cut and you can see the scar behind his ear from when he was injured in Iraq.

"Life's too short to change. I live like I want and if you don't like me, oh fucking well."

"Such a charmer," I playfully respond.

"Listen, I know it's not my place and all, but . . ." Quinn runs his hand down his face. "I'm happy for you. I wasn't at first. I mean, we have a code about wives. But, I think Aaron would be glad you found someone like him. If it helps you at all."

I place my hand on Quinn's. He doesn't know that what he said matters. Or that maybe in some small place in my mind I needed to hear that. I do believe Aaron would be okay with it, it's a matter of whether I'm ready to move forward. If I can live the life of dating a SEAL. Knowing what could happen because I've already had my worst nightmare take place.

"Thanks, Quinn."

"Enough of this . . . you need another beer!" he exclaims and motions for the waitress.

"Natalie?" I hear my name and Brittany is standing behind me.

Okay, maybe I need shots.

"Yes?"

"I just wanted to say I'm sorry about Aaron," she looks away and my stomach drops. Liam's eyes cut to me and he stops dancing. I'm confused because I thought she knew Liam. Why the hell is she talking about Aaron?

"You knew Aaron?"

I've seen this girl. I know her face and it's driving me insane. The way she looks at me as if she knows me too. Her eyes fill with tears and dread spreads through my veins.

Why would she be crying?

"Yes. I mean, I did. I-I met him and . . ." She stops talking and looks at the ground as a tear falls.

"Okay . . . I don't understand why you're so upset if you only met him." I try to figure this out.

Suddenly, Liam's hand is on my shoulder. "Brittany, you should go." Liam steps forward and pulls me to the side. "I don't know what shit you're trying to pull."

"How did you know Aaron?" I ask and push past him.

"Aaron?" Liam asks, sounding as confused as I am.

She sways slightly and I see Quinn stand and move behind me. "I didn't really. I mean . . . I did . . . but it was . . ."

"Either you did or you didn't," I snap.

"I wanted to say I'm sorry. We were friends."

"You said before you just met him."

"You have a daughter, right?"

She's lying. Woman's intuition rings loud in my head. Something isn't right. Something deep inside my soul is telling me not to trust her. Her face though—I've seen it.

"I've seen you before." And then it hits me. "At his memorial." My eyes flash and I remember the blonde that stood off to the side at his memorial. She rushed out before anyone could talk to her. I saw her crying in Pennsylvania. Why would anyone from Virginia drive up there if they'd only met. "You were there."

"I don't know what you mean." Her voice is shaky and she starts to back away. "I shouldn't have come over here."

"Lee, let's go." Liam is trying to command the situation. I feel dizzy and anger starts to take over.

Reanell's at my side, pulling me back, and my hands start to tremble. "You were at his funeral. I saw you! Why?" I yell. "I-I remember there was a woman crying off to the side. I thought it was strange, but I was so distraught I didn't care. It was *you*."

Liam pulls me against his side and Reanell starts to push past everyone with Mason behind her. "Natalie, there were a lot of people there," she soothes as she turns to Brittany.

"I'm not stupid, Rea. She was there. Why were you there?"

"It wasn't me."

"Why don't you leave now?" Reanell suggests to her.

Brittany turns to leave but I need to know. "How did you know him?" I ask once more and her eyes are filled with hurt.

"It wasn't what you think."

"Is this what you do? You come to a widow and talk about her husband? I mean, it wasn't quiet that my husband was killed overseas. So when you were snubbed by Liam you felt as though you needed to do this?"

Brittany looks away and then back at me, "I knew Aaron very well . . . this isn't a game. I've wanted to meet you for some time."

"Why? Why would you want to meet me?"

"I wanted to apologize to you and meet his wife."

Ice shoots through my body, freezing me in place. "Were you involved with Aaron?" I blurt the question out, unsure if I want the answer, but I need to know. Every muscle in my body clenches in anticipation of her answer.

"We were in love," she says slowly and a tear falls as does my heart.

chapter twenty-five

"OH MY GOD!" I cry and Liam's arms are around me in a heartbeat. "Let me go!" I push him away.

"Lee, stop." Liam grabs my face and forces me to look at him. "Stop. You don't know anything. She could be full of shit."

"You're a liar! My husband would never cheat on me. We were having a baby! We were happy and in love."

Brittany steps forward, but Reanell pushes her back slightly, keeping herself between us. "I'm sorry. We were together for a few months before he found out you were pregnant."

"You couldn't get to my boyfriend, so now you make up some crazy shit about my husband?!"

"I wish I were making it up. But I loved him."

"Stop saying that!" I bellow. "You're lying. You don't know him." I say to myself, "He wouldn't do that." Liam holds me against his chest as I fight against him. "You have the wrong guy," I say defiantly.

"He had a tattoo on his ribs and he ground his teeth when he slept. I wish it was a lie. He lied to me."

My body shakes, and as much as I want to believe it's a lie, there's a part of me that knows it's not.

"This is low and fucking ridiculous," Liam says and he wraps his arms around me.

"I wanted to tell you so many times. And when I saw

you today . . ."

My eyes close and I want to wake up from this nightmare. It hurts to breathe.

"Natalie," Liam's voice is calm and measured, "All you know is what she's telling you."

I look at him in disbelief. "She was there, Liam! She was at his fucking funeral. Who comes to a funeral for someone they just met? Five fucking states away?" I turn and Reanell has Brittany backed against the wall. I head over needing answers. I want every fucking detail. The man who I've been grieving was a cheater.

"I knew that man and he wouldn't have touched you," Reanell says and points her finger in Brittany's face. The tears forming in Brittany's brown eyes, she looks at me with pity.

"How long?" I ask with rage and disgust piercing their way through me. "How long and how many times?"

Brittany steps out of Reanell's grasp and her face falls. "It wasn't like that. I swear."

"What was it like?" I demand an answer.

"I met him and it just happened. I'm so sorry. I-I just wanted to see you. I wanted you to know I'm not . . ."

"Not what?" I ask with tears falling down my cheeks. They burn and fuel my anger.

This night was supposed to be a step forward. A chance to feel alive a little and be a woman. It was my night with Liam and somehow this has turned into the night from hell. Each word shreds my world into pieces and burns them to ash.

"I loved him. We were together for months before I found out. I didn't want you to find out like this."

"You wanted me to know. You stupid bitch! You wanted me to know!" Liam's arms are vices around me as I flail toward her. "If you cared, you could've not come to talk to me!"

"When I found out he was married, I ended it. But

that didn't mean I stopped loving him."

I scoff, "I loved him. You're selfish, do you know that? Months you were together! We have a child."

"I saw her." She looks away ashamed. "I wish things were different."

"Don't look away! You need to see my face when I say this to you," I practically growl the words. I'm so angry! "You could've kept your mouth shut and let me be, but no, you had to come make sure I knew. You stupid, selfish whore!" I scream and I'm ready to punch her in the face.

"Natalie, enough," Liam says as he pulls me away. I'm quaking in anger and disgust. I hate her. I hate everyone.

This can't be real. I tell myself over and over again. I was starting to be me again, and now I find this out. It's not real. Still it is. The cruel joke is on me. The echoes of despair scream loudly through my heart. Hollowness overcomes any emotion and I try to shut down. My mind goes back to when I first found out Aaron was dead and how I trained myself to become numb. I search for that power again, but I come up empty.

"Let me go!" I cry out in Liam's arms.

"Come on, sweetheart." Liam's voice is calm and it enrages me.

"Let go of me!" He practically carries me out of the bar, sets me on the ground, and takes my hand. I look up and pull my hand back. "Did you know?"

"Are you fucking kidding me? No, I didn't know."

Liam extends his hand and I tremble. He looks at me waiting and I just stand there. I don't want to touch anyone. My mind starts to run crazy circles and the questions assault me. My heart is shattered and my life feels like a lie.

A man I would've lived the rest of my life loving is a lying piece of shit. He slept with another woman when I was pregnant with his child. I cried for months over losing him. I clutched his pillow and sobbed wishing he was home, only to find out he was doing this.

Reanell rushes toward us and places her hand on my shoulder. I look at her and tears continue to fall like rain. "Rea," my voice is barely a whisper.

The torrent of emotions flow from one to another and I can't seem to hold on to the anger. I could handle the anger.

"Let Liam take you home." She nods to Liam who grabs my shoulder and pulls me toward him. "I'll come by later."

"Rea," I say again, begging her to make this a lie. Make this all go away.

"I'll find out the truth. Just go home. Liam has you."

The entire walk to the car is a blur. I keep seeing Brittany's face and imagining my husband kissing her, touching her, and I feel sick. When we reach the car, I lean over and the nausea is too much. My stomach heaves, whether from the news of my husband's infidelity or the alcohol I've drunk, I couldn't say. I cry and let it out.

Liam holds my hair and my shoulders. I want to die. I feel like each bone in my body is shattering. The splinters of my wounds are open and I'm bared for the world to see.

"I hate him!" I cry out as I stand and Liam puts me in the car without saying a word. I hate myself for coming here. I hate Liam for touching her even if it was only her hand. I hate Aaron for his indiscretion and the fact that I'm left with my imagination.

Aaron, the man who wrote me letters. The one who made love to me so sweetly when it was my first time—was a fucking cheater. I made him promises of love and fidelity, to end with him dead and now a liar. I cried for him, wanted to put myself in the ground next to him so I could be close to him.

Did he love her? Was she better than me? When he held me at night and talked to my stomach, was he wishing it was her carrying his child? I can't stop thinking it. It flows through my thoughts over and over. Each memory feels tainted.

Next thing I know, I'm in front of my house and Liam is helping me out of the car. I close my eyes and sit on the deck. The warm air that used to give me solace makes me ill. Liam stands before me, and when I look up, he looks as lost as I am.

"I'm going to let Paige go home," Liam says and walks into the house.

I barely nod.

This day I want to forget.

Paige walks by and waves. I lift my hand and then I feel Liam beside me.

"I'm at a loss here, Lee. I'm not sure what to say or do."

"You think I know?" I say harshly. I'm sitting here crying about my dead husband's newly discovered year-old affair to my current boyfriend. There's no way to make this shit up.

"No, I don't, but do I hold you? Do I tell you that he's a fucking fool?"

I look at him ready to spew my anger, but he looks as enraged as I am. "I don't know. I can't get answers for any of this. Do you know how this makes me feel?"

"I swear to God, Lee. If he was alive, I'd fucking kill him right now."

"How could he do this to me?" If Liam can give me some answers, I'd really appreciate it.

Hesitantly, Liam moves closer. "I don't know, but I would never be able to touch another woman after you. I'd cut my fucking arm off before it would happen. So I can't answer you because I don't get it. I hate that you're hurting."

I look at him and I feel worse than before. Here's Liam, my boyfriend, consoling me over another man. The word "man" is being used loosely because right now, I don't consider him one.

"I don't know if I can do this with you."

Liam laces his hands behind his head and looks at the sky. "This is going to sound fucked up, but don't let what he did to you define what happens with us. I'm not Aaron. I'm here. I'm standing right here. I didn't touch her and I wasn't married to you. Fuck, we're not even sleeping together and I couldn't do it. So I'm not that guy."

I step toward the door and want to erase this entire evening. Before I open it, I turn to him, "I know you're not Aaron. I know you're here, but right now my heart is broken. It's like I'm back grieving all over again."

He steps forward and grips my face, and I beg him with my eyes not to do it. "You're not grieving. You're hurt and I get that. But if you didn't find any of this out, where would we be tonight? I'd be in your bed with you. I'd be holding you, touching you, showing you how much you mean to me."

"Make me forget him," I say desperately.

"Lee . . ." The apprehension in his voice tells me to stop, but I can't.

"Please, show me how you want me," my voice is dripping with need.

"Don't do this," he begs, staring into my eyes.

I want him to make this all go away. "Make love to me tonight. Please, I need you to show me I'm yours. Make all I can think about be you. Give me this." I try to lean up to kiss him but he backs away. The way he looks at me says it all. I cover my face with my hands. This night just keeps getting better and better.

Liam pulls my hands down. "When we make love

for the first time, when I claim you, it's not going to be because you want to forget. It's going to be because you want me. You're mine now." He pulls me close and kisses me. Every emotion Liam's feeling is passed through us. My stomach tightens as I experience them all—anger, hurt, fear, love, and desire. He pours himself into me.

Liam pulls back and looks at me.

My eyes fill with unshed tears. He kisses me gently and walks away, leaving me feeling worse than I did before.

I enter the house and I want to feel nothing. I deserve a break from every emotion that's haunting me. The bottle of Jack Daniels sits mocking me. I grab it and don't bother with a cup.

"Fuck you and your cheating self, Aaron," I say out loud as I take a drink. The burning down my throat ignites my anger. "I hope she was good, fucking bastard," I say at his photo and the flag on the mantel.

I drink another gulp and the alcohol flows through me. After getting sick at the bar and the amount I drank before, my body welcomes the numbness. "I guess I'm a real naïve idiot."

Reanell opens the door and stands there. "Oh, Lee . . . you and Jack don't need to have a date tonight."

"Jack, Johnny, hell, any man will do. Except for Liam, nope . . . he doesn't want me like this." I grab the bottle and pour more down my throat. Might as well, my life went to shit again anyway.

She walks toward me and takes the bottle. Before I can protest, she takes a long drink. "I figure we can both hate life tomorrow."

I snatch the bottle back from her and she glowers. "Mine. I need it more than you."

"Before you grab a straw, I think you should talk to me. Where's Liam?" Reanell looks around and I scoff.

"He left too. I threw myself at him and he left." I

see the disapproval through her eyes. Good. She can be pissed at him too. "Maybe he went back to the bar to find Brittany. She seems like she gets around."

"Now you're just being an idiot. Keep talking like that, I'll take your liquor away," she chastises me and I begin to cry. "Oh, Natalie..."

The tears stream and the numbness I was hoping for morphs into pain. "How could he do this to me?" I sob and she opens her arms. "I thought he loved me. I was pregnant!"

"I know, I know. Let it out." She doesn't try to console me more than hugging me and letting me drench her shirt.

"I gave him everything. I-I don't get it-t."

"You're hurting and drunk, so go ahead and cry," Rea says as she brushes my hair off my face.

I lie in her lap as she plays with my hair. I mumble incoherently about hating him to wishing I could kill him myself. All this time I thought I was married to a different man.

Once I've gotten to a point where I'm no longer hiccup-crying, Reanell helps me upstairs. She climbs into bed with me as I lie here wishing I could sleep so I could get a break from my mind. This is what she did after he died. Mason was away and she'd come sleep here so neither of us were alone.

"I wish I could go back in time," I whisper, holding back the sadness that creeps up.

Rea shifts onto her side, "Yeah? To when?"

"I wouldn't have tried to make him sleep with me..." My eyes close and I fight the sleepiness. "He didn't even want me."

Reanell shakes my shoulder, waking me. "Liam wants you. Liam cares for you and that's why he didn't sleep with you. You both deserve better than a drunken night of sex because you found out Aaron cheated. Now, shut up and go to sleep. I'm going to owe Mason a blow-job for sleeping here tonight."

My lips attempt to smile but I fail. I close my eyes, drifting to sleep where the hurt can't touch me. I welcome the reprieve and pray Brittany and Aaron don't haunt me in my sleep.

CHAPTER TWENTY-SIX

LIAM

MY HOUSE IS eerily quiet and I fight the urge to go back to her. I sat in my car for an hour after Reanell showed up. Fought with myself to knock on the door but instead I went home. Sitting there wishing I hadn't pushed her to come tonight. Selfishly, I'd wanted to force her to be with me outside of the walls of her home, to go public.

After two hours of staring at the walls, I need to see her and make sure she's okay. The way I left wasn't exactly how I'd planned for the night to end. I wanted to fuck every memory out of her mind. Show her that he's a prick for ever making her feel like this, but I don't want it to be because of him. When I take her for the first time, it'll be because she's ready, but I had to use every ounce of restraint I had to walk away.

What a mess this whole damn situation is . . . I can't really bash Aaron because he was my best friend. But I want to bash him because he's a fool. I can't push Natalie to be with me because the guilt of falling in love with my best friend's wife overwhelms me, but I want her so bad I can barely breathe.

I open the door with the key under the plant. I make a mental note to have her change that. She's asking for something bad to happen.

First, I see the half-empty bottle of Jack on the living room table. I shouldn't have fucking left her. There was no way in hell I was going to sleep with her tonight. Not that I don't fall asleep thinking about it every damn night, because she's the real deal. The girl you bring home to your mother because you want to spend every day with her. She's not the girl you fuck the night she finds out her husband slept around.

Anger boils inside because he's a prick. The Aaron I thought I knew wasn't so selfish. I can't understand how he could cheat on Lee. She's beautiful, smart, funny, and loving. He was so willing to throw it all away for someone like her? Thank God I never touched that slut.

I check on Aarabelle and see her sound asleep in her crib. I love this little girl. I mean, she's freaking adorable, other than the diaper thing. If she could use the toilet, we'd be golden.

Slowly, I creep open Natalie's door, unsure of what I'm going to find, but I need to see her. She's asleep on her side facing me, but doesn't stir. Her hair falls in her face and she looks perfect. I want to wake her and pull her into my arms. Hold her close. But I refuse to do anything tonight. I look over and see another person on the other side of the bed.

Immediately I want to punch something.

How the fuck can she have someone else in her bed?

Then I see the dark brown hair pulled up and realize it's Reanell. She must've stayed.

I head downstairs and look over at the mantel where the flag sits. I'm conflicted and angry. "Why, man? Why would you do it? After everything that you said about the guys who fuck around on their wives." I speak quietly but I'm pissed off. "And fucking Brittany?" I only met her once, but she was more than willing to do whatever I wanted after one night. Hell, she would've blown me in the bar if I asked her to. It makes no sense. You trade up, not slum it.

I sit on the couch and lean my head back. I'm drained, pissed, and a slew of other feelings I'd rather not think about.

The bottle of Jack sits there and I grab it, pulling a long gulp down. I close my eyes and wait for some brilliant idea to strike me on how to handle all this shit. She's going to pull back. I can feel it. I pushed her away when she threw herself at me, but I want her to be ready when we take the next step, because after that . . . there's no going back.

I relax and my mind goes blank.

Suddenly, I hear footsteps. I jump up disoriented and realize I fell asleep on her couch.

Shit.

I look over and see Reanell coming down the steps. She stops and her hand grips her throat until she registers who I am.

"You're here?" she asks with a knowing look.

"I came by late to check on her, but . . ." I feel stupid. I should've left after I saw they were okay.

Reanell steps forward and puts her hand on my arm. "You really do care about her, don't you?"

I let out a deep sigh. "I think that's pretty obvious."

"Do you love her?" She pulls no punches.

"I cared for her all those years we were friends. But I'm falling in love with her," I admit for the first time to anyone including myself.

She nods and looks at the bottle of Jack. "She's going to be hurting for a while, but don't give up on her. I see things in her that you've brought out. Her heart will heal, but you'll have to decide how much shit you're willing to put up with in the meantime."

We both sit on the couch and I look at the clock. It's six A.M. and it's way too early to be thinking about this. "I should get going."

"For what it's worth," she puts her hand on my forearm, "I don't think Natalie's willing to see the issues she and Aaron were having. In her mind their life was wonderful, but getting ready to have a baby had her rose-colored glasses firmly in place. When you're a military wife you choose to see things in a certain way. It's easier than dealing with your brooding asses when you go through another shift in attitude." Her face falls and she looks away.

"I can't compete with him."

She looks back and her eyes soften, "I don't think you have to. That's what I'm saying. Give her a few days and let her grieve the loss of the *real* husband she had. She's been mourning an idea . . . which I understand."

"I can't feel like I'm second best to him."

"I understand that. I think in a day or two she'll come to terms with it all. If you love her, you're going to have to realize this is like losing him all over again. The past slapped her pretty hard. And then kicked her a few times." She sighs and looks away. "I also don't think you were ever number two. Once she allowed her heart to let you in, you've been number one, even when you weren't."

"That makes no sense, but I'm exhausted and need some fucking sleep. Plus, I don't want her to see me here."

"You're a good guy. I like you," Reanell says and we both stand.

"Thanks. I think." I grab my keys and head out the door, careful not to make any noise.

I look at her window and decide I need to let her come to me. I can't keep pushing her and I fear I'll push her away. I love her and that scares the ever-living shit out of me. She needs to decide if it's me she wants. I sure as hell won't be the consolation prize.

chapter twenty-seven

natalie

MY HEAD IS throbbing. Between the crying and the copious amounts of Jack Daniels I drank on top of the beer, I'm lucky I'm not puking. I roll over and Reanell looks at me with a sad smile.

"Morning, sunshine," she says in a low tone. "Water and aspirin are over there. You should take them."

I groan and press my palm against my skull. "Aarabelle?"

"I already fed her and she's down for her morning nap."

I shoot up and immediately regret doing that. The clock reads eleven and I feel like the world's worst mother. "I didn't even hear her."

"That's because I woke up early and took the monitor out. I think you needed the sleep more than being super mom." Reanell sits up and puts the water bottle in my hand.

Memories from last night flood back and I immediately wish I was still asleep. I look around the bedroom and anger boils past what's reasonable. "I need to get out of this room," I mutter and take the pills.

"Do you want to talk?" she asks, knowing what I'm feeling. In the beginning of her marriage to Mason, he cheated. They're one of the stories in the teams that gave others hope that they could come out on the other side. Reanell and Mason worked hard to get through it and come out stronger. He paid heavily, but love was never their issue.

"About what? How stupid I am?"

"How the hell are you stupid?" her voice is full of reproach.

I stand and look at the dresser where Aaron's watches sit. I look at his side of the bed that still has his clothes folded neatly. Opening a drawer, I start looking for something. Anything that tells me this happened. The headache throbs on, but I don't care. There are answers here and I'm going to find them.

"Natalie, what are you doing?" she asks me as I start to throw his clothes out.

"I have to know. There has to be something here. Something that tells me my husband was fucking another woman," I explain as I pull a shirt out of the drawer. "I never bought him this . . . maybe she did."

Rea comes up behind me and her hand grips my shoulder, but I shrug it off.

"He wasn't that smart. There's something here," I insist. I grab the picture of us with him behind me holding my shoulders and kissing my cheek. I throw it against the wall with all my might and the glass shatters. "I hate him!" Everything comes flooding back.

Reanell sits back on the bed and crosses her legs.

The next drawer contains his pants. I pull each pair out and rifle through the pockets. Looking for God knows what, but I need something . . . anything. "Stupid bastard." Each time I come up empty, I grow more and more angry.

I rip open his closet door and start pulling more

things out. I find a pocketknife in his pants and rage consumes me. I want to tear every emotion out of me. Purge the hurt he's managed to cause from the grave. "I hope she was worth it!" I cry as I cut his favorite suit with his knife. The fabric rips apart and so does a part of my soul.

"You about done?" Reanell asks, while sitting on the bed.

"No!" I rear back and stab his uniform and tear it apart. "How? My entire life I was devoted to you!" The knife rips another shred. I drop it and the clattering against the wood floor is the only sound that penetrates the air.

I stand in his closet and inhale. It hits me like a brick to the chest, I smell him. It's as if he's standing behind me. The clove and musk scent is strong, and instead of sadness . . . I want to see it turned to ash.

"Okay, I'll just go make some popcorn," she leans back against the headboard.

"I hate this house! I want to set it on fucking fire," I cry out and Reanell sits quiet. "Say something!"

"What do you want me to say? Tear it up, burn it down . . . do what you have to so you can start to heal."

I look back in the closet where his shirts are shredded as if an animal tore through them. "Are you happy now?" I grab the shirt and grasp the hole, yanking it further. The pocket tears and I keep ripping apart anything in my sight. I taste the salt from my tears as I continue to assault his belongings. "Do you see me?" I cry out to the ceiling. "Do you see what you've done to me? I hate you! You've ruined me!"

Reanell touches my shoulder and I fall into her arms. "He didn't ruin you. I think he just freed you."

I wipe my eyes and let out a deep breath. "I need a shower."

"Yeah, you do. Go get cleaned up and we'll go get some fresh air and talk."

"GRANDE, NON-FAT, WHITE chocolate mocha please." I order my drink of choice and sit in the chair across from Reanell.

"She could be completely full of shit," she tries to convince me for the third time today.

I look out the window and try to find an answer that doesn't end in "fuck you." "You and I both know she's not. She was at his funeral."

"That day was a blur for you. Are you sure it was really her?"

Aarabelle plays with a smile on her face, throwing the toys out of her stroller as we sit on the deck. "I know it was, but I know it in my heart."

Reanell sits back and shakes her head. "Maybe. I don't know. I knew you and Aaron weren't perfect. I feel like you need to remember that. But I'm going to say this and you can punch me: he's not here anymore, Lee," she lets out a shaky breath. "You have Liam now. Are you willing to let him go?"

"Do you realize how fucked up this is? Legitimately, this is so insane I can't even fully comprehend it." I begin to ramble as it all comes out. "I married Aaron out of high school, followed him all over the place. Made it through how many deployments, work-ups, and all that other crap to have him get out of the Navy. Then, he goes to work for Jackson and somewhere in there he screwed someone else while I was pregnant. Oh, but wait!" I keep going with my hands moving as I speak. "He goes and gets himself blown the fuck up! Yup! That's my life. But no, it gets better, because it wouldn't be fun if I didn't keep going . . . I fall in love with his best friend," I say and then sit back.

Oh my God.

"Love, huh?"

"I said love."

"Yeah, you sure did." Reanell studies me over the rim of her cup and then takes a slow sip of her drink.

"I didn't—" I start to say "I didn't mean it," but the words get stuck in my throat.

"Dadadada!" Aarabelle screams as she throws her pacifier.

"Mamamama," I say as I try to get her to say my name. She laughs and raises her arms. I lift her and hold her close.

"You're going to try to deflect, but you and I both know you and Liam work. You make sense."

I hold my daughter close and kiss her. "How so? We've kissed a few times, so how are we working?" I ask while bouncing Aara up and down. She giggles and my heart that felt broken mends with the love of my child.

"Maybe I'm talking out of my ass. I like him. He's different than Aaron was. I know you think you guys had a good marriage, but do you remember all the bad? What about the nights he was being an asshole and angry at nothing? What about the way he'd go out with Quinn and the other guys and not come home? How easily you forget all of that."

"Aaron and I never had it perfect, but what was wrong is what made us right." I defend my life and feel foolish. He wasn't always great. In fact, if I'm honest, there were many times where I wasn't sure we would make it.

War changes a man. It causes what was once a light heart to become black and cynical. He'd been slightly injured in the firefight in Iraq that took out his team, and that loss affected him greatly. After that mission, he was never the same. I gave him time and space, but when he chose to get out of the Navy, things were bad for quite a while. He was angry, and when I got pregnant, there was a part of him that pulled away from me completely.

He wasn't happy, but he pretended. I guess I did a lot of pretending as well. If I avoided the issues I thought they would just go away.

"I know it's not easy, but give yourself some time."

"And you still like him after he left last night? I threw myself at him, begged him to sleep with me, and he said no and then left."

She huffs and looks away, frustrated with me. "Did you actually want to screw him on the night you found out about your husband's affair? Is that what you want to remember? I think he's a fucking hero for telling you no!" Reanell doesn't typically get loud with me, but here she is cursing at me.

"Don't judge me, Rea."

Her eyes narrow and her jaw falls. "Are you high? Because there's no way you would ever say that shit to me. I've never judged you, Natalie. Ever. You have no idea, and for that, you're an asshole."

"Gee, thanks."

My phone rings and I look at the screen and see Liam's name.

"Hello," I answer the call.

"Hey, I wanted to check on you."

Always concerned about me.

"I'm . . . I don't even know. Reanell and I are getting coffee."

"I think we should talk. Do you want to meet up?"

I draw in a breath and let it go. "I don't know. I'm not sure I can handle much today."

No response.

"Liam?"

"I'm here. Let me know when you decide."

"I will," I reply and hang up.

Reanell gives me the knowing eyes and keeps her mouth shut.

"Don't look at me like that. There's only so much one

person can take in a day."

Aarabelle demands my attention and I choose her. I'm a mother first and foremost. I need to decide if I'm ready to love again and if that person is Liam. It's not fair to either of us to go forward only to find out later.

"You know, he was there this morning," Reanell blurts out and then folds her arms across her chest.

My face is blank as I try to understand. "At the house?"

"Yup, sleeping on your couch while you were passed out. He came back. He stayed even though you pushed him away."

"I don't . . . I mean . . . why?"

"Why?" She throws her arms up and Aarabelle giggles. "Because maybe he loves you. He was worried about you, so he came to your house in the middle of the night and checked on you. Then fell asleep on your couch. But here's the thing and why you're an asshole . . ." she pauses and stares at me, "He left before you'd see. He could've stayed and made you face him, but instead he did the noble thing and left. He didn't want me to tell you. So yeah, you're an asshole."

He came back even after I made a fool of myself.

"Why does this have to be so friggin' complicated?" I ask the beautiful sky, waiting for some divine intervention.

She huffs, "I think you need to think about what I said and tell me: are you going to screw this up?"

I look back at her and I realize it's my choice. It's up to me. And if Liam and I can't make it work because of my truckload of issues, then so be it. But he's been here, day in and day out. He cared for me when I was sick, was there when Aara was in the hospital, and put me back together when I wouldn't acknowledge I was broken. It was Liam who mended my cracks.

"Can you watch Aarabelle? I need to take care of

something."

Reanell just sits back as if she knew this was coming and extends her hands. "I think you should go now." She grabs Aara from me and shoos me. "Go. Run. Now."

I grab my keys and get in the car.

Time to see if we really have a chance.

chapter twenty-eight

HE CAME BACK.

I keep saying it over and over again because it doesn't seem possible. Every time I think I've figured him out, he does something else to throw me off. I battle with what exactly I'm going to say when I do get to his house. There are a lot of things I'm dealing with, and it needs to be him who leads this relationship now. He's what I want, but I need Liam to take the reins. My heart is mangled and it's going to be his decision whether he wants to be the one to mend it.

His apartment is only a few miles away from mine and I wish it was further. I have no idea what to say. The words float through my mind: *sorry, I wish it was different, I want you, I'm a mess.* I don't know which is true, or maybe all of them are. I am a mess. I do want him—so much. I wish that this entire situation wasn't happening and I'm sorry this is where we are.

I park in the drive and try to collect myself. I know two things. One, I care about Liam deeply. Two, I'm going to have to process everything.

The walk to his apartment seems to take forever. It could be that I'm walking at a snail's pace. I go to knock and he opens the door.

Liam stands there in his tight, navy blue t-shirt and dark blue jeans. His light brown beanie is on his head and he leans against the door. "Hi," he says and looks past me.

"Hi, can I come in?" I ask hesitantly.

He opens the door and turns so I can pass him. Well, shit . . . now I have to talk.

Liam follows behind me and I look around. His apartment is modern and practically empty. The typical bachelor pad, complete with the biggest television I've ever seen. I stand in the middle of the room and he waves toward the couch.

"I'm surprised you're here," Liam says as he sits in the seat next to me.

"If I'm keeping you from something . . ."

"It's not important."

I tuck my hair behind my ear and try to decide where to start. "I'm going to talk and I'll probably ramble, but I need to say it." I look up and he nods. "I'm sorry about throwing myself at you like that. It wasn't fair to you or to whatever we've been doing. I care too much about you to do that . . . but I knew you could make it go away. It makes me selfish, and I'm so embarrassed that I did that. When you left, I drank so much and all I could do was replay how you looked at me when I begged you. I understand if you don't want to be with me or don't want m—"

"Don't even say it. Don't say I don't want you. That's not the case. I want you. Every day I want you," Liam cuts me off with his voice razor sharp.

My cheeks flush and my heart begins to race. "Okay, I just meant that I shouldn't have tried to get you to sleep with me last night."

"Look, if all that shit hadn't gone down and you wanted to take that step, I would've been all for it. Trust me, I want nothing more than to touch you, but not because you want to fuck Aaron out of your mind. I want it to be because you can't stand the idea of me *not* touching you."

He's right but so wrong. "I want to be with you.

There's something between us that is beautiful and I don't want to lose that. Even if you had said yes last night—it wouldn't have been that."

"That's exactly what it would've been. Let's be honest, because if we start with lies, this will fail before it even has a chance."

Fear of losing him begins to bubble up. "I don't know how to go from here because I feel like I've taken two steps back. I want to trust you, and I do, but I feel like this affair just destroyed whatever we were building. How could you want me knowing this?"

"Natalie," Liam says and his hand gently cups my face. He pushes me to look at him and I get lost in his eyes. "I've fallen for you and for Aarabelle. I'm not going anywhere until you tell me you're done. I'm done fighting with myself over having any kind of feelings for you. I want you, Lee. And his fuck ups have nothing to do with us."

"But they affect us."

"Only if you want them to. Look, every part of me battles with touching you. It's like I'm the fucking dirtbag here. You were his fucking wife." His hand drops.

"He obviously didn't hold that title very high," I say and grab his hand wrapping my fingers around his. "I'm angry, though, and hurt. He and I weren't perfect, but I didn't think he was capable of infidelity."

"Did you have any idea?"

"No, I mean, we were fighting, but I was pregnant. We had been trying for almost a year to get pregnant with Aarabelle. I could only sleep with him during certain times, and sex was tedious, but I thought we were making the best of it."

Infertility was a huge burden between us. Aaron felt his manhood was being challenged and I thought I was maybe not meant to be a mother. Even through it all, Aaron and I tried to stay close. He wasn't any more distant than normal, and I definitely didn't suspect anything.

"I wish I could take this away from you. I can't though. He was your husband."

I nod in understanding. Liam only knew the side of our marriage everyone saw. The happy, smiling couple that loved each other since they were sixteen. In many ways, it wasn't an act. I did love him, and if he were alive, we'd be together, or at least figuring out where to go from here. But he's gone, and I have Liam.

"In a way, it's also opened my eyes to how my life wasn't exactly what I thought."

"How so?"

"Do we seriously talk about this? Do I really tell you about good and bad in my marriage to your best friend?" I question because it feels almost unnatural. This is the guy who I'm sure listened to Aaron talk about me and now I'm sitting here about to make him listen to me.

"I can't say I'm going to enjoy it, but if we keep avoiding this shit, we're never going to get past it. Look, this is hard as hell for me. Aaron was my best friend. I would've taken a bullet for him, no questions asked. When things started happening with you and I, I felt like a dick." Liam plays with my fingers as we sit and talk. "You're off limits. No one fucks another team guy's wife. It's code. But he's gone and I don't know how we found our way here."

"I battle with the same thing. You were . . . well . . . *you*. I saw you as a friend. As Aaron's friend. I can remember sewing your patches on and painting your helmet when you were in BUDs. When my feelings started to shift, I tried to stop it." I twist my fingers in his as we both open ourselves up. "Do you know what I'm most upset about?" I muse out loud, but I need to say it.

"What?"

"This whole time . . ." I look away, but Liam's hand pulls my chin toward him.

Liam's eyes are tender but his jaw is tight. "Don't hide from me. Let me in."

My eyes blur with unshed tears as the words begin to form like acid on my tongue. "I've been so blind. In my mind, I blocked out everything bad and I've put him on this pedestal. When I told him I was pregnant, he shrugged and walked away. I forgot about that until last night. I wanted him to be so perfect. I didn't want to remember how we weren't always happy, but we were comfortable. I'm such an idiot."

He's rubs his thumb gently against my skin. I close my eyes to his touch and my hand touches his chest. I lean into his body and he holds me close. "You're not an idiot."

I let out a short, sarcastic laugh. "The hell I'm not. My husband was cheating on me when I was pregnant. I laid in bed crying for days over someone who could've been planning to leave me. My entire life was a lie."

"I don't know what to say. A part of me—the selfish part—wants to tell you he was a fucking moron and you're better off with me. I wouldn't cheat and would tell you how you shouldn't spend another minute thinking of him." I lean up and Liam lets out a deep breath. "The other part of me is fighting against defending the motherfucker. But I won't defend what he did . . . it's so fucked up."

This is what I worry about with us. "Will Aaron always be between us?" I ask and hold my breath.

"I don't know. Tell me . . ." Liam pauses and bends forward. His lips touch mine and he kisses me. His tongue glides across my lips and he pulls back. He waits for me to open my eyes, and the fierceness stops my breath. The tension in his muscles is clear as he gives me what I need. "Do you wish he was here instead of me? Right now, do you wish it were his arms around you? His mouth on yours?"

I hear him speaking, but I can't focus. When his lips touch mine, all that exists is Liam and me. He stops and waits . . . I bring myself back to his question and shake my head no.

"That's not good enough," his low gruff voice is demanding.

"Right now, I'm not thinking of anyone else." My lips ghost against his.

He just barely touches his lips to mine. Liam's head moves side to side as he brushes against my mouth. It's a game of who's stronger at this point. "I didn't ask that."

"I'm not sure how to answer that, Liam. I'm here with you right now. I'm in your arms. I want to be here—with you."

The air is thick between us and he doesn't relax. "He doesn't have to be here. This is you and me."

"I don't want to lose you." The honesty seeps through each syllable. "I'm scared."

Liam lies back on the couch and pulls me against his chest. I lie in his arms pressed against him with our fingers intertwined. "I'm falling in love with you, Natalie." His chest rumbles and I look up. "If I'm not already there. You're not the only one who's got something to lose. I don't want you to say anything back to me. I just want you to know." Liam's fingers roll mine as he waits for me to react.

As afraid as I am about being hurt again, I know I'm not alone. "I'm falling for you too. I just don't know if I can."

His eyes tell me he understands. He pulls me back down and rubs his hand against my back. There's a lot the two of us need to overcome. But right here and now, I'm safe. Liam's strong arms hold me together and I try to think of the last time I felt this way.

Aaron and I were married so young, but we'd had a good marriage. He was gone a lot, and that part sucked, but it made our reunions that much sweeter. Aaron had a temper, but he was never abusive or mean. Hell, half the time I was the one throwing things across the room. He provided for me and I became content. But there were times I could see him distancing himself from me. When he would become belligerent when I would try to talk about what happened overseas. The infertility, PTSD, and his disdain of no longer being a SEAL ate at us. He would spend hours in the garage working on his car and then go to sleep or go out. I put blinders on and thought when I was pregnant with Aarabelle it would fix everything. But the only time Aaron was happy was when other people were around.

Then I wonder about Liam. The fact that I'd be entering a relationship knowing the life I'd live with him and the possible outcome. But I was built for this. I'm a SEAL wife. I know the life, the struggles, and the joys that it can bring. I know I'm able to handle deployments and all that goes with it. I just don't know if I could withstand losing him. Loving Liam comes with a cost.

"What's going through your mind? I can feel you tensing up." Liam breaks the silence.

I lean on my hand that rests upon his chest. His blue eyes sparkle and I give a sad smile. "I'm thinking about all of it. The love, the loss, the affair. I think the fact that I don't have answers is the hardest part."

"Do you want to talk to her? Will that help?" Liam's hand continues to run up and down my back.

"I don't know. A part of me wants to forget it all and call her a liar. What does it even matter?"

Liam kisses the top of my head and lets out a deep sigh.

"Where do we go from here?" I ask.

Liam's hands grip my shoulders and he pulls me on top of him. I'm lying on his chest and we're face to face. "We decide. You decide because I'm here with you, but I need to know you're not there with him."

Pushing my hands up his chest, I rest against his shoulders. "I'm with you right now."

He sits up so quickly I'm not sure how he manages it. He flips me so I'm on my back and he's on top of me. My body warms from his touch and he glides his calloused fingers down my bare arm. "Liam . . ." I sigh his name.

"Tell me when you need me to stop," his voice is low and smooth.

I don't know that I'll ever be able to tell him to stop. I hope he has more control than I do.

chapter twenty-nine

HIS FINGERS GRAZE my pants where my shirt meets. I squirm in anticipation. Liam pauses and my eyes lock on his. I don't speak or move, but I grant him the permission he seeks. He knows how to read me, my body, my tiny movements that not many would be able to pick up on. It's a blessing and a curse.

The pads of his fingers float across my stomach and my breath stops. Lust flurries and builds as his fingertip moves higher. It skims my ribs and he traces the underside of my breast.

"Tell me if it's too much," his husky voice gravels in my ear.

"It's not enough," the words fall from my lips.

Liam groans and his tongue traces the shell of my ear. My eyes roll back in my head in pure pleasure as he pushes underneath my bra. When his finger grazes my nipple, I nearly buck off the couch.

"You're so perfect," he reassures me and rubs back and forth, my nipple pebbling beneath his adept touch.

Needing to touch him, I run my hands under his shirt, pushing it up. Liam uses one hand and rips it off. My fingers delicately press against his skin. I trace the tattoo on his ribs: *Dulce bellum inexpertis*. I outline the letters and he tenses. "What does that mean?" I ask as he kisses my neck.

He looks up and his blue eyes darken. "It means war is sweet for those who haven't experienced it."

My voice is barely audible, "I'm sorry. I know you've lost a lot."

"I've gained too. War takes from us. It robs us of so much, but if we let it . . . it can save us. You being here in my arms right now is reminding me that sometimes the victory is worth the battle."

Liam bows down as each breath passes between us. As much as he's breathing life into me, I'm doing the same for him. We've both lost because of war. Liam's lost countless friends as well as handling his own demons. "I shouldn't be feeling this way," I say as he brushes the hair out of my eyes.

"What do you feel?" his voice is rich and warm. It heats parts of my body that have been forgotten. "Describe it," he demands.

I close my eyes as his hand floats down my body and back under my shirt. I allow the sensations to overtake my mind and Liam's touch is what I give myself over to. "Your hands are strong, but when you touch me, it's tender." His thumb brushes my nipple and I sigh. "The scraping of your thumb against my skin." He does it again.

"Does it feel good?" he asks gruffly.

"Yes," I moan, as his hand cups my breast and he squeezes.

"Do you want me to keep touching you?" he asks.

Keeping my eyes closed, I stay in the moment. "Please," my voice is low and dripping with need.

His weight shifts and he pulls my shirt over my head. I look at him and his eyes turn to liquid as he appraises me, setting my nerves at ease. Liam groans in approval. "Perfect. Every inch of you is perfection." He pulls my straps down and waits. I tilt and unhook my bra, but leave it in place.

No other man has seen me like this besides Aaron. Aaron was my first and only. Liam seems to understand my hesitation and then he's on top of me again. His mouth fuses to mine and he kisses me eagerly. My fingers pull his beanie off and tangle into his hair. I want him so much right now. Every cell feels like it's on fire and I'll soon become cinders. Burning with need, I get lost again. No thoughts of anything but him exist.

My hands grip his ass as he grinds down on me. I feel his hardness against my core and I begin to throb. His hands start to drift down my side as he pulls the bra from between us, but keeps me covered with his body.

"I'm going to suck on your breasts, Natalie. Do you want that?" he asks and I practically melt into the couch.

I whimper as he reaches behind my back and pulls me with him. He keeps me shielded with his chest. I'm straddling his legs, feeling the exceedingly large bulge between my legs.

He holds me against him and stares into my eyes, "Do you want my mouth on you, or do you want me to stop?" There's no anger or hesitation. He wants me, it's clear, but he's not wanting to push me too far.

"Don't stop," I plead and his hands drift down my back ever so slowly. There's no hurt in my heart right now. I feel alive and adored. My heart races and my core clenches.

Liam carefully extends me onto my back, keeping his eyes on me. His head drops and his tongue circles my nipple. He lavishes it and caresses me. "Oh, oh God." My voice is husky and my breath comes in short bursts.

His mouth moves to the other breast and my hips move against him, creating the friction I'm desperate for. "Your skin tastes like heaven." He sits back and looks at me.

I fight the urge to cover up, and the way his eyes appraise me keeps me still. The tip of my finger slides to the front of him and his head falls back. I rock against him again. It feels too good to stop. "Liam," I sigh his name.

"Tell me to stop or I'm going to flip you over and not be able to control myself."

"Kiss me," I request and he acquiesces. Our mouths come together and my hand rests on his heart. I feel his life beneath my palm. He's alive, real, and he's good to me. Liam was there when Aara was sick, when I was sick, and any other time I've needed him. Liam's mouth never touched Brittany. His hands press against my back and he holds me tightly against him. There's nowhere else I'd rather be than right here in his arms.

We break apart and we stay chest to chest. "I'll never take you for granted. I'll never give another woman a piece of me once you're mine. I'll only be yours."

I look up with tears in my eyes. "I'm not ready, but I'm yours now. I want to give myself to you completely when it can be only about us."

"What makes you think I was offering myself to you?" Liam smirks and the mood shifts from raging desire to playfulness.

"Oh?" I raise my brows in question. "I think if I wanted you, I could have you."

Liam pulls me closer and I nuzzle into his neck. "Are you calling me an easy lay?"

I laugh and he kisses the side of my face. "Never. There's nothing easy about you."

"Well, except my banging hot body . . . I mean, that's just easy on the eyes."

"Arrogance is not sexy, darling," I tease as his finger makes designs on my back.

"I think you're very sexy," Liam says as his hands make their way to the sides of my breasts.

"Oh?" I reply as my lips press against his neck.

"Should I show you with my mouth?" he inquires while his scruff grates across my shoulder. It prickles my skin and ignites the lust that had dropped to a low simmer.

My phone chimes, interrupting where we were going. I groan and reach over toward my purse. Liam adjusts himself and sits back, looking at my half naked body with a smug smile.

"Shit," I say when I read the text. "I gotta go. Aarabelle is being super fussy and Rea has to run out." I grab my bra and Liam snatches it from my hand. "I need that."

"I'm thinking you wouldn't want to leave the house like that."

I don't want to leave. God knows I want to stay here with him. It's the only time I'm whole. There's no pity in Liam's eyes. When I see myself in him, I'm desired and beautiful. I lean down and kiss him and grab his t-shirt. I throw it over my head and smile.

"Keep the bra. I can wear your clothes."

Liam stands before he takes a measured step, slowly drawing me in. "I'm going to take the coldest shower I can manage. I'll somehow find a way to not think about you in my clothes. Walking around with my shirt clinging to your body and you smelling like my cologne."

I step back and grab my purse. "You may need to take two showers." I wink and open the front door. I turn back and glance at him over my shoulder. "You know, I might even sleep in it." I turn back and hear him groan as I close the door behind me.

Funny, I didn't think of the pain Aaron caused even once while I was in Liam's arms.

CHAPTER THIRTY

LIAM

"DEMPSEY, MY OFFICE now," Commander Hansen orders and I pop tall. What the hell did I do now?

"Sir," I say and stand at his desk.

"Take a seat," he instructs me and points to the chair. Commander is the kind of officer we all want to serve under. He's fair and doesn't think he's above everyone. He's a leader you want to follow and it makes taking orders from him pretty easy. "My wife is a pain in my ass. She meddles, and most of the time I'm able to handle her shit, but Natalie is a different story. Gilcher served under me for six years. I knew him and he was like family. So, me calling you in here isn't Commander to Chief. It's man to man."

I nod out of respect and bite back my response. It's no one's business what the hell happens between Natalie and I. The other night was a shit show. What was supposed to be a turning point ended up in complete disaster thanks to a stupid bitch.

"I'm sure you don't give a shit, and honestly, I don't care if you do. I care about Lee and Aarabelle. More than that, my wife makes my life miserable when she gets like this. Rea is worried, so if you need to take a few days and be there, go."

That wasn't what I thought he was going to say. I thought I was going to get the stay-away-from-her speech. To which I would've found a way to tell him to suck my dick . . . respectfully. "How long?"

"If you need to drop leave, I'll approve it. We have the next two weeks where there's nothing going on. Hell, most of you guys will leave before lunch anyway."

"I'll do that, sir. I appreciate it."

Commander looks away and huffs. "Natalie didn't smile, cry, or laugh. For weeks she just sat with no emotions. Reanell was in the delivery room with her and it wasn't until Aarabelle was born that she finally cried. She went back to that way a few weeks after Aaron's memorial." He scratches his face. "Then she started to open up when she thought no one was looking. I attribute that to your arrival."

"I don't know that I had anything to do with it."

"I don't either, but it's a hunch."

This is the most bizarre conversation I've ever had.

Commander stands and walks to the wall. "I suspected something was going on before he left for Afghanistan," he admits. "I think Natalie remembers a different life than what she was living."

Aaron was my best friend. I knew he was struggling with a baby coming and what it meant, but I never thought he was fucking around on her. He and I were living on opposite coasts, so we didn't talk as often, but he sure as fuck never mentioned another woman.

I think about Natalie and how she is already reconstructing her walls. I remember what she felt like, tasted like, and how long it took my dick to go down. Yesterday was another day I didn't expect to happen the way it went, but she opened up to me. The need to claim a part of her was so strong, I wasn't sure I would stop. I had to constantly remind myself that she was in control of how far we went.

She's worth the blue balls.

"I understand, Sir. I'm going to need those few days."

"I was hoping you were the man I thought you were." Commander stands and extends his hand.

"Commander."

"Chief, I'll see you in a few days."

I turn and start to form a plan. One that includes no way out and maybe rope.

"SO, YOU GUYS still together?" Quinn asks as we load the weights on the bar.

"Yeah," I reply and get aligned to lift. I'm going for a personal record and all this dick wants to do is talk about Natalie.

I line up my hands and Quinn pushes down so I can't move. "She's okay with this? The fact that her husband—your best friend—was fucking around on her and she wants to be with you?"

"I'm not sure where you got confused when I said 'yeah.' She and I are together. Aaron fucked up, but he and I are separate."

"If you say so," he scoffs and moves his hand.

He's always got something smart to say. It's irritating and I'm tired of his bullshit. "You know, you're not a part of my fucking life choices. If I want to be with her, I will. If she's okay with it and I'm okay with it, then what the hell do you care?"

Quinn steps back with his hands raised, "I'm just asking, dude."

I sit up, pissed off. "When you've fucked anything that walks, I never said shit. You've fucked up more than all of us combined." My hands tremble as I clench them into a ball. "Lay off about me and Lee."

He moves toward me. "I won't say another word

after I say this. You hurt her and I'll beat the ever-living shit out of you. She's not just some girl. She's his fucking wife and that's his daughter. I know the cost that comes with a single mother."

"I'm not stupid."

"The jury's still out on that one." Quinn slaps me on the shoulder. "I may not have been as close as you and Aaron were, but he was my friend too. I know you're not a piece of shit. I'm saying to make sure you're all in before you go any further." He gives me a pointed look and then morphs back into his normal, jackass self. "Now, let's see if your weak ass can lift this."

We've been friends for a long time. It's probably the longest speech I've ever heard. "You don't have to worry about me hurting her."

"All I wanted to hear. Are we going to work out or do you want to hug it out?" he jokes while waiting.

"Dickhead. Let's go." I get back on the bench and try to focus on getting through the rest of the workout.

Quinn and I finish and decide to go grab lunch. He's smart enough not to bring up my relationship or whatever the fuck this is with Lee. We talk about the upcoming deployment. Having our own squad means we work together but each manage a group of guys. We're hoping our squads aren't split since we understand each other. It's nice to know the guy who's watching your six.

"I heard you're taking a few days off," Quinn mentions as he grabs his drink.

"Yeah, I'm going to take Natalie and Aarabelle somewhere. I have to figure it out," I laugh. I've racked my brain trying to think of something close that she'd like. Just something for us to get away from all this shit and see if this is something or if it's a matter of circumstance.

"Why don't you take her to my beach house?"

"Where?"

"The one in OBX. I know she lives on the beach and

all, but it's a nice house and it's away."

"I gotta admit, man, I'm shocked," I muse and lean back. He's the last person I thought would be helping me out.

"I told you, I wanted to be sure. You care about her and you're taking the kid. I think that says it all. Here," he says and takes the key off his ring. "Take it. Go or don't. I don't care. I'll tell you all the info. It's a few hours, but Corolla is a cool spot. I've seen the wild horses a time or two."

"You're not such a dick after all." I smile as I put the key in my pocket.

"Don't tell anyone."

"Your secret's safe with me," I slap him on the back. "Until you piss me off. Then I'll tell everyone."

"Yeah, I'll tell everyone how you couldn't lift the bar today."

Now, I need to get my bag together and a plan to get Natalie to agree.

This should be fun.

chapter thirty-one

natalie

"Mamamama," Aarabelle repeats over and over, sitting in her highchair. It's music to my ears. She's growing up so fast. I wish I could push pause and freeze frame each tiny moment.

She's truly mobile now, which has been a huge pain in the ass. Plus, everything goes in her mouth, and I swear the child can find the tiniest things.

"Mamamama."

"Hi, beautiful girl." I smile and put another Cheerio on the tray. I've learned one Cheerio gives me time for about one dish to get washed. Timing is everything.

She grins and tries to grab it as I rush back to the sink to keep cleaning before she starts screaming again.

I look out the window and see Liam's car pull up. My happiness is automatic and the butterflies start to flutter in my stomach. It's only been a few days since we've seen each other, but I've missed him.

The time apart gave me a chance to come to terms with my emotions. I'm angry, but I won't allow Aaron's decisions to impact my future. He's gone. He made bad choices and I have to live with that. But he gave me Aarabelle, and in a way, he gave me Liam. The truth is, I have no way of knowing if it even happened. All I have is the word of some woman.

I hear Liam knocking at the door and Aarabelle starts to fuss. Looks like my Cheerio time has expired.

"Come in!" I yell toward the door and hear it open.

"Lock the damn door," Liam grumbles as he enters.

"I live in the safest neighborhood. I also have the nosiest neighbor who camps out on her deck. I think Mrs. DeMatteo would notice and beat you with a bat before you could get in." I smile and Liam squats down and kisses Aarabelle on the cheek.

"Hello, gorgeous," he coos at her and she grins.

"Mamamama," Aara says.

"Give her one Cheerio, please," I instruct Liam and almost get excited that I can do all the dishes while he feeds her.

"Sure thing, but first you better kiss me."

I turn and my arms wrap around his neck. "Hi," I whisper.

"Hi. You look beautiful," Liam says seductively.

"You're all sweaty," I reply as I lift up on my toes. I inch closer to his lips and he leans down slowly.

The tension builds between us and I savor the moment. When a kiss can leave your head spinning and your body tingling . . . I haven't had this in so long.

He stops right before his lips can touch mine. "I like sweaty," he grumbles and then he kisses me.

I hold the back of his neck and he holds me tight as he moves me backwards. My back hits the counter and he pushes against me. The kiss ends as quickly, but leaves me breathless.

"Maaaaaamaaaaa," Aarabelle screams from her chair reminding us of her presence.

I laugh and push against his chest. "No one forgot you, silly girl," I chide playfully and place a Cheerio on Aara's highchair.

She gives me one of her whole-face smiles. Where her eyes glimmer, her nose crinkles a little, and her lips are wide. You can't help but smile back at her.

"So, I have an idea," Liam says as he snakes his arms around my waist.

"Oh?"

Liam releases me and turns me so we're facing each other. "We're on training workups, so you know that the deployment will be coming at some point."

"Yeah, I figured." I know this. I can try to pretend that I'm ignorant, but I'm not. Years of being a SEAL wife has given me the knowledge of how they work. How I'm going to handle him leaving remains to be seen. This is one of my biggest worries. Can I cope with this again?

"Hey," he lifts my chin. "Do you trust me?"

I look into his eyes and my hands rest on his chest. I think it's the one question that I never have to think twice about. Liam has proven time and time again in the last nine months that I can trust him. "Of course I do."

"Okay, then go upstairs and pack a bag for you and Aarabelle."

"What?" I pull back looking at him confused.

"For a few days." Liam kisses the tip of my nose and turns me around.

I turn back but he starts to walk me toward the stairs. "Liam, stop."

"I knew you were going to argue," he mumbles.

Damn right I'm going to argue.

"What the hell am I packing for? Where are you trying to take us? I have to work this week. I have things to do," I start to ramble off without taking a break as my mind reels. "I can't just go away. There's no way I can drop everything. I have meetings and Aarabelle has a play date. I mean, what about . . ."

"Good God, woman. You trust me. So trust me," Liam stands against the wall as I stare at him with pursed lips.

"Go! Up the stairs."

"Don't 'woman' me. And don't order me around," I reply defiantly.

He bursts out laughing and I follow. Liam steps forward and grips my hips. My hands wrap around his neck. "Stop being so damn cute. Go pack. I want us to get away from here." He pulls me close and gazes with adoration in his eyes. "Give ourselves a chance to be free of all the shit here and see how we feel. Just us. No ghosts. No memories. Only the three of us."

When he says those last few words, my heart sputters. The three of us. It was never meant to be him in the three of us, but here we are. Liam doesn't just want me. He wants Aarabelle too—even with her diapers and drool. He's not asking to whisk me away on a getaway so he can seduce me. Instead, Liam cares enough to want to build something together and include Aara.

"You really know how to win a girl's heart, Dempsey." I tug on his neck while lifting myself up and press my lips against his.

Liam pulls back but keeps me tight against him. "Only yours. I only care about your heart."

I lean my head against his chest and wish I could stay here. With my eyes closed and holding on to this moment. In his arms where I'm secure and I know he'll protect me.

"What am I packing for?"

"A few days. Beach gear."

"Beach? Do you see what is off my back deck?" I ask confused.

"Zip it. Go pack." Liam breaks from my hold and slaps my ass. "I've got Aarabelle."

"Oh, that's comforting," I retort and climb the stairs quickly, hoping he won't chase me. Or maybe I do hope that.

I enter my room a little giddy. A vacation—with Liam.

It's kind of surreal and completely unexpected. Holy shit, we're going to have to sleep together. Like sleep—in the same bed. I mean, I wouldn't want him to sleep on the couch and we've been moving so slow with everything sexual, but I don't know that I'll be able to be in the same bed. Then, of course, I don't know that I want to keep going slow. I want him and it's clear he wants me. I know that my feelings for Liam are real, but still. I've only ever been with Aaron and it worries me that I won't be good.

Panic starts to bubble and I decide I need to focus. I'm getting way ahead of myself here. Packing. That's all I need to worry about. I'm going to have to smack him for this. Women need days to pack for a trip, not minutes, and that's when they know where they're going. I try to make a mental list of all the things I'll need for Aara and myself.

Piling different clothes on the bed, I start to feel a little better. I have outfits for whatever may happen, and I at least have the beach necessities. Aaron's closet has all our luggage in it. I haven't come back to this closet since the day I shredded his clothes. There's nothing inside of here that I want to open again, but I have to. My hand rests on the door handle and I draw a steadying breath, then open it. It still smells like Aaron. Spice and musk assail my senses and I fight the tears. He's hurt me so deeply, even from his grave. "Why didn't you tell me?" I ask aloud. "I won't let you destroy me. My heart was yours but you decided it wasn't good enough so I'm taking it back. I'll always love you but I'm not yours anymore." I lean against the door and hope he hears me.

I allow a solitary tear to fall as I grab the suitcase from the top shelf. When I pull it down, I see a torn piece of paper that sits on the floor.

Hesitantly, I squat and grasp the paper. I turn it over afraid of what I might find, but all that's written is "I'm sorry."

More questions begin to take shape. "Sorry for what, Aaron? Or to who?" I yell and kick the door closed. The loud smack of the door echoes through the room. Leaning my back against it, I slink to the ground and hold my knees. My head falls forward and I begin to cry. Dissolution of a marriage is always hard. Becoming a widow and having that marriage taken from you is the most difficult thing anyone can imagine, but finding out that marriage was a lie—inexplicable.

"Natalie?" I hear Liam call out. "Are you okay?" I feel his hands touch my arm and I slowly lift my head.

There he stands with Aarabelle in his arms.

"No. Yes. I don't know," I say in a hushed voice. I'm trying to hold back the tears. I don't want him to see me like this. Liam is who I want, but I'm still breaking from Aaron. It's not fair to either of us.

"Okay, well . . . let's get packed and we'll figure it out together." Liam stands and puts his hand out for me to take.

I place my hand in his and he lifts me up.

Aarabelle begins to clap her hands and I laugh. "You wanna go on vacation, pretty girl?"

She squeals as if she has any clue what I'm saying and I look at Liam.

"Together," he states again and kisses me on the temple. "Now," his voice shifts to be more animated. "Someone needs a diaper change and I call not it."

I shake my head as he holds her out toward me. "No way, you said you've got Aarabelle and if we're in this whole 'together' thing," I say with air quotes, "You're going to be doing diapers too." I cross my arms and give him a shit-eating grin.

"Over my dead body, sweetheart."

I walk over and my tongue glides across my lips. I watch the intake of Liam's breath, the way his eyes follow my tongue and linger on my lips. He shifts Aarabelle to his other arm and grabs my waist when I get close.

I lean close to his ear and whisper, "No diapers, no naked." Liam groans and I laugh. "Now, I need to finish. No rope!" I yell as he walks out the door.

"You can't make the rules," he yells back and I hear him talk to Aarabelle. "Now, where is Mommy's duct tape?"

chapter thirty-two

"OKAY, NOW WILL you tell me where we're going?" I ask for the thirtieth time. It's so easy to drive him crazy.

"You're trying to make me frustrated, but it's not going to work. I'm highly trained," Liam throws his arm over the back of my seat. "What can I say? I'm just superior like that."

I look at him waiting for the smirk or something to let me know he's kidding. "Superiorly stupid!" I retort.

"Jealous."

"Of what?" I ask with my jaw hanging.

I wait for him to answer.

And wait.

And wait some more. He continues to drive and looks anywhere but at me. Aarabelle giggles and plays with her toy in the backseat.

This man is maddening.

"Liam!" I shriek and he begins to chuckle. Which of course only fuels my irritation. Fine. I can play.

I lean back and put my feet up on the dash. With my eyes closed, I lean back into the seat and I can feel his eyes. *Yeah, this is going to be good.*

"Sweetheart," Liam says through his teeth.

"Hmmm?" I reply keeping my eyes closed and feet in place. My face stays stoic as I fight the urge to smile.

"Would you be so kind as to take your feet off of Robin," Liam's voice is strained but polite.

I open my one eye and look over. "Oh, I'm quite comfortable."

"That's great, but really, you wouldn't want to lose your foot if we crashed. I'm only thinking of you."

My head rolls to the side lazily and I shrug. "You'll carry me around. I'm good. Thanks for caring though." I bite the inside of my cheek to keep from laughing. I can practically feel the steam building in his head.

"Lee."

I look over coyly. "Liam."

"If I tell you where we're going, will you take your feet off my baby?"

Oh, the joy of winning. Some men are hard to figure out what their trigger is, but Liam is simple: his car. Robin, as he calls her, is his version of a child.

"Do you use rope on Robin?"

Liam tries to smother his smile, but I see his eyes crinkle. "Feet, Natalie."

"Where are we going?" I ask as I shift my legs a little.

No way am I conceding. It's too much fun, first of all. But secondly, it keeps my mind off not knowing where we're going, for how long, and whether or not I'm going to sleep with Liam. My type A personality is going a little crazy not knowing. I'm trying to relax and go with the flow, but that's not in my DNA. Everyone knows I'm the take-the-bull-by-the-horns-and-do kinda girl. I've had to be with Aaron always gone.

"Do you really want to know?" Liam takes my hand and laces his fingers with mine.

I look up and boldly meet his eyes, "Not really. I just like annoying you."

"Women."

"Men," I answer back as I take my feet off the dash.

"She's sound asleep," Liam notes while looking in

the rearview mirror.

Glancing back, I see how peaceful she is. Not a care in the world. I envy that kind of serenity. I'd be lying if I said that being away from home right now isn't a little bit of a relief. There's something to be said about leaving your worries behind.

"Thank you for this," I squeeze his hand gently.

Liam lifts our intertwined hands and kisses my fingers. "I'm glad I didn't have to tie you up and carry you out. Let's just focus on relaxing and seeing where this goes. No expectations."

"I can do that."

He laughs, "I'll believe it when I see it."

"Whatever. So, how many days do I need to call out of work for?"

"I already talked to Muff and Twilight. You're good."

I look over with wide eyes. "You did what?"

I'm not sure whether I want to slap him or kiss him. On one hand, it shows he cared enough about my job to even think of it. On the other, it's my job and I should be the one to handle things.

I've only been working for Jackson for a few months and I love it there. I don't want to risk losing my position. Although, I highly doubt that Jackson would ever fire me. I've increased their manpower and reduced costs in some areas. I've also been able to utilize my contacts through my time as a journalist. I did a lot of military reporting and knew a few people who worked in similar companies. They were all too happy to give me some new people looking to create some areas of opportunity for growth.

"I called Muff and told him my plan. He said—and I quote—take her for as long as you want." Liam pauses and let's that sink in. "So I'm taking you."

I let out a deep breath. Relax and enjoy. Relax and enjoy. I tell myself repeatedly so I don't go postal.

"I'm going to just say thank you."

"There's a first," he grumbles.

"Why does this feel so easy with us?" I ask out of nowhere. I don't know why it came out of my mouth, but I wonder it often. Our relationship feels like it went into hyperdrive. It's not instant because I fought him for months, but when I gave in . . . it just felt natural.

Liam looks over with his brow furrowed. "Easy? I don't know I'd call this easy."

"No, I mean being with you. It's easy and effortless. As if we've been doing it forever," I muse.

"I think it's because it's right. I don't know. Why? Are you wanting me to be difficult? Because I can."

I laugh and shake my head. "I'm sure you can. You already are difficult, but I mean us as a couple. I wonder if this is normal."

Liam's hand grips the inside of my leg. "I've never felt like this with anyone. I think it's because we've been friends for a long time. I know you and you know me. There's no getting-to-know-you phase. I loved you before we were ever more—just not like I feel now. You were one of my close friends, but you were off limits. Doesn't mean I wouldn't have done anything for you, though. Now, it's just different." Liam looks out the window as he tries to figure it out too.

"I loved you, too. That being said, I never thought about making out with you all the time. This is new to me so I wasn't sure if this is how it happens. To go from friends to lovers and feel as if it's the right choice." I grab his hand and lace our fingers together.

"I stopped fighting feeling wrong about us and it happened. Maybe that's why it feels so easy, because it's right. We're not two strangers who met at a bar. I know your family, friends, and I would've kept being a part of your life even if Aaron hadn't died." He pauses and scratches his jaw. "I never looked at you the way I do now and I can't honestly say when it happened for me. I can pinpoint when I decided it was okay though. In the hospital, after we were flirting, I decided I was allowed to feel for you. I think you were meant to be mine."

"Do you now?"

"I do."

"And how exactly do you think that's the case?"

I love this part of our relationship. We can go from serious to playful in a second.

Liam huffs. Maybe he doesn't love this part so much. "I don't fucking know. I think you were in love with me years ago."

"No, I thought you were hot though. Always have."

He smirks and nods his head. "I'm a catch."

"You know you wanted me."

He turns his head slightly to give me his sexy panty-melting smile. "Oh, I did. You've always been beautiful. Only now, you're mine and I will have you."

"Don't count your chickens before they hatch there, pumpkin. Maybe I'm going to meet a handsome stranger on this trip who's going to whisk me away on his yacht. Show me all the things I'm missing out with you," I joke and watch the muscle in his jaw tick.

Oh, alpha men are all the same.

"I'll fucking kill anyone who tries."

"So scary."

"Keep testing me, woman. Watch what happens," Liam warns and I grin.

Liam smiles and pulls off the highway toward the Outer Banks of North Carolina. I didn't even notice where we were going until now. I knew we were going south, but it didn't dawn on me that we would be going to one of my favorite beaches.

"Why are you smiling?" Liam asks.

I didn't realize I was. "I'm just happy. I love OBX."

"See? Superior."

"Oh, shut up," I laugh and smack his chest.

We drive north a ways and through all the quaint little towns that make up the Outer Banks. There are tons of little shops and restaurants. I love where I live now, it's the old feel of Virginia Beach, but these towns are homey. They have charm and scream beach living. Where my house is still has a lot of tourism. All of these towns thrive on the summer tourists, but they still keep their roots.

Liam enters the town limits of Corolla and I close my eyes and breathe in the salt air. The smell of sun and sand mixed with the sea. It's home to me. We pull into the drive of one of the most breathtaking houses I've ever seen.

"Wow," I say, looking up.

"It's Quinn's family's house."

I look over and Liam looks as surprised as I am. "Who knew?"

"No shit. Aara's still sleeping. Do you want to grab her and I'll get the bags?" Liam offers.

"Sure." He goes to exit the car, but I put my hand on his arm stopping him. He looks over with his mouth slightly open.

"What's wrong?"

I lean across the console practically into his lap. "Thank you," I say and press my lips to his.

The second our lips connect, something shifts. Liam's hands thread into my hair and he kisses me roughly. Our tongues move together and my body ignites. I'm euphoric in this moment as I give my appreciation to him. He holds my face to his and I feel his teeth nip at my lip.

There's no way he's sleeping on the couch.

Liam gently pulls my face back and kisses me tenderly. "You can thank me anytime you want."

My laugh is short and my breathing is heavy. "I bet you'd like that."

"Damn right I would."

"Go get the bags. I'll get the baby," I instruct and climb back over to my side.

I get Aarabelle out of the car miraculously without waking her and look closely at the house. It's a beautiful, blue, two-story house with white plantation shutters. The porch wraps around the left side and sits on stilts. Even though it's old, you can tell it's been well cared for. Through whatever storms it's been dealt, it's strong and stands proud. The front door is white and the sand dunes almost cover the wood stilts. I walk up the stairs and Liam's behind me.

He unlocks the door and allows me the time to take it in. "It's magnificent," I say hushed, careful not to wake Aara. She's napped for about an hour, but if she doesn't wake on her own time, she's a beast.

"Look around. I'm going to bring the bags up."

I nod and start to explore. The kitchen has been recently updated and has beautiful black granite countertops with country white cabinets. I walk forward and the windows make me stop short. Beautiful, cream, satin fabric drapes across the glass and pools on the ground making the blue ocean look bluer. I know I have the view of the ocean at home, but it's as if I've never seen *this* ocean before.

I hold Aarabelle who's fast asleep in my arms and look out at the sea before us. I hear Liam come down the stairs and feel him behind me. His arms wrap around my torso and we both stand looking out.

"Beautiful," he whispers.

"Yeah, it is."

"I was talking about you."

My heart is buoyant and his warmth cocoons me. I lean against his chest and cherish this moment. There's so much I want to say, but this is enough right now. Being in his arms, away from all the shit at home, just spending time with Liam and Aarabelle. This is contentment.

"YOU READY?" LIAM yells from downstairs. He's had Aarabelle for the last hour while I've gotten ready for dinner. I assume she hasn't peed or pooped since I haven't heard massive amounts of cursing or Aarabelle screaming.

"Almost!"

I have a white eyelet dress on with my hair in a low twist. I spent extra time shaving every inch of my legs and making sure I didn't miss anything. If we do end up where I hope we do, I want to be as perfect as possible.

Standing before the mirror, I look at myself and smile. This trip was everything I needed. I feel alive and refreshed. After we got settled into the house, we took a walk on the beach. Liam carried Aarabelle while I held on to his arm. Aara was giggly, especially when Liam started to run into the water with her. She would squeal and laugh, then he would run back out.

A part of my heart became his in that moment. I'm hoping tonight another part will be his as well.

"I'm going to eat baby food soon!" Liam's loud voice carries through the halls.

Men.

I grab my bag and head down the stairs.

"I'm ready. Sheesh," I chide as I enter the living room area.

Liam stands there with his khaki pants and navy blue shirt. The muscles in his arms tug at the fabric, stretching it so the shirt looks almost uncomfortable. His blue eyes are deeper than normal, but still mesmerizing. The scruff he usually has is clean-shaven and his beanie that I love so much is missing. He's ridiculously sexy.

"I'm not going to make it through dinner," Liam

grumbles.

"What?"

"Can't you wear sweatpants?" he asks, looking at my legs.

I scoff, "I'm not wearing sweatpants to dinner. I got dressed up, you're going to have to learn to control yourself, Mister I'm-so-superior."

Of course there's a part of me that's more than giddy that he seems to be having a hard time with my dress. I didn't wear it to drive him crazy, but it's a perk. I forgot what it was like to have a man's sole attention be you. How it makes you feel when you're desired. Liam awoke that inside me. He brought the woman in me back to life.

When I turn around, his breath hitches. The dress is a halter top, and the back drops to the small of my back.

"Fuck no," Liam says and gently grips my arm. "Please tell me you have a sweater or a poncho for that dress."

I turn slowly with a sly smile. "Nope. It's warm out."

"I'm gonna need a minute." He lets out a deep breath and holds Aarbelle out for me to take.

I grab her and laugh, "Come on, Dreamboat. Let's go eat before you lose your mind."

We head over to a small seafood restaurant, which seems to be one of the only places in town. Liam had to stop for gas and we grabbed a town map. Tomorrow we plan to use the beach cruisers that we found in the house and check out the other local spots.

They seat us at a table by the windows with an ocean view. Aarabelle sits in the highchair between us.

"Mamamamama," she says looking at Liam.

"I'm not your mama. I'm the fun one."

"Fun? You tied her up."

"And she lived and didn't pee all over."

I shake my head, "It's okay, my love. Liam doesn't know how to handle a little diaper," I mock him and

Aarabelle is her happy self.

Liam looks off and Aarabelle yells, bringing his attention back to her.

"Someone is just like her mommy," his playful voice is animated. "I see you." Liam gives Aara his hand and she slaps it a few times.

He gives her his attention and I sit in awe. They say the way to a man's heart is his stomach, but mine is Aarabelle. She's my world. There is nothing else that matters other than my daughter. A man can leave, die, cheat, but she'll always be my child. Loving and accepting her is not only important, but without it, no man will ever have me.

Our food arrives and we eat and make small talk. I tell Liam about some of the things I've been handling at work and he tells me about the stupid things the teams have done. I laugh at his new game with Quinn of who's the stronger one. It seems to be helping him with working out on a schedule again.

"Aarabelle's birthday is coming up. Are you going to do a party?" Liam asks once we've finished dinner.

"I want to do something fun. Jackson said he and Catherine would fly in and I know my parents will come too. I should probably start planning."

I have some time, but Liam's known me long enough to know that my parties are Martha Stewart on crack. I go overboard and love to have extravagant events with each minute detail planned. Usually it takes me about a month to hand-make all the decorations. I have issues.

"I would volunteer to help but . . ." he trails off. "I've been to your shindigs . . . and I'll bring the beer."

"I don't think so," I state with a smile. "You're with me, you have to help."

Liam mumbles under his breath as the waitress brings the check.

We decide to take another walk on the beach since it's beautiful out. Liam pays the bill and lifts Aarabelle into his arms.

"Come on, sweetheart." He stands with his hand extended.

I place my hand in his and we exit to the beach. Liam has Aarabelle in his one arm and wraps his other around me. I walk surrounded by him as his body shields me from the wind. This is one of the things I love most. We don't have to talk. Liam is okay with the silence and so am I. Neither of us has the need to fill the quiet, we can simply find comfort in each other.

As we walk, Aarabelle tucks her head onto his shoulder and he protects her. My heart fills with love watching him care for her. He loves Aara and I love him. I've always cared for him as a friend, but today there's no doubt that my feelings of friendship have formed into something much deeper.

"Liam," I say tenderly.

He stops and we face each other. I want to tell him. I want him to know how much I care.

"What's wrong?"

"Nothing," I say feeling awkward. I look down and move the sand with my toes.

"Hey," he says and pulls my attention back to him.

I take a deep breath. Liam isn't Aaron. There's no guarantee he won't suffer the same fate, but the bottom line is that he's different. Our relationship is much different as well. I was a kid when I met Aaron, we grew up together, and in some ways, we grew apart. The losses in his life caused him to put me in a different place in his heart. Maybe he didn't want to hurt anymore, so he chose to hurt me instead. I'll never know that answer, but I have to move forward.

I never planned to love again. But Liam . . . I can't fight him. I don't want to fight it either.

"I love you." I say the words and I see the joy reflected in his eyes. Tears fill my own eyes as I let the love free in my heart. "I do. I love you. You make me happy and you make me feel safe."

Liam steps closer and cups my cheek, "I love you, Natalie. I'll always keep you safe." My face tilts into his hand and he wipes a tear that descends down my cheek. "Don't cry, sweetheart."

"I'm not sad. I just . . . there are things that scare me with loving you," I admit.

"Like what?" Liam's voice is tender and curious.

He must know the fears that I face. Or maybe he doesn't. They immerse themselves in this world where they think they're untouchable. Even though they live and breathe death.

"You're an active duty Navy SEAL. I'm already a SEAL widow." The words seep out and so does fear.

"I can't make you promises. I'd be a liar and a fool to tell you it can't happen to me. I know you know that. You knew when we started feeling more than friendship what it would mean. Deployments, training, dangerous things I can't tell you about." Liam's words are measured, and his voice is strong and steady. He keeps his hand caressing my face, and my hand rests on his chest. "I can tell you all the bullshit you want to hear, but it'll just be that. I want a life with you, Lee. I want to build something with you and Aarabelle. I want to spend my days thinking about coming home to you. I want to feel your body beneath me when I make love to you."

I look up and my chest tightens.

"I want it all. I love you and Aarabelle, but it comes with a cost. I knew this was going to be something we have to work through. Loving me comes with the risk of knowing I might not come back home."

A tear falls from my eye as the image flashes before me. Another knock on the door telling me he's gone. Another flag on the mantel where I have to look at the only two men I loved taken from me. I can't. I don't think I could do it.

"I can't lose you like that."

"I can't promise you won't, but I can promise I'll fight everything to make sure it doesn't. I'll do anything I can so you never have to feel that way. That's the only promise I can make."

Aarabelle sleeps soundly on Liam's shoulder and I know the choice before me. Either I walk away from Liam now, save whatever is left of the heart I have left. Guard myself and be careful about who I let in, or give everything I have to him. Take the chance to end up with nothing or maybe the greatest love I've ever known. Liam and I have a chance to create a new love that I never had.

Aaron was easy and known. He was comfort and stability. I think even with his affair he wouldn't have left me. We would've maybe found a way to get through it. It wouldn't have been easy, but we have a kid, a life, a marriage together. I'll never know those answers or whether it would've been true, but I loved him. Even now, as hurt as I am, Aaron holds an intangible piece of my heart and soul. It'll always be his.

"If we do this," I hesitate, "You'll be careful?" It's a stupid question, and that word is abhorrent to them. They don't know how to be careful. It's a hero complex, but he needs to know I need that.

"Natalie, I'll do everything I can to come home to you."

"Then let's go back to the house. I'm ready for bed."

I take his hand and we walk back to the car.

chapter thirty-three

NERVES START TO take hold as we get back to the house. I try to tell myself it's only Liam, but then again—it's Liam.

"I'm going to put her down." My voice trembles. *Smooth, Natalie.*

"I'll come with you," he offers and places his hand on my back.

Great.

We climb the stairs and reach the spare bedroom where I've set up her portacrib. It faces the back of the house so the sun shouldn't wake her first thing in the morning. I hold her a little longer than normal and kiss her forehead. I'm stalling.

Liam kisses her cheek, then kisses mine. He leaves the room and I let out a deep breath.

I need a fucking drink.

"Here goes nothing," I say to myself and place her in her crib. "Sleep all night, my little princess."

Mommy's going to be busy.

Well, now where do I go? The bedroom? The bathroom? Do I have to slip into something? I feel like a dipshit.

I decide I really do need a drink and head to the kitchen. Liam is standing against the counter sipping a beer.

"Seems I'm not the only one," I say with a laugh and grab the beer from his hand.

He grabs my waist and pulls me against him.

"You don't have to be nervous. We don't have to do anything you don't want," he says against my neck. His nose trails from my neck to my shoulder, and I place the bottle down on the counter behind him. Slowly his fingers dip into the fabric where my back isn't exposed. He lingers there, grazing against my skin, while his tongue traces my neck up to my ear.

I shiver and heat pools in my core.

"I want to go slow. I want to savor every moment with you. I want to touch you, taste you, feel you, and then we'll do it again." His deep voice is rich and full of promise.

I melt in his arms.

"Liam, I've . . ." I stop speaking when his tongue traces the shell of my ear.

"You what, sweetheart?"

"I've . . ." I let out a shaky breath. "I've only ever been with Aaron," I admit and tense. To some this might be a turn off. I don't know. I only know how to do what Aaron liked and maybe I didn't do it well. Maybe that's why he sought another woman. "What if . . ."

Liam's hands drift up my back and grip my shoulders from behind. He pulls me back so we're eye to eye. "What if?"

"What if I suck?"

"I'm going to keep my first thought in check," he replies with a smartass grin.

I stand waiting for him to be serious.

"Natalie, stop it. You're perfect and we'll talk. If you don't like something, just tell me." Liam's eyes don't waver. He waits until I nod.

Then he scoops me into his arms and pulls me against his chest.

"Put me down."

"Hush."

"I can—" I start to say, but he silences me with his lips.

Liam carries me with almost no effort up the stairs. We enter the bedroom and he carefully kicks it closed with his foot. He holds me and kisses me nonstop as he lays me on the bed.

"I love you," he assures me.

"I love you."

"I'm going to show you how much," Liam's eyes don't leave mine as his hand travels from my face all the way along my body. He leans down allowing me to feel his weight.

I'm warm everywhere. I want him to touch me, kiss me, and I want to feel him inside of me. The want to be claimed by him is so fierce it rocks me to my core. He strokes the skin on my leg with his fingers. Gradually gliding up and down while staring at me. He inches higher and higher until he's at the hem of my dress.

"Kiss me," I request and he does.

Our tongues volley between each other and he pushes me deeper into the bed. His weight covers me and I want more. I hold his face and kiss him with everything I have. My heart thumps in my chest and my pulse races when his fingers skim across my underwear. Liam deepens the kiss and his hands trail higher until he's rubbing the underside of my breast. The fabric is too tight and he retreats.

He sits up and pulls me with him. Deftly he unties the knot behind my neck and the straps fall, leaving my bare chest exposed. Liam looks down before his hands cup my breasts. Leaning in close, his lips are at my ear. "I've waited to do this again. I've dreamt of you lying naked before me. I hope you're ready for a sleepless night, sweetheart." He rolls my nipple between his fingers and

I moan.

"Take your shirt off." My voice is desperate. I want to feel his skin against mine again.

I help him by pulling it up and he removes it. The pads of my fingers trace the tattoo again and I remember how much he's been through. Before I can think too much, his lips wrap around my nipple and his tongue circles it. My hands grip his head and hold him there.

"Oh," I sigh as his teeth gently bite down. "Liam."

He stops, "Say it again."

I look into his eyes confused.

"Say my name."

"Liam," I say it again.

He groans and then lavishes the other breast. His hand snakes to my back and pulls my dress off. He throws it on the floor and lies me back down. His mouth returns to my breasts and then he begins to sink lower. I tense as fear begins to take over.

Liam doesn't miss the change in me though. He knows too well how to read people. "Relax, sweetheart. I want to make you feel good."

I let his words wash over me and focus on staying in the moment. His fingers hook in my white simple thong and he leisurely pulls it off. I'm completely bared to him. I'm open and exposed, but all I see is awe in his eyes. He looks at me like I'm a prize, a gift for him.

With his eyes trained on mine, he lowers his head and kisses my stomach. Then an inch lower he places another kiss. Another inch receives the same attention before he's settling between my legs.

He watches me as I lean up on my elbows.

His head dips and mine falls back. Liam's tongue swirls against my clit and every part of me comes to life. He sucks and then his tongue enters me. I jump up, but he anchors me. My arms give out as I squirm against him, but he doesn't relent. Each swipe of his tongue brings me higher. I build toward my orgasm and he moans against me.

"So close," I start to chant.

It's been so long. I swear I've never come this quickly. I'm right there when he lifts his mouth.

My eyes fly open and my mouth is slack as I look at him in frustration.

"Not yet," is all he says and then he returns. He starts slowly and his tongue is feather light. I fight the urge to push his head where I need it most.

"Liam, please," I beg.

I feel his finger press against my opening and he slowly enters me. I don't know whether to cry or laugh. He starts to move and his tongue is exactly where I need it. I climb, and I swear if he stops, I'm going to bite him. He moves creating the friction I need. Heaven. This is fucking heaven. My nerve endings burn with the need to release. My muscles lock and I let go.

Each part of me tingles and feels heavy. I'm panting and still throbbing as Liam continues to draw out every ounce of pleasure my body can give. He pushes up and stares down at me. "You're even more beautiful when you come."

"Now it's your turn," I say flipping over and climbing on top of him. My fingers touch his lips and I trace all the way to his sternum. I travel over every ridge and plane of his six-pack. Sliding down his body, I admire the man beneath me. He's strong, sexy, caring, and I'm going to do everything I can to make this night memorable for him.

Touching him feels right.

Being with him feels like it's meant to be.

I loosen his belt and remove his pants. He lies there with a lazy smile as I take my time removing his boxers. I take a moment to admire him. His long, thick cock throbs before me and the need to be filled overwhelms me. I want him to take me. But first, I want to explore him.

"Natalie, if you keep looking at me like that, I'm not going to be able to control myself," Liam warns and I want to defy him.

I love that I can test his limits. It's a sense of power I've never known.

My hand wraps around him and I lean up and nip at his ear. "You're not the only one testing their strength," I say low and seductive. "I want you inside of me so bad I could cry. Make me yours, Liam."

A switch flips inside of him and he turns me onto my back. "You're already mine."

My eyes close and he waits.

"Look at me," he demands.

I open my eyes and see the love shine through him. "Do I need a condom?"

"No." I don't tell him that the chances of me conceiving are slim to none. The only way I can get pregnant is through infertility treatments.

"I want to feel you. Only you. I want you to feel me. Don't close your eyes."

Each breath I take feels like an eternity passes waiting for him to enter me. He goes slowly and I feel the tip of him. "I love you. I love every part of you. I wanted to fight it, but I can't fight you." He comforts me as he pushes deeper inside. My eyes stay on his and I give over all my heart. "You're supposed to be mine and I won't lose you." Liam's eyes close as he enters me fully.

My breathing is short as I try to adjust. He stays still and then presses his lips to mine. I relax and get lost in the kiss and then we begin to move together. Liam thrusts and I hold on to his back as he slowly rocks inside of me. I push against him and he groans.

I take everything about him in. The way his jaw is tight and his muscles are taut as he moves. His eyes shift from dark blue to light, his eyes open in pleasure. My hands memorize the way his ass fits in my palm as he moves with me. Pushing and pulling me apart. We fit together as if we've been doing this forever.

He flips me over so I'm on top and my hands trail his body. "You feel incredible," I say as I rock back and forth. "I don't want this to stop," breathless as I start to climb again. "It feels so good," I whisper against his mouth and he kisses me again.

His hand dips between us as he finds my clit. The pressure from his finger and the way his dick hits the spot inside of me . . . I'm a goner.

"I'm gonna come, Lee. You feel so fucking good," he warns me.

"Oh my God," I moan as my orgasm is so close. I close my eyes and free my mind. I focus only on the way Liam is touching me.

I shatter apart and I swear my body just exploded.

He flips me back over and pounds relentlessly as he follows my orgasm with his own.

Liam and I made love and I never want it to end.

We lie here trying to catch our breath and I start to come down from my high. I get up and head to the bathroom. I stare at myself in the mirror after cleaning up and try to notice anything different. My hair is a mess and I try to fix it, but I'm still the same. The insides of me are changed though. I'm no longer just Aaron's girl. I've given myself to another man—a good man. A man that I hope will be around for a long time.

I climb back into bed and he wraps the blanket around us. I lie there staring at him with adoration.

His head lolls over and his face lights up. "That was . . ." Liam struggles for words.

"Good?" I ask apprehensively.

He takes my hand. "No, sweetheart. That was better than good."

I beam and close my eyes. My mind drifts without permission to my first time with Aaron. It was nothing like that. We were both inexperienced teenagers who were trying to recreate a movie. I don't want to think of him. Liam deserves to have me here and not in my past right now.

"Liam?" I ask, trying to divert my thoughts.

"Hmmm?" He takes my hand and places it against his chest.

I don't know after this how much we'll see each other. I wonder if he's leaving soon for a deployment or if it's just training. Even before our relationship progressed, I missed him when he was gone. I don't know how I'm going to handle it now. I have to remember he's a SEAL and I'm back to that life. Previously, I wouldn't even notice when Aaron was gone, but Liam and I are so attuned.

"What's your schedule for the next few weeks? I'm not a needy person, but I want to know how much we'll see each other."

"I have to leave in a few days for about two weeks. Then I'm home for a bit. I'll be here for Aara's birthday and then probably have to leave after that."

"I'll miss you."

Liam shifts, pulling me on top of him. His fingers trace down my nose to the side of my face. My chin quivers a tiny bit thinking of him leaving for six months. We're so new and I don't want him to go. "I'll see you every day. When I close my eyes, I'll see your blue eyes, blonde hair, and your beautiful face. You've done this, you know it's not forever," Liam stops, catching himself on that phrase. "I'm sorry, I didn't mean it like that."

"I know you didn't," I reassure him and roll over. "But it can sometimes be forever."

Liam pulls me to his side and I close my eyes. He holds me close and I dare to hope that this forever won't be the same fate as the last man I loved.

I wake the next morning and my hand reaches for Liam, but all I get are cold sheets. Again.

No.

I sit up and look around. *Please don't let this be a dream.* It's definitely not my bedroom. I'm in North Carolina. "Okay," I tell myself, "Just take deep breaths."

Climbing out of bed, I feel the aches of the muscles I hadn't used in a while. I'm sore but I welcome it. It reminds me of the complete ecstasy I felt in Liam's arms. The sun shines through the window and I go to see where he is.

I walk past Aarabelle's room to check on her, but she's not there. I rush down the stairs and see them on the couch. Liam has Aara tucked into his side and she has food all over her face. She's elated and smiling, watching television with him. Leaning against the wall, I watch them.

She starts to wiggle and he places her on his lap. "Okay, Mommy's still sleeping, and I'm pretty sure you're going to need a new diaper after the amount of food you ate. We're going to keep that between us."

She stands on his legs and bounces.

"So if you could not poop, that would be really great," he tries to convince her. "I mean, I can buy you a doll or whatever it is you kids are into. Want a pony? There are wild ones running around. I'm sure I can snag one if you can keep up your end of the bargain."

"Mamamama," Aarabelle coos and Liam tries to occupy her.

"Your mama is way better looking than me. Can you say Liam?" he asks and she eats her fingers. "Probably not but you could try."

I stifle my laugh as she eats her hand and bounces, oblivious. If he's already bribing her with ponies, we're going to need to nip this in the bud.

"A pony?" I say as I come into view.

"Oh, thank God. I was worried she was going to shit and I don't have rope or tape."

"There's so much wrong with this situation." I smile and walk toward them. If this is a glimpse of my mornings with Liam, I'll be a very happy woman. He sits shirtless and I do my best not to ogle, but his body is hard to tear my eyes away from. His chest is broad and shoulders strong. I know what it feels like to have his strong arms wrapped around me.

In fact, I would like to have that right now. I saunter over, wearing his long t-shirt that I found on the floor. Remembering how much he liked me leaving in it the first time we fooled around, I figured he wouldn't mind.

"Good morning," he gazes at me as I stand in front of him.

"Morning." I scrunch down and kiss him and then kiss Aara. "Morning, Princess."

I lift her into my arms and make myself comfortable on his lap.

"My two favorite girls." Liam wraps his arms around us and squeezes.

"Thank you for waking up with her."

Aarabelle babbles on as I nestle her into my chest. She looks at Liam and her whole face lights up.

Liam shuts the television off and pushes the hair off my face. "I went for my run and when I got back I heard her talking in her crib. I must've worn you out last night," he says with pride.

Rolling my eyes, I snuggle into his chest. "What time is it?"

"Ten,"

"Ten?" I yell out as I jump up. "You let me sleep till ten? What the hell?" I ask and look at Aara. "Did you feed her?"

"Yes, I fed her," he scoffs. "I'm not a total idiot."

"What the hell is on her face?" I ask, swiping the dark

brown smear on her face. "Is this chocolate?"

Liam stands and ignores my question. "I'm gonna hop in the shower."

"Liam! You gave her chocolate for breakfast?"

"Feel free to join me," he says while walking up the stairs.

"You're going to change every shitty diaper she has!"

"Love you!"

"Ugh!" I groan and look at her all happy and clueless. It's hard to be mad at him since he let me sleep in, but still. He has so much to learn and hopefully he'll be around for me to teach him.

chapter thirty-four

"DON'T LET HER get too close!" I call out from my beach chair. Liam is letting Aarabelle play near the water and I can't help but get a little antsy.

"Calm down. I know how to swim—well!" he lets me know in an annoyed tone.

I've gotten to actually enjoy the beach for the first time since Arabelle's been born. I don't know what to do with myself. Plus, I get to look at Liam shirtless. Really, I'm winning anyway you look at this.

My phone rings and I look at the number. California?

"Hello," I answer.

"Natalie? It's Catherine."

"Cat! Hey!"

I haven't talked to her in so long. Between her working insane hours and the fact that my life is nuts, we just miss each other. I do get to talk to her through Jackson though . . . I guess that's something.

"Hey! I had a few minutes and was thinking of you. I think I'm going to come back east next time Jackson comes to Virginia and I'd love to see you."

I laugh as Aara throws sand at Liam. "Yeah, that would be great."

"You sound happy," she notices.

"I am. I'm actually away until tomorrow. Liam and I came to the Outer Banks."

She goes silent for a second. "Things are good then? With Liam?"

I sigh and the smile that forms is natural. "Yeah, things are really good. I'm content, Cat. He's sweet and he loves Aarabelle and me. It's strange and we're adjusting, but I'm in love with him."

"Oh, that's amazing. Seriously! I'm so happy for you. And after finding everything out?"

Jackson and Mark found out about the affair, I assume through Liam or Quinn. Jackson pulled me aside and assured me they knew nothing. He and Mark were both angry, but they've also seen it so many times. Cheating isn't uncommon in the SEAL community. I was grateful that I wasn't the only person who was blindsided by it.

"It sucked."

"Trust me, I know. I know it's awful, but I promise you, in time, the affair can even become a blessing. When I walked in on my ex cheating on me with his whore, I didn't think I could love again. It was the most horrific thing, but because of that . . . I met Jackson. Maybe Liam is your lobster." We both laugh at the *Friends* reference.

"I think he could be. I'm taking things one day at a time, but you know. Oh," I remember to tell her about Aara's party. "In about a month, I'm going to have Aarabelle's first birthday party. I know it's a little early, but I'd love if you and Jackson could be there."

"Oh, for sure! Jackson wouldn't want to miss it. Okay, babe, I gotta run. I have a meeting in a few, but I'm glad we could catch up a little," Catherine says, sounding rushed.

"Me too! I can't wait to see you."

"I can't wait either. Kiss that precious little girl and we'll chat again soon."

I disconnect the call and think about what she said. Her ex did a real number on her. At least I never had to walk in on Aaron and Brittany, but at least Catherine wasn't married and having a baby. It sucks no matter which way you slice it. Infidelity takes a part of your heart and tarnishes it forever. I can polish it up, but it'll always have a dull spot.

Liam and Aarabelle head back and I appreciate the way he moves. Even the way he walks is lithe. The muscles in his arms enlarge as he lifts the baby. I stand up and head over to them.

"Dadada," Aarabelle babbles and rubs her eyes.

Liam and I glance at each other and then down to Aara. She gazes at the house and I wonder if she is just making noises or if she seriously called him some form of Daddy. It would make sense. He's the only man in her life. Neither of us speak as I wait to see if she says it again.

"Did she?" I question aloud.

"We probably misunderstood."

I nod and blow it off. She might have said something else and we are being silly. We both stay silent for a few beats and watch her as if she'll say something again. After a few minutes, Liam reaches for my hand and laces his fingers with mine.

The sun warms my face and I close my eyes.

"You should really be wearing something else," Liam chastises, breaking me from my peaceful moment.

"What's wrong with my bathing suit?" I ask looking down.

I know it's not the body I had before kids, but I don't think I'm fat. I have on a deep burgundy strapless bikini. It hugs my new curves but hides the tiny pooch I'll never get rid of.

"Nothing's wrong. I'm just having a hard time not wanting to carry you over my shoulder and bury myself inside of you again," Liam says and I literally shudder.

My stomach tightens and I need a minute to think again. That was definitely not what I was expecting to hear.

"Okay," I manage to say. "What time are we leaving tomorrow?"

"I need to get some stuff ready before I leave, so probably after breakfast. And after morning sex."

"So sure I'm going to give it up, huh?" I play with him a little.

"I think I've proven myself."

"I'm not so sure."

He's more than proven himself, but it's not in my nature to let him gloat.

"I'd be careful. Aarabelle is yawning and I can think of something to do during her nap time."

I look at the baby and wonder if it's too early for her nap.

"I have some other things I really wanted to do, like catch up on my TV shows.

Maybe another time though."

Liam lunges forward and practically knocks me out of my chair. "I'd start stretching, sweetheart." He kisses the side of my neck and his warm breath causes goosebumps to form. "I'm going to make you come many, many times."

I try to manage my breathing and appear in control. "I'm counting on that."

He's going to make me suffer, but in the absolute best way.

An hour later, we pack the few things we brought to the beach and head back toward the house. I feed Aarabelle and get her ready for her nap. She's exhausted, and after her oh-so-healthy breakfast, getting her to eat lunch was not fun. Once everything's cleaned up and I get her settled, I'm not sure what to do.

Do I go and look for him? I mean, he alluded to what we'd be doing. Then I feel awkward because I'm not sure if this is normal. I feel like a horny teenager worrying about having sex all over again. I've never had an adult relationship where you date.

"Trying to avoid me?" Liam says and I leap out of my skin.

"What is with all of you? Do they train every one of you to scare the shit out of people? Fucking hell." I try to calm my heart, but it's been almost a year since he died . . . it's been a year.

It's a year.

Today.

And I didn't even realize it. It's been one year today since Aaron died.

I look at Liam with tears building. I'm here on vacation with Liam—making love, having fun, and I didn't realize it's the anniversary of my husband's death.

"I didn't mean to scare you. Are you okay?" he asks concerned.

"Liam," I say with my hand on his arm. "I don't know . . . I mean . . . today is a year. Today makes one year since he died." I look up with despair. I'm an awful person. I mean, I didn't even know. I didn't think about it or him. Yes, he hurt me, but still. Shouldn't I be in Pennsylvania? I suddenly want to vomit.

Liam stands there and doesn't say a word. Guilt for two men becomes too much for me. I'm standing here on vacation with my boyfriend crying over my dead husband. The day after we had sex for the first time. Oh my God. I'm going to lose it.

"I need a minute," I say and rush down the stairs.

There are no answers here to ease my mind. Nothing is right and yet nothing is wrong. I made my peace with Aaron. I made my choice with Liam, but at this moment, my two worlds are colliding and nothing fits.

I burst through the door onto the beach and fall to my knees. I'm more upset that I forgot. I don't know what the protocol on mourning is, but shouldn't I have remembered?

I think about the note I found with the apology. Maybe he was sorry about the affair. Maybe he was sorry he married me and was unhappy. Even though I don't think that. Sure, we had hard times—all marriages do—but we had a lot of happy. We had laughs, love, and we had a family. I take this time here on the beach to forgive him and forgive myself. If I go off his letter, he wanted me to be free and to love again. I want that too.

And I have that.

I look toward the ocean and there are three wild horses trotting along the water. I've never seen the horses when I've been on the beach. They're majestic and the three of them move a little slower for a moment.

The dark brown horse seems to be in charge as it leads the pack. There's a light tan horse who's in between the two darker horses. The other horse pushes past and is almost black. It's the tallest of the three. It moves in front and the tan horse perks up.

I sit and watch them and can't help but feel for the tan horse. I decide it's a she. She has two male horses vying to lead her. But she's wild and doesn't want to be led. Again, I decide all of this. She wants to love, but feels torn between the two horses. When I've written their entire story in my mind, the dark brown horse turns and leaves her.

"I'm sorry too, Aaron. You left me."

The two horses run in the opposite direction and I feel like somehow he just answered me.

Standing, I brush the sand off my legs and decide to find Liam. He deserves an explanation. When I turn, I see him standing a few feet behind me. His arms are at his sides and his eyes are sad.

"Liam," I say as a plea.

He puts his hand up and then pinches the bridge of his nose. "I didn't realize it either. I didn't fucking remember." He steps forward.

"I'm sorry I ran out like that. It's not your fault. I felt like I was an awful person. Here I am," I walk toward him, "Happy and in love. Falling asleep in your arms and wanting to be there again. It's overwhelming all on its own. And then when I realized what today is, I felt this pang of guilt. But I choose you, Liam. I want to be in your arms. I want to be here with you. It's you who has my heart."

His eyes meet mine and he pulls me against him. Neither of us speaks and I wonder if he saw the horses. The symmetry between those three horses and myself spoke volumes to me. One of them would always have to be alone. They had to make choices about who should lead and who she should follow. But I don't have to choose because one left, leaving my path clear.

I vow to myself to enjoy the rest of our trip together. To allow myself the break from the life that awaits me when I'm home. Liam is who I want to spend my time with. He's who I love. I look forward to him calling, coming over, and he gives me everything I need. Liam and I may have been friends but I can't help but wonder if this was how it was always meant to be.

"GOOD MORNING, SLEEPYHEAD." Liam's hot breath is against my ear. I curl into a ball and want desperately to be asleep.

"It's still dark out," I grumble. I open one eye and want to slap him for waking me. Last night we spent our time just the three of us holed up in the living room. We played with Aarabelle and then he held me for hours.

We didn't speak about what the day had held. I think each of us needed to process it on our own. A year changed a lot for me. I learned a lot about life, love, grief, and that there are no real answers for any of it. Love can hurt and heal. Aaron hurt me deeper than I knew was possible, but Liam showed me it's okay to forgive. Grief ate at me, formed pockets of guilt and anger so deep I didn't think I'd find a way out, but I did. There are still times I'm angry, but I won't let it define me. Each day I have to choose the life I want to live.

"I'm going to go for my run, but then I thought maybe we could exercise together," his voice penetrates deep into my core.

God, his voice is sexy.

"What did you have in mind?"

His lips glide over my ear and he pulls my hair back exposing my neck. He gently bites the skin there and I moan. Slowly, his tongue slides across the skin he just nipped. "Maybe some cardio?" he suggests. "Or stretching . . ." he says as he bites another sensitive area.

"I . . ." My voice is breathless when his hand snakes across my chest. "I . . ." I can't get the words out.

Liam's hand squeezes my breast as his mouth explores my neck and ear. "You what?" he breathes the words into my ear.

His fingers pull at my nipples and my ass rocks against him. I'm already wet. I want him so bad. "I want you," I say in a voice that even I don't recognize. I'm needy and begging for him, though he's barely touched me.

"How bad?"

I moan as his hand finds my other breast. I try to roll over, but his body keeps me where I am. Completely at his mercy.

"How bad do you want me, Natalie?"

"More than my next breath."

His hand dips lower and he pushes my legs apart. When his finger finds my clit, I moan out in ecstasy. He pushes and swirls while I lay panting. My hand reaches back and I push his shorts and underwear off. I want to lead this one.

My hand wraps around his dick and I pump him up and down as he swells beneath my touch.

"I want to do something," I say as he continues to insert a finger inside.

"Do anything you want," he offers.

I sit up and take my top off. Liam's eyes shine in the low light entering from the moon. Morning, my ass.

I pull his pants off and he shifts on the bed. Leaning down, I wrap my lips around his cock. Liam groans and his fingers tangle in my hair.

"Holy fuck," he moans.

My mouth glides up and down his length as I focus on every breath hitch and sound he makes. I focus on taking him deep and know he must enjoy it based on how his hand tightens in my hair. I slide back up and then take him deeper, and Liam moans again.

"Natalie, you need to stop." He pulls me and flips me on my back. "I'm going to fucking drive you insane."

I have no doubt.

He pulls my legs over his shoulders and wastes no time. Liam's mouth is on me in a moment and my head falls back. He licks and devours me. There's no finesse. It's savage and feels incredible. His finger enters me and he pumps inside of me, twisting his hand while his mouth sucks at my clit.

"I'm gonna come," I say as he takes me higher.

He doesn't relent and slips another finger inside that moves at the same pace as his tongue. My breathing is erratic and I'm growing closer to release. I can taste it. I need it. Liam sucks harder and I fall apart. I squirm and pant as he continues to draw everything I have.

"So fucking gorgeous," he says and slowly climbs his way up my body.

My hand grips his neck and I pull his mouth to mine.

Our tongues meld together and he slips inside me.

"Oh," I break apart as he pushes deep and waits. "Move. Please, move," I beg as he rests fully seated inside of me.

He waits with eyes closed as if he's memorizing this feeling. I'm full and want him to take me.

"I want to live inside of you," he says and then pulls back. "You're made for me." He continues to talk as he pushes deeper than before. Liam slides back and forth as he fills my heart and my body. "I want to love you all day."

My eyes close as I savor the sensations of him inside of me. When I look up, I rest my hands against his face. "You already do," I say softly. "You love me all day." He slows his pace but continues to move as I tell him how I feel. "You give me so much without even knowing it. You healed me. You gave me the strength to be the woman I once was." Liam's eyes stay locked on mine as he pours himself into me and I pour my heart out to him. "You showed me how to love again. So you do love me all day, and I love you."

We both stare at each other as we make love. A tear falls from my eyes as we both fall over the edge together without saying a word. Liam holds me against him as I cry, overcome with love and happiness. This is a moment I'll never forget. It's the moment I realized just how deeply in love I am with Liam Dempsey.

chapter thirty-five

"HEY, CAN YOU head into the conference room?" Mark asks. It's my first day back to work after our vacation. There were piles of papers on my desk and I saw on the calendar that Jackson is flying in again.

"Sure."

"Thanks," he replies, already gone.

I'm assuming something is going on because everyone is running around like lunatics. I grab my notebook and try not to notice the weird looks I'm getting. I wonder if I'm getting fired.

"What's going on?" I ask as soon as I enter the door.

"There's an issue with an account. Jackson is on his way here and then we're heading out. It'll be me, Jackson, and three other guys," Mark says, still looking at a paper.

"Where are you guys headed?"

"Overseas," he answers quickly and seems extremely distracted.

"Okay . . ." I trail off feeling a little out of the loop. "Did I screw something up?"

Mark's head snaps up. "No, not at all. This is fairly normal. Our overseas accounts are always a little strange. This account is in Dubai and the Navy wants us to provide asset protection. They want us to come out and see what's going on firsthand and give them an assessment on what we can do to ensure it doesn't get fucked up. Muff wants to make sure you can handle the office while I'm gone."

"I'm sure I can."

"Okay, we'll be out of reach most of the time, so you'll have to be able to figure out anything while we're away. I wanted to give you these files before I leave in a few days. Plus, go over a few of the financial things."

It says a lot to me that they want me to handle the office in their absence. It doesn't make sense why they'll be unreachable, but far be it from me to understand everything that goes on here.

Mike knocks, "Charlie's on the line for you, Twilight."

Mark looks over at me, "I need to take this. We're leaving in a day or two, but I'll shoot you an email with everything in case things are hectic beforehand."

"Okay," I stand awkwardly and head out of the room. Mark is usually a pretty calm guy but he seems keyed up. I hope he's being honest and that I didn't do something wrong. I handled the Dubai account and made sure they had the manpower they requested.

Heading back to my office, I see I have a missed call from Aaron's mom. It's the first time I've heard from her in a year. She cut me and Aarabelle off completely, and no matter how many times I've tried, she never reciprocates.

I sent out Aarabelle's birthday invitations the other day. Maybe she's going to come.

I dial her number and someone picks up.

"Patti?" I ask.

"Lee," she says my name with a sigh. "I'm so sorry. I've been an awful mother-in-law. I should've called. It's just been so hard," Patti starts to ramble and my heart aches for her.

"There are no guidelines on grief. I wish you would've let me grieve with you, but I understand." I want to ease her mind. It's a hard place to be and I can't begrudge how she chose to live with it.

"I got the invitation with her photo. She looks so much like him."

"She does," I agree.

"How are you doing?"

We chat and catch up. She tells me she wants to come out for her birthday party and would love to talk again. I've missed her. She was like a mother to me since I was sixteen.

"Are you happy?" The question stops me short. I want to be honest with her, but I worry she's going to hate me.

"I am. There's a lot that's happened in the past year, but I'm moving on. I don't have any other choice." I choose not to tell her too much. She doesn't need to know about Aaron's affair. I decide to let her memory of her son stay unsullied.

"I'm glad for you. I think he'd be happy too." Patti sniffles but holds it together. "I'll let you get back to work and I'll see you in a few weeks."

We disconnect the call and I sit back in my chair. I've got a lot to be thankful for.

The rest of the day passes without any issues. I go over all the files Mark emails over. Reanell texts me and asks me to meet her for lunch. She's been so busy with the command side of the team that we haven't seen much of each other. I'm excited to get to spend a little girl time with her, and since everyone in the office is nuts, no one will miss me.

I pull up to our favorite restaurant that serves breakfast all day. Citrus always has a wait, but we're good friends with the owner. I called her and let her know we'd be coming, so she saved us a place at the bar.

"Hey, sexy mama," Reanell says as she finds me on my stool.

"I've missed you!" I exclaim and pull her into a hug.

She hugs me tight and we act as if it's been years rather than a week or two. "How's everything? Vacation seems to have agreed with you."

"Yeah, it was great." I smile thinking about the time with Liam. It really was great. I know Reanell well enough to see the wheels turning in her head. I give it five seconds before she goes from chewing on her nail to berating me.

"Seriously? That's all I get?"

Or maybe less.

I laugh and grab my drink, giving me a few extra seconds and also giving her frustration a little nudge. "I'm happy, Rea. He makes me feel like I can do anything."

"I'm happy. How are you with the whole SEAL thing and the thing with Aaron?"

She's the first person to bring it up. She's also the only person who watched me go a little crazy and shred his shit.

The truth is . . . I'm not sure how to handle either issue. Aaron isn't here, so I can't get answers from him. Liam is a SEAL, so I can't do anything about that either. My choices aren't really favorable.

"They are what they are."

"You are a liar." Reanell laughs and puts her head on her hand. "It's me. No need to fool me."

"I can't do anything about either. I'm still upset about the affair. I was pregnant and he slept with someone else. We'd been trying to have Aarabelle for so long and I know it took a toll on us, but still," I pause as it all comes boiling back up. "I can't even pinpoint when things might've happened."

The hair on the back of my neck stands. I can't explain what has my senses heightened, but I look around, trying to see if I'm being watched.

"What is it?" Rea asks and looks around too.

"I don't know, I just got a weird feeling." I look around again but I don't recognize anyone.

We enjoy our lunch and I tell her about Aarabelle's birthday party. She laughs and tells me I'm going overboard, but knows there's no stopping me. I want to celebrate where we've come in a year. Aara may not know the life she's had isn't exactly sunshine and roses, but she's had a life filled with love.

"I gotta get back to work," I say and put a ten-dollar bill down. "The guys are all leaving and I need to make sure everything is in order."

"First, you're going to sit here and tell me about the sex." She crosses her arms and waits expectantly.

I thought I'd gotten away with it, but apparently not.

"I really don't have to tell you anything." My smile fades almost immediately when I look at the end of the bar and Brittany is sitting there. "I'm leaving," I inform her and start to grab my bag.

"Why?" Rea looks and sees her.

Brittany looks over and stands.

Anger flows through my veins. I walk over to her and she averts her eyes. "Don't look away. Are you following me?"

"Following you? No!" she says and goes to gather her things. "I swear, I don't want to cause trouble."

"What do you want?" I ask, because this is the part that still gets me. She wanted me to know about her and Aaron. She could've let me go on living my ignorant life, but instead, she made me aware. "I'm trying to move on from all of this, but it's obvious we're going to see each other."

Brittany leans against the chair and sighs. "I want to move on with my life, but there's a lot causing me not to."

"I feel the same."

"Look, I didn't want to tell you. I didn't set out for you to find out, but don't you see? I'm the same as you.

I'm in pain." She nearly chokes on the last word.

"I wish I could say I care . . . but I don't."

"I know you don't care and I wish I wasn't the other woman. I just don't know how to move on . . ." she admits and her eyes fill with tears.

Reanell stands behind me and places her hand on my shoulder.

"Can you answer some questions for me?" I ask. I can't even believe I'm entertaining the idea of talking to her, but maybe we can both find a way to move past this.

"I can try."

"When did you start seeing him?"

She looks away and then back to me as she tries to collect herself. "We were together about a year before he died. We met at a bar and started talking."

"Wow." It's as if I've been punched in the gut. He was seeing her when we were trying to get pregnant. "When did you find out about me?" I look at her and wait for the answer that has bothered me since I found out.

Brittany pushes her blonde hair behind her shoulder. "A few weeks before he died. When I found out I was pregnant."

My eyes snap up and I fight back the nausea that threatens to escape. "Pregnant?" I ask looking down at her stomach.

"Yes, I was eight weeks pregnant when I lost the baby." She looks at me with sadness in her eyes.

I grasp my throat and try to breathe. "I-I don't . . ." I'm not sure what to say. "When?"

"I lost the baby a week after he died."

And the hits keep coming.

So she would've had a baby with my husband. Awesome. After three failed pregnancies and countless months of infertility, I find this out. Each time I start to think this can't get any worse, it does.

"I think I'm going to be sick." I turn to Reanell and

she pulls me into her arms.

"I love him. I wasn't just some girl."

I turn and look at her. "Yes, you were. He didn't tell you he was married. He never told me about you. The man you loved was a lie. I've known him since he was sixteen. I went to his senior prom, was at his boot camp graduation, married him. You weren't his life." I spew the words out.

"You weren't either," Brittany rebuts.

I wish I could argue with her. I wish I could yell and scream, but she's right. I wasn't his life. I was his wife who got pregnant and maybe trapped him.

Brittany wipes her eyes and rights herself. "I'm sorry. I should go."

Reanell steps forward. "I know you're hurting, but this," she points to me, "Isn't the right way."

Brittany starts to walk away and I grab her arm. The words taste like vinegar on my tongue. I fight with myself whether to say them, but I've lost a child. I know the pain and how hard I held on to each loss as my own personal failure. Each baby that didn't make it ate at me. "I'm sorry you lost a child," I say as tears fall.

The tears she had stopped start to flow and slide down her cheek. She doesn't say a word as she gathers her bag and leaves.

"A baby," is all I can say as Reanell pulls me into her arms. "She was going to have his baby."

chapter thiry-six

TWO WEEKS PASS and I do my best to put Brittany and her bomb to the back of my mind. Liam has been gone, so it's given me time to grieve the news in my own way. I've come to some kind of peace regarding it, although I don't know I'll ever completely be at peace with it. I hate myself for being relieved she lost the baby. It's not something I'm proud of, but Reanell has been great with helping me understand my feelings.

This last training session was supposed to be three days, but they extended it to seven so they could get some shooting qualifications. I don't miss this shit.

He came home late last night and had a lot to finish, so we agreed for a late dinner tonight.

"Hey, sweetheart," Liam says as he comes in the kitchen with a bag of Chinese food. I can smell the yumminess.

"My hero." I give a dramatic sigh and clutch my chest. "Did you get me an eggroll?"

"Do I get a prize if I did?"

"You get a kiss and maybe I'll get naked for you."

"Maybe?" he asks with a raised brow.

"Fine, you'll get nookie if I get an eggroll," I acquiesce.

Liam digs through the bag and his face says it all. They forgot the eggroll. Ha! I'm so going to make him pay for this.

"Eggroll, Dreamboat." I put my hand out waiting. He continues to dig.

"If I don't get laid because there's no fucking eggroll, I'm going to kill someone," he says out loud and I smile.

There's no eggroll and he's going to be upset. Oh, how I enjoy late dinners.

"Is that all I am to you?" I quip. "Sex?"

He looks over and grimaces. Looks like someone isn't happy. "I'm not even going to answer you. I'll be back," he says and starts to walk away.

"Oh, stop!" I say laughing. "Don't be an idiot."

Liam's arms cage me in as he leans down. "I'll make it up to you." His voice is full of promise.

"I'll be sure you do."

"I missed you," he says as his lips barely touch mine.

"I'd miss me too."

"And you say I'm arrogant." He smiles against my mouth.

I smile back and kiss him gently. "I just know how lucky you are."

He kisses me again and laughs.

We eat our dinner and fill each other in on our time away. I miss hearing the field stories. Things that happened and all the dumb things they do. Liam tells me about Quinn and the pranks he pulled on some new guys who checked in this week. I laugh and tell him about work and then I fill him in on my talk with Brittany.

"She was pregnant?" he asks with his jaw hanging open.

"Apparently. I don't know what the hell to believe anymore. It's all ridiculous."

Liam pulls my chair so I'm sitting with my legs between his. "Are you okay?"

I know it's not easy for him to shift into this conversation. I mean, here we are again, talking about Aaron in some way. Even I grow annoyed with it. The flip side is that Aaron wasn't just some ex for me and he wasn't some guy to him. There's a lot of history for both of us.

"It was a shock. It was a big shock," I say in a hushed tone.

"I'm sure, but that doesn't answer my question."

"I'm fine."

"Oh, good. You're fine again." Liam throws his hands up and they come down with a slap.

I look up as I hear the chair grate against the floor. He moves away from me and starts to eat again. I sit here stunned.

"Why are you pissed?" I ask, a little pissed myself.

He drops the fork and looks over and huffs. "You're fine? We're going back to that? You find out your husband was having a baby with the woman he was fucking behind your back—and you're fine?"

Fuck him. I can be fine or whatever else I want to be.

"I've had a few days to process it all, Liam. I'm sorry I don't want to tell you all the shit that went through my mind. I'm fine with it now—is that better?" I sneer the words and shake my head.

"I have a lot on my mind."

"That's no excuse to be an ass to me. I didn't have to tell you about Brittany and their love child. But I'm trying to be honest with you. You said we should talk about this crap."

"I know."

"That's your cue to say 'I'm sorry,'" I instruct him.

He looks over and pulls my chair back. His eyes sparkle in the light and he gives a dramatic sigh. "My darling, Natalie," Liam pauses and then lifts my hands between us, "I'm forever sorry for being an ass. I promise to only fight with you when it's acceptable and you grant me permission. Will you forgive me?"

"I hate you."

"No, you don't."

"I'm pretty sure I do."

"You'll live."

"You might not," I threaten.

Liam's lips rise as he fights his smile. "I'll take my chances."

He could probably kill me in half a second, but he'd have to catch me first. We both sit in silence and I allow myself a few moments to gather myself after our argument. I wonder how long we can seriously go like this.

Liam starts to shift a little and I notice he seems to be somewhere else. Normally I would push him, but it's unlike him to be uncomfortable. Liam exudes confidence. He knows how to handle most situations before they even happen. Maybe I really upset him with our disagreement.

"Are you okay?" I finally ask after a long bout of silence.

"Yeah, I told you I have a lot on my mind," he explains. I sit and wait for him to expand on that. He lifts his head to the sky and lets out a deep breath. "We got our deployment orders today." He looks over at me and waits.

I know what this means and the fact that he's this unhappy tells me all I need to know. It's soon and I'm going to need to start preparing for it. I try to dig deep into my old ways. Think later—smile now. I need to lock down my own concerns and be his support. He can't see my fear, he can't see my sadness. He has to hear the words that will keep him safe. Time to rely on my own training of being the one who gets left behind.

"When do you leave?"

Liam grabs my hand. "Right after Aarabelle's birthday."

"Oh, really soon," I say and try to fortify myself behind the wall of indifference. It's been a long time since

I've had to deal with deployments.

"I'm sorry."

"For what?" I ask surprised. He didn't do anything wrong. This is the life. It's time I get used to it again because Liam is in for a long time.

He stands and begins to pace. "I know you're not okay about this. Fuck. I'm not happy either."

"Am I happy? No. But it's your life. I understand."

"I think we should go away for a week before I leave. I have stand-down leave before. We can go back to Corolla and just be us."

The picture he paints is something I can't refuse, but I took off work not too long ago. "I don't know. I mean, I have a lot going on." I chew on my nail and battle my own wants. Another trip would be great to be able to just be us again. But I'm trying to move forward in all parts of my life, including working.

"Lee, I think it's important for us to do this before I go."

"We just got back though."

"I know, but I want to spend a week together. Just the three of us. I want to soak up as much time as I can with you and Aarabelle."

The pleading in his eyes makes it almost impossible to resist him.

I stand and put my arms around his waist. "Liam, I'm not going anywhere. I don't need some trip to reaffirm how much I love you." I wait for him to look at me. "I don't know that I can get away again."

Liam's hands glide down and he grips my thighs, lifting me. I hang on to him as my legs wrap around him. "I'll just steal you."

"I'm not stealable," I joke and make up the word.

"I've already stolen you." He kisses the tip of my nose.

And he has. He knows it too. I don't want to fight

tonight, and I think I can talk him out of the trip later on . . . but tonight, I want to be with only him. I don't want to think about babies or deployments. I want to just be us.

"Where's my eggroll?" I ask and he smirks.

"In my pants."

My eyes widen as I try to keep from laughing. "Is it a big one?"

"I'd say so," he retorts with a smile.

"I may have to see for myself."

"I can arrange that."

I press my lips on his and he carries me out of the kitchen. I keep kissing him as he moves with me in his arms. A tiny pang of stage fright hits me again as I realize this will be the first time Liam has ever been in my bed. The bed I shared with my husband.

He slowly lowers me as we get to my door. "I don't have to stay," he somehow reads my mind.

"Don't be stupid. I want you here." I take his hand and open the door. He holds my hand as we enter my bedroom.

There are a lot of memories in this room, but I want to make new ones. I deserve new ones. Corolla was beautiful, but this is where our life is. We need to be a couple in our real life.

Liam holds my hand as I pull him to the bed. I look around at the room and am grateful for my tirade. It allowed it so there aren't any pictures other than of Aarabelle. I didn't want to look at him after I found out about Brittany. I sure as hell don't want to feel like he's looking at me now.

His hand holds my face as he slowly inches close before he kisses me. I lie back on the bed and pull him on top of me. Pushing the beanie off his head, my fingers slide through his hair. The scruff I love so much is back and it scratches my neck as he begins to move his mouth there. I could fall apart so easily in his arms. He gives me such comfort and security.

"I hate the idea of leaving you," he says against my skin.

I hate it too, but I focus on the words floating around before speaking them. I have to tread carefully before I say things. I'm in the tiptoe stage where I have to guard his heart and my own.

"It'll be okay."

Of course I don't know that. Our lives are constantly hanging on a precipice, ready to tip over the edge and shatter. He could die at any point. I could decide it's too much stress. But if we can love each other enough, we have a chance.

Liam pulls my shirt over my head and holds me close. It's like he's holding on to more than just this moment. Unease begins to build and I start to question what we're doing. If he's dreading it already, do we even have a chance?

His lips trail down my collarbone and I try to alleviate my worries. I want to stay in the moment with him. Give myself over and let him take me from my own mind.

"Stay with me," he orders in his deep, husky voice.

I close my eyes as his mouth wraps around my nipple. He sucks and nips at it as I writhe beneath him. His hand travels down my body beneath my shorts. He moves slowly, and I catalog each movement he makes. The way his finger brushes against my hip. Each swipe across my clit as he toys with me.

Liam strips me of my defenses so I'm open and exposed to him. He can see through my layers of bullshit and straight to my heart. "Liam, kiss me." I want to hide back behind my walls.

"Let me love you. Let me in." His voice leaves no room for question. He knows I'm scared. He knows me. I close my eyes and he pushes his finger inside me. "I've got you. I won't let you fall."

"Feels so good," I moan as he uses his thumb against my clit.

Suddenly his hand retreats and I'm left feeling empty. My eyes fly open and I whimper. He gazes at me as he removes his clothes.

I sit up and push his hands away, "Let me."

My fingers gently pull at his shirt. I go slow, savoring him and knowing what lies beneath his clothing. A man too beautiful for words. I trail down his now bare chest and use my nails to scrape at his skin. He hisses as I run my finger across his stomach.

"No other man has my heart," I murmur. "No other man has my body." My eyes lock on his as I remove his pants. They slide down and he moves me back beneath him.

"And no other man will ever have them again."

His lips crash against mine and his tongue presses into my mouth. I kiss him with everything I am. He commands my body and I allow him. Liam is claiming me and I'm claiming him. We are each other's and no matter what happens, I can't go back.

I don't want to go back.

He pulls my pants off completely and hovers above me.

"I love you." My voice is strong and I need him to know. "I'm yours."

He enters me in one push and I nearly cry out from the feeling. His eyes stay trained on mine and he rears back and slowly pushes forward.

"Liam!" I cry out as emotions and physical sensations become too much.

"No other man will be inside of you," he says aloud but I can't tell if he's trying to convince himself or me.

"No one . . . only you," I say.

"No other woman will have my heart," Liam assures

me. "No one else ever had my heart. Only you, Natalie." His eyes close as he slides back and forth.

From the words and the feelings, it's too much. Liam has stolen every resolve I had to keep something for myself. He knows what I need and he gives it to me. With his body and with his words.

I soar high as he flips me onto my stomach. His hand wraps around and he applies pressure on the bundle of nerves. He pounds me from behind as I push back against him. I need him to lose it. I want to drive him so hard that he can't think of anything but how good this feels.

"Fuck me," I cry out as I push myself back to meet his thrusts.

He nearly loses it as he grips the back of my neck and the sound of skin slapping overtakes the room. Heavy breathing, moaning, and our love making echoes. I close my eyes as he grips me tight and fucks me relentlessly. It's heaven and hell. I fight my orgasm off, as I want to go over the edge together.

"Let go, goddamnit," he says angrily. "Let me feel you lose it."

He swirls his hips and circles my clit and I'm gone.

I moan and let myself go. Liam kisses my back and follows me over the edge a minute later. I fall flat on the bed, sated and exhausted.

"You're incredible," Liam says as he rubs my back.

I roll over and smile lazily. "You're pretty incredible yourself. I'll be right back."

I sit up and head into the bathroom. I wrap my robe around me and look at the left side of the sink. Aaron's old razor and toothbrush. They've been a part of the house and I forgot to get rid of them. I pick them up and hold them in my hand. I don't feel anything though. No sadness, no anger just resignation.

Liam opens the door and sees me. He looks at my hand and then closes the door.

"Liam!" I call out and rush toward him.

"I'm going to go."

"No! Please, it's not like that," I try to explain. I wasn't mourning or anything, I saw it and picked it up. "Please, stop. Let me explain."

He's throwing his clothes on and tears start to form in my eyes. "I'm sorry. I need to go."

"Stop!" I cry out and he turns. "I wasn't upset. I wasn't crying over his razor. I just saw it and I don't know . . . I picked it up. It wasn't like that."

"What was it like?" He looks away, but I see the hurt in his eyes.

"I don't know. I can't explain it."

Liam grabs my hand and I look up. "Try."

"I saw it there, but I didn't feel anything. I won't feel bad though. You can't expect me to be so unfeeling. You're the first man to be in my bed other than him. You have to have some sympathy for that." I wait for him to fully register what I've said.

"You think I don't have sympathy for what you feel? You're fucking kidding me. I've never said a word, but I'm fighting a damn ghost." Liam's words are sharp and he's clearly upset.

"You're fighting something on your own. I've never made you feel that way."

His eyes meet mine before he turns away again. "Maybe not, but seeing you with that razor. Clutching it to your chest wasn't my imagination."

"You have two choices," I say determined to end this, because he's making it something it's not. "You can either trust me when I say you have nothing to worry about or you can leave."

"So easy for you?"

"Don't." I say with no room for an argument. "Don't you dare make this my fault. This is all you."

Liam steps toward the door and my heart sinks. His

hand rests on the doorknob and he turns to me. "I just need a minute. I'll be right back."

I nod, understanding. "I can handle a minute."

He steps toward me, and in an instant, I'm in his arms. He holds me close and breathes me in. "It'll never be more than that," he vows and then releases me.

I climb into bed and wait for his minute to pass.

chapter thirty-seven

"NO, MOM, I hear you," I say while trying to put the food we need for Corolla in the bag. I figure if we're going for a week, we should pack what we can.

"Are you going to be back in time for her party?" she asks.

She's flying in three days before Aarabelle's birthday party to help. The flight from Arkansas isn't cheap, and no matter how many times I explain I'll be back a full week beforehand, she isn't grasping it.

"Mom, everything will be fine. It's a two-hour drive and Liam has to be back to work after that anyway."

"I'm ecstatic you guys are going away again," she admits. My mother has been extremely supportive of my relationship with Liam. She's always loved him and knowing how great he is with Aarabelle is enough for her.

"Liam pretty much demanded it. I feel like shit taking off work again, but I'm going to do some stuff from there. I think it's important though."

I'm really looking forward to the trip. After about a week of arguing with him on how I didn't think it was fair to request time off again, Liam made a valid point. I work with a team of former SEALs. All of them have had deployments and work ups, they all know what it's like to be the one leaving and wouldn't begrudge me a chance to spend the time with him.

consolation

Of course Mark gave me no argument and said he didn't even need to run it by Jackson. I still felt guilty and almost hoped they would say no.

"Well, I can't wait to see you and that beautiful granddaughter of mine."

"We can't wait to see you either. I'll call you when I get back from Corolla." I grab some snacks to throw in the bag. We leave in three days and at least this time I've had time to pack.

"Okay, have fun. Love you."

We disconnect and I hear a car pull in the drive. The purr of the loud engine lets me know it's Robin. Great, now he even has me calling the stupid car by its name. I head out toward the deck to see why Liam's here. He told me he was super busy with training before the leave periods start.

"Hey," I say, pulling the blanket I grabbed off the couch around my shoulders.

"Hey, sorry I only had a few minutes and I figured you'd rather hear it from me." Liam looks pissed and determined. He pulls the brim of his uniform cover lower, so I can't see his eyes.

"Okay? What's wrong?"

He kicks his foot and I can already tell I'm not going to be happy. "I'm leaving tonight."

"What?" I exclaim.

"I have to head out for a few days. We have a mission and they need us to go."

"But your leave starts tomorrow. We were leaving for Corolla," I say and pull the blanket tighter.

He looks up and I see the resolution. He doesn't have a choice. "I know. I'll try to be back . . . they said it's a day or two. If we can't leave on Friday, we'll go as soon as I get back."

"I'm not taking off more time. I was having trouble with taking the five days."

Liam steps forward and places his hands on my shoulders. "I know. I'm not happy either, but I have to go. It's a small team of guys."

"And you can't give it to the other chief?" I ask, knowing he couldn't.

Life of a military girlfriend. Job comes first and we come second.

"Natalie," he says my name and he grips tight. "I *have* to be the one to go."

"Okay, I mean, I don't have a choice. I hate this. I'm pissed, but it is what it is."

Liam pulls me close and his lips press against mine. He holds me tight against his body and keeps his mouth fused to mine. This kiss is desperate as if he's memorizing me. His hands hold like vises around my arms. He doesn't let up and I can't help but think how this feels like goodbye. It's like that kiss where you're not sure you'll ever have another one. I fight the urge to cry because I feel it in the tips of my toes. It's hurting and I try to break away, but Liam keeps me against him.

Finally, he pulls back. My breath is coming in short bursts. "What was that?" I ask.

"I'll see you as soon as I can. I'll try to make it back before we were supposed to leave." He brushes his hand across my cheek.

"Liam," I try to stop him but he keeps going. "Liam! Stop!" I start to jog after him and he stops. "You can't kiss me like it was our last and then leave like that." I hold my arms across my chest and he turns and looks at me.

"I've never had to leave someone behind. I don't know how this works," he explains.

I haven't thought about how this would be for him. He's been single.

I step forward and wrap my arms around his stomach. "Well," I say sweetly, "You tell me you love me and that you'll see me soon. You kiss me tenderly and feel free to tell me how every minute you're away from me will suck." I grin and Liam's arms encase me.

"Oh, is that all?" he relaxes a little.

"Well, any compliments will work."

"How about this . . . every second I'm away from you I'll feel like my heart is missing."

"You can do better . . ." I smirk.

He looks behind me and chuckles, "I will think of you every moment of every second."

"Better, but I could use a little swooning."

"Oh, Natalie, love of my life . . . I will hold my breath until I can breathe the same air as you and even then it will not be good enough because my lungs will be dead."

I laugh and pull him close. "Now you're just being silly."

"I love you."

"I love you, more," I say and lift up on my toes and kiss him. "Hurry back."

He doesn't say another word and releases me. I stand here and watch him get in his car. The sound of the engine makes me jump and I fight the tears. I won't let him see me cry. He waves and I wave back as he drives out of sight.

I can do this. He'll be back. I can handle it.

DAYS PASS AND I don't hear from him. I should be in Corolla right now, but instead I'm working from home while Aarabelle is at the sitter. I hate not being able to hear his voice. The training missions were different because he would call.

Instead, now I sit and wonder. I worry that I'm going to turn on the news and see something has happened.

God, I didn't miss this part.

I head out to the deck to get some sun. It's still funny to me how we take this view for granted. I stare out at the horizon and get lost in my thoughts. My life is in a wonderful place. I have a beautiful daughter who makes my life worth living, a man who loves me and who I love, and a great job.

My family will be here soon and then they can all see just how great things are. Faith works in mysterious ways. A year ago, I was unwilling to think I could be here. I thought I was destined to live alone and sad.

I stand here looking out at the ocean, feeling a sense of serenity until I hear the sound of a car pulling into the driveway and I turn. The smile is instantaneous. He's home. I need to lay eyes on him. I want to kiss him and hug him.

I rush down the driveway and see Jackson and Mark walking up first. They look at the ground and walk slowly as if they're about to destroy my world.

No.

No.

Not again.

No.

My heart falters as they approach without looking at me. "No!" I scream out and begin to step backwards. "I can't." I begin to shake, but Mark moves to the side and I see Liam.

He's okay. "Oh my God, you're okay!" I scream and rush toward him with tears falling. "I was so scared!" I begin to run and then Liam puts his hand up to stop me.

My feet don't move as Liam approaches, but doesn't say a word. He just looks at me with so much pain in his eyes, I'm afraid he's going to break.

Oh, please tell me they didn't lose someone.

"Liam?" I ask hesitantly and take his face in my hands. "What's wrong?" I feel his scruff against my palm and lean in to kiss him, but he jerks back slightly. I stare at him with wide eyes trying to figure out why he's so forlorn. "Hey," I say again. Still, he doesn't speak.

He closes his eyes while pulling my hands from his face. My fingers fall as he steps to the side, and then I see him.

"Aaron?" my voice shakes.

My chest heaves and I stare at his dark brown eyes and long hair. My husband . . . Oh, God.

Aaron steps toward me and my heart stops beating.

"Hi, baby."

TO BE CONTINUED . . .

Acknowledgements

YOU'D THINK BY the third time I'd have this down pat, however, it still is the hardest part. If I forget you, I'm sure I'll hear about it but know I love you.

My betas: Mandi, Jennifer, Melissa, Holly, Roxana, Megan, & Linda—I love you all and I couldn't do this without you. Each time I send you the mini cliffhangers you come back for more. I love torturing you and making you smile. Thank you for your friendship!

Christy Peckham: I couldn't do this without you. You put up with all my crazy and still stick around. I'm so blessed to have you in my life and I don't take that for granted. You make me smile when I want to cry, laugh when I'm already crying, and if I'm really gone, you get me pissed which helps. I love you!

Melissa & Sharon: Melissa, thank you for not wanting to kill me or at least not actually doing it. I'm blessed to have a publicist like you. Every author should be so lucky as to work with you. Sharon, oh my love! You make me laugh and keep me anchored. Love you both Maleficent & Satan.

Claire Contreras: They say people come into your life for a reason . . . I think it was to teach me the kind of woman I want to be. Your strength is astounding, your friendship never wavers and each day I'm grateful to know you. Love you to the moon!

FYW: You're the first place I go, the last place I go, and my in between. I'm so blessed to know such a fantastic group of women. You're all fun, beautiful and Funk-y and I love you.

Bloggers: Without you, our books would never get seen. Thank you for taking the time to read and review, promote tirelessly, and for all your love and support.

Stabby Birds: You girls are my rocks. I couldn't imagine a place without each of you.

Corinne Michaels Book Group: You guys are so much fun. Thank you for loving me and all my crazy. You truly make me smile each day I come in to check on the group. The words of encouragement and friendship overwhelm me each day.

My test readers: Thank you for dropping whatever you are reading to let me know how you feel. You can't imagine how much I appreciate you.

A huge thank you to my editor, formatter, proofreader, and cover designer for making this book all that it is.

Thank you, The Rockstars of Romance, for hosting everything for Consolation. I love you girl so much!

Lauren Perry: Ahhhh thank you for finding Ben and Hannah! Your photos are the reason this book isn't a standalone. Your art inspired me to make this story so much more than I planned. Thank you!

Rinny, Melanie, Krissy: We've been friends since we were babies it seems like. We've had bad boyfriends, weddings, love, hate, friendship, sisterhood, and babies. Through it all, we've kept our friendship strong and it doesn't matter that we go months without uttering a word. If I called tomorrow, I know you'd be here. It's a friendship many will never be fortunate to experience. I love you so much.

Crystal: Even when we bring out the most hostile parts of each other, we are able to find our friendship. I think it's something special and unique that, no matter how ugly it gets, we see the beauty. Thank you for loaning me your husband to kill off. It was fun and we should totalllllly do it again!

Lucia Franco: Without your convo this book would've

never happened. Thank you for cheering me on and being as excited as I was.

Tammi Ahmed: You are a graphic queen! Thank you for making me such beautiful art! I love every creation you come up with.

My children: You two have no idea the depths of my love for you. Thank you for my great big hugs, my fun snuggles, and making me remember there's more to life than books. You are my world.

My husband: I met you when I wasn't sure who I was. You loved me and helped me become the woman I am today. I may want to smack you but there's no one else I'd rather build snowmen with.

conviction

CORINNE MICHAELS

To my mother, you always believed in me even when I didn't. Your love, friendship, support, and courage made me the woman I am today. Without you, none of this would be possible.

chapter one

TIME ISN'T SOMETHING I ever thought much about.
It ebbs and flows, but it never changes. I can't make it stop—no matter how much I want to. There's no way to rewind the clock or halt it. In this moment, all I want is to make the world stop and go back to when I was happy and ready to tackle the world. Just two short minutes ago, there was no worry about how my day would go. I was going away with the man I love, the one who healed me. But time isn't my friend. It slaps me in the face and laughs as I stand here wondering how the hell any of this is happening. I don't want to move forward, and I sure as hell don't want to slow it down.

"Aaron?"

He stands before me—alive. The man who I would've sold my soul to have back again a year ago is here. I take a hesitant step forward. I'm aware of the people around me, but my mind can't focus on anything else but him.

"Hi, baby," he rasps.

"Oh, my God. You're alive?" I ask and step closer. His dark brown eyes glimmer with hope and happiness.

"I'm here," he says, and I rush forward. My arms wrap around his neck while the tears fall. He's alive and here. In my arms, I hold my lost husband as he rubs my back. My heart races as I fully start to process what's happening. Aaron holds the back of my head as I sob into his chest. "I missed you so much," he murmurs and rocks.

"You're alive." My heart stutters while I struggle to catch my breath. I hold him closer and squeeze just to be sure.

He winces, and I step back. Aaron comes forward with a smile, and I place my hand on his face. He has bruises on the side of his cheek and neck, his hair is long, but it's really him. The man I loved for so long and the father of my daughter is home. It's unbelievable.

"I-I thought . . ." I choke on the words, as my breathing grows shallow. "You're . . . I don't know what—"

My mind spins as the last year of grief, sadness, and devastation crashes around me. He was alive and we didn't know. We didn't look. Or maybe it's just a dream?

"Shh." He takes my hand in his. "It's okay now. I'm here, we're going to be fine, baby. I'm home."

The words filter through me and my gaze shifts as I notice movement to the right.

Liam. Oh my God . . . Liam.

I look over to the side where he stands with his head bowed. My heart thumps out of sync. Tears well in my eyes as the enormity of this moment comes down around me. Liam still doesn't look at me. The pain lances through me as I beseech with my eyes for him to turn and look at me.

Please, just see me, I beg him, but he doesn't lift his eyes.

My feet move toward him, but he still doesn't move.

"Liam, please," I plead with tears falling.

His eyes lift, and while his face is stoic, his eyes give it away. He's hurting.

"Natalie?" Aaron's voice breaks through the small moment I was having with Liam.

I turn around and try to get a hold of myself. Jackson

and Mark stand to the side, watching the mess unfold. There's so much confusion rolling around within me. I don't know what to do, where to turn, or how any of this is happening. I was packing my car to go to Corolla. I was going to spend time with the man I love. The man I was building a future with. And now my husband is here.

I step back and my body begins to shake. This is too much. No one can endure this and come out on the other side. I'm losing it. Shock rolls through me like waves on the sand. "I can't breathe," I say aloud.

Mark takes a step toward me. "Lee, it's okay."

I laugh sarcastically. "No. None of this is okay. None of this makes any sense!" I scream as my heart implodes. "I can't! I mean, this isn't real."

I feel someone close in behind me and Mark shakes his head. "It is real."

Turning around, Aaron is right there. "I'm here, Lee. I'm home." He sounds so hopeful as if this is everything I could want. Of course I had wanted this for so long. He was my world and now he's back, but what does all this mean? Liam is the man I love. How am I going to do this now?

Aaron's hand reaches out then he touches my arm. My body locks as Liam watches with sadness in his eyes. I look at Aaron, and the past comes down upon me. This isn't my husband I dreamt of. This isn't the man I loved with every part of me. This is the man that a few months ago I found out had an affair. The same man who almost had a baby with someone else. His hands feel foreign, and as he goes to embrace me, my hand rises and I stop him. I'm no better than he is in this moment. "Please, just, I need . . ." I trail off.

Liam is here, watching me go into another man's arms. Five minutes ago, I was relieved Aaron's alive and Liam saw the joy in my face. I'm killing him. I see it.

"No!" I yell and step back. "Please, don't touch me."

My hand flies to my mouth as shock locks my body in place.

Aaron's hand drops and his breath hitches. "You're my wife, Lee. I know you're confused and this is a lot to take, but I'm here, baby."

I move toward Liam, his blue eyes meet mine as I rush toward him. I take his hands in mine, but he releases them. My heart shatters as he steps back.

"Don't pull away from me," I demand.

"I think you need some time," his voice cracks. "You need to talk."

"I don't know what I need," I acknowledge.

"Lee," he says and looks at Aaron, but then he returns his gaze to me.

I see it in his eyes, the resolution forming and masking over this pain. "You're going to walk away from me, aren't you?" Tears fall relentlessly as I wait for his answer.

Liam's hand lifts, and he tenderly cups my cheek. "I'm not walking away. I need a minute."

Aaron clears his throat. "I missed a lot more than you filled me in on. I guess I understand why you've been so quiet now."

The loss of Liam's touch registers immediately.

Anger boils within as the hurt and betrayal at Aaron's hand over the last few months comes flooding forward. "You should stop," I demand.

"My wife?" he yells and steps forward. "You've been fucking my wife?"

"You were dead!" I scream, and my legs give out. I fall to the hard ground as the gravel scrapes my skin. Liam's arms are around me in an instant.

"Get your hands off of her! You son of a bitch!" Aaron continues to raise his voice warning Liam. "I'll kill you!"

I look up, and Jackson and Mark are holding on to Aaron, dragging him to the back of the house.

I turn into Liam's embrace allowing his strong arms to hold me close. "Take me to Corolla. I'll grab Aara, and we can go," I plead. "Please, take me away."

"Lee," he says with regret laced in his voice. "I can't. I wish we could, but we can't."

"No," I reply defiantly. "You and I had plans."

"And now your husband is home."

"My cheating husband?"

Liam sighs while pushing me back slightly. "You both need to talk. I can't be that man."

We both stand looking at each other before I speak. "What man? The man I fell in love with? The man who told me he loved me? Because that's the man I need."

Liam wipes his hand down his face. "He's your fucking husband, Lee! Not to mention he was my best friend. I saw the way you looked at him. It was clear in the second you saw him how much you love him. You ran to him, and I get it," he says despondently. "I get why you would. You loved him. I mean, what the hell do you want me to do?"

"Fight!" I slap his chest and push. "Fight for me. Fight for us. So what, you're going to walk away? Just hand me over like I mean nothing?" The question hangs in the air as I wait for the bomb to drop.

"You want me to fight?" he steps closer. "You think I'm not? You think this is what the hell I wanted? To deliver your husband back to you when I'm so fucking in love with you that I would've rather cut out my own heart? I hate that I brought him home to you."

Anger stirs between us as the weight of the situation descends around us.

"I can't believe this."

Liam's shoulders sag in defeat. "You both have a lot of things to work through. I should leave before this escalates. I won't be that guy."

I huff and look away. Unreal. "I can't believe you

think so little of us."

With my pulse beating rapidly in my chest, Liam grips my shoulders pulling me close. Our noses touch while we both breathe heavily. "I would give my life for you. I would go in there and pummel his ass to a pulp if I thought that would help. But it won't. You're married to him. You're his wife. Right this minute, I'm the other man. Do you understand that?"

"I belong to you."

"No, you belong to him."

I need him to understand me. My life changed when Liam came. He made me feel again, loved me like I've never known. I don't know that I'll survive if he leaves me. I close my eyes and press my lips to his. Gripping his shirt, I yank his body against mine.

Kiss me, dammit.

Claim me.

He stands unmoving as I pour myself into him. He doesn't respond, and my anger grows.

Pulling back, I glare at him as his eyes shut. My hand rears back then I slap him across the face. I take pleasure in watching his eyes snap open, hoping this draws him back to me.

"What the hell was that for?"

I slap him again. I see the fight coming to life inside of him.

"Fuck you. If I mean this little to you, then go. Go. Run. Leave! Go be the man you're not because of whatever bullshit you'll feed yourself! Go!" I raise my hand again, but he grabs it.

Liam's control snaps, he grips my arms tighter jerking me against him. I breathe one deep breath before his lips crash against mine. I savor the feel of his mouth pushing against mine. I get lost in the brute force of this kiss. His fingers are a vice around my arms, and I don't care. I want him to bruise me. Leave his mark so I have proof of what we shared. My lips mold to his as I give him back all I am.

I escape the moment we're both drowning in when our tongues touch. His grip loosens as his hands glide to my neck until they cradle my head. The mood shifts to sadness. My fingers thread in his hair as I try to hold him against me. Liam's hands tighten, and he breaks us apart.

"I need a minute. I need a few of them. I love you, but I have to go."

My heart shatters all over again. I've lost him.

"If you leave me, I don't think you're coming back," I say, hoping he'll refute me and give the comfort I'm desperate for.

Liam rests his forehead against mine. "I'm never far. You need to get through this without worrying about me."

"You think I can do that? You think right now as happy as I am he's alive. That I'm not distraught? That I'm not worried about how the hell you and I will survive this? I'll worry every day about you and us." I beg him to stay. I need him to stay.

"Aaron and you had a whole life together. We had a few months."

"Don't you dare downplay what we have!" I fight the urge to slap him again.

Liam runs his fingers the length of my arm. "I need you to see this from my side. I never knew if you'd have chosen him, but now I don't know if you should choose me. I need to get my fucking head on straight. Right now, you have to let me go." Liam's eyes mirror mine with the agony of this moment.

I fight the tears that build. As much as I know he's right, I wish he were wrong. I don't know how to navigate this. It's too much. My heart had healed, and instantly I'm raw all over again. There was a time that Aaron was everything I wanted. Now that he's back in my life, I no longer want him. If any prayer I wish went unanswered, it was this one, only because now I have to endure the pain of breaking a man I love. But my life doesn't work that way.

"I want you to know something before you walk away from me. I need you to know that I want you. You are the man I'm in love with. Yes, he's my husband and Aarabelle's father, but I love you, Liam. I love you so much more than I want to, but God, I love you. Please, hear me. I love you."

"I love you too, but I have to do what's right."

"Right for who?" I scoff.

Liam leans back and waits until I look at him. His blue eyes shimmer with unshed tears. "For you. For Aarabelle. For all of us. I can't be the man who destroys a marriage, and sure as fuck not yours and Aaron's."

There's no convincing him, and all I can hope for at this moment is that he heard me.

Before I can respond, I hear someone approach from behind. Liam looks up, and by the flash in his eyes, I know it's Aaron.

"I hate to break up this touching scene, but I've been gone more than a year and this isn't exactly the reunion I anticipated." Aaron's voice is on the edge. "If I could have my wife, brother."

I don't miss the way he enunciates "wife" or "brother."

Liam doesn't say anything, but his arms fall, as does my heart.

He walks away without a word. I face my husband, my first love, with tears in my eyes as the man I love more than anything leaves me behind.

I want to die.

chapter two

AARON AND I walk toward the back of the house where Jackson and Mark are standing. Jackson shifts, and I smother the urge to punch him in the face. "No one thought a heads up would be a good idea?" I spit the words. "No one thought I should know this? Did your cell phones all die? Because I can't think of any reason why you all wouldn't want to tell me."

"Natalie," Mark steps toward me. "First of all, none of us knew if it was definitely Aaron. Secondly, we couldn't compromise the mission. This all had to happen very secretly and very covertly. And what, did you want us to call on the way over? No one knew how to handle this."

Jackson takes a hesitant footstep. "I know you were getting your life together. I know you were happy, and for that, I'm sorry. No one here would want to hurt you. Least of all me."

"Sure, you're sorry." Anger flows through me, tearing me apart.

His head bows then he turns to Aaron. "We should let you guys talk. Remember what I said about a lot changing in a year. But I'm glad you're home."

Aaron looks at me before turning back to Jackson. "I appreciate it. I'm happy to be back with my girls."

The last few months rush back. I remember how I felt finding out about his transgressions. How he loved another woman. My mind starts to wonder if he means me and Aarabelle, or me and Brittany.

I can't listen to this. I need to get a grip on what the hell is festering inside of me. There are so many things I'm feeling all at once. I walk down onto the beach, the sand burning my feet, and I welcome the pain. I stand still, lifting my head to the sky. *Why?* I ask the clouds. This should be a happy moment. One filled with hugs and tears of joy, but I'm left feeling as if a gaping hole was punched through my chest. Just when I thought my life was on track—boom.

My mind drifts to Liam and how devastated he was. His eyes lost the spark I loved to see. I don't know where my life will go—once again. There are no easy answers in this situation. I have a husband, a baby, a boyfriend, and suddenly a shitload of problems. But I need him to see that I meant what I said. I want him beside me.

"Are we going to talk?" I hear Aaron ask from behind me. The raspy voice that once made me long for him now makes me want to cry.

I turn as he stands still, waiting for something from me. "No, I'd rather not. I feel like I'm about to wake up any moment, so I'm just waiting for it to happen. All of this is so confusing," I reply and wish I could slap myself.

Aaron steps forward. "Lee," his voice trembles, "I'm here."

"You keep saying that. But how? How is this happening?" I take a moment to look over his face. His brown eyes are dull and lifeless, there's a large gash on the side of his neck. My eyes travel down his arms where there are a few scars from what look like burns, and he's missing a finger on his left hand. He looks broken and alone, but then he smiles at me and I try to stop my heart from swelling a little.

"All I could think about was seeing my girls," he steps closer. "I fought to be here for you."

"For me? Really?" I question, not actually wanting an answer. Aaron looks at me with confusion. *Well, I'll be happy to clue him in.* "Are you sure it's me you want, Aaron, or do you want me to call Brittany?" I ask, shooting daggers at him. I stand watching his reactions. I catalog the way he shifts to the side and the way he grips the back of his neck.

I see the fear flare in his eyes, and if I hadn't known him for most of my life, I'd have missed it.

"It's not—"

"Not what I think?"

Aaron takes another step closer as his face pales. "I love you. I've always loved you."

"You love me?" I scoff. "That's rich. You have a funny way of showing it. God, this whole situation is so insane," I say in disbelief. "I mean, you were dead. I buried you. I stood and wept for you. Then I go through hell finding a way to put myself back together. Only to find out you cheated on me for months! Months, Aaron!" I move forward this time allowing him to see the anger on my face. "You betrayed me. The man I married wouldn't have done that. But the man who held my hand and told me he'd die before touching another woman did exactly that."

"And you fucked Liam!" he bellows before sinking into the sand. On his knees in front of me, I see the hurt all over him.

"You have no clue."

Aaron looks at me and tears form in my eyes. "We have a lot to work through, Lee. I know I fucked up. I know I made mistakes and I wish you'd never found out about them. Can we please give ourselves a few days?"

A tear falls and my heart breaks. "And then what?"

"I don't know," he admits. "But I've thought about you every day that I was gone. Every fucking minute of the day, I fought death to come home to you. All I wanted was to see you and the baby." His eyes flood with tears and every part of me aches.

I don't want to hurt him. I don't want to cause him pain. That's not who I am. This is the man I thought I'd spend every day of my life with. The man I struggled to have children with. Agonizing months of shots and treatments because I wanted to give him a child. A part of me is pulled to him, but I don't trust myself. He represents every memory of our twelve years together, and we have a child. It's taking everything inside of me not to collapse.

I sink in the sand beside him. "I'm in love with Liam." My voice is a whisper. The way his hands clench tells me he heard.

Aaron tenderly lifts my chin. "I'm begging you, Lee. I'm on my knees begging you to give us some time. Let's wait a few days before we decide anything. There are a lot of things we have to discuss regardless."

The words catch in my throat as I think of Liam. I don't know how to feel in this moment. Who am I loyal to? Aaron was . . . is . . . my husband. But Liam has my heart. He brought me to life in a way Aaron never did. He's good to me, loyal and faithful. There's no mistrust between us. It's not Aaron's fault he's been gone a year, but it's not Liam's either. Now, all of us have to pay the price.

"I don't know that a few days will change my feelings," I warn.

"I think you should know everything."

His hand drops, and I look back at the house. So much has changed in a matter of a few minutes. I sit here, wishing I could go back in time. I would've made different decisions. Maybe I'd have seen the writing on the wall with Aaron and left him. I don't know that I'd be with Liam if that were the case, but I could've started over.

"I missed you so much, Aaron. So much that it broke

me, and now . . ."

He takes my face in his hands. "I'm here now, and I'll fix the broken, baby."

My heart shatters because in this moment, I don't think he can. I'm destroyed by what we've both endured. I'm wrecked for what Liam is feeling. I'm devastated for what's about to come down the road for both of these men—and me. We will all have blood drawn and be left to try to heal after this.

Aaron and I stare at each other as so many emotions flow through me. I'm so happy he's alive, but with that comes sadness. The flame that was once so strong I could feel him in my soul is barely a flicker.

His thumb brushes my cheek, and I try to catch my breath. "I'm so sorry, Lee."

Another tear falls as I start to shut myself off. I have to hold my child right now. I have to have her in my arms because she's real and what I need to focus on. "I need to go get Aarabelle."

"Aarabelle? Is that what you named her?" Aaron's demeanor shifts, and he smiles for the first time. Oh, how I missed his smile. "I thought we decided on Chloe?"

"I wanted her to bare your name always." The pain shoots through me. "I wanted her to know you in some way. I needed her to know how special she is because her father was a hero."

Aaron's body leans closer. "She has you. She was always going to be special. I want to see her."

My throat goes dry as I fight the tears threatening to fall. "I don't want to confuse her. I know she's your daughter, but I don't know what to do."

"I'm your husband too," he reminds me.

"You and I may be married right now, but there's so much we have to talk about, Aaron. This isn't an easy place for either of us. You haven't been a husband for a long time." I give Aaron my own reminder. We're both victims here. "I'm going to pick her up from the sitter. I need time. There are a lot of things we need to decide on to press forward."

"Where does your boyfriend fit into all of this?" he sneers. He's lucky I don't punch him.

I stand, giving myself the height advantage. He doesn't get to degrade me for something he did. I won't let him taint the love I share with Liam. If he wants to be an asshole, I'll show him how much I've grown.

"I'll let you slide on this. I didn't date Liam behind your back. I didn't betray you. I thought you were *dead*." Aaron looks at me, and I know this is killing him. I didn't fall in love with someone random. I fell in love with his best friend. The immense pain he must feel is something I can't understand. Brittany was bad, but I didn't have to lose two people I care about.

I know this isn't easy for him. I hate that now I'm the one holding the knife to his chest.

"But I'm not gone."

"No, you're not, and I'm so happy you're alive. I'm glad Aarabelle will have her father. But Liam is the reason I smiled again and found a way to muddle through the days. Liam is the reason when I found out about your affair I didn't go off the deep end. So that was the one dig you get. I'm not the liar or the cheater—" I let that hang in the air between us.

Aaron stands then grips my shoulders. "I came back to you. I lived to see your face again. Not hers—yours. Every moment, I thought of you, dreamt of you, needed to touch you again." His hands graze my arms as he speaks. "I need you, Natalie. I need you, and I'm not letting you go without a fight. I lived for you and our daughter. I'll be damned if I'm going to let anyone take that from me again."

I stare into his amber eyes and choke back the sob that threatens to escape. "It's not your choice anymore."

"No one is going to take my family from me. I'm going to win you back. And I'll be sure to let Liam know that as well." Aaron's hands fall, and he heads toward the water.

I stand in shock at the promise he made. My heart races while the nausea bubbles up. I don't have any idea how I'm going to handle this. All I know is right now I want to be wrapped in Liam's arms in Corolla, away from all of this.

chapter three

"THANKS, PAIGE," I say as I lift Aarabelle into my arms.

"No problem. I hope you have fun in Corolla," she smiles and I nod. I can't say the words because they will break the carefully constructed front I've managed to build.

I buckle Aarabelle in her seat while she smiles at me. "Dadadada," she babbles and then I fall apart.

My muscles go limp while I lie with my head in her lap and sob. I think about how she called Liam "dada" and how much it made a part of me happy. Now, the sound of her saying it makes me break. I drown in the sea of pain as each sound of my own cries takes me under.

She plays with my hair as I lose it in the back seat of my car.

Breathe and you'll figure this out. You're stronger than this.

I look at Aarabelle, and brush the side of her face. "So much has changed, baby girl. So much. Mommy's going to be a mess, but I'll do everything I can to protect you from it all. I love you so much," I tell her then close the door.

When I left the house, Aaron was sitting on the deck. He asked if we could talk more tonight and try to find some kind of middle ground. I don't even have a clue as to what kind of agreement we can come to, but I at least have to try. If I want any shot in hell with Liam, I need to know where things stand at home first.

There are so many issues flying through my mind: where he'll sleep, clothing, do I file for divorce, what about all the money from him being declared dead? I sit in the driver's seat and put the music on. I don't want to think about any of this. I want to take a moment.

I pay no mind to where I'm going, because I'm singing as loud as I can with tears streaming down my face. Life is cruel. Love is a joke. And not even death is final.

I'm not ready to head home. I know I should because he's waiting for her. He's waiting for me. I'm being uncaring, but all I want to do is head to Liam and beg him to take me into his arms. Looking back in the rearview mirror, Aarabelle stares out the window, and I wish things could be different, but I'm grateful she'll never remember all of this mess. I turn into my driveway and sit. The turmoil boiling through my veins makes it impossible to move. There's not only the fear of him with Aarabelle, but also me too. I'm a match next to a canteen of gasoline, ready to ignite at any moment. We haven't dealt with anything and I reluctantly agreed to let it rest for a few days.

A few days that I can't go to Liam.

Time to get your shit together.

Aarabelle smiles when I get her from her car seat. I walk slowly with her to the deck where Aaron is standing with his back to me.

He turns slowly and casts his eyes on Aarabelle for the first time. I hold her close as she looks around. Aaron takes a slow step forward and smiles. "She's beautiful."

Words fail me, so I nod.

"She looks just like you, Lee." Aaron's eyes swim with love as he stares at my—our—daughter.

"I always thought she looked like you," I say looking

at her while she smiles at me.

"Can I?" he asks, his arms extended.

I shouldn't pull her back, but I do. I can't stop the fear that festers. He's her father, he wanted her, and he will love her, I know all of this. But she's only ever been mine. It makes me harsh and selfish, but I don't really care. She's *my* daughter. I've been through it all with her. Well, me and Liam. He's practically been a parent to her, and I feel as if I'm betraying *him*. Which is insane.

"Lee," my name rolls off his tongue.

Tears pool and one lone bead of moisture escapes. It slowly descends down my face before landing on my lip. "I j-just . . ." I stutter. My hands grip Aarabelle as she squirms to get free. Aaron moves closer, keeping his eyes trained on her as if he can't look away.

This was the culmination of years of heartbreak. Years of both of us feeling inadequate and alone together. She's the beauty in all the heartache. She's the prize from all the desperation we endured. And she's his. Not Liam's.

No matter where Aaron and I land, Aarabelle is the glue that will hold our lives together. Forever we will be tied to each other. I slowly extend her, and his arms meet me halfway. Our hands touch as his eyes fill with tears.

"Hi, Aarabelle," he says adoringly to Aara. The way he looks at her, like she's the air he breathes, makes my chest tighten.

The arms I'd wished would wrap around her, protect her, love her are now holding her. She looks at Aaron with her signature smile. My body goes stiff as it all settles around us.

Aaron somehow lived and is home.

He's holding our baby.

"God, she couldn't be any more perfect," he laughs and looks at me.

I sniff and try to rein myself in. "Yeah, she really is

perfect."

"You look just like your mommy." He bounces her and wipes his eyes. "I dreamt of you. I wondered if you were okay," Aaron talks to Aarabelle, and I have to take a few steps back.

Father and daughter are united.

"What's her birthday?" he asks.

"August ninth." She looks at me, and I walk over to them. I place my hand on her back while she touches his face.

Aaron just stares at her. Aarabelle squirms again and begins to fuss.

"She's almost one. She just wants to move around," I explain, reaching for her. "Do you want to go for a walk? She loves the beach." I offer the olive branch to him. The confliction on how to handle this entire thing is too great to make things any harder.

His eyes soften, and he nods. "That would be great."

I lean down, place Aara on the chair, and then remove her shoes. "You'll need to hold her other hand. She's a little unsteady."

Aaron holds his hand out to her, and she wraps her fingers around his. With me on the other side, we begin to head toward the water. Mother, father, and daughter. It's a picture perfect vision of how our lives could've been. My thoughts wander to the man who's been at my side the last year. How would he feel about this?

"Lee?" Aaron asks as we walk along the water line, breaking me from my reflections.

"Yes?"

"I really do love you." Aaron's voice doesn't waver.

"Mama!" Aara yells demanding my attention. I'm grateful for the distraction, because I don't know how to respond. Do I love him? I'll always love him. But because of Liam, my life this last year has been different.

"She's getting hungry."

"Okay," Aaron says then looks away. "I should probably lie down. I'm exhausted."

We start to walk back to our home, but I don't speak. The silence says everything.

After I get Aarabelle to bed, and Aaron hovers watching everything I do, we both head toward the living room. It's the first time we're completely alone. I don't know how I'm going to last days without talking about all the crap between us.

He sits on the couch, but he's not relaxed. The muscles in his arms are coiled tight. His head rests on the back of the seat, but everything in his body shows his distress.

"Aaron? Are you okay?"

Immediately his eyes fly open. "Hey," his voice is like ice. "I'm fine. Just got lost for a moment."

I'm a fairly empathetic person, but how to navigate this is beyond my understanding. I have no idea what it's like to be held captive. I don't know how someone can endure that and resume their old life. Especially one that everyone has spent the last year moving on from, so that it doesn't even exist anymore. "Do you want to talk about it?"

Aaron shakes his head. "I can't yet. I'm trying to figure out a way to make it through this. I came home to a world I don't have a place in. I lost you, my house, my life."

"I know you want to give it a few days. I don't think we can. How are we supposed to sit here and have all this just hanging? It's putting us both on edge."

Aaron shifts forward so that his forearms rest on his knees. "I don't know. I'm in agony, Lee. It feels like you wish I'd stayed gone, and I don't know how to feel about that. I'm your husband."

"You were dead. You were gone. I had to live."

"I fucking know that." Aaron stands while his eyes

focus on flag sitting on the mantle. "I see it in your eyes though, baby."

"Don't," I warn. "You told me to move on, you made me promise. You can't hate me or blame me for doing what you asked."

My heartbeat falters as he kneels while gripping my hands. "I can't. I've loved you my whole life. I can't look at you right now and think of my fucking best friend touching you."

I pull my hands back. He's suffered and I know this. I can't begin to imagine what the last year has brought him, and then to add insult to injury, I wasn't here waiting for him. "You ruined me. I trusted you, and then to find out you had an affair . . ."

Aaron's gaze drops, and he sucks in a breath. "I know. It was never like that."

"No?"

He looks back up as I search for the man I once loved. Not because I want to be with him, but because I need to know he's there. I implore him to tell me the truth. If he lies, there will never be a way for us to move forward.

"I was the broken one. I needed you so much, and all you cared about was getting pregnant. We didn't talk if it wasn't surrounding infertility. We didn't touch if it wasn't a part of your schedule. I couldn't have sex with you because it would diminish my counts. I hated coming home. I volunteered to go on missions just because I needed a fucking break."

His words cut me deeper than I ever imagined. They tear through any whole part of me that remained. He and he alone made these decisions for our family. My emotions and my needs were secondary in every way. I had to go through hell because he was too much of a chickenshit to fight. "You volunteered when I was already pregnant?"

"No, the ones before. When I would go on those trips, it reminded me of how it felt to be in charge of *something*. I failed at every fucking turn. Being your husband was exhausting."

"So she was just some way to escape the horrors of being my husband?" I ask with disparagement dripping from my tongue.

"Natalie, it was a way to escape the horrors of not being man enough. It wasn't about you. Don't you get that?" He waits, but I don't say a word. "It was me who wasn't able to give you, my wife, the woman I would've laid my own life down for, a baby. I was inadequate on every level. She didn't see that in me. She saw the strong, virile male who wasn't a failure. I needed her to take the pain away."

"Was she worth it?"

"It wasn't about her."

"Would you go back and do it again?" I ask with raw pain drowning my words.

Aaron looks away and then back again. "She gave me something you weren't willing to give anymore. She looked at me like a man. She looked at me like a hero. In her eyes, I was someone worth loving. I needed that. I deserved that."

"Would you do it again?" I ask again.

"I don't know!"

I look at him, and he knows me well enough to see the hurt, anger, and despair in my eyes. He knows that was the end of any chance he had.

He just lost me.

Completely.

CHAPTER FOUR

LIAM

"FUCK!" I SCREAM and throw the glass against the wall. It's been forty-eight hours since I last saw her face. Two fucking days. I haven't slept. I can't eat. I want to rush back to her house and take her and Aarabelle. I need her like I need air.

But I have to stay away.

He's my best friend.

He's her husband.

I'm a piece of shit.

"Dempsey, open the fucking door!" I hear someone, but I'm not moving.

"Suck my dick!" I yell back and reach for my glass. Oh, yeah, I broke it. The bottle will be just fine. I grip the neck of the bottle as the vodka pours down my throat. I need the numbness that won't come.

"I'll knock it off the goddamn hinges. Don't think I won't," I hear Quinn on the other side threatening me. He's the last person I want to see. Like I need a talk about why loving her was a bad idea.

"Go away," I reply, taking another swig of what I'm hoping will give me a break from the hell I'm living.

I hear the wood splinter as Quinn kicks the door in. Asshole.

"You're going to pay for that," I inform him.

"If you'd have opened the damn door, I wouldn't have kicked it in." He looks around the room, and I sink into the couch.

"Good to see you're taking it well."

I open my eyes then flip him off. "If you've come here to gloat, you can see yourself out the door. I don't need anyone's shit."

Quinn pushes my leg and sits next to me. He grabs the bottle from my hand and puts it on the table. "No one could've seen this coming, man. You didn't know."

"I brought him to her. I had to sit on that fucking plane and listen to him go on and on about her." I want to throw something again. "He wouldn't shut up about being with her again. I just sat there, and Jackson and Mark didn't know what to say either. None of us could tell him. None of us could talk. How fucked up am I that I wished it hadn't been him?"

Quinn sits there quiet for the first time in his life. I reach for the bottle, but he moves it before I can grab it.

"Give it to me."

"You've had enough, Demps."

"I'm on leave! Give me the goddamn bottle," I growl as I reach again.

Quinn smirks and I stand, ready to fight him.

"You wanna hit me, buddy? Go ahead. I'll have your ass laid out before you get your first hit in," he taunts and sits there lazily.

"Fuck you!"

"Nah, you're not really my type."

"Are you enjoying this?" I ask and head to the kitchen before he can answer me. He may have taken my vodka, but I'll grab the whiskey.

I try to be as quiet as possible while I grab the Jameson. I get the top off and take half a swig before Quinn grabs it from me.

My fist clenches, I go to take a swing, but Quinn's hand goes up and grabs my hand and twists it. "You wanna kill yourself? You want to be a pussy and drink yourself stupid, or do you want to be a man?"

I don't say anything. I'm drunk, angry, and I want my girl back.

My other hand flies up, and before I know it, I'm face down on the ground with Quinn holding my arms behind my back. "Pussy it is," Quinn laughs and uses something to secure my hands behind my back.

"Untie me, you son-of-a-bitch." My voice is borderline murderous. "I'll kill you when I get out of this."

Quinn squats in front of me while I lie on the ground. "I'm not worried." He pats my back and grabs the whiskey. "Now that you can't do anything stupid let's chat."

I lift my head while glaring at him.

"You have two choices here. You can either let Aaron claim his wife back, or you can show her why you're worth her time. It's clear you love her and she loves you."

I look at him incredulously. This was the same guy who told me to stay away. "She's married to *him*. She's not just some guy's wife."

"Did she tell you to leave?"

I close my eyes and see her face. She was so angry and slapped me, but I couldn't be that guy. I can't be the one who breaks up a family. It's not just about Aaron . . . there's Aarabelle to think about too. She may not be mine, but I love her as if she were. I can't be the reason that she doesn't have her father. If Natalie wants me, she'll have to decide that on her own with no influence from me. I'd never stop wondering.

"No, but she was in shock."

"You're clairvoyant now? Wow, okay," he pauses. "What will the winning lottery numbers be? I could use some serious dough."

"Untie me," I demand as I try to move my hands.

"I'm not done talking," he states as if there's no issue in this.

"Quinn, I promise I'll kick the shit out of you if you don't untie me."

He laughs then moves to the chair, making himself comfortable. "You can try, but first you'll need to get out. Here's the deal. I don't think you're capable of making a rational decision right now. You need to sober up and figure out how the hell to claim your balls back. Right now, you're waving a white flag to a man who cheated on his wife. Yeah, he was your friend. I get it. Are you willing to fight for her? If you're not . . . then you don't deserve her."

Quinn stands and places a knife on the floor, clear out of reach. "You better run," I warn him.

"You should be chasing someone else. Think about that and then clean this shit. You're better than this," he says and walks out the room.

I start to slide against the floor toward the knife.

Each inch I get closer, I think about what he said. The alcohol fog I was hoping for is lifting as the anger sobers me. Natalie begged me to take her away and fight for her. And all I wanted was to whisk her away and run. But the part everyone fails to understand is that this isn't my fight. It's hers.

I'll never be able to push her away. I'll wait forever if I have to, but I can't fight this battle.

She has to be the one to choose me.

If she loves me like she says, she knows where to find me.

chapter five

natalie

"THANKS, REA," I say as I place Aarabelle in the porta crib at her house.

I haven't heard from Liam in two days. I've tried to get a hold of him multiple times, but he doesn't respond. He's starting to worry me.

"No problem. I love waking up at two a.m." She yawns and nudges me.

Aaron was asleep on the couch tossing and turning. I literally snuck out of my own house. Since the first night, we haven't spoken much. There's not much for me to say. He tells me repeatedly that he wants to work on us, but it's two people fighting to have the other let go. He wants me to let go of resisting him, and I want him to let me go. "I just need to see him. I won't be long."

Reanell takes me into her arms and holds tight. "Go. I'm sure he needs you."

"I don't know what to say to him," I admit.

"Just talk to him. How are things at home?"

Reanell and I haven't been able to talk except through text messages. Aaron hasn't left my side except to sleep. "I don't know. Rocky at best. He's on the couch, which he's not happy about. He keeps saying he's going to prove how much we belong together."

She looks at me with empathy. "I know this is hard. I can't even imagine what you're feeling, but I can say I've seen you with both men. I know the Natalie you were with Aaron and who you are with Liam. Neither was wrong, but one was definitely happier. I'm here no matter what." Rea kisses the side of my cheek and swats my ass. "Now, go."

I turn and head toward the man I'm desperate to see.

As I drive, I debate whether I should let him know I'm on my way. I worry that he won't want to see me. The pain in his eyes haunts me. The need to see Liam as he was before all this is my only goal.

Guilt over leaving Aaron at home chews at my heart. It wraps around and squeezes me tight. My chest hurts, but I keep heading toward Liam. He's who I need right now. I miss him, love him, and long to touch him.

I park and check my reflection, already hating the dark circles forming under my eyes. The red, blotchy marks on my skin from all the tears I've shed. The acid marks on my skin matching my insides.

I knock twice but he doesn't answer. It's the middle of the night and I didn't call. I shouldn't be surprised. Regardless, disappointment swells over me. I rest my head against the door, hoping to feel some sort of connection to him. If he can feel me here, he'll open.

But instead the door shoves forward.

"Liam?" I speak quietly as I enter.

The hinges are broken, but look as if someone rigged the door back up. What the hell happened? I flip the light on in the living room, suddenly unsure if I'm in the right place. It's a mess. Papers, bottles, and shattered glass is everywhere. There's a hole in the wall by the television and a bloody towel lying on the floor.

"Liam?" I call out more loudly, but no answer.

When I reach his bedroom, I'm floored at what I find. Liam is passed out in the bed, wearing only his boxers. "Oh, Liam," I whisper and move toward him. Crouching down by his face, I gently brush his hair back. "I've missed you." He lets out a long, slow breath as if he's been holding it. "Why haven't you called me? I don't want to lose you. I feel so alone, Liam." My eyes prick as a tear falls. He sleeps as I confess my pain. "The tension is so thick, and I can't breathe without you. I close my eyes and pretend you're next to me. I feel your arms wrap around me, but you're not there. I wish I could be with you and not feel like I'm dying inside. We could be away, making love, holding each other, but you're passed out, and I'm sobbing on the floor. How did we get here? How do we go back?" My breathing becomes difficult as I let it all out. My fingers rub the side of his face, letting his beard scratch the pads of my fingers.

I need to be closer to him, so I strip down to my t-shirt and climb next to him. I lift his arm and drape it over me, allowing his warmth to blanket me. Tears continue to fall as I cocoon myself into him. I need to be close to him. Liam adjusts onto his side, and pulls me flush against his chest. He's still asleep, but it's as if he knows I'm here.

"I miss you, sweetheart," his deep voice trembles.

My eyes stay trained on his, but he keeps them closed.

"So fucking much," he says as his hands move down my back. "I need you, Lee."

"You have me. Take me," I murmur and press my lips to his. He kisses me with reverence and tenderness. Liam lets out a moan as his hands glide up my back.

He flips me onto my back while his delicious weight holds me beneath him. I'm where I belong. "Are you real?" he asks then crashes his lips back against mine. Our mouths stay fused as his fingers scrape down my sides. Liam doesn't break, he doesn't stop touching me, as if I'm going to vanish. His eyes stay glued shut as he gives me all of him. I breathe in every touch and every moment that I'm here with him. He brings me back to life.

My heart feels light, and it's as if I'm floating.

He stops and gazes at me with so much emotion in his eyes I can't move. Words fail. My heart stops. And time doesn't move. All that exists in this world is us right now.

Liam's strong hand presses against my face. He gazes lovingly at me as I begin to cry. The connection we share is more than I can explain. It bonds us stronger than ever before. I'm his and he's mine. This one look has cemented our love and forged an unbreakable bond. Even if we will never be together again, I'll never be anyone else's.

His voice is thick and husky as he refuses to break from my eyes. "Tell me you're real."

"I'm real."

"Tell me you're really here."

"I'm here with you." My hand rises, and I press my thumb to his lips. "I'm here for you. I'm here with only you. I need you so much."

His eyes close as I rub my thumb, savoring the rough feel on my skin.

"Stay with me," he pleads.

Liam's hands rest on each side of my face as I drag him down further. "There's nowhere else I want to be." Our lips meet, and I lose myself.

I may be married.

Aaron may be alive.

But my heart belongs to Liam.

My body is his, and I want him to take me.

My hands roam his thick back, memorizing each dip and ridge along his taut muscles. He hovers above me and his tongue brushes with mine over and over. I feel his hardness against my core, and I need him to fill me and bring me back to earth. To him.

My fingers trail his spine and hook in his boxers, dragging them lower. He becomes frantic and pulls me on top of him. Liam rips my shirt off and then discards my bra.

"I don't want to wake up," he says as he squeezes my nipple. I writhe on top of him, wishing I could convince him this is real.

"You are awake. This isn't a dream."

His hands slither down and cup my ass. "You're my dream." His eyes slam closed, and he groans as I grind down. Only the fabric of my underwear separates us. "But in my dream, you'd be fucking me already."

My head falls back as he grips my hips setting the pace. Liam rocks me against him. I feel his length rub against my clit. The friction drives me higher and then he stops. I moan in protest. But he rises and his hands hold my face.

Liam stares at me for one beat.

Then two.

Then three.

I need to feel him. I lean forward and kiss him. Our tongues tangle and he bites my bottom lip, holding it between his teeth as he pulls back. My God. He's killing me. His head drops to my breasts as he runs his tongue along the top of one and then repeats on the other side. My fingers grip his hair, and I tug him closer, needing more. For the first time in two days, my body has come to life. Liam latches on, and I cry out, feeling his teeth, tongue, and the warmth of his mouth.

"Liam, I need you inside of me." I don't recognize my own voice. It's thick and heavy with a need only he can fulfill. "Take me, sweetheart. Take me," I beg.

He responds with a throaty groan and flips me onto my back. He tears my underwear off and stares at me, blinking a few times. I see the moment he realizes this isn't a dream. Awareness registers and his hand travels down my side. "You're here."

I grip his cheeks. "I'm here. I'm yours. Now prove you're mine."

Liam settles between my legs, and our eyes stay locked as he slowly enters me. I refuse to break the connection we share as he fills me. I stretch and savor the feeling of being complete.

We stay together as he glides back and forth. Liam brushes my hair, rubs his thumb across my lips, and keeps his gaze trained on me. My hands gently trail his spine, his shoulders, and down his arms. He sucks in a breath when my nails scratch across the tattoo on his ribs.

Liam thrusts me forward, and the sound of our lovemaking echoes in the room. Our tangled bodies and heavy breathing mixed with the smell of sex and sweat fill my mind. I want to bathe in this moment. Drench myself in the happiness and love I feel, because I know all too soon that it will end.

"Don't," he commands.

Confusion sweeps over me.

"Don't go there. Stay here. Stay right here with me, Natalie."

I crush the thoughts that were chasing me and focus on him. My thoughts only memorize his frame that's covering me, the connection we share right now, soul to soul and body to body.

My orgasm comes out of nowhere and I fall apart in his arms. "Oh, oh my God."

Liam stops moving and watches me burst into pure ecstasy. I wriggle and he reaches between us, putting pressure on my clit, drawing out all pleasure from my body. "I can't," I say, needing him to stop. It's too much.

"You can," his voice is strained.

He milks each ounce of bliss my body holds. It lasts forever. My limbs are limp at my sides when he begins to move again. "I'll never grow tired of watching you come apart." He pounds harder and I slide up from the force. "I want you to think of how I make you feel when you're away from me." Liam slams into me again, and I claw my nails into his shoulder. "When you move, I want you to feel me right here." He rears back and the slapping of skin rings loudly through the air. "You belong to me. Not him. Not anyone else."

I can't speak as Liam sets a punishing rhythm. He growls as he pushes harder and harder. Each time he hits a little deeper, and I bite my lip to fight from crying out. This is rough, but it's exactly what I need. We had our sweet lovemaking . . . now we're fucking. There's no finesse, no love. Just primal and urgent. The need to sink our bodies so deep that we don't know where I end and he begins.

"Do you understand?" he asks and pushes so hard I can't control the cry. I welcome the pain from his body. I'd rather feel him hurt me than all the other forms of agony I'm in.

"Hurt me! Make it stop!" I scream out.

Liam stills and looks down at me as tears build in my eyes. "I'll never hurt you." His voice is calm and unlabored, as if all of that minutes ago was nothing. He flips me on top and grips my hips. "I love you," he says tenderly.

Tears fall from my eyes and splash against his chest. "I love you," I reply.

He moves me slowly and I rock, allowing his cock to fill me. "Stay tonight," he requests.

I don't reply because I can't. He knows it, but it hurts. Liam forces me to pick up the pace but still stays affectionate. "I'm gonna come, Lee," he tells me as he begins to pump from below.

I lean down against his ear. "I love you. Fill me."

He grunts and releases. Liam's arms wrap around my body, holding me close. I close my eyes and wish I could stay here.

But I can't.

No matter how much I don't want to . . . I have to go home.

CHAPTER SIX

LIAM

UGH. MY FUCKING head is throbbing. I feel like shit. I roll over and fight the spinning.

That was one hell of a dream. I scratch my head and look at the bed in disarray. I must have really gotten into that one. I haven't had a wet dream since I was twelve.

I get up and head to the bathroom, reliving each moment. She felt so real. I could touch her, taste her, and feel her body beneath me, but there's no way it was her. Natalie's with her fucking husband.

Once I'd gotten myself out of the rope the bastard tied me in, I passed out in bed. I let the alcohol-induced coma take me over. Quinn was right, I need to pull myself together and man the fuck up. So she's gone . . . I have a deployment coming and a team of men who need me to be present. Not some lovesick puppy licking my wounds.

I rub my neck and notice the nail marks on my shoulder. What the fuck?

I turn in the mirror and see them extending down my back. No way. It couldn't have been real. But I can smell her. The smell of lavender filters through the air. I remember the taste of her lips and the way she kept telling me it wasn't a dream.

Well, then where the fuck is she?

The room is cleaned more than I could've done last night. I rush out to the living room to find it picked up as well. Son of a bitch. She really was here. The night comes flooding back, and I slap myself for thinking it was a dream. She kissed me before she left and told me she loved me. I was already half dead between the intense sex and extreme hangover I was nursing. Within seconds, I was passed out again thinking I dreamt it all.

I grab my phone and text her.

Me: When can I see you again?

Natalie: Soon. I promise.

I hope it's sooner than later. I miss her already, but I can't say that. She's got a whole host of bullshit on her plate.

Me: We should talk about what happened.

Natalie: I'll call you tonight.

Me: Okay, sweetheart. I'm glad you came over last night.

And I am. Even though I wasn't sure if it actually happened, it means a lot to me. She was thinking of me enough to sneak out and come over. Of course, I feel like a monumental shitbag for sleeping with her when her husband is home, but he lost her. At least that's what I'm telling myself.

Natalie: Me too. No more drinking like that. I'm on my way to work. I need to get a break from my mind.

I decide not to respond. I need to figure out what the hell to do. I'm on leave, so I don't have to be anywhere.

I grab my keys knowing exactly what I need to do today. Aaron and I need to talk, and since he's home alone—looks like it's my perfect opportunity.

Of course my luck runs out when the lights flash behind me. Motherfucker.

The cop strolls over to the driver's side door with his aviators and I'm-bad-ass walk. I would like to dropkick this guy and he hasn't even spoken. I must remain calm since the last thing I want is a ticket.

"Good morning, do you know why I pulled you over?" Officer Brock asks.

Yeah, because you saw a bright red hot rod.

"Sorry, Officer. I must've been speeding?" I say more as a question. I seriously have no fucking clue what I did.

"You were speeding. This is a thirty-five. I need your license, registration, and insurance."

I pop open the glove box and grab the papers, handing them over along with my military ID. The officer looks them over and nods. "You're active?"

"Yes, sir."

"I don't think you meant to hand me this," he says and hands me over an envelope with my name on it. I look at it and realize it's the letter from Aaron. "I'll let you go with a warning. Just slow it down. Thank you for your service." He hands the rest back and walks back to his cruiser.

I sit here stunned and I feel like I got hit by a bus. Well, fuck. Do I read it or shred it? I pull into the parking lot right across the street from his house and stare at it. What he had to say is irrelevant now, but curiosity gets the best of me.

Liam,
Hey, man. I'm sitting here before heading out on this deployment and I have this weird feeling. I can't explain it, but I don't

think I'll make it back. I know we're not supposed to think like that, but, well . . . it is what it is. I have a few things I want to ask of you and you're the only person I trust.

Take care of Lee. I haven't talked to anyone about this, but things have been hard for her. We've lost another baby and it's killing her. I'm watching my wife dwindle to nothing, and I can't stop it. She used to be full of love and light, but now she's miserable. Make her smile and help her find happiness. I can't give her the life she's desperate for. So please, watch her, help her, dry her tears, and be there, because I don't know how she'll handle it. If you realize the gift she is and you fall in love with her, treat her right or I'll fucking haunt you. There's no woman in the world like her, and if she has to love anyone else other than me, I hope it's you. I want her to find someone worthy, so if it's not you, make sure he's not a prick.

If by some stretch of a miracle she's pregnant now, I want you to be like a father to him or her. You're like a brother to me, and I need to know they won't grow up not knowing anything about me. Tell them about all the trouble we caused and protect them from doing the same stupid shit.

I've thought a lot about some of the things we've talked about. How this life will eventually destroy you and a family, and I think you're right. I'm not the same guy I was. I've seen too much, and while I'm proud of the things I've done, I carry guilt *about Natalie. I'm a piece of shit. I don't deserve her, but for some reason she loves me, and I keep hoping she never sees the bad in me.*

Anyway, be good to her. And even in death, I'll have your six.   —Aaron

Once I pull into the drive, I grab on to my anger. He fucked around on her, got another girl pregnant, and then has the balls to be pissed at me. I respected her, loved her and his daughter. He even asked me to do all this and then he wants to act like I broke some damn man code. He can fuck off.

Aaron steps off the deck as I close the door.

"Didn't think you'd be back so soon."

I step closer. "I thought we could use some time to discuss the last year."

He nods and turns toward the back deck. "Seems I've missed a lot."

We sit in the chairs and we both stare off. I'm not sure if I should start or let him ask the questions. My training kicks in and I decide to let him go first. Typically, it's the best way to get answers you want.

I wait, but he doesn't say anything or move, just stares.

Then I remember the fucker is trained to do the same thing. It could be hours before either of us budge. The thing is, he's not a terrorist, he's a friend and deserves to be treated like one.

"I'll go first," I say and he turns. "What do you want to know?" I give an inch but still try to maintain control of the discussion.

"How long have you been playing house with my family?"

So this is going to be how it is.

"First of all, I wasn't playing house." I make sure I

keep my eyes clear so he knows that's not what the fuck this was. "Second of all, how long were you making a new family while you had yours here?"

His eyes shift the slightest amount, but it's enough for me to notice. "You don't know everything."

"Neither do you." I give it right back. He didn't see Natalie at her worst or when we were both trying to figure out how we felt. He wasn't here, so he better not fucking judge me.

"Brittany was a mistake," Aaron says and then stands. "A big fucking mistake."

"Yeah, well, your mistake doesn't think she is." This is the part that pisses me off.

"You think I care what she thinks?"

"I don't know what you think. You fucked around on your pregnant wife! Brittany told her everything, and now you come back spewing your shit about me and Lee? Fuck you, man. It wasn't behind your back. It wasn't to shame you. You even told me to love her. You said you wanted me to raise your kid as my own and now you're acting like this?" Once I start talking, it all comes out and I can't stop. "I love her. I helped pick her up when you died. I was at the hospital when Aarabelle was sick, I held Natalie's hair when she was puking, and I fucking defended you!" I push his chest and he winces.

Aaron takes a few steps back rubbing his chest, and I feel like a dick.

"Aaron, I'm sorry, man," I try to apologize, but he turns before I can say anything else.

"I deserve it. I know I was wrong, but I fought to live for them. I don't want to fight you, but she's *my* wife. That's my daughter, and I won't let them go just because for the last year you decided you love her." He steps closer puffing his chest. I clench my fists and release them. "I've loved her almost my whole life, and if you're the man I think you are, you'll walk away."

I step closer and weigh my words. I could be a prick and let him know I fucked her last night. I want to, but I won't. The depth of pain I could cause my closest friend right now is all in my hands. But in the end, Lee will be who is hurt. And I'll fucking slice my veins open before that happens.

"Just know how much you hurt her. She may not want you. And if she walks away, I'm not going to push her back to you."

Aaron nods and pauses. "I'm going to ask you this once, for the sake of my child." He waits and I already know where he's going. "If you love Natalie and Aarabelle, then don't do this shit. Don't be the man who ends a marriage and a family."

"You're unbelievable. Don't you think you ended your own marriage when you fucked around? The guy who I knew would've manned the fuck up and fixed it before it got that bad. You and I aren't going to battle over this. It's her choice."

Aaron steps closer, and I swear I've been nice, but he pushes me and I'll knock him on his ass.

"What about your word, Liam? Huh? What about the fact that you swore to have my back no matter what?"

I look at him wondering if he sustained some kind of traumatic brain injury, because he seems to have forgotten one key issue—he's the one in the wrong.

"Have your back?" I'm going to punch him. "I had your back. I had your back every fucking day. I didn't do this to you!" I draw a deep breath and try to stop the pulsing in my neck. I can feel my rage boiling over.

"I told you to love her, but . . ."

"But what? You didn't mean it? You know, I read that fucking letter today. I didn't even know what was in it. I fought day after day with feeling anything for Lee. I would tell myself it was wrong and ridiculous. The first time either of us acknowledged anything, we struggled.

Being with her was never easy. I always had you in the back of my mind, but I prayed you'd know that I would never let her forget you or let Aarabelle not know the man I knew."

"So you just went forward with her anyway?"

"None of us knew you weren't dead!" I throw my hands up and fight the urge to shake him. "You're missing the entire point. I'm not wrong here, and neither is Lee. You are. You made your choices, and now you have to handle the fallout."

He looks at me with fury burning in his eyes.

"I didn't expect to come home to this shit! You didn't say a word on the plane."

My mind spins as I try to find a way to not go to blows. "What did you want me to say? I couldn't believe it was you. When we were told about the mission, I thought it couldn't be you—you were dead. We had a part of your body as proof. So when we get to Afghanistan and I realize it *is* you . . . I'm not sure what the fuck you expected from me, man." I walk around in circles because there's still a part of me that's processing the fact he's standing here. My brother in arms, my friend who I would've traded places with to die instead, is here.

I hope he takes a swing at me. I'll get a good one in for the dumb move he made screwing around on Natalie. But then I look at him. He's been home a few days and looks a little better, but the bruises still cover the one side of his body. He's been broken.

"I love her. I thought about her day in and day out."

There's two sides to me, and both are so screwed up I don't know where to turn. One, he's alive and he thought he'd come home to the life he left. Two, he doesn't deserve her. I do. I'm the man he couldn't be and she loves me. She came to me last night, and I made love to her while he slept. I'm not perfect, but God, if I wouldn't do anything to make this situation different.

"Look, man, you've been through more than I'm sure you'll ever admit. I get that. But let me be clear: if you'd come home from that mission and Natalie would've found out you'd been screwing some froghopper behind her back looking for the next SEAL to hop to, she'd have thrown your ass out."

"If Natalie chooses because of whatever I did, then I'll let her go. No matter how much it'll kill me. But don't pursue her. I'm asking you as my friend. Give her and I a chance to see if we can mend our family for Aarabelle's sake."

The responses roll around in my head. So many things I want to say, but out of respect for Lee and the fact that this man saved my life on more than one occasion, I simply nod. "You really don't get it?"

"Get what?"

"This isn't up to you. You don't get to make demands or requests. I'm not walking away for you. But understand this: I love her. I love Aarabelle. And I'm going to be the man in the end that has them. I don't think you realize how bad you screwed yourself. So, I'll give her the time she needs, because I don't think she knows what end is up. I love her enough not to push her . . . do you?"

"I know her."

"Not anymore. She's changed, Aaron. She went through hell and then got kicked when she was already at her lowest. I was there. I saw it, and I won't let her go down that path again."

This is the best I can do.

He steps forward. "Fair enough." Aaron extends his hand. "Thank you for being there for them. I'm grateful."

No, he's not. He's hateful that I got his girl. I grip his hand and we shake. I don't respond because I'm not sure I can be civil at this point. The urge to tell him to take his request and shove it so far up his ass he sneezes it out is on the tip of my tongue—but I don't. We have history, and ultimately, I can't force Lee.

She's who matters here. And Aarabelle.

I have to sacrifice a part of myself for her and pray in the end she'll come to me. Even if it means my closest friend will be fucked in the end.

chapter seven

natalie

"HEY SPARKLES, CAN I come in?" Mark asks apprehensively.

"I figured they'd send you in first." I grin as I wave my hand to usher him in. "You'd be the one I'd be more likely to forgive."

"It's because we both like to glitter." Mark flops in the chair and slaps his hands on the side.

"Must be that."

You can sense the tension in the air, but Mark is probably the best at masking his discomfort. Coming in here today was difficult, but I needed a sense of normalcy. Aaron didn't notice I'd been gone all night, or if he did, he never said a word.

After I left Liam's house, I grabbed Aarabelle and cried myself to sleep. I didn't mean to sleep with him. I honestly just wanted to see him. But once he touched me, it became impossible to stop and there wasn't even a part of me that wanted to. The lines in the sand are becoming blurred.

Walking in the office was far more difficult than I could've expected. Knowing prying eyes and Aaron's friends surround me makes me want to cower, but I've done enough of that. I work here now, and I needed a reprieve.

People's lives are in my hands—at least that's my excuse.

"What can I do for you?" I ask after a few moments of awkward silence.

Mark grows serious as he shifts forward with his elbows on his knees. "I'm worried about you. I know you may think you can't talk to me, but you can."

I believe that he cares for me. I trust that he has good intentions, but I also know if push came to shove, their whole "bros before ho's" bullshit would be in full effect.

"I'm doing fine." The last word trips me a little. I immediately think of Liam.

"How's Aaron?"

I glance out the window and mull over my words. "Adjusting, I guess—we both are."

Mark waits for me to look back at him before speaking. "I know this is hard on you more than anyone. You moved on, you found out about the affair, you were happy, and now he's back. It can't be easy. Hell, I can't even pretend to know what you're feeling. But he's been through fucking hell. If you're in pain, imagine what he must've gone through in the year he was being held. I'm not asking you to forgive him," Mark pauses. "I'm just asking you to let us help."

My eyes widen at his last request. "Help? How do you plan to help?"

Mark tilts forward. "Jackson and I are your friends, Lee. Aaron can stay with me for a while, you can take some time off, or whatever you need. But all he could talk about on the plane back was seeing you. He never mentioned the other girl."

I huff, "Like you'd tell me anyway." I wait for him to refute me, but he won't.

The stories of infidelity run rampant in the teams, but we all ignore it. We look the other way, because no matter what, they'd never tell the wife who's blissfully ignorant. So many of my friends found out, after their husbands returned, that while they were holding down their homes, their husbands were fucking everything that walked. Some even after they'd made love to them again. It's the worst slap in the face, and I thought I'd been immune to it.

"No, I wouldn't have told you ... but I would've made sure you knew."

"What the hell does that mean?" My hands come down on the desk with a smack, and Mark looks a little startled. Good. "I'm so tired of these riddles and rhymes. You all talk of honor, valor, and code, but you're all hypocrites!" I stand and the chair flies out from under me.

"Lee," he says hushed.

"No!" I yell and walk over to him. "You don't 'Lee' me ... I'm tired. You can all tell me that in all the time you spent with Aaron for that year, you never suspected it? You can honestly sit there and tell me you had no clue? I'm sure more times than you know he said he was with you. How does that make you feel?"

Mark stands towering over me, his hands gripping my shoulders gently. "I didn't know. I would've told him to knock it the fuck off or tell you. He made mistakes and he's paid his penance."

"And that's supposed to comfort me?"

"What do you expect?"

What do I expect? I don't know. That's the part that gets me. I can't tell him what I want, because if it were Reanell, I wouldn't run and tell Mason. But there was a baby involved. And it wasn't a one-time thing.

I flop in the chair and hang my head. "I expected it to never happen. But none of that matters because I'm over it. I'm over the affair and all the other bullshit. I was genuinely happy with Liam."

Mark sits beside me. Wrapping his arm around my shoulder, he pulls me close. "Were you happy with Aaron? If you hadn't believed he was dead all this time, would you be with him?"

I rest my head on his shoulder. "I can't answer that. We weren't happy, but we were happy about the baby. Who knows if after Aara was born if we'd have gone backward?"

"Yeah, that's the thing . . . you don't know. But what I do know is you have great friends who love you. And you have Aarabelle. As for the rest, it's up to you."

I lift my head and look at him. "Is it? My choices affect everyone in this."

Mark kisses my cheek, "I think you need to give yourself a chance to breathe before you choose anything." He heads out of the office and then pops his head back in. "Lee?"

"Yeah?"

"Do you think we could give Aarabelle the call sign Moonlight?"

My smile is automatic, and I throw the box of tissues from the table next to me at his head.

He ducks and it misses him, but he smiles. "I'll take that as a no."

Only Mark.

I head back to my desk and get back to work. The people overseas matter, and I need to focus on their lives instead of my own. At least for a few hours.

My phone rings and I answer without looking.

"Hello?"

"Natalie," Aaron's scratchy voice sounds nervous.

"What's wrong?" I ask quickly.

"It's late. I'm just wondering if you're coming home."

I look out the window and then at the clock. Shit. It's almost seven.

"I'm sorry. I got caught up in these projects," I explain.

"Right. Work," Aaron replies disbelievingly. "I figured you might be somewhere else. I don't have a car or anyway to get anywhere. I just wanted to know what to do."

"Aaron," I say softly. "I'm really sorry. I'm leaving the office now and I'll be there soon. Let me call Paige and see if she can keep Aarabelle overnight. Then we can have dinner and talk?"

We need to figure out the logistics of all of this, and I need answers. I need to know from him what exactly happened and how we move forward for Aarabelle's sake. I don't want to move out of my house, but I don't want to throw him out either.

"I'd like that."

"Okay," I smile. "I'll see you soon."

"I love you, Natalie."

"I—" I choke on the words. "I gotta go," I mutter quickly and disconnect the phone.

There's no traffic on the road and Paige was happy to keep Aarabelle. I'm not sure how to handle things with Aaron, but I need to know a lot of things. Where he was for the last year, for one. I'm assuming if Aaron went on that rescue mission, it hadn't been by choice, but I'd also assumed he wasn't sleeping around.

I park in the drive and a text bings.

Liam: We have to talk.

Me: I know. I need to handle things tonight with Aaron.

Liam: Okay. I'll wait to hear from you.

Me: I love you.

The text was easy to say. I didn't stumble over my words because my heart is where Liam is. No matter what my past holds with Aaron, my future belongs to Liam. I need to figure out how to make my present match up with all of this now.

I wait for a text from Liam but it doesn't come. My finger hovers over the call button. How can he not say it back? I'm trying to prove to him that he's my choice. I'm being honest and faithful to him. Hell, I snuck out of my house just to see him.

"Lee?" I drop the phone and cover my mouth to avoid screaming. I look at the window and Aaron is standing there. "You okay?"

Gasping for breath, I look over. "I'm fine. You scared me."

He opens the door and extends his hand. "Sorry, I was worried." Hesitantly, I place my hand in his. I wait for a spark, a zing, anything, however, there's nothing but familiarity there. "I ordered food. I figured it would be easier than either of us cooking."

"Yeah," I laugh. "You and cooking don't really mix."

Aaron places his hand on the small of my back, and I move faster.

"Some things never change," he muses.

"And some things do."

Aaron lets out a breath. "I guess they do." He pauses as we make our way to the deck. I look at the table with candles, roses, and pizza by the side. "I thought, maybe . . ."

I turn and look at him with so much anger and hurt. "You thought what? You would make this a date? This isn't a date, Aaron. This is figuring out how the hell to make this less painful than it already is. I can't just forget that you cheated on me . . ."

"So you're going to take her word as bond? You're not going to give me the chance to explain anything?" he explodes and softens his stance. Aaron lowers himself to the ground at my feet. "You loved me once. We had a love that others prayed for. You and I made vows." His voice is feeble, and it's as if the ground is swallowing him.

I drop my purse and perch myself on my knees in front of him. "Vows that were broken. And yes, we loved each other once, and we lost ourselves somewhere on that path." Aaron's eyes meet mine, and I want to cry. "Let's not do this to each other. Please," I plead.

"Let's just enjoy dinner and talk."

I nod and we both shift. "There are things I need to know. Like, what happened in Afghanistan?" I decide we have to start there. I need to know about the affair, but at the same time I don't know it will make a difference. I need to put each of our issues into their appropriate box. *Again with the damn boxes.* But I think it'll help me keep each of the mounds of bullshit contained so I can handle them better.

"I know you have questions, and I'll answer the best I can. I'm still fuzzy on some parts." Aaron says and stands extending his hand.

I stand on my own, knowing I need to keep my composure and appear in control. We sit in the chairs illuminated by a soft candle glow. I fight the urge to blow them all out. This isn't a date. But I need him to be honest, not set him off.

"Tell me about the explosion." My voice is low and calming.

Aaron puts a slice of pizza on both our plates and then he grabs my hand. "Is this okay?" he asks looking down.

It seems like he needs this from me. Like my hand is the lifeline that will ground him. "Yeah, you can hold my hand." I speak the words and squeeze his hand.

"Thanks, baby."

"You can't call me 'baby,'" I reply more harshly than

I meant to. Aaron's eyes drop to our joined hands.

"But I can hold your hand?"

"I think you need a friend. I think you need support to talk about what's going on and what happened. I've been your friend since we were kids. I'll always be your friend."

Aaron nods and let's out a deep breath. "I don't know how much will make sense. But I remember getting in the caravan to head out to the site where we were having issues. There were four of us in the truck just talking and laughing." His eyes glaze over as he retreats into his story. "There were a bunch of kids throwing their arms up screaming. They were trying to stop us—I guess. I don't know what they wanted. I was sitting in the passenger side and urged the driver to keep going. I know better than to slow down, but instead of listening, he let up on the gas. As soon as we slowed a little, the explosion happened. It hit my side of the vehicle, and I remember feeling like I was flying. Everything was weightless but chaotic at the same time."

He takes a deep breath and his hand tightens. "What happened then?"

"There was screaming and blood everywhere. I remember being dragged by the neck, and I assumed it was one of the guys in our car. I was going in and out so much, I honestly don't know much more than that."

As a tear falls down my face, Aaron releases my hand. "Who was pulling you?"

"They did."

"Who's 'they'?" I encourage him to tell me more.

"Who do you think, Lee?" Aaron says as his jaw tightens. "I was losing a lot of blood. I thought I was dead. They made sure I wouldn't die, but I wouldn't tell them anything. Not my name, not anything. They knew I was American, even though I only spoke French so they'd be confused. I would go unconscious for long periods of time. I honestly don't remember much. When Charlie came to the site, she apparently was following around some high ranking terrorist pretending to be his new toy."

"Is that the agent that found you?" I ask.

"Yes, she literally stumbled on the camp I was being held. When she realized I was American, I started to get the care I needed and got some information. But I wasn't sure any of it was real. I'm still not sure what was reality versus not."

I sit quiet and try to absorb all he's telling me. It was a year and we never looked. None of us searched for him. "They told us there was no way you could've survived the blast. It was so bad that no one would. There weren't many remains of the others. Did they survive?" I look at him and he shakes his head.

"I shouldn't have. The blast was bad, but apparently, I got pulled out before the secondary explosion of the vehicle. I was mangled and in bad condition when I woke up the first time. I would wake for a few hours and then go back out for who knows how long. There wasn't exactly good medical attention. Charlie was the only thing keeping me alive. It took her months to gain my trust. I wasn't sure if she really was CIA or if she was full of shit. I couldn't rely on my training because nothing made sense."

"I hate this for you," I admit.

He tangles his fingers with mine. "All I knew was that if there was any chance, I needed to stay strong. I would let her help me so that I could come home to you," he says, hushed.

"Aaron," my voice shakes. I hate that he's been hurt. I know he won't tell me, but I care. "Did they . . . ?"

"I've been through worse. I'm alive, so all of that shit doesn't matter."

"I can't tell you how much your death affected me.

I was a mess. Each night I would pray it was a lie. I refused to get rid of your things for almost the full year. I can't tell you what it was like when Mark came to the house to tell me," I let out a shaky breath. "I latched on to every good memory we had. I held them like lifelines, praying they would keep me afloat. When I went into labor, Reanell practically had to carry me to the car. I knew once Aara was born, things would be different for me." I stop and take a gulp of wine. "I did it though, I gave birth to that beautiful little girl, alone. Each time I'd push I would think of you. How you went through so much and always stayed strong. When I held her for the first time, it was agony. I hated being alone."

"You think I didn't want to be there?" he asks incredulously.

"No, of course I don't think that. Let me finish." I wait for the vein in his neck to stop pulsing. "There was this baby we fought so hard for. She was everything I wanted, but you weren't there. It was the end of me feeling sorry for myself. I found strength and determination. I was still sad, lonely, and missing you terribly, but you were gone. When I had the memorial, it was horrific, but again, I did it. I had to get up each day because she needed me, but that was about all I could do. Then Liam came to Virginia."

"No," Aaron cuts me off. My eyes snap up, and he rips his hand back. "You're not going to sit here and tell me about how Liam put you back together. Natalie, you're my wife." He leans forward with determination in his eyes. "We have a child. We have a life people only dream of. You and I are meant to be together."

"You slept with another woman. You keep forgetting that. And I don't think we had a life people dream of. I think we were comfortable and content. You were seeking what I wasn't giving you! You said it yourself."

"It was a one-time thing, a fucked up night," he says,

and my retort dies on my tongue.

"One night? You can look me in the eyes and tell me that?" I ask hesitantly.

Aaron stands and comes around the table. My heart falters as I look at my husband, my best friend since I was sixteen. He stands over me and pulls me to my feet. "One horrible night after we'd lost the baby. After I had to watch you lie on the bathroom floor begging for God to kill you. You held your stomach and prayed that someone would just end it all because you weren't good enough. I was broken after that. I didn't know what to do, so I left."

"I remember. I came out and you were gone. You left when I was in the middle of pure torture." I look at him recalling that night.

It was the last failed procedure, and I was distraught. I thought that baby was the one. I was ten weeks, we were so close to the safe zone. I started cramping and then I saw blood. I sat there trying to convince myself that it wasn't really blood. That it wasn't a sign that we were going to lose the baby, because I was so close. The pain was unlike anything I'd ever felt. I would cry and clutch my stomach as the life I'd been desperate for left me.

I told myself that if the pregnancy didn't stick, I would stop trying. I needed to move forward and stop hoping for something I wasn't meant to have. We'd spent so much money and energy. I was consumed by everything regarding fertility.

Aaron's hands hold my face. "I couldn't watch. I felt like I failed you as a husband. I couldn't watch you like that. I went to the bar, got drunk, and I fucked up."

Turmoil boils in my body as I try to figure out if he's lying. None of this makes sense. "Brittany said it was months. She said . . ."

"She lied," Aaron says, so sure.

"Why would she lie? What does she have to gain? We all thought you were dead. So it makes no sense for her to be vicious and mean to me. But you lying right now would make sense," I say, feeling angry that I don't know what the damn truth is.

There's so much between us, so much history, and throwing it all away isn't something I take lightly, but I think about Liam. How far we came. How much we loved. And how hard it would be to lose him. I've already lost Aaron once, I know I can endure it. Besides, this man in front of me isn't the same man I loved. I look at him now and see betrayal and deceit.

"Why would I lie to you, Lee? I always told you the truth!" he exclaims and turns his back.

"You didn't lie? You think for one second even if it was only one night with her, that's okay? Do you not see how disgusting that makes you? On the night we lose a child, you sleep with someone else. The night I had to crawl into bed on my hands and knees because the cramping was so bad, you were fucking someone. While I was in horrific pain, you were enjoying the night of your life?" I spit the words, hoping he feels the knives embedded in them. I hope they tear into his heart and shred him to pieces. "Some man you are. Some love and honesty we have."

Aaron stands behind me unmoving. I feel the heat radiating from his body. But he doesn't touch me, and if he'd like to keep his hands, he won't try to.

"I never told you because it meant nothing. She means nothing and neither does the affair."

I spin on my heels and slap him in the chest. "Fuck you. It meant everything to me! *You* meant everything to me! I hate you right now. You stand here smug as if *I'm* doing *you* wrong. You were a coward."

"I deserve that." He steps closer, but whatever emotion is showing on my face causes him to retreat.

"You don't deserve me." I step closer. "No matter what your relationship was with *her*—which I don't believe for one second it was a one-time deal." Another step.

"What does it matter? I'm here right now trying to fix things."

"You then came home that day saying you slept at work. Two months later, we found out I was pregnant with Aarabelle." Aaron takes two steps back as I vibrate with anger. "So you did whatever the hell you did and came home and then made a baby with me."

He looks away. "You're not going to listen to me at this point. Apparently, what I've been through doesn't matter. You're no better than me, Lee."

"Unreal," I huff. "You went through hell over there. I hate that you were hurt. I hate that you ever had to endure one ounce of pain," tears stream down my face. He's been through so much. We both have. Now we have to hurt even more. "But it doesn't erase our past. There are no free passes because you're holding up the argument that what I did is the same. Me moving on and finding love again doesn't equate to cheating. I can tell you don't want to tell me everything. I see it in your eyes that there's more."

Aaron steps closer and grips my shoulders. "Damn right there's more. But it's in the past. She's in the past. I went through more hell than you can fathom. I didn't think I'd ever see you again. You. Not her. *You!*"

Confusion sweeps over me as I soak in what he says, conflicting emotions rioting within me. I have no doubt he went through a lot. I also don't doubt him when he says that it is me he loves. That's the part that kills me. But it's not enough.

"I know you love me. And if I'm being honest, I love you. I will always love you. You were the first man I ever loved. But you're not the only one anymore," I reply somberly. "I let Liam into my heart, and he and I share something special. I never meant for this to happen. I had no reason to expect you were alive. But things failed way before then, Aaron. Were you happy? Because I wasn't." I let out a deep breath. "We have to let each other go."

"So because of what I suffered, I get to pay even more? How is that fair? You even said yourself you love me."

I shrug out of his hold and walk toward the end of the deck. "I don't want to make you suffer. No matter what you think, this isn't easy for me. And there's no 'fair' here. I would never intentionally hurt you."

"But I am hurt."

"Well, so am I."

The silence lingers between us. Years of love and trust are gone. They've washed their way out into the sea, leaving behind shells of who we were.

Aaron blows out the candles, and I can't help but feel like the light inside of him just went out too. He walks over, grabs the dishes, and starts to head inside. I turn toward the ocean and wait for the calmness it usually brings, but instead, I feel cold and alone. Both of us have had to deal with so much in one year.

The plates crash to the ground, and when I turn around, Aaron is already in front of me. He grips my face, and before I can say anything, his lips press against mine. My mouth stays still and he pushes hard. It's painful, like this entire situation. He holds me against him as my hands shove against his chest, Aaron just holds me closer. His tongue sweeps against the seam of my lips, and I turn my head. As our lips break apart as he stares down at me.

"Why can't you love me again? I would do anything for you."

"Then tell me the truth."

"You want to know everything?"

I stare at him, waiting. "I don't think we can ever move forward if I don't know everything."

"I told you everything that matters."

"That's just it. Everything matters."

"I choose you, Natalie. I'd choose you every day until the day I die. I want you. I need you. And I don't know how else to make you see that. Everyone and everything else is in the past."

"And so are you. You're living in the past where I'm your doting wife. I lived the last year of my life knowing what it's like without you. I found out the truth about who we were—hell, who I am. I'm not the same woman you fell in love with. I've changed." I touch his arm and he flinches. "I'm not that girl anymore, Aaron."

"Fine."

"Fine?" I ask skeptically.

"It's done, Lee. You want me to go back to her?"

"I thought it wasn't about her?"

"That's right," he sneers. "It's about Liam."

I don't say anything as he turns and heads into the house.

chapter eight

WE DON'T MENTION the kiss. We barely acknowledge each other's presence. It's awkward and it's as if we're walking on eggshells. I cleaned the stuff from outside while Aaron looked through photo books of Aarabelle.

"Do you want to sleep in the bedroom? I can take the couch," I offer.

"No, I think I'm going to head to Mark's. Maybe spend the night there. Jackson offered the condo he owns as well."

"Oh," I reply. I can't fully explain why this bothers me at all. I should be happy, but it saddens me it's come to this. He just got home, and I've already displaced him. "You can stay here, Aaron. I mean, if you want to spend time with Aarabelle. I know things are . . . strained . . . between us, but this is your home."

"My home is where you are. You're not here with me," he says and then goes back to the picture book.

The reactions play out in my mind, but my mouth stays closed. I could tell him he's wrong, but he's not. I could give him false hope, but I won't. "I don't know what to say." Which is the only honest thing I can reply.

He closes the book and I sit next to him. "You can say you'll try. Maybe you can forgive me, see how much I love you. Are all the years of marriage worth so little to you?"

I look over as tears begin to fall, painting my face with the pain in my heart. "It was never easy for me to let you go. I struggled so much with it. Even at my angriest, I never wished you dead." Aaron brushes the tears from my face. "But you hurt me so badly. Even *if* you had only slept with her once, you did it on one of the worst nights of my life. She loved you, Aaron. I could see it in her eyes. She came to your memorial."

"She's irrelevant to me. It's you who has my heart. It's you who has my world."

I don't acknowledge his statement, because right now, I don't believe him. I know what it's like to be someone's world.

The bruise on the side of his face is starting to fade, and my hand reaches up to feel it. I try to remember what his skin felt like beneath my fingers. How his clean shaved face would allow the pads of my fingers to slide down with no resistance. The way our bodies would come alive at each other's touch. His head leans into my hand as if I'm comforting him. How long did he endure pain? How much was he awake for, and how did he suffer?

"Did they torture you?" I don't respond to his statement because all I can think about is his marred skin. The way the Aaron I knew is gone in every sense of the word. His body, which was once strong enough to lift me even when I was pregnant, doesn't look like it could lift much more than Aarabelle.

His eyes close. "I can't talk about that. I was badly injured and barely holding on. It wasn't until the end that anything really happened, and then Charlie got word out."

"But they hurt you. Why did she wait so long?"

Aaron grips my hands. "I think it looks worse. Remember I was in an explosion. Some of these are injuries that didn't heal right. There was a medic on site of the extraction and he said I'm really lucky. She had a job to do, exposing me would've sacrificed everything she'd worked for. Her helping me was a huge risk. I respect her mission. I feel like I need to tell you something."

I brace myself for whatever it might be. "I don't know how much more I can take."

"I'm going to fight for you. I didn't live for nothing. I'll be damned if you think I'm going to fade away. You and I are for life, Lee. You, me, and our daughter. We have a lot of adjusting and a lot to work through, but we make sense."

"I need you to stop and listen to what I'm saying," I plead hoping he won't make me say it. I'm battling everything inside of me to not tell him I went to Liam's last night. I'm fighting to not tell him I want to be there right now. But I know it'll break him, and no matter how badly he hurt me with Brittany, I know that this will wound him deeper.

Brittany was a nobody in my life. Liam is his friend. The man who went and rescued him and then brought him to me. They share a bond that I never had with her. I try to imagine what it would feel like if I still loved him the way he claims he loves me and it were Reanell. I would be devastated.

"I told Liam the same thing."

"What?" That stops the words that were forming on my tongue.

When the hell did he talk to Liam? Did Liam tell him we spent the night together? Oh my God, maybe he knows.

"Liam and I talked today. I told him the same thing—I'm not giving up. I asked him to step aside and let us have a chance to fix this."

The color drains from my face and my throat goes dry. "W-what did you . . . ? Why?"

"Because you're my wife. Because you've been my

girl since we were kids. He understands that this isn't just some relationship. You and I, baby, are the real deal. We don't quit because someone died."

My eyes snap open. "I didn't fall in love with him because you died. That might have been what forced us together, but I love him in a way you can't understand," I say and see the way his jaw ticks.

"You can't convince me you love him more. I know you. I know your heart and your soul. I can see everything you're feeling before you say it. So I told him to step aside before he destroys us all."

"How dare you?" I rip my hands from his and stand, needing to dispel some energy. "You don't get to make that decision for me."

"We made vows."

"You broke them."

"Is this your whole argument? That I broke promises? You did too, babe. You promised to love, honor, obey. You fucking fell in love with someone in under a year. What does that say?"

Anger rips through me as I clench my fists. If I were a violent person, I would've punched him by now. "What does it say, Aaron? It says we weren't happy. It says we had problems. It says that I met someone, fell in love, and moved on. It says that you met someone while we were married and did the same."

"Well, we'll see, because Liam and I have an agreement," he says smugly.

Fuck him.

"I hope he told you to go to hell."

Aaron stands and walks away. He stops and turns toward me. "He said he would give us time."

My heart plummets. "Of course he did." I nearly choke on the words.

"I'm not a fool to see that he loves you. But he knows we have a life, a child, a home."

Liam and I are going to have words. His text message now makes sense. He's giving up on us. After all we've shared and how far we've come. All the promises are lies, just like those of the man who stands in front of me.

"Had," I say and stare into his eyes. "We had. You keep forgetting what we had is now past tense. Right now, we have a mess to clean up. Do you even want to acknowledge the fact that you were going to leave me for your whore?" I bite back the nasty retort floating around in my mouth.

"I'm not with her now, am I?"

"And if we don't work out, will you go back to her?"

"Is that what you want?" he asks, watching my reactions.

I huff, "I can't even believe you. You sit here telling me you love me, spouting off how we have a love no one can ever understand, but you can't even answer me honestly once. Are you going to admit what your relationship was with her?"

His story has too many holes. There are too many nights I remember being alone or wondering. The times I pushed down my woman's intuition and smothered it. Ignorance is a beautiful place sometimes, but I don't plan to live there anymore. The hardest part in all of this is that I'm going to be the one to hurt Aaron. I was supposed to be his lifeline. Just as Liam has become mine.

Then I think about what Aaron said about him stepping aside.

Fuck them both.

I get a say in who I'm with, and they're both going to learn that quickly.

"Who knows?" Aaron says and then shakes his head. "What is the truth anymore?"

"Then I'll be sure to talk to Brittany tomorrow. She doesn't have any issues saying what happened between you two."

"You love my fucking best friend! She's nothing compared to that," Aaron's voice trembles.

"How can you say she's nothing? You were with her for a long time. You went to her many nights, didn't you? What about the time you stayed with Mark for two nights? What about all the times I would call your phone and it would go to voicemail? The late nights you'd come home so tired you'd fall asleep on the couch. I remember them all, Aaron. Clarity isn't something I'm lacking."

He can play dumb as much as he wants, but he's a master at deceit. I always believed he kept his work away from home, but as the truth unravels, it reminds me it's a part of who he is. He worked to get information from others, concealed himself and the truth from those he had to. Aaron can withstand torture, injuries, and this to him is probably a walk in the park. I was a lovestruck idiot, hoping my husband was the man I wanted.

"Jesus Christ," he groans and throws his hands up. "She means *nothing* to me! Nothing."

"I don't believe you. She sobbed and cried saying how in love you were, but you still can't be honest."

Aaron looks to the left and shakes his head. "You have no idea what you're talking about."

"Then tell me! Tell me the truth. You want your chance . . . this is it!"

His face becomes stone. "I told you what matters. I was with her more than I ever should've been. I hated myself. I thought I could stop, but I was too weak. I didn't deserve you then and apparently I don't now. But we've had a year that we've been apart. I can be better. I don't want her anymore."

Even though we're not together it hurts. The word 'anymore' hangs heavy in the air. I'm the runner up. When he wanted her, he had her. Now, for whatever reason, I'm his choice but what happens when things get tough? When our lives aren't filled with laughter, but we're swimming in tears . . . does he go back? Too much has happened.

His hand extends, but I move before he can touch me. "This is why I didn't want to tell you. I knew you wouldn't understand."

"Understand? I can't even look at you. I don't know how you can say this is what love is. I need to leave," I start to move back. "I'll be home later. Or maybe not," I say grabbing my purse. There's no way I'm staying in this house with him. I'm hurt, livid, desolate, and more than anything, I'm devastated that Liam would cast me aside so easily.

"Don't leave," Aaron begs.

"Don't lie anymore." I grab my keys and head out the door.

Once in the confines of my car, the need to scream overwhelms me, so I let it go. I punch the steering wheel and scream at the top of my lungs. Nothing coherent comes out, just yelling, trying to cleanse my body of all the confusion. I look at the window and see him standing there. He watches me lose it in my car and the contrast between him and Liam is glaring in this moment. Aaron chooses to let me go while Liam would've been at the car already.

Speaking of Liam, I turn the key and back out of the driveway while my husband watches me leave to go to my boyfriend's house.

The drive isn't long, but it allows me the time to form a plan. I'm so hurt that he would just toss me away. We need to talk and figure things out. I'm not either of their doll and they can't pass me off to the other. Aaron and I may be married legally, but he's been dead for a year. He and I aren't married in any other way.

I knock on the door and hear a woman's laughter.

Please, God, don't let him have another woman in here. I can't handle it.

Liam opens the door smiling and it falters when he sees me. "Hey," he says, closing the door behind him, pushing us out into the hall.

"Wow," I say in disbelief.

"Wow?"

"You're kidding me, right? You have someone else here? Not only do you tell Aaron you'll step aside, but you move on so quickly." I'm so beside myself I can't think. I push his chest and slap him. "I hate you all!"

Liam's arms wrap around me and stop my physical assault. "What the hell are you talking about? Calm down," he commands as I struggle to get out of his hold. "Natalie, stop."

"How could you? I trusted you!" I begin to cry.

"What the hell are you talking about?"

"I heard a girl laughing, and you pushed me into the damn hall." Tears fall like rain as he refuses to let me go.

"It's Quinn and the girl he's talking to." He releases me a little so I can look at him. "Did you think I had another girl in there?"

My eyes meet his with drops streaming down my face. "I don't know what to think anymore."

"Only you. I wouldn't be able to be with anyone else." Liam holds me close, and I try to melt into him. His words soothe me, and being in his arms allows me a sense of comfort.

"Don't give me up so easily," I cry against his chest and he lets out a deep breath.

"Let's go inside?" he offers.

I nod and he pulls me to his side.

As we enter, I see no broken bottles and everything is cleaned up better than when I left. It's been not even a day since I was here. So much has happened in the last few days, but my mind and body feel as if it's been a lot longer.

"Hey, Lee," Quinn says and looks at Liam then sits.

"We'll get out of here and let you guys talk," he offers and grabs his date's hand. She stands and smiles at me.

"I'm sorry to run you off."

"You didn't. Ready, Ash?" I look at her and she looks familiar.

Liam juts his head toward the kitchen, and Quinn nods and heads there. "I just need to talk to Quinn a second," Liam quietly tells me in my ear before kissing the side of my head.

She walks over and waves awkwardly. "Hi, I'm Ashton Caputo. We kinda met, but didn't really, because well, it wasn't the time for introductions. However, I think that may be our thing," Ashton rambles. "Anyway, I'm Catherine's best friend from New Jersey." It takes a second, but I remember she was with Catherine. She's absolutely stunning. Her long, red hair flows down her back and her eyes shimmer.

"I sort of remember."

"I'm visiting Mark, but he pawned me off on Quinn while they left for a few days to go . . . well, anyway, so we came here to meet Liam," she explains.

"Are you and Mark . . . ?" I ask with wide eyes.

"No!" she waves her hands animatedly. "We tried that and it was like putting the same person in the other and one trying to claw its way out. We're just friends."

"Ahh, so you're both smartasses?"

"Well, he's an ass and I'm smart." She pauses and I smile.

Ashton seems uncomfortable, and I instantly hate that I've ruined their night. "What brings you down here?"

Her eyes close and she shakes her head. "I needed a break from my life, so Mark suggested I come to Virginia for the week. Just so happened to be a busy week here as well."

"You could say that," I half laugh.

"I know you don't know me, but I feel like I know you. Cat talks about you a lot and she's worried about you. I don't know much other than what I've overheard, but are you okay?"

I sit on the couch and Ashton sits beside me. "Short answer . . . no. I'm so far from okay I don't even know what it looks like. I'm sorry, I shouldn't burden you on your vacation."

"Please," she scoffs. "This is an escape from my self-inflicted hell. Plus, with Cat gone, I don't have much girl talk, so please don't feel bad. I miss this. She's practically married to Jackson, and they're in a good place, so I get nothing." She grins, and I feel at ease with her. "You have a lot going on, and believe me, I only know what I'm overhearing from G.I. Joe over there. Mark told me that he had to go do something and then dropped me off at Quinn's. So I've pieced a few things together."

I smile and even if she knows everything, I'm grateful she's allowing me the sense of privacy. "Quick version . . . my dead husband isn't dead. Liam is his best friend and has told him he'll back off. I'm in love with him, and Liam deploys soon. Basically, I'm losing my friggin' mind."

"Well, who do you want?"

"Liam," I say without any hesitation.

"I'm not trying to talk you out of it. But do you think you should give yourself some time to really be sure? Again, you can tell me to eff off and I'd understand. I tend to give unsolicited advice." Ashton gives me an out, but I feel oddly comfortable. She reminds me of Reanell, and I almost wish I would've gone to her instead of coming to see Liam. I'm too conflicted and emotional to be rational.

"Aaron and I weren't in the best place when he died—well, went missing—I don't know if we could've survived it. He cheated, lied, and I'm not sure we can move forward. Liam has been my rock this last year. I know it sounds crazy, but our love is different than I had with Aaron," I explain.

It's true though. My love with Aaron was almost infantile. The way you adore something so much that you only see the good. We loved each other because that was what you do. It's all I knew and so I thought it was all there was. It doesn't diminish the time we were together, but when I fell in love with Liam, it was like a part of me clicked. I could've never told Aaron things that I can tell Liam. If I told Aaron why I was mad, he'd make me feel stupid. Put me down and tell me I was being ridiculous. Liam draws me out.

"Different is good. Trust me, I'm the last person you should be getting love advice from, but I'll be here for a little while, and if you want to grab a drink or whatever, let me know." Ashton stands as the guys walk into the room. "It was sincerely nice to meet you, and I hope I'll see you soon?" she asks.

Quinn walks over. "I was going to bring Ashton to Aarabelle's birthday party, if that's okay?"

Her party. I completely forgot. "Yes," I say snapping out of my head. "Of course."

"Great! I know Catherine and Jackson are coming too, so thank you."

"All right, man, see you at work tomorrow." Quinn slaps Liam on the shoulder and leaves with Ashton. I give a short wave and she smiles.

I turn to Liam and remember why I'm here. He stands there uncomfortable but I don't care. He's not going to play the martyr.

"You don't think I should get to decide?" I ask with venom dripping from each syllable.

CHAPTER NINE

LIAM

"I DON'T THINK you should have to," I state while glaring back at her. She comes here pissed off, hits me again, and then breaks down. "You're a mess, and you can't tell me it's me you want when he's waiting at home for you."

"He's only there because you won't come get me." She drops to the couch.

"Do you hear yourself? You need to give yourself some damn time. I need time too," I explain.

She doesn't see how this alters everything. Aaron being alive makes me the other man. I'm not Aarabelle's father; I'd be the guy that stole her mom from her dad. Besides the fact that it makes every family gathering the most awkward thing there could possibly be.

"This is impossible for all of us." Her body almost goes limp. "He's dealing with coming home after God knows what happened. You're not wanting to break some code with him, and I'm torn in the middle." She wraps her arms around her stomach and drops her head.

"Lee," I say and tilt her head with my fingers. "If we truly love each other, not time, another man, or distance will keep us apart. Do you trust that enough?"

There's so much at stake, and while I want to be a

selfish asshole, I can't. My loyalty has nothing to do with what I said to Aaron. Truth be told, I couldn't give a fuck less what he wants me to do. He lost her, but on my way home, I realized she lost herself too. I don't doubt she loves me. I don't think she doubts it either, but we need a minute. We both have to figure out the best way to handle it, and I can't be the one to tell her what to do. I leave for deployment in two weeks, and there's talk about leaving a week earlier. The deployment gives us the time and space to work through it all and really see if what we have is strong.

"I know I love you. I trust that right now all I have in my heart is you."

"I think we need to take my deployment as a break," I utter the words and instantly wish I could take them back.

The last thing I want is a break from her, but it's the only choice we have. I won't put her through trying to sort things out with him while I'm deployed. I don't want to worry about what she's doing while I'm gone. I need to focus on my men and keeping myself safe. This type of shit is what gets guys killed.

Her face falls and I see the pain spark in her eyes. I hate hurting her. "I seriously can't believe this."

I take her hand in mine and savor the feel of her skin beneath my fingers. "I love you, Natalie. More than I should, but I can't have this shit hanging between us when I go. We won't be able to talk a lot when I'm gone, and I already knew I would go batshit crazy when I leave, but now . . ." I trail off.

Her blue eyes pierce through me, and I see how hard this is for her. "Can I write you? Can I see you before you go?"

Every part of me disintegrates with her questions.

I hope to God there's a way we can find a way back through this, because if I lose her for good, I don't know

I'll ever go through this shit again. There's a part of me that always wondered if he was actually alive who she'd choose and if we can stand the test. This is the time to prove it.

"You don't get it. I don't want to be away from you. I don't want to do this, but I think we have to. I need to focus when I'm away, and imagining Aaron moving in on you will get me killed. Do you understand?"

"Please don't say stuff like that. He's not moving in on me and nothing will happen to you."

I bring her against me and close my eyes. If only it were so simple. If I were Aaron, I would fight to the death. Which is exactly what he'll do. Brittany isn't who he wants to be with. It's Lee, who happens to be who I want as well. I won't ruin myself in the process though. If she wants to be with him, I won't stand in her way, because he had her first. Even if it kills me.

"Nothing is guaranteed, sweetheart. Know that each moment I'm away from you, you'll be in my mind. There won't be a moment that you won't be what I'm thinking of."

We recline back in the couch then she wraps her arm around my torso. "I don't want you to go."

I sigh, "I know, but maybe this is what we need."

"No, it's not what we need, but it's what we have. I'm going to ache for you every day you're gone. I'm going to wish you were here so I could snuggle into your side and remind you why you should love me."

I pull her closer and rub the side of her arm. "Loving you was never the issue. It's keeping you when you're not mine to have."

She looks at me as a tear falls. "I think I was always yours to have. I'm just hoping you'll see that soon."

chapter ten

natalie

"LEE?" REANELL CALLS out from the back deck. It's Aarabelle's birthday party and she came early to help set up.

"In the kitchen!" I call out and wipe my forehead. The house is a mess. There's flour all over the floor, eggs on the floor thanks to my clumsy hands, and Aarabelle laughs at me from her highchair.

She opens the swinging door and stops. "Wow . . . I mean . . . wow."

"Yeah, can you help me?"

"Where's your devoted husband? Visiting his girlfriend?" she asks with hostility.

"Reanell!"

"Too soon? Yeah, probably too soon. Sorry." She bends down and starts to clean up the eggs. "So, where is he?"

"Mark picked him up and took him out for a few hours since the tension was enough to suck the air from the house." I point over to the newspaper that featured his rescue. "Read the last paragraph."

Considering I used to work for the local press, you'd

think they would've given me a heads up. Nope. They did a huge piece on him and how he's a hero. But the worst was how Aaron told them how determined he was to make his family whole again. How he loves his wife and child more than his own life and we're what kept him alive.

"He really laid it on thick." Reanell puts the paper on the table. "Mason seriously feels bad, but he couldn't say anything—not even to me."

I put the mixer down and huff. "I know. I'm not mad anymore. It could've risked Liam and the other guys' lives."

Still sucks, but I get it.

"What time will your mom be here?" Rea asks, tiptoeing around the mess. "Did you get anything in the damn bowl?"

"Shut up. I'm not a great baker, but I wanted to make her a cake."

Reanell laughs, "Maybe I should head to the store and get her an edible one. Jesus, you're like Betty Crapper—this doesn't even look like cake mix."

I drop the mixer and start to laugh hysterically. Tears drop from my fit, and I slide against the counter to the floor. "Oh, God, Betty Crapper . . ." I continue giggling, unable to stop. I laugh on the flour-covered floor as Reanell stares at me as if I'm losing my mind. Hell, I am. "I can't . . ." The laughter rages on.

"What the hell is wrong with you?" Her voice is full of concern.

"I mean . . . it's funny," I say, trying to calm myself.

"I'm not sure I follow. You're scaring me, Lee." Reanell hunches down and puts her hands on my knees. "I'm really worried about you. The last few days you haven't been yourself."

Her fear is valid. Since I left Liam's house and he basically told me we need to take a break, I've been a mess.

The only thing that kept me going was knowing I had him. Aaron hasn't said a word about our last fight. He's here trying to help and be a part of our lives.

We've met with doctors, psychologists, and he met with some liaison from the government. But I'm robotic. I drive him there and listen to everyone tell me how blessed I am to have him home. They tell me it's a miracle and how happy they are for us, but I feel no joy. I've placed myself back in my bubble of void. It's easier than feeling, and I'm emotionally drained. The only thing that gives me any light is Aarabelle. I try to keep her around me at all times.

"I'm broken."

I haven't told her about what Liam said, but I'm sure she notices.

She grabs my face. "Oh, honey. You're not broken. No one is. You have Aara, me, Mason, and so many other people who love you. This isn't easy. This is real life and it fucking sucks."

"Yeah," I reply dejectedly.

"Seriously, this isn't some movie where it'll all work out in the end. This is ugly and raw. No one has the answers, babe. The thing is . . . there's not really a choice. I feel like six months ago you made your choice. You let Aaron go when you allowed yourself to love again."

She's right. That's the issue. I can't go back not just because of the affair and the lies between us. But because I let go of that love. I forgave him. I found a place where I learned how to truly love and not have to see what I wanted. Will my love for Liam always be that want? No. We'll struggle and we'll fight but there's no one else I want by my side. He thinks he's giving me time to make the right choice. But he's a fool.

Reanell places her hand on mine. "I know something happened with Liam, but you won't let me in again."

"He doesn't want me," I mutter. "He said he wants to

take the deployment as a break. I need to focus on here, and he has to worry about the mission."

"First of all," Reanell's voice morphs into her serious tone, "He does want you. You're an idiot if you believe that he doesn't, and since I'm not friends with idiots, I'm going to say you don't. He wants you so much, but can't you see how hard this is for him?"

"Of course I do!" I push up off the floor. "I see it all, and I'm the one who has to deal with all of it! I have to deal with Aaron, Liam, Aarabelle, and last of all, how I'm coping." I throw my hands in the air and wipe my face. *I will not cry. I will not cry.*

She doesn't get it. No one does. This whole damn situation is ridiculous. Aaron and I agreed he could stay here until Aarabelle's birthday party. Then he's going to stay at Jackson's until we can make a decision. It was his idea to go there since the psychologist recommended we get a little space. His night terrors wake us with his screaming, he zones out in the middle of a conversation . . . he's definitely getting better, but it's a long road for him. But the worst is that Aarabelle hasn't been the same, and he wants to allow us both some sense of normalcy.

"Is Liam coming today?"

"I don't know. I can't imagine he would, but he loves Aara, so who knows?"

"He loves you too."

I scoff, "I don't know at this point. He hasn't called or shown any sign this is affecting him."

"Sit," she commands and points at the chair. "Natalie Gilcher, you are so much fucking stronger than you know. Liam is not the only man alive. If he gives you up so quickly, then fuck him. But I think there's more there. I think he's in pain and guys are idiots. They do dumb shit because they don't know how to handle these situations." She smoothes her hair. "Think about it. If he calls you, then he's breaking his own rules. He's giving in, and then he has to break you and him all over again. So . . ." I see the gleam in her eyes as a plan forms in her mind, "You make him break them." Her smirk forms, and she raises one brow.

"How the hell do I do that?"

"You go upstairs and make yourself irresistible. He seems to have a weakness for red, doesn't he? After all, you're the host . . . shouldn't you look presentable?"

I sit there with my jaw slack at her plan. But she's right. If he comes in and sees me a crazy mess, it won't help my cause. So I muster the strength I have left and stand. "Watch her please . . . I have some freshening up to do."

Reanell smiles as I head up the stairs and decide he's going to miss me no matter what.

○○○

I GIVE MYSELF a once over in the mirror before heading back downstairs. Thank God Rea came early. I made sure to wear my red dress from our first date. I have my hair in soft curls down my back, and I went very natural on my makeup, except for my cherry red lipstick. I'm not sure how to handle this. I don't want Aaron to think there's a chance in hell we're getting back together, but at the same rate, I need to wake Liam up. Make him see that giving up isn't what he wants.

I slip on my heels and head to see what Rea thinks.

"Holy shit!" Reanell says as she holds Aarabelle. "Sorry, I mean . . . hi there. Are you trying to give him a stroke?"

"If that's what it takes. My mom said they're on their way. I figure the mommy should look good, right?" I no longer feel sexy and in charge . . . I feel stupid. Maybe this isn't the best idea.

"Do not even think about changing," Reanell chastises as she walks over. "You own this man. Now remind him just how much."

"Gimme the baby," I say with arms outstretched. "I'm going to get her in her party dress before anyone gets here." I bounce her and she smiles, turning to Reanell, I give her something to do. "Everything should be set up, other than the cake, which my mother called and said she's bringing one since she figured I botched this one. If you can make sure my mother never sees the kitchen, I'll love you forever." I laugh and shake my head. It's the running joke that baking and I do not mix.

She nods and waves her hand. "Go make that baby shine for her first birthday!"

Aarabelle is in her pastel pink dress complete with little jewels on the bodice. I went a little crazy on this party, but I wanted to celebrate her birth. The reminder that something so perfect came at a dark time.

"Lee," I hear Aaron's voice as he knocks. "Wow. You look incredible, ba—" He catches himself.

"Thanks."

"Hi, my beautiful girl," he smiles and makes his way over to Aarabelle. He extends his hands, but she clings to me. "Mama's girl through and through." Aaron laughs it off, but I see that it hurts him. I'll give it to him that he's been trying. He spends as much time as he can with her and offers to help. "Who all is coming?"

I hear the undertone to his question. He wants to know if Liam is going to be here.

"A few of our friends, and you know my parents are here. Is your mom coming back down?"

Aaron shrugs and winces. I hate that he has some residual pain, but his right arm took the worst from the IED. The scars are more prominent. He explained the weather has a lot to do with his pain as well.

"She said she couldn't stay this long. I'm going to

visit her in a few weeks."

"Okay, what about Brittany?"

He huffs then looks away. "I haven't seen her since I've been here."

"I'm only asking." I try for nonchalant, but I'm sure I fail. There's a part of me that wishes he would choose her so that I didn't have to be the bad guy here. Yes, he cheated, but according to him it meant nothing. He says he wants a life with us, and even if I want to dismiss him, there's a part of my life that belongs to him. "I'm sorry. That was out of line. I'm just nervous about the party."

Aaron steps forward and brushes the hair off my face. "Can we ever get back to us?" His voice trembles with hope.

I look at him and let out a breath. "I don't think so. I can't explain what learning about your relationship was like, but it opened the door to seeing what our marriage truly was, and I can't forget that. And I may not have been with Liam for very long, but I don't know that I could go back. I know that hurts you, and I hate it. I don't hate you, Aaron. I'll always love you in some way."

"I'm not giving up. I won't let you walk away so easily," he warns as he heads toward the other room.

He knows me better than anyone. Aaron can twist my heart so that it's unrecognizable, and it scares me, but it wouldn't be out of love. Loving someone is being unselfish and sometimes relinquishing your own wants for that person. It's being noble in the face of knowing it would obliterate your world—like walking away. Like the man I love is doing now because he loves me.

I head down the stairs, and my mother and father rush over.

"Hi, sweet pea!" she yells and holds her arms out. She beelines straight for Aara and ignores me.

"Hello, Mother," I chide, laughing.

"Hi, baby girl," my dad says and pulls me into his

arms. "You look like you're going on a date." He appraises me in a fatherly way.

"Nope." I decide not to elaborate. My dad was always very protective. Hell, Aaron wasn't even allowed in the house until I was eighteen. My father was the one sitting around talking about a black belt he never had and cleaned guns that I swear he only bought once I turned fifteen. He's all bark and no bite.

"Wouldn't you be more comfortable in jeans?" he asks and I laugh.

"Give it up . . . how's the hotel?"

"Fine. Your mother wanted to stay another night sightseeing in Williamsburg. I couldn't get out of there fast enough. That woman can spend money like no one else." He shakes his head and my mother slaps him in the chest.

"Where's Aaron?" she asks.

"He was upstairs last I saw."

She looks at my father and sighs. It's got to be killing her to keep her mouth shut. There's no way she doesn't have an opinion on what I should be doing.

"Well, I think for Aarabelle's sake, you should be trying to find a resolution."

"Mom—" I cut her off.

I didn't want to tarnish Aaron's memory for my family or his, so I kept his infidelity a secret. To them, Aaron is still husband of the year. But now that he's back, I'm glad I chose to keep it hushed. It's between us regardless, and our mistakes don't need to be broadcasted.

"No. I'm saying that he's your husband and her father." She raises her hand as if it's just her friendly advice.

I reach out for Aarabelle and decide I've had enough pleasantries. "We're going to make our rounds." I smile and walk toward Reanell, who's laughing at my discomfort. Some help she is.

The party is in full swing, and I can't help but look over at the door for him. How can he not show up for her birthday? He's been a father to Aarabelle since she was a baby. He was the man in the hospital with her. Liam cared for her when I was sick and held her in his arms. For him to not be here breaks me in two.

"Hey, there's my goddaughter!" Jackson calls out and Aarabelle smiles. He pulls me and Aara into a hug. "You both look stunning."

"I think she's a little young for you, babe." Catherine chuckles from beside him. He rolls his eyes as he takes Aarabelle into his arms. "Hey!"

"Catherine, you look amazing!" I say and we hug each other. "California agrees with you." She's cut her hair to her shoulders and it's pin straight. She looks so much more a classic beauty now. Her skin is bronze and she has this natural aura around her.

"Please, you would never know you had a baby. You look insane, and that dress . . ." We both smile knowingly. "Anyway, I'm glad we could be here. Muffin told me all about everything, and if you need anything please call me. Is he here?"

"I'm going to take this one and make the rounds. Women love a man with a kid," Jackson says and heads into the kitchen with Aara.

"Such an idiot," Catherine scoffs. "So . . . is he?"

"Which one?" I ask.

"Either, I guess."

"Aaron's here somewhere. Probably with Mark."

She nods and we walk over toward a quieter corner. Jackson has Aarabelle and is probably feeding her God knows what, but right now, I don't care.

"I'm sure he'll be here." She pats my arm.

I wish I could be sure. I've fought the urge to text him all day, but I need to keep my strength. He needs to come to me, because I keep running to him but he's shut me out. I miss him.

A few more guests arrive, and my hope dwindles. Reanell and Catherine keep me busy and try to stop me from spinning into a downward spiral. This isn't the Liam I know. There would be nothing he wouldn't do for us.

"I'll be right back," I say to Reanell and she nods.

As I head into the hallway, I run into someone. "I'm so sor—" The words die on my tongue as I look up and see him. My heart rate accelerates as he holds my arms.

"Hi," he says, still not releasing me.

I focus on breathing and try to ignore that he's touching me. I want to kiss him so bad it hurts. "I wasn't sure you were going to make it."

"I had to help a friend first. I wouldn't miss her birthday." His warm, rich voice washes over me and I shiver. "Cold?" he asks, not missing anything.

Liam releases me, and his eyes travel my body. He gazes over my skin then to my dress. His breath catches as he makes his way back up to my lips. Deciding to make this a little more difficult for him, I slowly lick my lips. He watches my tongue and presses his body against mine.

I'm flush against the wall, and his warmth is blanketing me. "Are you trying to fucking destroy me?" His voice is low against my ear. "Do you want me to lose my mind, sweetheart?"

I whimper softly at the term of endearment he uses. "No."

"Really? Because that's exactly what you're doing."

I straighten and stare at him. "You're doing that on your own."

"You're making me hate the one person who I shouldn't. You have no idea how torn up I am. How I fight the urge to come here at night and rip you out of his house. How I had to smash my phone to stop from calling you. I'm begging you . . . go change." Liam's plea is full of bitterness, and as much as it makes me want to ease his pain—I won't.

I push against him and he backs up. "I've got guests waiting. You could've been here." I step toward him and he retreats. "You could've been in my house every night, but you need space. With space comes this." I turn on my heel and head toward the party, hoping he's watching my ass the entire time.

Liam stands to the side of the party by Quinn and Ashton. They talk, but his eyes never waver from me. I can sense the way he watches me and almost feel his hostility when Aaron is around us.

Aaron does his best to give me space, but I try to include him. He's different though. It's almost like he's not really here with us. Everything feels forced and uncomfortable. While he may not have always been overly social, he would've been at least engaging in conversations, but now he only responds to questions he's directly asked.

I can't help but be concerned that this is all too much for him. "Do you need a break?" I ask him quietly.

"I need to lie down," he admits.

"Go ahead upstairs. We won't do cake until you come back." I place my hand on his arm, but he flinches.

Immediately he tries to soothe me. "Sorry, I just . . ."

"You don't have to explain."

Aaron turns, but then looks back. "I'm sorry, Lee. For everything."

"I'm sorry too." And I am. I'm sorry our lives have come to this. I'm sorry that we can't go back in time to a place where there was no affair, no other people, just us. Maybe if I hadn't been desperate for a family, things would've been different, but the bottom line is, sometimes sorry can't fix the hurt. Sometimes the pain is so deep that no words can heal the damage, and knowing the man you spent months grieving slept with another woman . . . is one of those hurts.

chapter eleven

JACKSON WALKS OVER looking nervous. He keeps wringing his hands and wiping them on his pants. I can't remember a time I've seen him looking frayed. "Hi," he says glancing around.

"Hi?" I reply skeptically as I smile a little.

"So, I'm going to propose to Catherine. I wanted to do it after the party, but I have something set up on the beach for ten minutes from now. I wasn't sure how long these kid party things last . . ."

My eyes alight and I'm so happy for him I could scream. "So go. Don't be stupid. Where are you taking her?"

"The lighthouse," he smiles and checks to make sure no one is near us. "I would love for everyone to come in about a half hour, but I don't know now since I apparently have shitty timing."

The joy in my heart is overwhelming. He deserves this so much. After he lost Madelyn, none of us were sure he'd recover, but when you see him with Catherine, you can't help but be happy. They've been through a lot of troubles, but in the end they endured. There's nothing more I'd like than to be a part of their special moment.

"I'll have my parents watch Aarabelle and round everyone up." I place my hand on his forearm. "I'm genuinely happy for you."

He smiles down at me. "Thanks, Lee." Jackson kisses my cheek and then nudges my arm. "I'm gonna grab Cat and head there."

I nod and watch him walk off. My eyes drift to Liam who's looking at me. Our gazes stay connected, and I suddenly wish we were that happy. He's the man I want to come home to, wake up next to, and fall asleep with, but for some reason he's trying to be noble.

Jackson and Catherine walk off to the beach while I head over to our friends. Mark, Ashton, Quinn, and Liam all look over as I approach. "Did Jackson fill you all in?" I ask, and they nod. Liam looks away for the first time, and my anger builds at his dismissal. "Okay, I'm going to change my shoes."

"Are you sure you want to walk on the beach in that dress?" Liam asks seemingly annoyed.

I smile at the fact that my plan is working. "Yup. I'm *very* comfortable."

"Glad someone is," he mutters under his breath.

Mark and Quinn give each other a look and slap each other on the chest. Apparently, they notice his crappy attitude.

I climb the stairs and check on Aaron. He's sound asleep and for once not thrashing around. I decide not to wake him and grab my shoes. Liam is waiting at the bottom of the stairs. I stop on the bottom step and have to restrain myself from either leaping into his arms or slapping him again.

"You can't be mad at me because you don't like your decision."

Liam steps closer and we're eye to eye. "I don't like the situation. This is fucking impossible."

"What is?"

"Not touching you," his hand lifts and he holds my cheek. "Not talking to you," he keeps me captivated with his voice. "Not kissing you," Liam leans in and our lips are almost touching. "Is it killing you, Lee?"

I don't answer. I hold my ground for a second before I can't hold back any longer. My lips press against his and I melt. His arms drop, he grips my hips, holding me tight as my arms wrap around his neck. I won't let go . . . I can't let go. I need him to fill my lungs and awaken me again. There's a house full of people, but right now there's no one else but us. His lips mold to mine and our tongues meet. Liam pushes me back against the wall, hiding us from anyone's view. He kisses me languidly, and I find myself in his touch.

Someone clears their throat, and we break apart. I look over at Reanell who has her hands on her hips. "At least find a spare room." She shakes her head and walks away.

"We should go," I say, feeling conflicted. He tilts back against the railing, wipes his mouth, which smears the lipstick even worse. "You have lipstick on your face," I say moving closer. I wipe his mouth, relishing the way his lip feels against my finger. The smell of his cologne filters around us.

He grips my wrist before it drops, "I won't lose you."

"You're damn right you won't."

Liam releases my arm, takes my hand in his, as we head toward the lighthouse. Everyone is ahead of us, and I savor the fact that we're alone. Neither of us fills the silence, we just walk hand in hand. Liam's thumb rubs the back of my hand, giving me comfort in his touch. Once we're out of view of my home, he drags me close, and wraps his arm around my waist. He pulls me tight against him, and dips me back. I watch his blue eyes shimmer as his mouth slowly moves toward mine.

Our lips touch and there's no rush. He kisses me like I'm a treasure in his arms. He cradles my head as he holds his mouth to mine. I could stay like this forever.

Liam pulls me back but keeps his arms wrapped

around me. "I'm sorry."

"For kissing me?"

We start to walk again and I wait for my answer. "No, sweetheart. For how this is for all of us. I hate that you're hurting and that I'm hurting you. The deployment got pushed up."

I stop moving. "You're leaving sooner?" I thought we had another week or two. Time to mend a little, or at least find a better resolution than him stepping aside so my husband can have a go at this.

"Yeah, I got the call earlier today. We leave in three days." Liam's voice is resolute. You can tell he's going into what we call deployment mode. They close off the world around them and start to focus on the mission.

The lighthouse is within view, and I still can't respond. My mind is going a mile a minute with how to handle this. Liam stops me before we reach everyone else. "I want to see you before I go."

I nod with tears in my eyes. "I'm going to miss you."

Liam gives a sad smile, but before he can respond, Quinn whistles us over.

We head toward our friends right as Jackson and Catherine exit the lighthouse. Catherine is smiling, and then she sees us and her face falls in confusion.

She looks back to Jackson as he drops to his knee. I watch with tear-filled eyes as she clutches her chest.

"Catherine Pope, you've given me more love in the last two years than I've ever known. You taught me how to love again, how to be a better man, and how to forgive myself. I want to spend every day of my life making you happy. I will cherish you, protect you, annoy you." She laughs as tears fall down her cheek. "I'll give you everything you could ever want. Will you marry me?" Jackson's voice is full of promise, and we all stand with smiles and love for them.

He's gone through a lot of hell to get here, and I have

faith I'll survive just like he has.

Catherine falls to her knees and grips his face. "I will marry you today if you want."

He holds her close and kisses her passionately. Jackson leans back and places the diamond on her finger and wipes her tears. "Tomorrow we leave for Hawaii."

She laughs and he pulls her close. "Always so damn sure of yourself."

"You can't resist me, baby." Jackson smirks and kisses her again.

We all join in their joy and hug the happy couple. Ashton squeals over the ring and the guys joke with him about losing his touch. I stand off to the side sharing stolen glances with Liam.

Fear that he won't make it home consumes me, but more than ever, I'm terrified we won't make it back to each other. There's so much at stake for both of us, and six months is a long time. Part of me understands his need for a break, but I worry it will be too much.

Liam walks over after the group disperses. "Do you want to walk with me?"

"Sure," I reply.

"I don't know how this works, Lee. If Aaron weren't here, I would be with you on my last night. I would make love to you and—"

"Don't," I lift my hand to stop him. "Don't tell me how you would be doing things if he wasn't alive. Because you could be doing them now, but you don't believe me. I chose you. I came to you and told you."

"And he's living in the house. What do you want—family dinners? I'm doing the right thing by staying away. I'm giving you *both* a chance to figure out what the fuck you want."

"He's moving out soon, but I can't just throw him out. He's Aarabelle's father. Jesus, he's been tortured and God only knows what. It's our home," I try to explain to him. This isn't easy on me or him, but Aaron has it the worst. Sure, he screwed up and there's no going back, and at the same time I can't be cruel. I know Liam isn't asking for that, but I'm at a loss here.

"Your home with him. Do you get it now? It's not our home. It's the home you made with him. Where you share a child. Where I would come crash for the night on the couch when I would visit while you two did whatever upstairs. I'm always the outsider."

I turn and fire burns through my veins. "I think you want to believe that. It's easier for you to walk away this way. Make me the bad guy so you can deploy and carry out your life without having to worry about me. I'm not the bad guy here. None of us are. Aaron is moving out soon. He wanted to give me and Aara some space so we can adjust and figure out a life."

"Did he tell you he'd let you go?" Liam fires off.

"No."

"I'll never know for sure, Natalie. I'll always wonder if you really loved me or if I was just the consolation prize. So take the six months and figure it out. Know that no matter what, when I get back I'll be hoping you're there. If you are, I'll marry you. I'll do anything you want to prove how much I want you."

My heart rate quickens, and I wait for him to say more.

"This isn't about me fighting for you. I know you keep saying I'm giving you up, but I'm not. I'll never stop hoping you'll still choose me when this is all over. I just can't watch you decide. I see the way he looks at you. He's made it clear he wants you back. I never wanted to lose you in the first place."

I grip his shirt and pull myself to him. "You never will."

"I hope that's true. You have no idea how much I want that to be the case."

"Have faith in us, Liam."

He presses his lips to the top of my head. "I do, sweetheart. I just need a minute."

Liam walks me back to the party with his hands in his pockets. Both of us keep our heads down. I don't know how I'll endure six months of not knowing. But I do have faith in us, and I won't let that falter. I have to make him believe me. As we approach the deck, Aaron is standing there watching us.

"Hey." He looks at both of us and guilt eats at me. "I woke up and your mom said you all headed to the lighthouse."

"Yeah, I came upstairs but you were asleep. Jackson proposed to Catherine and he asked us all to come," I explain, hoping he'll drop it.

He looks toward the ocean. "Where's everyone else?"

"They're coming. Do you feel better?"

Aaron looks at Liam with hate in his eyes. "I did until now."

"Stop it," I chastise him. "I've been honest with you. I'm not sneaking behind your back and doing God knows what while we were still married. I'm not keeping half truths or secrets."

"I thought you would give us time before you moved in on her again?"

Liam steps forward, pushing me behind him protectively. "I wish you'd seen the wife you love so much when she found out about your girlfriend. The pain in her eyes, the way she cried and then drank herself stupid. Or maybe you could've seen the way she wanted to kill Brittany after she found out about her pregnancy. My word means something to her . . . does yours?"

chapter twelve

I NEVER TOLD Aaron about the baby. I wanted to see if he was really lying about his relationship with Brittany. *So much for that plan.*

Liam stares Aaron down, and I push him back, but he doesn't budge.

"What?" Aaron asks.

"You didn't tell him?" Liam turns to me with his jaw slack.

The blood drains from my face leaving me colorless. As much as I wanted to not mention the baby because I wanted him to tell me, I also didn't want to acknowledge it. Aaron and I had a host of fertility issues, but the main one was me. I have PCOS, therefore I was the biggest contributing factor. Polycystic Ovary Syndrome causes my hormones to constantly be unbalanced and renders me practically infertile. My doctor explained even if I could get pregnant, I needed to be aware I was very high risk.

"I didn't know how," I mutter.

"Lee, look at me." Aaron steps forward, and my heart begins to sputter. It hurts all over again.

Liam's eyes implore me to tell Aaron. "Acknowledging the baby to him is a reminder that it's me who couldn't have a baby. I didn't want to face that so soon."

He nods and then I turn to Aaron. "I know it all. I know about your relationship you keep telling me is nothing. And I know about the baby you and your girlfriend were having." I look at the now practically empty home except for my parents and Reanell. "Now's the time to be brutally honest because there's nothing that can hurt me more at this point." Aaron sits on the step and now I wait.

"I think this is something you and I should discuss privately."

I half laugh. "I didn't get that luxury finding out. I had to be in a crowded bar with all of our friends when I found out that you, the man I would've never imagined, cheated. I had to stand there and have her tell me about how much she loved you. And while you may not have loved her the way she did, I saw her pain." My voice is low, but he cringes.

"All I could think about was you," he says, not fully admitting what he did. "So you're going to throw it all away? Our whole life?"

And there it is. For the first time, he's not denying or circumventing how deep their relationship was. "Did you know she was pregnant?"

"Yes," Aaron says, barely audible.

No matter how much I love Liam, this still hurts. Aaron wasn't just some guy. He was my partner and the one person who promised to love me and honor me. I was guilt-ridden after he was gone about having any kind of feelings for another man.

"So was all of what you said a lie? Were you in love with her?" I ask him unsure if it matters at this point.

Aaron stands, and Liam's arms hold my shoulders from behind. Here I am between them both. "No, I loved her. It wasn't even an inch of the love I have for you. Being held over there reminded me of that. I made vows and promises to God and anyone who would listen about the man I'd be when I came home," he says looking straight into my eyes. "I love you, Natalie. I always have and I always will."

"You broke the very core of our marriage."

"I can fix it," he pleads with me. "I fought for you. I lived for you. Please, give us a chance."

We stare at each other, and I see the man I promised to love in sickness and in health, for better or for worse. I'm torn in half and burnt to ash. Everything inside of me is dead. How do I do this? How do I break him when he's already broken? I know that my answer right now will kill him in some form, and if I spare him it'll be in false hope. Then, the added pressure of knowing Liam will hear whatever I say.

"I can't do this with you both," I finally reply exasperated and overwhelmed. "You're literally killing me. Inside I'm a mess. I cry all the time, I can't remember the last time I slept without waking in a pool of sweat. You broke me when I found out. I literally tore everything you touched apart. I don't know who you are anymore," I say and clutch my stomach.

I turn to Liam and prepare to unload on him. "And you. I love you so much it is physically hurting me to be away from you. But you keep pushing me into someone else's arms. You leave in three days and I'm dying inside. How can you push me away and then know you could get hurt or worse? All I want to do is curl into your arms and you tell me it's all going to be okay, but you won't give me that. Instead you tell me we need to spend time apart?" I ask as the tears fall. "I hate what you're all doing to me. Am I the only one here that sees how fucked up this is?"

I look to them both and they stand there. I want to throw something, scream, cry, and lose it for once. I'm always the one holding it together. Trying to make our lives easy. I'm a mother, friend, daughter, and lastly I get to be a woman. Well, this time . . . I'm a woman first. I have to give myself a chance to come through this.

"Sweetheart," Liam steps forward.

I put my hand up. "I need a minute," I say the words that I've been biting back. I see the flash of pain across his eyes, but right now I'm going to save myself.

"No, there are no more minutes." Liam's entire body is tight and ready to fight. "I'm done with us taking time. I love you. I would never betray you. You and I make sense. So I'm done shoving you away."

These two men have the ability to destroy me, and I won't let that happen. I push past them and head inside. My mother stands with Aarabelle in her arms. Tears fall from her face, and I know she heard it all. I walk over and wrap my arms around them both. Her arm holds me close and Aarabelle puts her head on my shoulder.

"Dada!" she yells, and I turn to see Liam walking in the house.

Aaron's face falls, he turns, and then walks out the door. "Aaron!" I call out and rush onto the beach after him. "Aaron, stop!"

He turns and pain lances across his face. "You let her call him Daddy?" There's no judgment in his tone, only hurt and disappointment.

"No," I shake my head quickly. "And he never encouraged her. It's just what she called him."

"I can't . . ." he begins and then stops talking. He walks closer to the water and stops and screams.

I wait in silence, unsure of what to say or do. You can feel the turmoil rolling off him.

"Everything I hoped for and lived for is gone," his voice breaks at the end. Aaron turns and his brown eyes cement me to the ground. "I wanted to die so many times. I could've begged at the end for them to kill me, but I lived because I kept seeing your face. Each night I closed my eyes and saw you and imagined what she looked like. Now, I come home and you're in love with another man. No, not just another man. Liam. My best fucking friend and my daughter is calling him Daddy!" he yells, and it's my turn to break.

I step closer to him, the urge to comfort him overwhelming me. "It wasn't like that. You died in my world, Aaron. There was a paper that said you were gone. No hope of a return. We said our goodbyes, and I grieved." My hand touches his. "I was dead inside. Then he came to Virginia and made me live again. He brought joy, laughter, and love back to us. Liam didn't steal anything." Aaron's eyes close and I go on. "In your letter, you told me to move on. I wasn't sure I could at first, and then when things shifted further into more with Liam, I found out about Brittany."

"You'll never know how much I hate myself for sleeping with her." I touch his face softly and he squeezes my hand. "It was my worst mistake. I felt so incapable of making you happy. Everything was about the baby and I couldn't cope. Then, I convinced myself while I was gone it never really happened. If I could deny it over and over then maybe, just maybe, we could find a way again. But once again . . . can you see how fucked up I am? Can you see how I don't even know who I am anymore?"

"You're in there, Aaron. You're not a bad guy, but you can't keep doing this. You have to deal with everything."

"Please, Lee. Save me," his voice is desperate.

There are two options right now—I can hold on to the hate and anger toward him or forgive and try to move forward. He made a horrible mistake, but it's not within me to make him suffer. "I can't save you. But I forgive you."

His eyes snap up and I see a small piece of relief. "Does that mean we have a chance?"

"Please don't ask me that. I may have forgiven you, but I don't want to hurt you. So please, don't ask unless you're really ready for the answer," I implore.

Aaron reaches his arm out tentatively and we embrace. He needs this, and in a way, so do I. The life we shared together was filled with happy times. There was love and passion, but the end was where we failed. It's both of our faults the marriage was where it was. I know he wants a chance, but my heart is with Liam.

"I know what your answer is." Aaron looks away. "I'm going to stay here for a bit."

"Okay," I reply. "I'm going to make some arrangements for Aarabelle. Liam deploys in three days, and I want to see him off. I want us to do what's best for her, so I can ask my parents to stay here so you can spend some time with her or they can take her?" I give him a little, hoping he'll see that while I'm not asking for permission, I'm taking into account his feelings. He is Aara's father, and I won't begrudge him the time with her.

"I'd like to spend some time with her, so if they agree to stay here . . ."

"I'll ask," I smile.

Aaron nods and looks off toward the water as I head to the house.

Liam stands on the deck as I advance. "He okay?"

"I think he's getting there. That hurt him a lot," I explain.

He looks at the sky and then back at me. "I never wanted that to happen. I should get going."

"Don't leave yet," I request. "I'm going to have my parents stay here with Aaron and Aarabelle. You and I are going to spend your last days here together."

Liam's lips lift as his eyes brighten. He steps closer hesitantly before his fingers graze my cheek. "Are we?"

"We are, and if you're a good boy, maybe you can break out that eggroll," I raise my brow and for the first time it feels normal.

"I'm not sure you deserve my eggroll," he jokes.

I lean close to his ear and use the tip of my fingernail to scrape down his chest. "I think you and I both know you can't resist me. So, you can go home, and then I'll be over with a bag soon."

Liam's lips just barely touch my ear. I shiver involuntarily as his breath wisps across my skin. "Don't bring any clothes, you won't need them."

I close my eyes and try to get myself under control as I now need to get the rest of my plan set. "I'll see you soon."

"I'll be waiting." He kisses the side of my cheek and walks off.

God, I love that man.

MY PARENTS WERE all too happy to stay at the house with Aarabelle. I explained the situation briefly, and they seemed to understand. Aaron was surly but didn't say much when I left. Once I arrive at Liam's, I grab my bag and head to his apartment. He opens the door before I have a chance to knock.

"I was beginning to think you weren't coming," he grins and leans against the door. His dark hair shines in the sunlight, and his white shirt accentuates his muscles. My mouth waters at the sight of him as my body burns to see it all.

I lick my lips and drag my bottom lip between my teeth. "Well," I say pushing my hand on his chest. He doesn't move, but I shove him a little harder and back him into the apartment. "What are you going to do with me now that you have me?"

Liam grips my hips and then kicks the door closed. He lifts me into his arms while pressing me against the door. "Do you know how much that dress made me fucking crazy?"

I nod and tangle my fingers in his hair. "I hoped it would. Nothing else seemed to get you to stop being so stupid."

His head rests on mine as we both breathe in each other. "You came to me. You're here instead of there."

My hand pulls his head back so he can look at me. I watch the turmoil flicker through his eyes. "I choose you. I just wish you'd believe me."

"Let's skip the heavy shit. I have an idea."

"Now I'm intrigued."

"As much as I'd love to strip you down and make love to you for hours," he pauses.

"I'm good with that."

He laughs and kisses me, but before we can get hot and heavy he shifts back. Liam glances at his watch and puts me down. "We gotta go now."

"Go where?" I ask confused.

Liam smiles and holds me against him. "Trust me?"

"Always."

He takes my hand and grabs a bag by the door. I reach for mine but Liam grabs it before I can reach. I smile at him and he winks. "We gotta hurry."

We sit in Robin, and Liam starts her up. My mind starts to wonder if we're going to Corolla. I would love to spend time with him completely alone and enjoy having that house again. Instead of bugging him, I let him surprise me. We only have a few days before he has to leave, so it's not like we can be going very far.

I notice we're not heading south, and now I'm really curious. We continue to head in the opposite direction, until we pull into the airport parking lot. He's got to be kidding me. How the hell can we go anywhere requiring a plane ride? It's not feasible.

"Why are we at the airport?" I can't hold back any longer.

"Because we're going on a plane."

He parks the car in the garage and exits. I sit here wondering what in the world he has up his sleeve.

"Lee?" he opens my door and looks at me. "Are you

going to get out?"

"Where are we going?"

"Jesus, you're killing me. Just get out of the car." Liam grabs my hand and lifts me out. He kisses me quickly and then hoists the bags.

"Did you plan all this from the time I told you I was coming over?"

"I did . . . are you impressed?"

More than impressed, I'm in awe. He trusted that I would come to him. So as much as he says he doesn't know if he can believe me, this gives me the assurance he does.

We step up to the ticket counter, and we hand over our identification.

"Welcome, Mr. Dempsey. I see you have two in your party traveling to Charleston."

I look over at Liam with a smile. He knows how much I've always wanted to go there. The cobblestone streets and little romantic restaurants are all Reanell talks about. She and Mason go there every year, and in passing, I mentioned how much I'd love to have a getaway there.

"I love you," I say, feeling overcome with emotion.

Liam wraps his arm around my back and holds me close. "I love you."

"Your flight will be boarding in about thirty minutes so you should head to your gate immediately," the woman smiles and hands us our boarding passes.

We head through security, and it dawns on me that I didn't pack for this. I didn't grab cute clothes and shoes. I don't even have enough toiletries. I figured we'd be in his apartment. "I'm not prepared for this."

"What?"

"The trip. I didn't bring anything I need."

Liam smiles and we make it to the gate as they begin the boarding call. "Relax, they have stores in South

Carolina. I doubt I have everything either, but all I need is you, and I've got that." He leans in and our lips touch. Everything I was worried about fades away.

"Yeah," my hand rests on his chest. "You do."

chapter thirteen

WE CHECK INTO the HarbourView Inn. It's magnificent with its old, historical, brick exterior and plush interior. Everything is upscale and pristine. Liam opens the door to our room, and I can't find my lungs. A four-post, wooden bed takes up the middle with white linens. The opulence is in every detail. The suite features a balcony that opens to a view of the water. It's stunning.

Liam stands behind me as I take it all in. His hands brush my shoulders and he sweeps my hair to the side. I close my eyes as his lips touch the edge of my neck.

"Are you happy, sweetheart?"

"More than you can imagine." I turn into his arms and kiss him.

Our mouths connect and Liam deepens the kiss. His tongue swirls with mine and my hands wrap around his torso. In all of this mess, he's the only person I want, and right now, he's all mine.

Without breaking, he walks us backward, and I feel the bed hit my knees. He lowers me slowly and tenderly. I devour every moan and sound he makes as our lips stay fused. His hands graze my body, and I squirm beneath him. I'm desperate to make love to him. I want to show him how much he owns me. Give him every part of me and let him take whatever I have to give.

His teeth tug my bottom lip and he pulls back. My eyes roll back as his hand finds its way under my dress. "We're going to go very slowly," he rasps. "Do you understand?"

I nod, unable to find my voice. He lifts my back up and glides the zipper down. My hands move of their own accord and trace his body. I lift his shirt and tear it off. He watches me, and my fingers touch his face. The scruff is longer than usual and almost a beard. I inhale the sea air mixed with the sandalwood scent of Liam and commit it to memory. I allow my fingertips to trail to his neck then to the hard lines of his chest. I trace the muscles and feel each dip and mountain. Lower I go until I reach his abs. I stare into his eyes as the pads feel his satin skin tense as I slide down the middle of his stomach.

"We can go slow, but I want this to be equally torturous for you," I whisper. I want to drive him as crazy as I'm sure he plans to drive me.

I reach his belt and slowly undo it.

"Seems you're a little overdressed," he grins while he pulls the straps of my dress off, exposing my fully lace, white bra. It's one that I can only wear with certain fabrics. Everything is visible and Liam appears to be fine with that. "God, you're magnificent."

His mouth descends on my breasts, and he licks me through the fabric. The heat from his tongue against the friction from the lace is too much. I moan and quiver as he moves to the other. The cool air breezing through is blissful agony as it hits the wetness on my skin.

"Liam, please." I beg for what, I don't know . . . more of him, more of us, more of this.

He doesn't let up as he drags the strap of my bra down and alternates between each breast. Bringing me higher and higher. His teeth scrape across my nipples, and I claw at his back. I'm going out of my mind. Finally, he removes my bra and sucks hard, pulling my taut nipple into his mouth.

I'm so lost to his touch that when his finger presses against my clit, I cry out. He pushes and swirls, applying pressure at the right times.

"I'm gonna come," I say, breathless.

"Not yet," he replies and lifts up.

I nearly weep with need. He sits on his knees and removes my dress, leaving me in my underwear. My eyes travel his body until I meet his eyes. Liam looks down and tears my underwear off then removes his pants. He stands there at the edge of the bed with his erection begging to be touched. I shift onto my knees and press his lips to mine. My hand travels down and grips him. I pump him slowly while we devour each other's mouths.

Liam's hands travel my body as he fondles my breasts, paying extra attention to my already sensitive nipples. I moan and his mouth moves to my neck as he nips at the skin by my ear. My hand releases him, and I press against his chest as I climb off the bed. He looks at me before I drop to my knees.

He groans before I even touch him. I smile and keep watching him watching me. My mouth opens, and I take him between my lips. Liam's head falls back with a deep sigh. His fingers thread in my hair as my hands grip his ass.

"Fucking hell. Your mouth . . ." he mumbles as I glide his cock to the back of my throat. Every muscle in his body tenses, and I repeat the motion. "Natalie, I can't. You're going to make me. I-I . . ."

I take joy in the fact that he can't form a coherent sentence. My fingers snake around and grasp him while using my mouth to perform the same motion. His hand grips my hair harder, and he pulls my mouth off him.

"The only place I'm going to finish is inside of you. Get off your knees."

I stand, and he lifts me into his arms. Even though

we're only a foot away from the bed, he carries me there. Liam places me down and crawls on top of me. My love for him swells and overwhelms me. "I love you, Liam Dempsey."

Liam stares at me and closes his eyes. When they open he looks at peace as if the world just righted itself. "I love you, Natalie. More than my own life."

"Make love to me," I request.

As if abandoning his plan, Liam settles between my legs and then enters me. The emotions engulf me. I never want this to end. He's going to leave soon, and I'll have to hold on to this in the days where it's hard. I try to take myself back years when this was the life I lived. When the last kiss could be my last kiss. The times where loneliness could annihilate me if I let it—and I can't let it. I have to hold on to this feeling when he's gone.

"I'll never be able to leave you again," he tells me. "Now that I've had you again, I can't walk away."

Liam thrusts harder as I cling to his shoulders. "Good."

"You fucking own me and you're mine."

He pushes deeper inside of me and my orgasm builds. "Liam," I whimper.

It astounds me how attuned we are in every way. He knows my heart, soul, and body. He can elicit pleasure from every fiber in my body. He flips us so I'm on top.

"Ride me, sweetheart."

I rock back and forth, my hands resting on his chest. I climb higher with each bit of friction. My eyes close as I lose myself in the moment. My orgasm takes me over the cliff and I fall. Liam holds my hips as he follows me over, and we ride out the moment together.

My chest falls to his and I smile against him. Being in his arms is everything I want.

But he leaves soon.

I stop myself from going there. If I start preparing

for goodbye, I won't enjoy the time we have.

Liam's hands glide up and down my back as we remain connected. I lift my chin and rest it on my hand. "Hi," I beam.

"Hi yourself," his smile mirrors mine.

"This was quite a way to welcome me to South Carolina."

He chuckles and pushes my hair from my face. "I'm happy to welcome you any time."

I start to get up, but he pulls me back against him. "I need to clean myself."

"No point. I'm going to enjoy making you dirty again," he says as his hands drift to my ass. He lifts a tiny amount and rolls me onto my back. "I told you this was going to be a long day."

His lips press against mine and we get lost in each other once more.

"WHAT TIME IS our flight tomorrow?" I ask Liam as we walk along the harbor with his arm slung around my shoulder.

He sighs and kisses my temple. "Too early. I'd like you to stay with me and see me off. I know that's asking a lot, but if it's possible, I want your face to be the last thing I see before I get on that plane."

We stop and I turn into his arms. "I don't know if I can."

Aaron used to ask me the same thing, but I never could. There was something about having to say goodbye in front of everyone that was too much. I tried once and driving home was a nightmare. I ended up sitting in my car for almost an hour sobbing as the plane took off. You feel so helpless watching the one thing you want more than anything possibly leaving you forever. It's heartbreak and fear on overload.

"I don't understand."

"I can't watch you leave and then have to keep it together. I don't know if I can handle it," I admit. I hold back the rest of my concerns because I know he can't worry about it. He needs to be focused, and my fears will only weigh him down.

Liam rubs my arms and stays quiet. "Then we'll say goodbye at my apartment. I don't want you to drive if you're going to be upset."

"Of course I'm going to be upset. You're leaving for six months. We're barely at a secure place in our relationship," letting more out than I planned.

Liam grabs my hand as we sit on the bench with the water behind us. "There's a lot I worry about with leaving. Aaron is living in the house and I won't be around. I worry it'll be easy for you both to fall back into your old life. I wonder if when I'm gone you'll think it's too much." He looks at our hands, and I follow his gaze.

His fears are valid. We have a lot of obstacles in our way, but small holes of doubt will only leave gaping issues. There are no guarantees. Neither of us can assure the other that the fears we are struggling with aren't real.

"I worry you won't make it home. That I'll be dealing with this all over again," I huff. "We're quite a pair."

"I'll do everything I can to be sure I come home to you."

"I promise to handle things with Aaron so we can move forward."

We both stay silent as we make the only promises we can to each other. They aren't concrete and I can only assume mine doesn't give him great comfort. I refuse to make things worse for him, but I can't lie.

"How do we do this, Lee? I may sound like a fucking idiot, but I don't know how to do a deployment with someone at home."

I sometimes forget that in a way we're both learning all over again. Liam hasn't ever had to think about the consequences of his actions at home. I've heard from Aaron and Quinn how he's the risk taker. While he never gambles with anyone else's life, he's more than willing to put himself in danger for the success of the mission.

My head rests on his chest while I try to form the right words. "Well, you focus on coming home, I guess. We email, Skype, write letters, and you call when you can."

"Do we get to naughty Skype?" he asks and raises his brow.

I start to giggle and slap his leg. "You're so stupid."

"Imagine how fun it would be . . ." he trails off with a glimmer in his eye.

"We'll have to see how well you behave," I toy with him.

I nestle back into his chest and try not to let my worries get too far ahead of me. *He'll be safe and he'll come home.* That's going to be my new mantra, because otherwise I'll lose my mind.

"I'll do my best to keep in touch with you. You know once we go to wherever we're needed, I won't be able to, but I'll do everything I can to let you know it's coming. It just depends on how long we'll be in Germany before heading to whatever hellhole we're needed in," he says before kissing the top of my head.

"Yeah, last time Aaron went to Germany he was only on a mission for two weeks. It's so hard for most wives to understand these new deployments. I mean, just send you guys from here. I hated when he'd be gone for what felt like no reason." Liam stays quiet and I wonder if I've upset him. I lean up and see him looking off. "Liam?"

He looks back and gives a small smile. "I know you were married to him. I get it, but right now, it feels different when you talk about your life with him. Maybe I'm a prick, but before when we thought he was dead, it didn't feel like I was competing as much as I am now."

"You weren't then, and you aren't now." My voice rings strong with honesty.

"I'm having to adjust to the fact that when you think of him, he's sleeping in your house."

"I can't just kick him out. Regardless of what he did and who I choose, he's Aarabelle's father. He's been through hell and back, and he was my husband," I speak the words measuredly. I know he's not asking me to kick him out, and I can't imagine how hard this is for Liam.

"This is why I thought we should take a break during the deployment," Liam says and lets out a heavy sigh.

I sit up and wait for him to turn his gaze back to me. "Is that what you need?"

He waits and closes his eyes. "I don't know. I don't want that. I honestly don't know how the fuck I'm going to be thousands of miles away and not wonder."

"Do you trust me?" I ask.

Liam grips my hand and tangles his fingers with mine. "I trust you, Lee. But I'm a guy and you being in a house with another guy—one that wants you back—is a lot to carry. Imagine knowing I was going to be with someone I loved once."

I glance at our intertwined fingers and decide that I have to make this easier for him. We both have a lot of fears we're dealing with and the only thing worse than not being with him is having something happen to him. I would never be able to handle that again. If he were to not make it back home, it would be the end of my heart.

"Maybe we can have tomorrow's goodbye be easier on both of us?"

"How?"

"Know that I love you and every moment you're away you have half my heart with you. And when you come home, you'll make me whole again. I don't want you to worry about Aaron, and we'll handle everything so when you come home we can move forward," I say with conviction. I need him to believe me, because it's the truth.

Liam links his fingers with mine. "I'm a lucky son of a bitch."

"Yeah, you are," I joke with him. "There's a part of me I never knew was missing until you came along. I thought I had it all. I really believed my life was perfect because it was easier than seeing the cracks. If things hadn't happened the way they did, I wouldn't know a love like this exists. I wish we could be . . ." I pause as I remember how hard this is for him. "I just want you home already."

"And when I come back, if you still want me, then I'll do everything in the world to make you mine."

I press my fingers against his cheek. "I look forward to that."

"Me too."

CHAPTER FOURTEEN

LIAM

"READY, ASSHOLE?" QUINN slaps my back as Natalie and I stand here looking at each other. "Wheels up in ten."

I nod and grip her hands. Even though she didn't want to come to the airport, she said she couldn't leave me at the apartment. This is the first time I'll leave someone behind. Even though we are in a good place, it feels like I'm leaving my life behind. She's everything I need. I love her more than I can ever explain. All I can do is pray when I get home, she'll be fully ready to move forward. And if she chooses *him,* then I'll know what six months apart feels like. Maybe that'll make it more bearable.

I'm fooling myself, but I know we'll be called up and I need to be ready. It's not just my ass on the line, it's the men in my team.

"Hey," she says drawing my attention back. "I'm going to miss you." A tear forms, but she wipes it before it can fall.

"No tears. You'll make me have to kiss you." I try to joke and lighten the moment.

Her laugh is short and then she looks down. "Maybe I should cry then."

"Lee," I pull her chin toward me. Her blue eyes look

gray and hollow. "You have no idea how much I'm going to wish I was here with you. Usually, I love deployments, but I can already tell I'm going to hate this one."

Her perfect lips attempt to smile. "I need to say this," she hesitates. "If you . . . I mean . . . if you get lonely . . ." She gnaws on her bottom lip and looks away, but I turn her face back.

"If I get lonely?" I know what she wants to say, but I'm going to make her say the words. First, it's keeping my mind off the fact that I'm going to touch her lips for the last time in a few minutes. Second, it's kind of cute.

"Just tell me. Please don't let me find out the other way. If you meet someone and you fall in love or whatever . . ."

"If I get lonely, how about I call or email you?"

Her eyes snap up. "That would work."

"Good," I say and lean down so she hears me clearly. "No one is going to fill the void of you. There's no woman in the world that will be able to make me forget you." I hope she hears the conviction in my words, because there's no one else. Selfishly, I want to add on, "Unlike your husband."

The announcement comes over, "Three minutes. Say your goodbyes."

Natalie's chin quivers, and her hands grip my shirt. "I hate this."

"I do too, but remember our trip. Remember what I said. I love you."

She pulls me close against her and my arms are locked around her. I want to hold on to how it feels right now. When the nights get long and I need to feel peace, I want to have this moment. And if God forbid she decides she can't do this again . . .

"Be safe, be smart, and please come home to me," Natalie says quickly. "I love you, Liam. You can't even begin to know how much you own my heart. I wish this were different right now. I wish you had no doubt that you're who I want, but I'll prove it. I'll show you that in six months when you come home, I'll be standing here waiting for you." Tears fall and once again my heart breaks.

"And then I'm going to marry you."

"I'm going to hold you to it."

"I'll call you as soon as I can," I promise.

She nods and presses her lips to me. "Okay."

"And then we can naked Skype," I smile.

She shakes her head and kisses me again. "You can keep your eggroll in your pants."

"And I'll be home as soon as I can," I assure her.

Natalie eyes lock with me as I bend to kiss her. "Not soon enough." Another tear falls and my throat dries.

Fuck. How the hell am I supposed to get on that damn plane? This was a bad idea and I should've listened to her. Walking away is going to break me. It's my job, and usually I'm the first on that plane, but I can't get my arms to release her.

I look over and see my men grabbing their bags and a few guys starting to head toward the plane. It's time. I have to let her go.

"I gotta go, sweetheart," I say gently.

I expect a scene. Her crying or unwilling to let me go, but I watch a shift happen in her face. She straightens a little straighter. Natalie's entire demeanor morphs into strength and determination. It's the same as when we're ready to head out. We shut down the emotional side and are ready to battle. There's no place for pussies during missions.

"I know," she smiles and releases my uniform then pats it down. "Okay, we got this."

I pull her hips closer one more time and kiss her with everything. I press against her lips as she opens her mouth and I dive in. I need to taste her, feel her, and make her remember how much I belong to her. Her arms wrap around my back and she moans. I'm kissing her like she's the only thing here. I hate myself for making her think we should be apart. I wish everything were different, but it's not, so I give her all I can right now.

"Let's go!" I hear Commander call out.

We break apart, and I rest my forehead on hers. I can't look at her eyes again or I'm not going to be able to get on that fucking plane.

"Come home to me, Liam. Please, just come home," she pleads and I nod.

I bow down and grab my sea bag. This is it.

"I'll see you soon."

I keep my eyes on the ground, and I hear her breath catch.

Don't look. Just get on the plane.

"I'll count the days." Her voice is soft and quiet, but I hear her. I think I could hear her voice even if there were a crowd of people yelling. She calls to me on every level.

With my arms full, I turn and head toward the plane. Two other guys are beside me with the same faces. We're ready, but this blows. There's no happiness getting here, but this is our jobs. We signed up for this, and we serve with pleasure. But no one ever told me this is the other side of this shit.

I'm leaving the woman I love in the arms of her husband. This is so fucked up. But she's not mine fully. I have to use this time to figure out if we have a chance. The life we're both entering into if we stay together is complicated, and there are a lot of people's lives at stake. Aarabelle being number one. I know she's Natalie's primary concern.

As I round the corner, I can't stop myself from looking back. She stands with her long, blonde hair pulled over her shoulder, her arms are clutched in front of her as she watches me walk away. I lift my chin and her hand lifts a little. Then she presses her fingers against her lips and blows me a kiss.

Right there . . . she just broke me.

chapter fifteen

natalie

I STAND HERE as he turns the corner before allowing myself to truly feel what just happened. My body is stiff, and my chest heaves. His desert camouflage uniform is taut and he adjusts his cover. How I wish I could trade it for his jeans and beanie. It would mean he wasn't putting his life in danger. But that's not who he is, and I knew this. Doesn't make it any easier because my heart is sitting on a plane.

This is pure hell.

Reanell walks over and places her hand on my shoulder. "Each time I promise myself I'll stay home, yet I can't stay away." I turn with tears in my eyes as we both grab each other and hold on.

"I hate this. I forgot how much I hate this." I cry against her shoulder, and she stains my shirt with her tears.

She sniffs, "I never really forget, I just block it out." Rea pulls back.

"How can I miss him so much already?"

"Because you love him. As soon as Mason walks away, I start to yearn for him," she says longingly.

I know what she means. "It's like we know we *can't* have them, so we want them even more."

She nods, "I always want him home, but it feels like even when he's home we're gearing up for our next deployment."

"Sometimes even when they're not active it feels like that," I muse. I think my life was worse once Aaron chose to separate from the military. While he wasn't deploying anymore, a part of him was missing.

Rea turns to me and points to the plane. "Those men, they're built differently. They love differently, and they need different things. We're the same way. This is the life we know, and while some may not understand it . . . we do. Our love is stronger than most couples, and you and Liam are no different."

I see Liam enter the plane and the door shut behind him. I want to run and kiss him one more time, but I know it won't ever be enough. There will always be times of missed moments we could've had. She's right though, we love differently, and we accept that our lives aren't up to us.

"How do I do this as the girlfriend?" I ask Reanell. I've always been the wife. I was privy to the information and the support. As a girlfriend or whatever I am, I have no rights.

She snorts, "I'm the Commander's wife, Lee. Any information, you know I'm not going to keep it from you."

"I need to go," I murmur. She looks at me perplexed. "I can't watch the plane leave. There's no way I can."

Reanell nods in understanding. It's one thing for me to be here to see him off, but watching his plane take off, that goes beyond my limit. I've tried in the last hour to put myself back to what I used to be. The military wife in me is rusty, and I know I need to dig deeper. I need to be the strong, silent partner and keep his mind as free as I can. It's one of the parts I loathed. Being angry or upset, but needing to be happy and cheery when they call.

I learned very quickly how to mask my feelings and all the things that went wrong when Aaron was gone. I had to be a somewhat less creepy version of a Stepford wife.

I smile as I unlock the door to Robin. I sit in the driver's seat and find myself grinning. He drove her here, so I get to drive her home. My eyes close as I inhale deeply. It smells of Liam, and if I try hard enough, I can almost feel him here.

"Okay, Robin . . . let's see why he's so protective of you," I say to the car and decide I need therapy.

I look over at the passenger seat and there's a note with a rose. I smile and try not to break down in tears.

Sweetheart,

You have my heart and now you have my car. Take care of both until I get home.

love,

liam

A small laugh escapes me as I start the car. The drive back to my house is a blur. I try to focus on the joy that awaits me. I haven't seen Aarabelle in seventy-two hours, and I missed her desperately.

I open the door and she looks up. "Mamama!" she calls out and my heart swells with love.

"Hi, baby girl!" I call out and rush toward her. I scoop her in to my arms and nestle her close. "I missed you so much."

"Hey," Aaron's voice is low and gruff. "You okay?"

I turn, wondering if he's being serious or sarcastic. I decide serious. "I'm okay, thanks." The small act of kindness means a lot to me. This is the Aaron I always tried to remember.

"The team get off okay?"

"Yeah," I smile.

Aaron shifts his weight as Aarabelle pushes against me to get down. "Good. I'm glad." He looks away awkwardly, and my chest hurts. This is hard for him, and I wish it didn't have to be. It's hard for me too if I'm being honest.

None of these issues are easy for anyone. It really sucks being an adult.

"How was she?" I ask, looking at her as she runs over to her toys.

He smiles and gazes at her. "She was great. Your parents left about an hour ago. They said they needed to get on the road. She's amazing, Lee. You did such a good job with her."

I try to fight the tears, but they come flooding forward. Between Liam's farewell and then this . . . it's too much. "I'm sorry," I say trying to gain control.

Aaron's arms are around me in a heartbeat. "It'll be okay," he comforts me, and I push back gently.

"Aaron," I pause, "You don't have to comfort me. This isn't fair to you. I'm so sorry."

I shouldn't be crying in his arms. I won't be that girl. This is no place for the weak. My emotions need to be better managed.

"I did a lot of thinking this weekend," Aaron says as we move toward the couch. Aarabelle lifts her block and then shows me the other ones.

"Yeah?" I ask, watching my daughter in admiration.

"I realized how bad I fucked up. Lying to you, cheating on you, it isn't the way it was supposed to be."

This isn't exactly the conversation I feel like we've been having lately. "What are you saying?"

"I'm saying I get it. I sat here this weekend knowing you were with him, and it fucked with my head. But if I didn't know and thought you were on some girls' weekend or something and found out, I'd kill someone."

I sigh and wish this could've waited a little, but it's the first time I feel he's being sincerely honest. "The issue was the lies. You lied about Brittany. You lied about the baby, and then you went so far as to tell me it was a one-time thing. That's not the man I loved. You and I had issues, big issues . . . but they weren't something we couldn't have tackled. We didn't talk though, and it cost us everything."

Aaron looks at Aara. "She's the best thing we ever did."

My lips turn up as I look at the reason for my existence. "Yeah, she is." My eyes prick in sorrow. "It's hard for me to know you were willing to throw it all away." I look over at him and see him nod.

"You and I fought so much. It wasn't a good time for either of us. Do you remember how much you hated me?"

Both of our guards are down, and we owe each other the honesty. "I didn't hate you, I just didn't like you. You were so angry all the time. Everything I did or said turned into an argument. Right now, you love Aarabelle and for that I'm so happy, but when I found out I was pregnant with her . . . you walked out."

He stares at her and then turns to me. "I wanted her for you. But there was a huge part of me that worried how you'd ever survive the loss of another baby. So the pregnancy was another way I thought I'd lose my wife. And in a small way I didn't think we deserved her."

It's heartbreaking how two people who genuinely loved each other can go so far off track. I had my fault in this. I pushed him away and made everything in our world revolve around getting pregnant. It was the only thing I could focus on most of the time. But I did try to be there with him. I never stopped loving him, and I couldn't imagine seeking out another person. Aaron isn't a bad guy, he made bad choices.

"Instead of talking to me though, you sought out

another woman?"

"You know how you're torn apart right now? You probably feel like you're split in two. I know you love me, Natalie. I see how you want to hate me, but you can't. We have a child, a life, and memories." He takes my hand in his.

I look over at Aaron with watery eyes. "I'm begging you, please don't do this to me today."

My emotions are everywhere and today . . . I just can't. It's a conversation we could have tomorrow or the next day, because today my heart hurts. I miss Liam. I had to see him off, and it's too much to process this heavy of a discussion.

"I've spent a year away, baby. I know who I want, and maybe with Liam away, we can find our way back. He's not able to interfere and you'll see I'm where your heart really is."

"You couldn't give me today? You had to say it . . ." I'm not even angry just hurt.

It was selfish to come at me about this today. He knows my defenses are down, and he's fighting dirty. I don't need selfish . . . I need strong. I deserve someone who's going to take my feelings into account. With Aaron it's all about him. He saw the opportunity before him and tried to break me. Liam may not be here, but that doesn't mean my heart and soul aren't filled with him.

"Lee," he squeezes my hand and I pull it back. "I just figured . . ."

"You figured he's gone and you have an opening. Knowing what it feels like to leave behind people you love and what he must be feeling. You've spoken to me the day after you left. You know how sad I was. This," I point between us, "isn't what we're discussing today. I can't even possibly think about us. So please, don't be a self-centered asshole for today and let me put myself together."

I stand, grab Aarabelle, and head into the kitchen. Too bad it's not even noon or I'd contemplate a damn drink.

THE ROUTINE OVER the next few weeks after Liam leaves is exhausting. I email every morning, usually I can catch him online and then we Skype. Seeing his face makes those days a lot easier. I don't have to imagine the angles of his face or the way his jaw curves at just the right place. His blue eyes are the perfect color of crystal blue and the full-blown beard he sports makes me melt.

He's there on my screen, alive and smiling.

"Hi," I smile coyly.

"How are you, sweetheart?" Liam asks rolling onto his side. His shirt is off and he's been doing that a lot lately. Not that I mind.

"Better now." I sound like a lovesick twit. Which I guess I am.

Liam smiles and stretches, giving me a full view of his chest and abs. "Me too. Seeing you is the highlight of my day."

"Put a shirt on."

"Take yours off."

I deadpan and wait for him to laugh, but he just raises a brow. "Fine," I reply playfully and take off my top. I have my cute bra on and he leans in close as if that'll help him see better.

"Bra . . ."

"Not happening, buddy."

He huffs, "You get to see my chest, it's only fair."

I reach behind my back and then Aarabelle screams on the monitor. I laugh and sit up. "Looks like Aara has other plans. No dirty Skype session for you."

"Ugh," he groans and flops back. "Go get her, I want

to see her too."

I smile and get my shirt back on, "I'll be right back."

Liam nods and I rush into Aarabelle's room. Aaron usually sleeps in the spare bedroom off to the right, but the last two nights he hasn't come back. He's been sleeping at Mark's, or so he says.

"Wanna see Liam?" I ask her as she bounces holding onto her crib. She smiles and gives me my morning kisses.

"Aarabelle!" he exclaims and now is suddenly in a shirt.

She smiles and presses her hand by the screen. "Dadada," she calls him and looks at me still beaming.

"Hi, beautiful! She's getting bigger."

"Yeah, she and I are both apparently gaining weight," I laugh. I swear I've always been an emotional eater, but this is ridiculous.

"You're both beautiful," Liam says as Aarabelle tries to touch him through the computer.

"Dada, up?" she says with her arms raised.

"Awww, she wants you to pick her up." I smile at how much Aarabelle connects with Liam. She calls Aaron the same name but she still won't lie with him.

He tries and he's a good father. Aaron is always here to put her to bed with me. He's genuinely trying to be a part of her daily routine.

"I wish I could, pumpkin." Liam's face drops a little like the air was let out. It's hard for all of us, but I can't imagine knowing your family is home and living their lives while you're gone. I hear some commotion behind him. "I gotta go, Quinn and Barnes just got here. I'm going to be down-range soon." He looks at me, and I get what he's trying to say.

He's going on a mission and won't be able to talk.

"Okay, stay safe."

"Always, sweetheart. I'll be in touch soon. Bye,

Aarabelle."

She waves goodbye and he blows her a kiss.

"I love you," I say with my hand hesitant over the disconnect button.

"I love you, we'll talk soon," Liam says and ends the call.

I look over at Aarabelle who stares at the screen with her head tilted. "Dada," she says looking back at me.

"Liam had to go bye-bye. Let's go baby girl. Mommy's gotta work."

I take her into my arms and get ready to start our day. On the days I do get to see him, it's harder to pretend I don't miss him so much. When he's on the screen, I don't feel like he's so far away. He's in our house, in my room, but I wish he knew that he's always in my heart.

chapter sixteen

"COME ON, LEE. I need a reliable gym partner." Reanell tries to pry me off the couch. The last thing I want to do is work out.

"Not this again. We barely lasted a week the last time."

"When Mason gets back, I want him to see I have a nicely toned ass."

She's ridiculous. Reanell has one of the best bodies out of anyone I know. She eats like crap and yet somehow manages to stay looking like a swimsuit model.

"Go away." I lie back down on the couch so she can't get me up so easily. I'm not sleeping well again. I have horrible dreams of Liam being hurt where I wake screaming. Last night was so bad that Aaron came in to check on me. I was crying and flailing around.

Reanell lifts my legs and sits under me. "Still not sleeping?"

"Nope. Last night was the worst."

"You know if I knew anything, I'd tell you. OpSec be damned. Mason told me all the cocks would soon be in the henhouse. So that's good."

We all speak in code. Operational Security is top priority when they're gone. It's one thing for the enemy to catch them because of whatever, but if it was because they heard somehow from our end, it would be unforgivable.

Previously, Aaron and I had words that would alert one of us to where or what was happening.

It gave me a sense of solace through the dark times. It's hard not knowing where or how long, and many of us have our ways of giving just enough information to keep each other calm. When they are deployed to Germany, you know they'll be called out. But when you talk daily and then nothing . . . you can't help but be scared.

"Mason needs a better phrase than 'cocks in the henhouse,'" I giggle.

"He knows I like when he talks dirty to me."

Aaron heads down the stairs slowly. "Hey."

"Good morning." I look at the clock. His schedule is completely off course. He can only sleep in small intervals, so he naps throughout the day. The doctors told him to rest and take it easy. He has counseling three times a week and physical therapy the same days.

"Mark is on his way over and we're heading out for a while."

Reanell slaps my leg and hops up. "I'm going to run. I'll swing by and grab you tomorrow for the gym since you're obviously not going today. But tomorrow—no bullshit."

"Fine. Whatever." I watch Aaron as he stares out the window. Sometimes he looks so lost and it shreds me apart inside. I wish I wasn't responsible for some of it.

Reanell opens the door and gasps. "You're fucking kidding me, right?"

I turn to look and see Brittany standing in our doorway.

I don't move or speak. I wait to see what he does. I've made it abundantly clear that we're not together, so Aaron has a right to do what he pleases. But I can't deny this hurts. For the first time, I can truly empathize with what he must've felt seeing me with Liam.

They're both standing there looking at each other.

Brittany has tears in her eyes and she waits.

"I'm sorry. I heard and I just needed to see if they were lying," Brittany tries to explain as she looks at me, then Aaron again.

"You shouldn't be here," he says from behind me.

"You're alive and . . ." The hurt rings loudly in her soft voice.

I grab my cup sitting on the table and start to head into the kitchen. I don't want to watch this, and I don't want to hear their conversation. It's too much. I may love Liam and want to be with him, but I can't sit here and look at Aaron with another woman.

Aaron grips my arm as I pass by stopping me. "Stay," he demands. I look at him and he doesn't take his eyes off me. We stand here as she waits at the door of our home.

"I can't."

"Because you still love me."

"Because I don't want to watch you with her. Because she represents the tear in our lives."

His hand releases my arm but travels to my wrist. "I didn't call or get a hold of you because I'm trying to win my wife back." Aaron's voice doesn't shake. He's strong and in control for the first time.

Brittany whimpers slightly, "I heard and I waited for you."

I close my eyes and try to fight back the urge to scream.

"I'm sorry I hurt you."

"Sorry?" she screams. "Sorry you loved me?"

Aaron releases my wrist. "No," his voice softens a little. "We shouldn't have been together. I fucked everything up for both of you."

"So you're going to choose her? What about the fact that she was with someone else?"

I keep my back turned because I'm barely holding on. All of the pain resurfaces. The lies and mistrust that hang heavy between Aaron and me. The nights I spent sobbing on the floor and waiting for him to come home. Times his aloofness left me wondering, but now I know—he was with her.

"She always would've been my choice."

"You two need to talk," I say and Aaron grabs my arm again.

"You're a liar! You told me we were going to build a life together! You promised you'd leave her, and what? Now you want to play the doting husband?" I turn and see her face. Her hands are in tight fists hanging at her side. She looks at me and then back to him. "Was it her name you were screaming when you made our baby? No. So, fuck you and your bullshit apology," Brittany cries and my pain streams down my face.

"Am I at your house?" Aaron yells at her.

"God, you selfish prick. You told me we would get married. You told me she was cold and barren. You said I was the warmth you needed and that I gave you something you never knew you were missing. I loved you. I gave you what you said you couldn't live without." Brittany's voice is loud and full of hurt.

I hate her. I hate her for making me hear this. I hate Aaron for holding me here against my will.

"You two are the most selfish people I know. You deserve each other!" I cry out and Aaron's arm drops. "How dare you come to my house? How dare you hold me here and make me hear this? This isn't love. This is destruction. You don't hurt people you love over and over," I spit the words at him. "And you," I turn my attention to Brittany. "You just can't stop, can you? It's not enough to ruin me twice, you needed to come back for the knockout punch? Is there a place you won't hurt me? You slept with my husband, you got pregnant, and then when he doesn't choose you . . . you come here. You want him? Have him!" I say and run up the stairs.

"Natalie, wait!" Aaron calls after me, but I keep going.

In the confines of my room, I pray I don't have to hear anymore. The baby is what gets me every time. It's the one part of everything, no matter what, I couldn't forgive him for. I know it's not for lack of trying that we didn't conceive naturally, but they did.

A few minutes later Aaron opens the door. "Get out," I say dejectedly.

"Lee, please."

"No, I didn't need to see that."

He steps further into the room that was once ours. "I needed you to see. She isn't my choice."

"Aaron, you don't get it." I look out the window and let out a deep sigh. "She isn't the issue, it's us. Yes, we were going through so much with trying to get pregnant that I think somewhere in there we both broke apart. I wasn't the woman you remembered, and you weren't the man I needed. We failed each other. But instead of either of us talking about it, you went off and slept with her."

He sits quietly at the edge of the bed. I'm not angry. I'm just over it.

"Not only did you have sex with someone else, you had an affair. A full blown I'm leaving my wife and having a baby affair." It reminds me of the second part of my argument. "Then you lied—again. You got back and told me it was *one* time."

Aaron turns slightly and grabs my hand, but I snatch it back. "I knew I'd lost you."

"Don't you think we both deserve to be happy?"

"That's all I want. I want us to be the way we used to be," Aaron admits.

I wish he would understand me.

"We can't ever be those people again. I'm not the same woman you married. I've gone through a lot. Learned a lot about who I am and what I want in life. I want a man to stand beside me and walk through the fire holding my hand. I want a man who, even though we're not even dating, will leave a woman to come to my side at the hospital. Who will sit with me when I need it. Hold me when I cry and give me love even when it hurts us."

I stand and walk to the nightstand. I see the scrap of paper that came out of his clothing during my rampage. "I found this," I say as I hand it over.

Aaron takes the paper and his eyes darken. "I was leaving you."

"And you did that day." I hold on to the back of the dresser feeling a little dizzy. Today has been crazy and I still haven't eaten.

"I never gave it to you. I couldn't."

The words hang in the air between us, but they have to be said. The guilt of being the person to say them weighs heavily on me. "We need to separate. I need to move forward with my life."

Aaron stands and takes my hand. "I never did this to hurt you."

"How did you think it wouldn't? Being pregnant while you had your mistress pregnant? Or sleeping with her and then coming home and telling me about how our child would finally be here? If you didn't want to hurt me, you shouldn't have kept going back. But here's the thing—I love Liam. I know that's so incredibly hurtful to you, but he's who I want to be with."

I could go further to tell him all the reasons why Liam and I are meant to be, but it wouldn't help heal us. And for Aarabelle's sake, we need to be civil, and truth be told, he's been my best friend since I was a kid. Aaron knows about the first time I snuck out of the house and drank. He was the one who taught me how to drive a car. He carried me down the street when I fell and broke my leg. In his arms I remember thinking how we'd always be together.

I was young and naïve. It doesn't diminish my memories, but it was an immature way of thinking.

"And if you and Liam weren't together?"

I take his other hand in mine. "I would still be saying goodbye. I can't get past the images of you two. I can't forget the pain I endured alone during all of that. Wondering if you left after I told you about Aarabelle to go to her. These are the thoughts I play over and over. I can't live like that. Then there's the fact that even when you had all the time in the world to come back, be a different man . . . you didn't. You lied to me—repeatedly."

Aaron releases my hands and holds my face. "I'll never know how I was able to do it to you."

I hold his wrists and pull his hands down. "I'm not angry. I will always be your friend."

My head starts to spin and I wobble a little.

"Whoa, are you okay?" Aaron asks, but everything sounds far away.

"I don't feel good." I sit on the bed and the room spins a little. "I think my blood sugar is low."

"I'll get you some juice." Aaron leaves the room and I lie here thinking about all that's happened the last few weeks. Him being alive, Liam and I dealing with the aftermath, Liam deploying, and now Brittany.

He returns and I sip the juice. I need to do better at taking care of myself. All of this stress is going to wear me down.

"Aaron?" I pull his attention back to me. "I want you to know I don't hate you. Maybe if things had unfolded differently we wouldn't be able to talk like this. But in a way, you being gone might have saved a lifelong friendship."

He sits beside me. "I lost myself before the explosion. I loved you, but it was almost hard to come home. I would look at you and it was like we weren't Aaron and Natalie. Does that make sense?"

I nod, "I get it. When you died, I blocked it all out. I literally couldn't remember how bad things were. I needed to only remember how much I loved you and how wonderful you were. Then, it all came undone."

"I think I'll move out this weekend. I've been putting it off, but I can't keep doing this. I'll always love you, Natalie." Aaron lifts his hand and then drops it.

I smile sadly. This is harder than I expected. I know where my heart lies, but having this conversation is immensely sad. The strings that tied us together will be snipped by our own choices. This isn't death where you feel robbed of your decisions. "You'll always have a place in my heart. And you'll always be a part of Aarabelle's life."

He leans in and kisses the top of my head. The pain in his eyes breaks me a little more. Aaron doesn't speak as he exits the room, and when the door shuts, I grab my pillow and cry for the marriage I just lost again.

chapter seventeen

"I'VE GOT A few things on the calendar I need to make sure we're ready for," Mark says in his command voice.

We had a small issue on the mission in Kuwait. Some of the guys had rounds missing that I know for a fact I ordered. It reminds us all of the problems that led to Aaron's explosion and Jackson's shooting. All of us are on edge and double-checking everything. There've been two more things that seemed fishy, but we caught them before anything could happen.

"I don't know what the fuck is going on, but until we do, everyone is on their 'A' game. I want nothing overlooked, and if you have to check it ten times, then do it. I won't have another life lost on our watch."

Everyone nods and starts to filter out.

"Lee, can you hold up a minute?" Mark asks.

"What's up?"

"I want to run a few things by you and make sure we're all on the same page."

I tilt my head wondering where he could be going with this. "Okay?"

"We want to bring Aaron back to work. His doctors think he needs to establish some kind of consistency, and I know it could be uncomfortable for you both, but . . ."

"I get it." I glance away and try to think about Aaron.

These are his friends and this was his job. I shouldn't feel disappointed, but I love it here.

"No, Sparkles . . ." Mark smiles and I roll my eyes. "I'm not asking you to step down."

"He deserves to be here," I say and place my hand on his arm. "I can find a job somewhere else."

"Fucking hell, woman." He grabs my shoulders and shakes me gently. "Are all of you this damn dense?"

"I know you're not talking to me like that." I widen my eyes and he smirks.

Mark has been strange the last few weeks. I haven't taken too much notice because I've been so out of it myself, but he's been irritable and very unlike him. He even mentioned going to spend time in Washington D.C. for a meeting with some top officials.

He speaks but everything suddenly goes tunnel vision. I feel lightheaded again and I try to grab the table. I'm going down.

"Lee?" I hear Mark call out.

But my hand is weak, and I fall to the ground. Then, everything goes black.

"We're on our way to the hospital." I hear Mark talking as I start to wake. "She's fine, she passed out."

I open my eyes and I'm being loaded into an ambulance. What the hell? "Mark," I grumble. I'm so tired.

He puts his phone in his pocket and grabs my hand. "You know if you wanted some attention, you just had to tell me."

I think I smile but I'm not sure. "What happened?"

"You went down. It wasn't long, but we want you to get checked out. And since the ambulance happened to be a block away, they got here really quick."

The EMT pushes Mark back a little then starts to take my vitals. "I need some information." He asks me all the basic questions and continues to ask about the frequency of the dizzy spells. He checks my sugar levels and asks if

I'm diabetic.

Once we arrive at the emergency room, I answer some questions before they start running some blood tests. I've been poked and prodded more than I care to know.

"So," Mark puts his feet on the edge of the bed and reclines back. "We can avoid burning vacation time if we talk work, and I'm all about making Jackson pay, so let's chat."

I shake my head and try to rest.

He nudges me with his foot. "I'm not kidding. I'm planning a giant vacation and I need all the time I can get. You're not dying, so it's billable hours."

"I'll call Jackson now if you want," I say as the room spins slightly.

The doctor walks in and smiles. "Hello, Mr. and Mrs. Gilcher. I wanted to go over the results of all your tests."

"Oh, he's not—" I start to say but Mark cuts me off.

"Comfortable in hospitals. My wifey here is concerned I will end up in a bed with her."

He's lost his damn mind. I stare at him, waiting for him to correct himself, but he grabs my hand and smiles. "For the love of God."

"She's just tired . . . please, Doctor." He pauses and kisses my hand.

I yank my hand back and slap the top of his. Idiot.

"Well, your blood tests came back and showed your blood sugar is low, but it also showed that you're pregnant."

My mouth falls slack and my heart rate accelerates. "No, that's not possible."

"Congratulations," she smiles.

Mark laughs loudly, snapping me out of my trance. "It was all my super sperm. Glitter and Sparkle, baby."

"Doctor, please can you run it again. It's not possible for me to be pregnant," I say urgently.

She looks at the chart and walks over to the side of my bed. My blood pressure is rising and she checks the wires. "I need you to calm down."

"Lee," Mark's voice morphs into concern. "It's okay."

"I can't be pregnant. You don't understand . . . I can't get pregnant. I had to go through five rounds of IVF to conceive. I lost four babies because of my PCOS. Please, I'm telling you it's not possible." The panic bubbles in my throat, and I start to hyperventilate.

The doctor places her hand on my shoulder. "Focus on breathing, Natalie. I can do a secondary blood test, but your HCG levels are high indicating you are in fact pregnant. I can have the OBGYN on call come in and check you over as well. Just rest, stay nice and calm, and we'll get everything settled."

I nod and try to do as she says. My hands settle on my stomach and tears form. I look over at Mark and he looks unsure. "All joking aside, are you okay?"

"No, I mean, if I'm pregnant . . ." I trail off thinking about what it means. Liam and I would be having a baby. Two men . . . two babies . . . one broken heart.

"I'm happy that we'll have a little Starlight." Mark tries to go for funny.

I look over unimpressed. "You do know we're not married and this is not your baby, right?"

Mark smirks, "I think you need to be happy and laugh. You went through hell trying to get pregnant before, and now you are without even trying. I know it's the worst timing possible, but maybe this is your time. Liam's my friend too, and all of this shit is going to be ugly, but you all need to do what's right so everyone can move forward." He grabs my hand, and the kind and compassionate jokester becomes the strong man. "I know I fuck around a lot, but I'm worried about all of you. You're passing out, Liam's overseas, and Aaron is a mess. He wasn't right before he went to Afghanistan, and Jackson and I failed to handle it."

"What do you mean?" I ask as he sits by my side.

"He wasn't himself. We all chalked it up to the fertility stuff or other stress at home. He didn't talk to us much on a good day," he laughs.

Aaron was always quiet. He lived in his head a lot because of the Navy, but even before that, he wasn't overly social. With me, it was a little different. We both knew what buttons to push and how to make the other lose it.

"After we got back from the mission where we lost Brian, Fernando, and Devon . . . I don't think any of us were right. I'm, you know . . . me," he pauses and I smile. "Jackson had Maddie, and we know he didn't handle it well, but Aaron was just quiet. I figured it was him dealing with it. I feel like we all failed each other."

Mark pours his heart out, and for the first time, I really try to see when it all happened. That mission destroyed and bonded the three of them. Aaron, Mark, and Jackson all left the Navy after that. Aaron was injured, but he finished his enlistment. He went through his therapy and never spoke about it. I just assumed he was dealing with it.

"I think I'm as much to blame for that. After all of that, having a baby became my only goal. If he died, I would have something of him," I sigh and look away.

"Forgive yourself, Lee. We all make choices and some of them aren't the best, but in the end, none of us are perfect. Aaron made some pretty shitty decisions, but you don't have to bear his demons—he has to," he squeezes my hand. "Now, about our beautiful bundle of joy . . ."

My hand rubs my stomach and I get choked up. "I don't even know if I can be pregnant, let alone carry. You have to promise me you'll keep your mouth shut." I look at him as fear begins to swirl. *If* I'm pregnant by some miracle, there's no guarantee I can carry full term.

He raises his hands. "I won't say a word."

"I'm serious. Liam has been out of touch a few days, and again, I don't think this is possible." I start to tremble.

"Hey," he wraps his arm around me. "Relax. We'll see what the doctor says and go from there."

I focus on staying calm and wait for the OBGYN to come for a consult. My mind wanders to Liam and how he'll feel about me being pregnant. We never used protection because I never thought this was a possibility. Mark stays with me, and of course, continues to drive me insane.

We talk about the investigation into Cole Security Forces and how he found something suspicious in the files. He explains how he'll be heading out of town a little more often to check on things.

"Charlie and I are working together on some leads," Mark says absently.

"Mrs. Gilcher, I'm Dr. Wynn." He enters and heads over with my chart. Mark stands and shakes his hand.

"I'm going to step out and call the office . . . let them know you're alive," Mark winks and I nod.

"Do you want to wait for your husband?" the doctor asks, looking perplexed at the fact he left.

I scoot up and shake my head. "No, he's just a friend."

"Okay, I ran your labs again and you are in fact pregnant," he confirms.

My lips turn and my heart races. I'm going to have a baby—Liam's baby. "I have a lot of history." I attempt to rein it in. The bottom line is that I've lost a hell of a lot more babies than I've given birth to. I know the pain that comes along with getting excited or being hopeful. I need to make sure I don't get too far ahead of myself.

I go over my past fertility issues and miscarriages. He listens patiently as I give details and start to get slightly emotional. I explain that the baby's father is overseas and how I need to be certain everything is okay. The big mystery is how pregnant am I. Because I don't have regular cycles, I could be a few weeks, or I could be a few months.

Dr. Wynn steps to the side of the bed. "Well, I'd like to do an ultrasound and see how far along you are. Then we can get you set up with your doctor, but at least we'll get a good idea today. Sound good?"

I brace myself and let out a deep shaky breath. This is it. "Let's do this."

CHAPTER EIGHTEEN

LIAM

"I'M JUST POINTING out you're whipped," Quinn razzes me as we unload the gear. It's been two weeks since I've heard her voice. Two long weeks where I've wondered and worried. All the damn shit I swore I wouldn't do.

Our simple in and out mission was of course delayed once we got boots on the ground. I'm tired, irritable, and need to see her.

"At least I'm not calling and going to voicemail."

Quinn shouldn't talk shit considering he's called Ashton at least five times and she refuses to answer. But the asshat keeps trying.

"She'll come around."

"Whatever . . . I'd rather be whipped than a pussy who can't get the girl."

He snuffs, "I am what I eat."

We both laugh and finish with the offload. Unfortunately, I still have a ton of shit to do before I can even be close to calling home. There's a stack of paperwork with my name on it.

After about three hours of mindless crap and a debrief with the Commander, I head back to my barracks. Luckily, I have my own room and don't have to deal with anyone. I want to sleep for days, but tomorrow we have another meeting for an upcoming mission and need to prepare.

I grab my phone and pray to God the Wi-Fi isn't going to give me shit today.

"Liam?" her voice is sleepy, and I would give my left nut to be able to touch her.

"Hi, sweetheart."

"Hi, are you okay?" she asks disoriented. I look at the clock for the first time and feel like shit. It's three a.m. her time.

"I'm sorry I woke you. I just got back to my room and missed you."

She groans and I picture her stretching. "I miss you. I'm awake."

"Go back to bed," I give her an out.

"Liam Dempsey, shut your face and talk to me."

"Kinda counterproductive there, isn't it?" I joke and smile, lying back down.

If I close my eyes, I can pretend I'm with her. The silence stretches between us as I imagine myself holding her.

"Everything okay?" Her quiet voice soothes me.

"Now it is."

The mission was one thing after another. And I'll be gone a lot more frequently as there's movement again in Africa. My team is the most ready to handle that region and the other team is already tasked to another area. I don't want to fucking think about it.

"Good." She sounds wary. "How long will we be in touch for?"

"Not long. I swear this deployment is going to destroy me," I admit to her. "I can't fucking handle the bullshit. Every time I get something in place, something goes wrong. My mind is all over the place, and I'm snapping at everyone. I swear one more person adds something to my plate, and I'm going to lose it."

"You seem overwhelmed." Her voice rings of defeat. But why?

"What's wrong, Lee?" Her long pause does nothing to calm me. I hear her sigh and my adrenaline spikes. "Natalie," I say, sitting up.

"Nothing's wrong. I'm fine."

"That word again." My voice is harsh, but I hate this. "Talk to me, sweetheart." I calm myself because she doesn't need to deal with my shit.

She lets out a deep breath. "I'm just missing you. Aaron moved out this week, and there's some stuff going on at the office."

Just the news of Aaron moving out of the house is enough to make me feel better. I would've never been the one to push it, but knowing he's gone will help me relax a little. The idea of him being there when I couldn't was killing me.

"How's he doing?" I wonder. No matter what, our friendship will never be the same. I could never look at him knowing he got the girl and I can't imagine he'll be calling me for a beer anytime soon. There is no way this can end well enough for either of us to the point where we can go back to what we were. If she picked him, I could never go around there. Looking at her with him would destroy me. Aaron will always be tied to Natalie through Aarabelle, and I respect that. She's his daughter, and though I may love her like she's my own, she's not. The loss of his friendship weighs heavily on me.

"He's good. I hope he is at least. He's in counseling and Mark is helping a lot. Is this weird?" she asks.

"It's not pleasant, but he's a part of our lives."

"Yeah," she sighs.

"I was thinking of Krissy today." I mention my sister for the first time in a long time.

"Oh? You never mention her anymore," Natalie

notes with her voice sounding more alert.

I feel like a dirtbag for not talking about her. Krissy was my younger sister, and I doted on her. When we were kids, we were best friends and later I protected her from asshole guys who wanted to fuck her. Which, considering we were Irish twins and only ten months apart, meant I broke a lot of my friends' jaws.

"Just wishing she could see me now . . . changing diapers and shit."

Natalie laughs and I smile. I love the sound she makes and how her eyes brighten. I can see it in my head. "You don't change diapers. You massacre them. But you'll have a lot of time to learn."

"Fuck that. I'll let you handle all of it." My eyes close, and I could pass out.

"I don't know . . ." she trails off.

"I hate to cut you off, but we just got back and I'm exhausted. Can we talk later? I'm beat and I have another shit day tomorrow. Let's hope everyone steers clear because I'm liable to snap."

"Of course. Get some sleep. I love you." Her voice is low and my eyes keep closing.

"Yeah, I need a nap. Love you. I'll call soon." We say our goodbyes and I swear I'm asleep before we disconnect.

chapter nineteen

natalie

"YOU STILL HAVEN'T told him?" Reanell asks as we sit at the Plaza Azteca. She grabs another nacho and pops it in her mouth, waiting for my answer.

"No, I don't want to stress him out, and when I miscarry, I don't want to have to tell him. It's easier this way."

It's been a month since I found out I'm pregnant, and whenever I talk to Liam, he seems stressed beyond his max. Each time I go to the bathroom, I'm terrified. It's like I know it's coming and I just wish it would happen.

"I think he deserves to know," she says, grabbing her giant fishbowl-sized margarita.

"I fully plan to tell him. But if I tell him now and then lose the baby, he'll be devastated and still be deployed. If I tell him and his mind goes elsewhere and he gets hurt—then what?" I ask her and stare. She knows I'm right. He's been stressed, crabby, and he leaves again for another time down-range, as he calls it. So, for now it's better for me to keep this quiet and keep him focused on the task at hand.

She nods and sits back. "I get it. You have a good

point. There are so many things I don't tell Mason when he's gone."

"Like?"

"Well, he doesn't know about how the stupid, piece of shit hot water heater went again. He'll get upset that he didn't fix it, and then I'll have to stroke his ego about how he's so amazing. And really, I'd rather buy myself some Jimmy Choos and say it was my reward."

I laugh and snort, "I don't know how that man deals with you."

Rea smiles and throws back her drink. "I promise that Mason has more cracks than the San Andreas Fault. He spends more money on his stupid sports memorabilia than I do in shoes and purses. We even out and we don't have kids."

Reanell's eyes fall and I know what she's feeling. She and Mason tried for years, and instead of killing themselves over it, they just resolved that if it happened, it happened. I admire that they put their marriage first, but I couldn't possibly imagine a life where Aarabelle didn't exist. My hand drifts to my stomach and I think about the baby inside. If I lose him or her, it will wreck me. I know the pain both emotionally and physically. The agony of not being woman enough gnaws its way up my throat.

"Lee?" Rea's hand touches my arm.

"I can't lose this baby," I admit with tears forming.

"No matter what happens . . . I'm here. I'll hold your hand, rub your back, and then we'll get drunk, but I think this baby is a miracle." She raises her glass, and I raise mine. "To Dreambaby."

"Dreambaby?"

"Well, he's Dreamboat, so he has Dreambabies."

"Oh, Jesus."

We both laugh and talk about my doctor's appointment. According to them, everything is on track and I conceived while we were in South Carolina. I'm only six weeks pregnant and my plan is to let Liam know once I make it through the twelve week period. I've lost two babies during the first trimester and the other was at fourteen weeks. I can't worry him, and I don't want to have him distracted.

Reanell sits back in the booth with a look that I know too well.

"What?" I ask.

"How are you handling Aarabelle and Aaron?"

I sigh and look away. "It's hard sharing her like this, but it's the way it is. Aaron is trying really hard and we're getting along surprisingly well. He's going to therapy and he loves her."

Right now he's taking her for short periods of time and nothing overnight. He said he's not ready with his sleep schedule and the nightmares being as bad as they are. I'm proud that he's aware of his PTSD and how it's affecting him. The decision not to keep Aarbelle overnight is his decision instead of something I have to fight him on. Our lives have drifted through rougher seas, but he's trying to calm them.

"How do you think he's going to handle . . . ?"

"Not well. But he knows I'm moving on. I filed for divorce and he signed it."

"Wow, that's surprising."

It was a shock, but I was glad it wasn't drawn out. Aaron and I had tears in our eyes when I gave him the papers, but nonetheless he didn't fight me. It was probably one of the hardest things I've ever had to do. It was truly admitting that the marriage was dissolved on our own choice.

"He said he loves me and he wants us both to be happy." She nods and looks around. "You don't think so?"

Reanell smiles. "I think you both are handling this difficult situation the best you can. I keep trying to imagine how I'd act if this was me. I think the divorce was more than a long time coming. I just want you all to be happy and in a good place. I know he was in a bad way when he got back, but considering he's in counseling, it should help when he finds out about the baby."

Since the fertility problems were basically the beginning of the end for us, I know this will kill him. I've thought about it and how to handle telling him, and I come up empty each time. Mark is the only person other than Reanell who knows. I owe it to Liam to let him know before anyone else. While having more children has always been something I wanted, I never thought it was a possibility. Now here I sit, pregnant with Liam's baby.

"Do you think Liam will be happy?" I ask the burning question.

"Did you guys ever talk about it?"

"No, not really. I mean, he loves Aarabelle so much, I assume he won't be upset, but . . ."

It's the one black cloud that looms over me. I worry that he'll think I tricked him before he was ready, but then knowing Liam, I doubt that at the same time. He loves me and we weren't some one-night fling. He's already made mention of marrying me and moving forward together.

Reanell grabs my hand. "I think Liam and you have a love that's real and true. He's patient, kind, loyal, and most of all, he adores you. He's chosen you over a friendship that lasted far longer and he loves Aara. I mean, not many men would do what he has. Liam is your forever love."

A tear falls as I allow my wall to come down for a minute and think about him. I miss him and can't imagine my life with anyone else. Liam fills the cracks that formed in my heart. He makes me whole again, and gives me something I didn't know I was missing. Just the sound of his voice can calm or excite me. I fall asleep thinking of him and wake up wishing he was next to me. I don't think I could ever get over him. He would forever exist inside of my soul.

"I'm such an emotional mess. Damn hormones," I laugh and wipe under my eyes. "I think Liam allowed me to see the difference between a comfortable love and a love that shatters your world. I loved Aaron, don't get me wrong . . . but it was just something I think we did. We dated, got married, then having children became what we should do next. When we couldn't, I felt like we were broken. Does that make sense?"

It's Reanell's turn to wipe her eyes. "It does."

My heart breaks for her. As much as she puts on the front about her purses and shoes, she wanted children. "I'm so sorry, Rea."

"I didn't want to go through it. I couldn't after watching you. My faith in God broke each time you'd call me and say it didn't work or you lost a baby. You're so much stronger than me, sister."

I come around the other side of the booth and hug her. There's a sisterhood we share. One of understanding, support, and unending friendship. When half our hearts leave, we bind our remaining pieces to get through the days. Not everyone can understand what we do. They say they can, but it's not all sunshine and unicorns. We put our fears aside and wear plastic smiles because that's what you do. Military wives aren't strong because they want to be. They have to be. I know the chance that Liam can be returning in a box is real, but I love him regardless.

Reanell returns my hug and sniffles. It's not often she breaks down, and she never shares this with Mason. "You have no idea how strong you are." I pull her close and we both cry out a little of the pain we share.

ANOTHER TWO WEEKS pass.

Another two weeks of Liam being gone.

I hate deployments.

I look at the beach filled with happy couples, and I want to scream. Aarabelle and I are playing in the sand. Liam hasn't called in a week, and I keep having horrible nightmares. I woke up last night and ran to the front door thinking someone was there to tell me he died. It was so real. I was already crying hysterically when I ripped the door open.

"Hey," Aaron's voice calls out from behind us.

"Hi." I smile as he looks at Aarabelle.

In the last six weeks, Aaron has started to look like the man I fell in love with. We haven't really spoken about anything deep, but he said he understands my need to move on.

"How are you?" he asks as Aara gets up and runs to him.

"Daddy!" Her tiny arms wrap around him and he kisses her.

"She just . . . !" I trail off as he smiles with his whole heart. We've been saying Daddy more and more to her in regards to Aaron. It warms me that he's being such a great father to her. She's lucky that she'll know the love of two men.

"She did! Hi, my beautiful girl." He lifts her into his arms and I hold my heart. Even with everything we've suffered, there's a small measure of healing through Aara. She is the glue that holds us all together.

Aaron carries her over and sits next to me. "That was amazing."

"Yeah," I grin. "I've been working with her on Mommy too. I'm glad she said it with you here."

"Me too. So, how are you?" Aaron asks and starts to play with Aara in the sand.

"I'm hanging in there. You?"

He looks at me and lifts his hand, but drops it before touching me. "I'm doing okay," he admits.

"Good, I'm glad." And I mean that. I don't wish anything bad on him. Aaron has suffered enough in his life, and I know the man he was. He was happy, loving, and fun. I want him to find that again.

"I wanted to ask you if you thought we could have dinner this week? There's some stuff I want to talk about and I owe it to you."

My heart sputters and I'm not sure what to do. Aaron hasn't done anything to make me wary, but I remember the last dinner we had.

"Is something wrong?"

"No, I just want to talk about going forward."

"Okay, I can get a sitter for Aarabelle."

"Great."

We play with Aara for a while and talk about work stuff. Aaron has been working with Mark on a lead outside of the office on what's been going on in Cole Security Forces. This will be the first time he's back in the office for more than a day or two. They both have been steadfast in checking every clue as to who could be behind the issue that caused Aaron to go over there in the first place. Jackson is flying back this week and wants to have a staff meeting. It's hard to believe anyone is intentionally messing with all of these guys, but it seems that way, and Mark is all too happy to work a little closer with Charlie in D.C.

After we discuss work, we transition into how he's handling everything. Aaron's been working hard in therapy and seems to be doing much better at opening up. His therapist has urged him to talk more about what he went through.

"Seeing Charlie this week was good I think," he muses.

"Why is that?"

"She was able to fill in some of the gaps of time and how she was able to get me the hell out of there."

Aaron looks off at the waves and I place my hand on his. "Can you tell me about the rescue?" I ask.

We start to pack Aarabelle's toys and head to the house. It's already getting dark and we've spent the afternoon talking and laughing. It was nice to spend time with him like two old friends. There wasn't anything awkward or uncomfortable. We just enjoyed the day with our daughter.

"What do you want to know?"

"How did it all go down?" I really want to know how they knew where to find him and what happened.

Once we reach the deck, I can tell by the way Aaron stiffens and the way he keeps clenching his hands that this is difficult for him. I reach out and touch his arm. "You don't have to tell me." I offer him the out.

"No, it's fine."

"Do you want to stay for dinner? I have chicken in the crock pot."

"Are you sure that's okay, Lee? I'm not saying I don't want to, but you need to be sure. I don't know if I can really be friends with you like this. You chose him."

My stomach clenches. "Aaron, I wasn't trying . . ."

"I know. You asked me to leave. You asked me for a divorce. I don't know how Liam or Brittany would feel."

"You're back with her? Even after all the shit you said to each other?" I ask.

"Do you hate it?" he asks and steps closer. "Do you wish I wasn't?"

I shake my head. "No. If you were willing to ruin our marriage over her, I would hope you cared about her enough to try. You were planning to leave me."

I thought we were making progress, but it seems not. I don't know if he's playing a game or what.

"I would've never done it."

"You'll never know that."

"I do know." He lifts Aarabelle in his arms. "I don't want to fight with you. I came here to see if we could talk."

My phone rings and it's Liam's number.

"I gotta answer," I explain.

"Liam?"

"Hey, Lee." He sounds exhausted and worn. "I only have a minute, but I needed to hear your voice."

"What's wrong?" Fear starts to course through me. This doesn't sound like the man I know.

He huffs and something crumples behind him. "Everything. I'm ready to be out of this hellhole. It's going to be a long deployment, and I've never been like this. I'm the guy who's counting down the fucking days, Lee. I'm not this guy. I don't do moody bullshit. The whole damn time I was away, all I did was worry about you. This isn't normal. I don't care about being away. It's money and fun, yet here I sit all pissed off and ready to come the fuck home."

"Lee, I need the keys," Aaron says loudly and I know it is on purpose. I hand him the keys and give him the nastiest look. Asshole.

Liam goes silent and then his voice morphs to anger. "Aaron's there?"

"Yes, he came to see Aarabelle."

"But he needs the keys?"

"Don't make this a fight because you're looking for one. It wasn't anything you need to worry about. Our divorce paperwork is submitted, but he's going to be a part of our lives. You're pissed off because you're gone, and I get that, but there's nothing here."

"My mind goes crazy. I think about him being there

when I'm not. I wonder if he's telling you how easy it would be with him. I'm going out of my mind, Natalie."

I wish I could take his worry away, but I know if it were me, I'd be the same. I don't blame him for it. He's away and my husband who I loved for more than half my life is here. One who made it abundantly clear he wasn't going to give up.

I look back as Aaron and Aarabelle enter the house.

"Listen to me," I say as I walk down by the beach. "You have my heart. You have my soul and you have my body. No one else. You have to trust me and know that I would never betray you. I love you, and you're not getting rid of me so easily."

"When I get home, I'm going to show you how much you mean to me. I'm going to marry you, Natalie. I'm going to give you everything I have. Just wait for me."

"You already give me everything. Now, come home soon."

Liam disconnects the call. I close my eyes and I rub my stomach. "You've given me more than you know."

chapter twenty

"YOU'RE NOW SIXTEEN weeks," Dr. Contreras says as she smiles and grips my hand. I've been with her from the beginning of my very first failed pregnancy, and she knows more than anyone how I've been terrified. Each week, I start to gain a tiny flick of hope this might be okay. "You are still high risk, but right now you're on track."

"I keep waiting," I say aloud.

"Don't live like that. Everything looks great right now, and you've made it through the most trying time." She walks over and gives my hand a squeeze. "Have faith, Natalie."

I need to harness my faith that no matter what, I will be okay. I can't be worried because the stress won't be good for the baby either. "Can you give me any insight about how this happened? Years I went through hell, and now when I'm not even trying . . . it happens?"

"Sometimes after you have a baby, your body resets itself in a way. Kind of like 'been there done that.' Your cycle restarted after Aarabelle, and while you might not have been regular because PCOS doesn't go away, you were ovulating when you did happen to get pregnant. It's a good sign." Dr. Contreras smiles and writes some things in her chart. "I want to see you back in four weeks."

"Are we doing this like we did with Aarabelle?"

During my pregnancy, I was considered high risk. My visits were more frequent and they monitored me very closely. I also was on a very light lifting ban. We were very careful, and I felt like I should've covered myself in bubble wrap.

"Most of it, yes. I don't want you doing anything strenuous. If you can keep off your feet then do it. I know that's hard with an eighteen-month-old, but try to take it easy. Do you have help from the father?"

I look away and shake my head, "Aaron has been helping a little with Aarabelle, but he doesn't know. Liam is deployed, and I can't tell him while he's gone."

She laughs, "I'm sure that'll be a fun homecoming."

"It'll be interesting for sure."

She pats my hand. "I'm sure you will get everything worked out. We'll keep you monitored and next appointment will be an ultrasound. It's all good things, Natalie."

"I have so much stress right now, between Aaron and Liam, I'm not sure what the hell to do. I'm concerned all of this is going to affect the baby." This is my worry I battle each day. I've been doing so well with keeping myself calm and in check so far though.

Aaron and I get along, but I'm sure that all could change very quickly. Liam will be home soon enough and then the dynamic shifts again. Plus, there will be an even bigger sense of betrayal. Liam was able to get his wife pregnant when he couldn't.

"I know this is a difficult time for you, but I want you to focus on you for once. Not Aaron and all the issues in the situation, but really give yourself the best care possible. Can you do that?" Dr. Contreras asks.

"Yes, this baby means everything to me. No matter what happens, it's a miracle and I'm happy."

She smiles, "Good. Now, I'll see you in a few weeks and then we can see your baby."

I leave the office feeling buoyant and hopeful. I

dreamt of having more children, but I never expected it to happen, and I sure as hell didn't think it wouldn't be without help. Liam and I have a tiny miracle growing inside of me. I don't know how he's going to handle it, but I can't stop the joy that builds.

I'm going to have another baby.

Once I arrive back at the office, I float around in a daze. I was so sure by now I wouldn't still be pregnant that I didn't really allow myself a chance to process what it all means. Aaron will need to be told delicately and not until Liam knows. God, I hope I don't show early.

"Earth to Lee." Jackson smiles waving his hand in front of me.

"Hi! Sorry." My cheeks flush as I realize I've been staring off into space.

Jackson laughs and leans back. "How are you?"

"Good. I'm good."

He smiles knowingly and I wonder if Mark told him. I'll kill him.

"Dempsey doing okay?" he asks.

"Yeah, Liam is out doing . . . well . . . you know," I sigh. "It'll be a few more days until he's back in touch."

Jackson nods and steeples his fingers. I forget sometimes how far he's come. The man who used to play beer pong as a sport is now a company owner. He took all of the bad things that happened to him and used them for good. "How are you handling his deployment?" he asks.

There's no judgment in his voice. He must know how difficult this is for me. I may do a good job of masking my fears, but they're there. They lurk in every shadow, waiting to jump out at me. The fear that someone will come to tell me he's died weighs heavy. It's the reality of loving him, but he's worth battling my demons.

"I have good days and bad days. When he's in Germany, I'm fine. We talk more often and it feels like he's just down the street, but he's been out of touch for a while now."

"It won't be too much longer."

"No, we're half done. It's that last month that's always the most agonizing," I laugh.

"For us too." His warm smile and blue-green eyes light up.

"So, you didn't come all this way to just talk about me . . . what's up?"

Jackson sits forward and explains what's been going on in their investigation. It affects my job because that was the initial issue. When Aaron went out to Afghanistan, it was to see why supplies were going missing. The issue seemed to die out after Jackson got shot, but when they started to delve deeper, they found something was amiss.

"Anything you need and I'll help," I offer.

"I was hoping with your journalism background, you'd be able to look into a few things, but I want you to be comfortable."

"As long as I don't have to travel, I can help. I don't know how great my contacts are and what I can find out, but I still have some friends."

Jackson nods, "Great. Thanks, Lee." He looks around awkwardly and I can tell this isn't the full reason he's here.

"Is there something else?"

"Aaron will be in the office more. I know you guys are talking and both moving on with your lives, but I felt you should get a heads up. I don't condone all the shit he did, but he's been my friend and saved my ass. If you want to cut back here or work from home more, I'll do what I can to make this as comfortable as possible."

Aaron and I have found a way to cope through all of this. We're civil and kind, but I'm not sure working together is the best idea. Especially with me being pregnant. But Aaron isn't responsible for supporting me, and

I don't expect anything from him. I need to produce an income.

"Can I think about how to handle this?"

"Of course. I just want you to know I'm your friend too, and I won't let you and Aarabelle suffer either." Jackson gives me a pointed look. "I mean it, Lee."

I grin and nod, "I know. Now, how's wedding plans?"

Jackson and I talk about their upcoming nuptials and how happy he is. It's nice to see him come full circle and with someone like Catherine. They may not have been each other's first loves but they are truly made for each other. Which is how I feel about Liam.

It may not have been the plan I had, but he makes me impossibly happy. Liam sees into the parts of my heart I never knew were there. He's the clarity in the darkness that brings peace to my soul.

MY COMPUTER RINGS and I fluff my hair. I haven't seen Liam in weeks and I want to look stunning.

"Hi!" I squeal as his face comes into view.

"God, I missed your eyes," he says and smiles.

My eyes start to water as I look at him. His dark brown hair is longer than he usually wears it and the scruff I love so much is a full beard. He still takes my breath away.

"I missed every part of you."

"You look beautiful. How are you?" he asks and leans back on his pillow.

"I'm good. I miss you," I say again. I wish I could find better words because missing him doesn't seem strong enough. I yearn for him in a way that's probably not healthy.

He chuckles, "I miss you too, Lee. Where's Aarabelle?"

"With Aaron."

"Ah," he says and his face falls slightly. "I got an email from Mark the other day."

Panic starts to churn, but I try to mask it quickly. "Oh?"

"Yeah, wanted to check in and see how things were. Let me know you were being watched and were doing good."

"Watched?" I say a little pissed.

"You didn't think I wasn't going to make sure you had someone looking out for you?" Liam smirks.

"I think you forget I've done this a time or two there, Dreamboat." I missed our playfulness. It's one of the things I love most. He makes the most serious of situations easier to tackle.

"Yeah, but I haven't. I needed to make sure my girls were okay." The way he includes Aarabelle makes my heart explode with love. He's going to be an amazing father to our baby.

I bite my lower lip and debate if I should tell him now. I decide to test the waters. "How did the last trip go?"

"Let's not even talk about me and here. I swear I'll never be happier to be stateside," Liam huffs and then continues. "There's been stupid fucking mistakes made over and over. I mean, you'd think I'm with a bunch of newbies this time. My frustration level is beyond high, and I'm going to have heads roll if there's one more screw up. I thought someone would be coming home in a body bag this last one."

Nope. Not going to tell him now.

"I'm sorry," I shrug, partially disappointed. I want to tell him about our baby. Of course I wish it was in person versus over Skype or the phone. "The divorce should be final soon, by the way."

"You okay with it?"

"I'm ready to start our lives with no more ghosts," I reply earnestly.

Liam pauses and then his eyes get serious. He leans in and sincerity rings in his voice. "I'm going to make you happy, Natalie. I'm going to give you all the things you want, and I'll never betray you. As long as we're together, you and Aarabelle will be what I live for. I know she's not mine, but I'll love her like she is. I'm going to make sure you never know what it feels like to be second best."

My heart soars and tears begin to fall. "You have no idea how happy you make me."

"We're just right, Lee. I'm not saying we won't have ups and downs, but I'll be by your side the entire time. Even when I have to be away from you, I'm with you."

I shift forward and blow him a kiss. This man has shown me love when I never thought it would exist again. He gave me faith to open myself to him and that he'd protect me. Even when he pushed me away, it was to protect us. The love we share is once in a lifetime. It may have taken a tragedy to bring us together, but it's true love that binds us.

"I love you, Liam Dempsey."

"I'm thinking you should prove it," he winks.

"Oh, and how do I do that?" I smile as his eyes begin to smolder.

"I want to see you, sweetheart."

I smile and shake my head.

"I want to hear you, watch you come apart with my voice. I need you so bad and this is the best we can get."

If I ever planned to do this with him, there's no other time possible. I'll be unmistakably pregnant soon and then I definitely can't.

I grab my laptop, shut off the light hoping to hide the bump I have now, and head toward the bed. "I've never done this."

"Me either, sweetheart, but I'm dying and I want to

do this with you. If I can't touch you, I need to see you and feel you in my mind."

With just the dim light from the setting sun, I glow. I smother my nerves and take my top off. I watch his pupils dilate and hold on to that to keep my confidence up. My heart races as I watch him settle into his bed. "I'm not going to be the only one naked, am I?" I ask.

Liam grins and removes his shirt. My mouth goes dry as I see the sinews of his muscles move. I want to touch him so badly. My hand reaches toward him, but all I can do is close my eyes and imagine the feel of his skin beneath my fingers. "Remove your bra, sweetheart." Liam's voice is hushed but full of heat.

I watch Liam as I move my hands behind my back and stop. Instead, I move my hands to my shoulders and slowly drop the straps down. "Like this?"

"You're so beautiful," he rasps.

Slowly, I remove my arms from the straps and then reach back and undo the clasp. When my bra falls, the moan that escapes him causes heat to flood my core.

"If I was there, I'd touch you. My hands would be everywhere. Do you wish I was there?"

"Yes," I breathe and my eyes flutter. This is the most erotic thing I've ever done. He's thousands of miles away and still makes me feel sexy. Liam's voice drops low as he groans when I push my hair back, giving him a full view.

"Show me how you want me to touch you, Lee. Where do you want my hands on your skin?"

My fingers move from my stomach to my breasts. I close my eyes and listen to his voice as I imagine it's his hands on me.

"I'd latch my mouth on your breasts. Suck each one and let my tongue roam over your gorgeous tits." His husky voice drawing out a moan.

"Liam," I whimper.

"My mouth would be over every inch of you. I'd kiss

you, touch you, lick you . . . I'm so fucking hard imagining how you taste."

I open my eyes and need to see him. I don't care that we're through a computer. All I need is him. "Show me," I request.

Liam stands and removes his shorts and boxers. He doesn't move, allowing me to see every bit of his body. I long to touch him, feel his body in my hands. "I wish . . ."

"I'm there with you now, Lee. I'm right in front of you. Tell me," he commands.

"My fingers would be on you." My voice is breathy as desire courses through my veins.

"Where?"

"I would trail up your arms," I close my eyes and mirror the movement on my own skin. "Making sure I feel every muscle. They remind me how strong you are and how safe you make me feel." Liam moans and it emboldens me to go on. "My fingers would glide across your shoulders and to my favorite part of you—your chest."

"You're killing me, sweetheart."

I open my eyes and look at him as his hand grips his cock. He pumps it slowly with his eyes closed and his head back. I want to crawl through the screen. I've never been so turned on in my life. Watching him jerk off to the sound of my voice and the promise of what I'd do is the sexiest thing I've ever seen.

"I would kiss each part of your chest. Slowly trail my tongue down your torso but keep my hands on you. I'd go slow over each ridge and dip in your skin. Feel how your muscles tense when I touch you before taking you in my mouth." Liam stops and his eyes are molten lava.

"Take your clothes off, I need to see you."

I remove my pants and underwear. We're both naked and so far apart, but right now, we're together in every way.

"Are you wet for me? Show me," he prompts. The

heat in his eyes makes me want to give him whatever he wants. I lie back on the bed and hope the camera angle allows him the visual he wants but still trying to hide a little. "Fucking hell, Lee. What I would do to you right now."

My skin is on fire. I slowly touch my breasts as they're weighted and very sensitive.

"That's it. Touch yourself for me," Liam encourages. "Go slow and pull at your nipples. Yeah," he moans and I imagine him touching himself. "Glide your fingers down to your pussy, sweetheart."

I hesitate for a second, but the need to ease the build is too much. My hand moves from my breasts down past my stomach. I pause, thinking of the baby for a moment, thinking I should tell him, but Liam speaks again.

"I love you, Lee. Let me love you with my voice."

It's not the time and this would surely kill the mood. "Tell me, Liam."

"I'd go slow, driving you crazy with need. I'd push your legs further apart so I could see all of you. Watch you pulse as you crave me. Then, I'd lower my mouth to your pussy and take one long lick."

I swear I see stars. His voice is thick and full of promise and I could come apart right now. My finger presses against my clit and I rub small circles.

"It would just be beginning as my tongue would push inside of you and I'd fuck you with my mouth first. There'd be no finesse, just pure passion. You taste like heaven and I'd want to stay there forever."

"Oh my God," I groan as I climb higher and higher.

"When I feel you tighten around my tongue, I'd stick my finger inside and twist until you were gripping me so hard that your body is begging for my dick."

"I'm begging now," I moan.

"I know. Make yourself come. Show me how bad you want me."

My pace quickens as I listen to his grunts and groaning. I lie on my bed imagining it's his hands, his mouth, and his touch.

"Only you, Natalie. Only you can make me this fucking hard. Make it this impossible to do anything but think about being with you," Liam coaxes me as I writhe. "I'm touching you. Wishing it was my hands on your beautiful body. My tongue would be in your mouth as I sink into you, claiming you with each stroke as you come apart on me."

I explode. My body shakes as I have one of the strongest orgasms of my life. I cry out and my breath comes is short gasps. I turn my head and catch Liam last second as he follows me over the edge. He moans my name and cleans up.

"Well, that was the best fucking Skype of my life," he smiles, and I flip onto my stomach hiding myself.

"It was interesting for sure," I blush.

"Hold on, someone's knocking," he says and gets dressed quickly.

I suddenly feel very naked. I grab my robe and throw it over me. I hear him arguing with Quinn for a few minutes before the door slams.

"Hey," he looks irritated. "Sorry about that."

"No worries. Kind of glad he didn't come knock a little earlier," I giggle.

Liam doesn't respond right away. He wipes his hand down his face, "I don't even know how to tell you this, but I have to go back out. I'm going to be gone a few days or more, again."

"I thought you guys were on a short break."

I know he has no control. But these missions are killing me. I worry and wonder when I don't hear from him. So far, I've been able to keep my mind from running rampant, but at the same time, the fear can come out of nowhere.

"We were supposed to be, but Quinn just came here to let me know we needed to start gearing up. This isn't like me." He looks off and lets out a deep sigh.

I'm not sure what the hell he means. "What's not like you?"

"This stressed out, pissed off, ready to go home guy. You broke me," he laughs. "I worry about you and Aarabelle. I wonder if you're okay and if you need anything. It consumes me. You consume my world. I don't know how these married guys do this."

He seems so forlorn I wish I could take it from him. I give him my best shot. "I know the job you have. I have a very small advantage than some new SEAL wife. I've walked in these shoes. You have to remember who you are when you're there. You're not Liam Dempsey. You're Dreamboat. If you don't do your job, you don't come home to me. So do your job and do it well. Then when you come home you can suck up."

"How did I ever get so fucking lucky?"

"You loved me at my lowest. You healed me by being the man you are. I'm the lucky one."

"I'll call you when I'm back and we can start planning another Skype before homecoming," he grins and leans in close. "And I mean a repeat of today, sweetheart."

"You better earn it," I smile and scoot forward. "Or next time I'll point the camera at the ceiling."

"You wouldn't."

"Oh, wouldn't I?"

"I'll be seeing *all* of you very soon," Liam smirks.

"We'll see about that."

"Kiss Aarabelle for me and get her potty trained," he smiles.

"I will. I love you."

"Love you more. We'll talk soon."

I nod as my throat becomes thick with emotion. I miss him and I don't want to hang up. But I know he has to go and I need to be strong for him. Liam disconnects the call, and I hold my stomach and start counting down until I can talk to him again.

chapter twenty-one

"AARON, IT'S FINE," I say to him for the tenth time. He's upset that I've decided to work solely from home. But this was the best choice. I don't want to work side by side with him every day, and this gives me a chance to stay home with Aarabelle and the new baby. I'm now nineteen weeks and starting to feel self-conscious around everyone.

"Something's going on with you." He walks over to where I am and looks at me.

Shit. He's going to know. I've been extra careful about dressing in baggy clothes and keeping everything hidden.

This is Aaron, the SEAL interrogator. The one who knows every trick in the book. He and Liam are cut from the same cloth. The last two weeks, Aaron and I have gotten along really well. Our divorce is now final and we're both free to move on. We've promised each other, for Aarabelle's sake, to not be hateful. He knows where my heart lies, and I know he needs to find his.

He's not a bad guy and he never was. He was a confused man who made some bad decisions. Unfortunately, for him, it cost him greatly. Cost all of us. Even with us not being together, he's proven to be a phenomenal father to Aarabelle. Each week he comes and has dinner with us, and every other weekend he takes her.

"Please don't Jedi mind trick me. I just have a lot on my mind." I try to brush him off.

"No, that's not it."

"I need you to stop, please," I implore him. I don't want him to know before Liam. I don't want him to know at all, but there's no avoiding that. I'm starting to show a more defined bump, but today I have a sweatshirt on. There's no way he can see my stomach.

"I'm just worried." Aaron stops and waits.

My cell phone rings, stopping this awkward and very uncomfortable conversation. I look at the number and I don't recognize it.

"Hello?" I answer.

"Natalie?" A man's voice I don't recognize asks.

"Yes, who is this?"

"This is Aidan Dempsey, Liam's father. I have your number from Liam's emergency file he sent before he left."

"Oh, hello, Mr. Dempsey." Concern sweeps in. "Is everything okay?"

Liam's father sighs and takes a long pause. "I'm sorry to call like this," he stops again and sniffs, "I just—I don't know what to do," he says and my heart plummets.

I clutch my throat and Aaron is at my side in a moment. "What's wrong?" I barely get the words out.

"My wife," he stops and catches his breath. "She was in an accident. And the doctors . . . they aren't saying anything yet. But the accident was bad." The pain is evident in his voice and I feel both relief and tension. It's not Liam, but this won't be any easier.

"I'm so sorry."

"I need him to come home." He begins to cry and my heart splinters into a million shards. My legs start to shake. I need to sit. "She's not going to make it, and they said to get the family here, but it's just me and Liam left." His Irish brogue grows thick as his emotions swell.

"Is he?" Aaron says, and I shake my head.

"I can help. I need some information from you. He's out on a mission, but I'll do everything I can." Tears well in my eyes as I think of how badly this is going to wreck Liam. His sister died and that was horrible, now his mother is barely hanging on.

Liam's father gives me all the information about his mother's condition and where she is. I write everything down, and Aaron rests his hand on my shoulder in silent support.

His father lets out a deep breath, "I can't tell him."

"It's okay, Mr. Dempsey, I'll get Liam home."

We disconnect and Aaron looks at me with empathy. It gives me a tiny amount of hope that we can all find a way to get along. "This is going to break him, Lee. When Krissy died, he almost lost his mind. I was there." Aaron reminds me.

He went with Liam to his sister's funeral. Aaron told me when he got back from Ohio how bad he took it. How the guy who would laugh and joke could barely smile. Even now, it's difficult for him to talk about her. She developed a blood clot that killed her in her sleep.

I look at Aarabelle and my emotions flood like a dam that opened. I imagine being that mother and entering her room. Seeing her asleep and knowing I was right there. It becomes overwhelming and I start to sob.

"It's too much," I cry out.

Aaron crouches down and grabs my hands. "I can't believe I'm saying this . . . but you need to be strong. He's going to need you. I can handle Aarabelle for a bit if you need to go. I would offer to go, but I don't think we're quite there yet." Aaron looks away.

"Are you sure you can handle her for that long?"

He sighs, "I'm sure, and if not, I'll get help."

"I'm not trying to be a bitch, but I don't want *her* around our daughter."

Aaron looks away and then back at me. "I was never with her. I said it to piss you off."

"Great."

"I'm sorry," he says with shame painting his face.

He lied. Again.

"I need to get an AmCross in." I stand and head over to my binder. The American Red Cross has to put the information in and then it goes to his command. Being that it's his mother, I can't see his command denying him the chance to come home.

Once I get the message in, Aaron and I sit quietly. Aarabelle is asleep and I wait for Liam or his father to call. He'd fly into Virginia, and then I don't know where we go from there.

Aaron clears his throat and I look up. "I can stay here if that's okay with you," he offers.

"I appreciate you helping out." Throughout these past few weeks, we've grown as friends. There's no spark or connection, at least for me, but the friendship that was always there is still strong.

"Why don't you get some sleep? I'll stay here and if something happens, at least I'll already be here."

I nod and look at my phone. It's been hours and still no call. I know these things can take some time, but it's not something we have the luxury of. Every minute is precious and I feel like we're waiting for the clock to stop ticking.

Once in my room, I lie down and my mind won't quit. I'm distraught over the fact that Liam will have to endure any pain. I love him and know what it feels like to lose someone you love. I would never wish that on anyone. The hands of time haven't been fair to either of us. We've both endured immense pain, but through it found the beauty in each other.

I close my eyes and clutch my phone waiting for his call. I don't know how much they'll tell him, but I hope

Mason knows enough to let him call me after. Hopefully, in less than twenty-four hours, we'll be together, where I can be the rock he needs.

I awake with the sun shining and leap out of bed. Glancing at my phone, I see there are no missed calls. That makes no sense. He should've called home by now. It was an emergency. No matter if he was on a mission or not, he would have communication with the base unit.

Aaron will know. I rush down the stairs where he's drinking coffee while Aarabelle plays with her toys. "Morning," he says and takes a sip.

"Hey, I'm worried. He didn't call." I waste no time explaining my fear.

"If they're out in hostile territory, he won't be able to. He may have to finish out the mission and then come back. He'll get in touch when he can. Sucks he was out and not at base," Aaron tries to reassure me. "I know this sounds fucked up, but we know the risks when we deploy. We know we may never get to say goodbye to someone dying. We miss births of babies and a lot of holidays. It sucks but it's also the way we live."

"Do you miss it?" I always wondered this.

When he got out of the Navy, I always felt it was more for Mark and Jackson. Jackson was the leader and he was the first not to take another commission. Mark was enlisted and he followed suit. But Aaron wavered. He wasn't hurt in the firefight like they were. Aaron came back different though.

"No, I'm not going anywhere again. I have my daughter, and I wouldn't ever put you through something like this again," he says and looks away. The tone in his voice makes the underlying message clear.

"What does that mean?" I can't help but ask anyway.

"It means that I wouldn't choose deploying over you. I'm here, Lee. I'm not going to leave, or get injured, or die. I'm here." Aaron's voice is low and pleading.

"You did leave, get injured, and hell, you died too. You weren't active then. Don't use this against me," I warn.

He stands and looks at the ceiling. "This is our house, Natalie. It's where we made a home. We conceived a child here, had fights here, made love here, and I thought we'd grow old here."

I don't know where all of this is coming from. He hasn't tried to make a move in months. We've been friendly and I've never lead him to believe there was a chance at more.

"I did too. I didn't choose for our life to fall apart. I know you made mistakes. I've forgiven you for them, but it doesn't change how I feel. I don't want to fight with you about this," I plead for him to stop.

"I don't want you to have a baby with him," Aaron's voice cracks at the end. He stares at my stomach and tears fall from his eyes. I follow his gaze and realize I'm in my shorts and a tank top with a very clear baby bump. "I thought maybe you were, but I didn't want it. I've really lost you. Haven't I?"

"Have I led you on?" I ask with hesitation. I tried hard not to ever let him think we were going to get back together.

He looks at Aara and back at me. "I hoped, Lee. I'm getting help. I know I fucked up . . . God, I know it . . . but I've always loved you. I would do anything to prove to you how good we could be. I'm doing everything the doctors want. I'm not seeing anyone because they're not you. We can get back and we can be better."

"Aaron, please don't do this now. First, Liam is deployed. His mother is on life support and I'm pregnant. I love you, I always have, but our love changed. It became friendship and comfort. We let it slip through our fingers and then the choices each of us made defined our future. You will always have my past, but Liam holds my future."

"We define our futures."

"So do our pasts," I say hushed.

Once again, he glances at my stomach and rests his head in his hands. I give him a minute because I can't imagine this is easy for him. The pain of finding out about Brittany was horrible for me, and I certainly didn't want him to find out this way.

"Were you trying? Were you going to tell me?" he asks gruffly.

"Not before I told him, and no, we weren't trying," I reply honestly.

"Un-fucking real. I couldn't get you pregnant after *years* of trying and . . ." he trails off.

Aaron stands and walks over to Aarabelle. He places a kiss on the top of her head before turning back to me. "I'll never stop loving you, but right now I can't look at you. I'll be back later, but I need some time."

I don't want to hurt him. It was never my intention. "I'm sorry you found out like this. I'm sorry you're hurting."

"I guess we're even now," he sneers.

I know he's angry and upset, but it stings. Instead of going back at him, I stay silent. This won't end well for either of us, and I won't break him further.

He looks at me once more and the pain rolls across his face. Aaron cups my face with his hand and then drops it.

Without a word, he walks out the door and the loud sound of it closing slams the door in my heart.

∞

IT'S BEEN THREE whole days. Seventy-two hours that I've yet to hear from Liam. I'm growing anxious and frustrated. I called the Red Cross again, ensuring the message was delivered to his command, which it was. His father called me this morning asking if he was going to make it home, and I couldn't answer him.

I don't know what to do, but I need to do *something*. Paige arrives to watch Aarabelle so I can go get some answers. I grab my purse and rush out the door. It makes me sick that I'm going to go this route, but I have no choice.

Aaron called this morning to find out what was going on. Even he seemed concerned that Liam hadn't gotten in touch. He apologized again, but said he needed some time away to get his mind straight. Then he offered to still keep Aarabelle if I needed. If anyone's lost the most, it's him. He lost his wife and his best friend and the life he thought he was coming home to.

My phone rings and my pulse spikes. "Hello?" I answer immediately not even looking at the caller I.D.

"Lee, it's Jackson."

"Hi," I say depressed.

"I'm guessing you still haven't heard from him?"

"No, nothing, and I'm getting worried."

"I'm sorry, I just wanted to see if there was anything you needed. I can call a few people and try to get some damn answers."

I know he'll do whatever he can, but there's really no way he can get answers. He's not active anymore. He's a contractor. Sure, he has connections but they're not going to hand over information on an active mission.

"Thanks, Jackson. I wish there was something you could do, but we both know it won't help."

He lets out a deep breath. "I know. I hate this, Lee. I'm here no matter what you need. I'm here."

"Thanks, Muff. I'm at the only place I can get answers now. I'll keep you posted."

We hang up and I look at my best friend's house. Where hopefully some of the answers lie. I grab my bag, let out a deep breath, ring the doorbell, and my stomach drops.

"Hi," Reanell says and looks away. "I figured it was a matter of time."

"You know?" I ask with my mouth agape.

"Come in," she opens the door then steps back.

I want answers.

"What's going on?"

Reanell sighs while she chips at her nails. "I can't tell you, Lee. You know I can't, but I can't not tell you either."

My chest tightens and my mouth goes dry.

Please, if there's a God anywhere, I'm begging you to not do this to me. I can't handle it.

Something's wrong and I'm going to lose it all again. Only this time there won't be any coming back.

chapter twenty-two

WE BOTH LOOK at each other as her face falls. She doesn't want to hurt me, it's clear in her eyes, but she's going to. Reanell, who usually has no problem saying anything, shifts her weight back and forth as she waits for me to say something.

"Rea?" I ask with dread. "You have to tell me."

She lets out a long breath and then her eyes flash with resolve. "Fuck OpSec. I talked to Mason today and he figured you'd be here already," she pauses and I bite back the bile threatening to choke me.

My breaths come in short bursts, "I-I . . . please don't." I heave and put my hands on my knees.

Reanell is at my side rubbing my back. "Lee, calm down. Listen to me, please." I stand slowly, and she walks with me over to the couch. "They're out on a mission. It wasn't supposed to be a long one from what I understand. All Mason said is they've gone dark for some reason. They can't establish coms and can't get in touch with him to relay the information. They've missed the last three checkpoints, but they have one more window. If they don't answer by then, Mason is sending a team in."

I close my eyes and try to focus on breathing. He has to be alive. There's no way he'd leave me like this.

"He'll be fine," I say with defiance. "He knows what

he's doing." I stand and grab my bag.

"Lee, talk to me." Reanell stands and clutches my hand.

"I have to go food shopping. I'll see you later." I squeeze her hand and look for my keys.

"Food shopping?" her voice is high. "What the hell are you talking about?"

"We need food in the house. We didn't have food in the house the last time, and I need to make sure we can eat," I explain as if it should be obvious. "When Aaron died, I remember wanting some chips and we didn't have any. I need to get food. And chips. Maybe some chocolate or ice cream. I should probably have a variety of things, because I don't know what I'll crave this time. If I leave now, I can get home in time to do some other errands."

"Natalie," her voice is soft. "Stop."

"No, you stop!" I can't take anymore. "I need to go grocery shopping. I have to *do* something, because if I stop, if I take a minute to pause, I'm going to go insane. Do you not see the irony?" I pause. "I'm pregnant—again. I'm having a miracle, and I'm going to lose my other one. I need food in the house. I need to clean so that the next time I see you, I'm prepared."

As much as I want to cry, I can't. The tears sit on the cusp, but they won't come. I need to keep moving and get ready for what seems to be inevitable in my life. Hope that was springing to life dies before it blooms. I should've known better than this. Liam warned me that his life would always be like this. He told me before we started this that he could die.

"Okay. You just don't know anything yet. I'm here though. I trust in Mason and Liam. Don't let fear lead you down a road you don't need to be on."

"I'm not scared. I'm just ready for the inevitable."

I lied to myself over and over that I could handle that possibility. I can't lose him. I can't stand by his casket and relive that again. Respecting death is his deal, because if this plays out poorly, it'll be my heart that never beats again.

"Lee..."

"No, I should go. I shouldn't have asked you to tell me."

Rea steps closer, "I would've been at your house in about five minutes. I promise I'll call if I know anything. I have hope, Lee."

She pulls me into her arms as I block out the fear. I can't let myself go down this road. There's too many variables and too much at stake. Hope doesn't grant you wishes. It doesn't paint you pretty pictures or give you a place of relief. It's something we hold on to when we need something to believe in. I believe in truth and facts. Right now, the only thing I know is he's missing and could be dead.

Once in the car, I head to the grocery store. I'm in a fog. People move around me, but I don't notice. I just know that I need to keep going. My cart squeaks against the floor as I head through the aisles. I place things in the cart all the while desperately trying to feel a connection to him.

"Ma'am?" A woman in her early forties places her hand on my shoulder.

"Yes?" I ask.

"Are you okay?" The concern in her voice is soothing.

I look around and nod. "Yes, why?"

"You've been standing here for a few minutes and I don't..." she trails off, and I look in the cart.

I've been just loading jars of peanut butter into the cart. There must be about fifteen of them. "I didn't..." Embarrassment is laced in my tone.

"I wanted to make sure you were okay," she explains.

I'm definitely not okay. I'm back almost two years ago to when my world crumbled around me. Sure, I made it through and I can do it again, but I'll never recover. I won't ever love again. There will be no healing, just being a mother to my two children. I'll give them everything of me because they will be all that matters.

My hand presses against my small bump, and I pray this baby will know their father.

"He doesn't even know," I say aloud.

"The father?" The woman is still standing here concerned.

Tears flood my vision, and I nod. "He doesn't even know I'm pregnant," I say as they fall.

Her Navy Wife t-shirt lets me know she probably understands in some way. She doesn't say a word as she pulls me into her arms. This stranger I've never met before comforts me in aisle three. I couldn't cry before, and I don't want to now, but I lose it. She rubs my back and lets my tears stain her shirt.

"Is he over there?" she asks and I tilt back.

I nod and look at her shoulder. "I'm so sorry," I say and wipe under my eyes.

"Don't be." The kind woman smiles and waits a second before I nod. "Do you want me to stay for a minute?"

"No," I smile. "I'll be fine."

She pats my hand, "I think I'll just check this shelf out, I'm Lisa by the way."

"Natalie," I try to smile but it won't come.

Lisa stands with me for a few minutes and helps me unload my cart of the jars. If something happens to him, I need to be prepared.

"Thank you," I say hoping she knows it's for more than helping restock the shelf.

"Sometimes we all need a little help," she smiles and heads down the aisle. I watch, wishing I could say more. But she helped me more than she can imagine.

I arrive home with bags of God knows what, and Aaron is in the kitchen. "What are you doing here?"

He takes one look at me and his face falls. His brown eyes shimmer with fear, as he knows I went to get answers.

"What happened?" he asks worriedly. "I got a call from Reanell asking if I'd seen or heard from you. She told me I should talk to you."

"They've lost coms," I say with no emotion in my voice. I can't muster anything. I'm a blank canvas on the easel. One call will define the color that gets painted and whether it's filled with joy or sorrow. "I don't want to think about it. I need to put this away and clean the house."

Aaron begins to pace and it does nothing for my nerves. "Lee, I know you don't want to hear this, but I can't tell you how many times SEALs go dark for one reason or another. Sometimes it's for safety and other times it's because the equipment goes bad. It could be nothing."

Something in Aaron's eyes tells me he doesn't think it's nothing. "But you don't think so, do you?"

"What did Rea tell you?"

"Just that Mason knew I'd be there and that was all she would say. You should go. I should probably make some meals, maybe get his car detailed, and start to get his stuff together." I make a mental list.

There's a lot to be done as I learned the first time.

"Don't get ahead of yourself. Just wait it out. This is the choice you made, and you have to be ready to deal with it. If something didn't happen to his mom, you'd never have known this." He looks away.

"I did. I chose him. It doesn't mean that if I lose him, I'll regret anything. It means I'll hurt and grieve all over again. Now, I need to make some meals and be ready."

I start to walk away, but Aaron grabs my arm. "Goddammit, Lee, don't you see? Don't you see the life that you have to endure again? I can give you and Aarabelle the life that you deserve. I won't leave again. You'll never have to worry about any of this." Aaron's voice softens. "I won't leave you. I'll never hurt you again."

"You're doing it right now." I rip my arm from his grasp and walk away.

Aarabelle runs into the kitchen to me, and I hoist her up. I hold on to my lifeline and anchor myself. I have to be strong. I need to believe that Liam is okay and that it's only a problem with the equipment. Aara grips my face and gives me a kiss.

"It'll be okay," I say to her. "Mommy will be fine. Liam will call soon and then we'll be okay."

She lays her head on my shoulder, and I rub her back. I rock her back and forth, almost as if we're dancing. "I love you, Aarabelle."

"Yuv you," she says in her tiny voice.

I inhale and memorize the baby smell that's starting to leave her. This moment, in all my turmoil, Aarabelle is the light. I press my lips to her head and she sighs.

We stay like that for a few moments. I close my eyes, and enjoy this fragment in time. Suddenly, a cramp hits me hard. White blurs my vision as the pain radiates across my stomach. Every muscle tightens and then releases. I start to fall but catch myself right as another flash of pain hits.

"Aaron!" I let out a mangled scream and he rushes in.

Another one hits, and he barely grabs Aarabelle before I fold over. "Lee, what's wrong?" The fear in his voice is clear.

"Oh my God, the baby!" I cry out as I hold on to the counter while my abdomen clenches. I lose my grip and fall to the floor holding my stomach protectively.

Aaron puts Aarabelle down and then I'm in his arms. He carries me tenderly with his eyes locked on mine. All the while, I watch the color drain from his face. Very gently he lays me on the couch as I pray another cramp doesn't hit. The terror is splayed across his face because we both know what this could mean.

I look into his brown eyes, and he sweeps the hair off my face. "Just stay still. I'll call the doctor."

I grab his arm as tears spill down my face. "I can't lose this baby today. I can't."

His eyes close and he nods.

I fight the urge to go to the bathroom. I pray I won't feel anything more. No pain, no blood, because it'll put me over the edge. I'm barely hanging on to the ledge now. I have to muster any amount of courage I have, because this . . . this will kill me. If I lose Liam's baby while he's missing . . . I can't let myself go there.

"No, she just crumpled over," I hear Aaron explain over the phone. "I'm not sure if she's bleeding." A pause. "No, she's not, but I'm with her now." Aaron comes back into view and then heads back into the kitchen. "Okay, I'll call again. Thanks."

My voice isn't there when I open my mouth. We both know what they said and now it's up to my body to decide. Even if I am miscarrying, there's no way to stop it. I'm too early and all I can do is stay off my feet.

He crouches down and rests on his knees. "Lee, you tell me what to do."

"Stay and be my friend. Call Reanell and someone should call Liam's father."

"I'm sorry about before," he says and shame is reflected in his eyes.

"You can't keep doing this to me. I love him, and I'm going to be with him."

"I wish you didn't, but I won't hurt you anymore."

I grip his hand and try to get him to hear me. Right now, I only have enough strength to worry about one thing. "If you love me, you have to let me be happy. You signed the divorce papers and said you understood. And right now, I can't talk about all of this. It's too much."

"I know. I thought if I let you go willingly, you'd find your way back." Aaron's hand falls as do his shoulders. "I want you to be happy. I love you enough for that and for Aarabelle. As much as this sucks, Liam is a good man and he'll be a good father."

My hand rests on my belly and I pray he'll get to be a father to our baby as well. I already know the kind of man he is and how he treats Aarabelle when she's not even his. He loves her with his whole heart. "I'm scared," I admit.

"He'll be okay. I know him better than anyone. If they went silent, it's for a reason. I know it seems like you knew a lot of what happened on our missions, but you didn't. There were plenty of times we had close calls. He's one of the smartest guys I served with and I'd let him lead me any day." Aaron stands and looks at Aarabelle. "And if something happens with the baby . . ." He looks at my stomach. "You'll tell him, and if he's less of a man than I think he is, I'll beat the shit out of him. Just rest for now. Rea is on her way."

I close my eyes, try to relax, and pray this doesn't end the way so many have before. I love this child. I love that man. And I want them both.

"LEE." SOMEONE SHAKES me. "Natalie, wake up."

I open my eyes and Rea is sitting on a cushion pushing my hair back. "Hi," I croak. "Have you heard anything? Did Mason or Liam call?"

She looks away and I fight the urge to scream. "Mason said they're still not responding. He won't tell me anything else, just that he's in control of the situation."

"Right," I sigh. To be honest, I'm lucky I'm getting this much. "I need to get up," I start to rise and my stomach clenches.

"You okay?"

"No, I'm not, but I need to go to the bathroom. I can't hold it in anymore."

Reanell helps me stand and walks with me to the bathroom.

"I'll be here if you need me."

"Where are Aaron and Aara?" I ask holding on to the wall.

"They went to the park so you could sleep. You were thrashing in your sleep, so I woke you," she pauses. "I know you don't want to go in there, but you can't stay standing here either. I'll be right outside the door." Rea puts her hand on my shoulder, and I fight back the tears.

She's right.

I don't want to look. I don't want to see blood again. The fear floods through me, leaving me paralyzed in a sea of unyielding pain. I'm drowning in my unshed tears, but I have no choice. There's no one that can change the outcome either way. If it wasn't meant to be, then I'll grieve the loss of another child and what could've been. Or if I make it through this with a baby, we'll celebrate the life that was born.

Entering the bathroom takes every ounce of willpower I have. I close the door and say a silent prayer while I muster up my courage.

I know I pray a lot asking for things. I'm not asking for anything any mother in my place wouldn't ask for. I know you're busy, but please don't take them both from me. Don't let me lose him and the baby. I won't be able to function for Aarabelle. Any ounce of hope I've ever had will be gone. So, I'm begging you to please bring him home and don't take another baby from me.

chapter twenty-three

I OPEN THE door and start to head to the couch.

"Seriously?" she asks incredulously. "You're not going to say anything?" Reanell helps me lie down.

"No blood, but I'm still crampy." It's relief and then terror all at the same time. No clear signs that I'm miscarrying, but then a cramp hits. I hold my stomach as a tear rolls down my face. "I can't do this."

"You can and you will."

"What am I going to do if this keeps up?" My chin quivers as the question hangs in the air.

Rea crouches down with empathy in her eyes. "You'll fight. You'll fight with every ounce you have to come back to us the way you are now. It'll be hard. It'll take all the courage you can find, but you have it. You have Liam, Aarabelle, and you have me."

"Liam's missing, Rea. I may lose him and this baby."

"I wish I could take this for you. I won't fill you up with bullshit, but know I'm not going anywhere."

I need to take my mind off of all this. None of it can be controlled. I can't make Liam come back, or this baby happen, but I can control how I handle it. Once again, I'm being tested. "One day I'm going to be able to be the rock in our friendship."

"You are," she kisses my cheek. "Now, is there anything I can do?"

"Can you clean the house for me?" I ask Rea.

It may seem like an odd request, but she nods. Reanell picks up the toys and starts to get some things organized. We make idle chit chat about nothing, and I see through her ruse. I know she wants to keep me busy and talking, that way my mind doesn't go in a million directions.

Like how my boyfriend is missing. I could lose a baby that said boyfriend doesn't know about. My ex-husband is spouting love and other bullshit. And Liam's mother could be dying at any moment and he won't make it home.

"I need to call Liam's dad and get an update," I say reaching for my phone.

"Here," she hands it to me. "Please, lean on me. I know this entire situation sucks, but I'm here."

"I love you for it too." I try to smile but it fails.

I hover over the keypad afraid to call and give an already horrific situation more bad news. He called me for help and here I am about to tell him that the other reason he stays strong is in trouble as well.

"Hello?" he answers.

"Hi, Mr. Dempsey . . . it's Natalie."

"Have you heard from Liam?" he asks straight away. I can hear the exhaustion in his voice. I've been there.

"No, not yet. He's still on a mission and they're not able to compromise it by sending a message."

I tell him a half-truth, but I don't have it in me to break his heart. I don't know all the facts either, so making him suffer for maybe no reason would do more harm than good.

"Oh." The disappointment is evident. "I don't know how much time we have. I hoped he'd be on his way by now. Will you call me if anything changes?"

"Of course," I say immediately. "I'm doing everything possible. I want him home for you just as bad as anyone. I have everyone I know doing whatever they can as well." I hope to assure him.

We talk a little about his wife's condition and how it happened. I wish I could do more for him, but we're both a mess. Once I hang up, I will the phone to ring. He has to be okay. Liam has my heart and my soul. He needs to call me. He needs to come home, and I need him to know about our baby.

"Lee," Rea draws my attention back to her. "Mason knows what he's doing. I have to have faith in him."

Before I can say anything, I hear a knock at the door.

All the blood rushes from my face and fear chokes me.

"Hey, it could be UPS," Rea says and puts her hand on my arm.

"I can't answer."

"Natalie," she chides.

"I've answered that door before. I know what comes on the other side. You've never had to be me. You have no fucking clue what this is like. The fear. The terror that eats at me with him gone. I'm pregnant—again. He's in a hostile area with no coms. Don't you dare judge me," I spit the words like razors to cut her.

Yes, she's my best friend, but she doesn't get it. It's the crippling fear of déjà vu that eats at me. But I have to move. I don't get a choice. I have to answer that door.

Knock. Knock. Knock.

I lift myself and count the steps to the door. My mind starts to check off all the things that I'll need to do.

My heart rate accelerates with each step, but I keep moving. I remind myself that I'm strong, resilient, and have my babies to think of.

I've done this once. I lived. I have to be strong for his child.

I open the door but no one is there. There's a package on the ground.

The phone rings, and I close the door without even grabbing it. I rush over to the phone.

"Hello?" I don't even look at the caller ID. I'm just grateful there's no one at my door in a uniform.

"Lee," Liam's voice is thick and scratchy. Tears fall immediately. My hand clutches my chest and a sob escapes.

"Liam," I say his name and sink down.

"It's okay, it's okay, I got the AmCross. I'm getting on a plane in a few hours."

"I'm so . . . I can't even talk," I admit. "I was so scared."

"I know. I'll talk when I get to Virginia. Is she . . . ?" he asks hesitantly.

"She's not doing well. You need to get home, and we'll head to Ohio."

"I love you, Lee."

I smile with the taste of tears on my lips. It's bittersweet, his return. It's not the happy reunion we dreamed of. It'll be getting off the plane and heading to another. We need to get to his mother as fast as we can.

"I love you. So much. Please don't scare me again," I request.

He lets out a deep sigh. "I gotta go. I'll see you soon."

"Yes, you will."

The call disconnects and I sit there trying to muddle through my emotions. Relief, joy, sorrow, and fear all come flooding at the same time. It's so many things to try to process at once.

Reanell sinks down next to me and pulls me into her arms. I lose it. I sob as she rubs my back without saying a word. It's cathartic and draws new worries with each one I let go. I worry about the baby, Liam, Aarabelle, Aaron, Liam's mother and father, but more than anything, I worry he has to go back.

"I'VE GOT HER," Aaron tries to reassure me—again. "I've been here almost every day and Paige will be here two of the days. I would never hurt her."

"I know that," I say exasperated. "I just want to make sure you're sure."

"It's either I watch our daughter or the babysitter does. So I'd like to have this time with her. I missed so much of her life."

Aaron has been great with Aarabelle, and he's been trying so hard. Paige said she'd stay at my house to make sure Aaron didn't need help. I've just never left her for so long before.

"Okay, thank you."

He walks over and holds my shoulders. His light brown eyes stare me down. "I may wish we could've worked things out, but Liam was my best friend, he needs you, and I may be a fuck up, but I don't want to watch him burn in hell. I hate that of all the people it was you two." His hands drop. "I hate that he's what you need and I'm not, but I did this to you. I deserted you when you needed me most and Liam loves you." Aaron looks down at my stomach and closes his eyes. "He can give you things I couldn't."

"We'll find a way for all of us. I know this is hard on you, and I don't want to hurt you. I never wanted to."

"One day, and for Aarabelle, we will."

I look at her eating her breakfast and I nod. I'd sell my soul if it were for her happiness. Aarabelle is the one thing keeping all of us grounded. That little girl has saved us all. I walk over and kiss her cheek.

"I'll miss you. Mommy has to go get Liam." She smiles and looks away, oblivious.

"Go, Lee." Aaron grabs my bag and heads toward the

door.

I went to the doctor yesterday and she said everything was fine. She told me to go but to take it easy. At this point, there's nothing we can do to stop a miscarriage, but she wants me to rest as much as I can. Considering we're heading to a hospital, at least I'll be close to medical attention.

Now to tell Liam and pray he's happy about it.

"Thanks again," I say to Aaron as I open the car door.

"Give him my condolences. He was really close with his parents. Also, tell Aidan I'm sorry for his loss. I know how much it . . ." he trails off. "Drive safe and I've got Aara."

"I'll tell him," I lean in and embrace him. He flinches and glances at my stomach once again. It's awkward, but Aaron is still my oldest friend.

My hands drop, and I rush out the house. Once I get in the car, I smile and head to see the love of my life.

chapter twenty-four

WAITING FOR THIS plane to land is more painful than shoving bamboo splints in my nails. Each time I hear the engines, my heart speeds up. I think it could be the one and then it's not and my stomach drops. I sit in the most uncomfortable chair at the Navy airfield. Mason called ahead and got me access to be able to pick Liam up.

My phone bings with a text.

> Liam: You'll know I'm close when this finally goes through. I'm on the plane and counting down the seconds until I see you.

I smile and realize he's within cell phone range.

> Liam: My entire body is aware I'm going to have you in my arms soon.

> Liam: I love you more than my own life.

> Liam: I hope you know how much it means to me that you're coming to Ohio with me.

They keep coming in, and each one causes my smile to grow.

Liam: I'm hoping security doesn't care that I'm going to maul you.

The blush paints my cheeks as I picture him attacking me. Not that I'm far off wanting the same.

Liam: God, seeing your face is going to be the only good thing about this trip. I miss you so much.

I close my eyes and try to respond but another one comes in.

Liam: Look up.

My eyes lift, and he stands before me. He drops his bags and the loud thump echoes in the terminal. I get on my feet and rush toward him. He's here.

Liam's arms open as I approach. I close the gap between us with a smile and wrap my arms around him. As soon as our bodies connect, I feel whole.

"Hi, sweetheart," his deep voice grounds me, and I look into his blue eyes. His lips lower and he kisses me.

My mouth molds to his as his arms keep me flush against him. All the fear disappears like a puff of smoke, and I know I'll survive no matter what. If I lose this baby, I know we'll make it through. Liam won't turn his back on me and seek out another. He's the man who will hold me and love me regardless. We're reunited and all is right in the world. There may be a lot of hell waiting for us, but we're together. He's alive and I'm in his arms.

He breaks the kiss and stares into my eyes. "I missed the shit out of you."

I laugh, "I missed you too." He pulls back a little as I bite my lip. He's going to see, and I want to tell him before he does. "Liam, I have to tell you something," I blurt out.

His face falls, "I didn't make it in time . . ."

"No," I stop him before he thinks he lost his mother. I practiced and rehearsed this all day, but now I'm choking on the words. I take his hand in mine and place it on my stomach. "I'm pregnant."

He looks up with wide eyes, and his breath catches. "You're . . . ?" he stumbles on the words. "We're . . . ?"

I nod with unshed tears forming.

"A baby?"

I sigh while touching his cheek. "I'm pregnant with a baby. Your baby."

He takes me into his arms again with such tenderness. "I wish I could say something, but you have no idea how I feel right now," Liam says against my hair. "Are you sure?"

"Yeah, I'm sure."

His eyes return to my stomach as his hand rubs the small bump. "Lee, I didn't think you could."

"I didn't either . . . apparently, you and I worked." I don't know how to explain it other than a miracle.

Liam smiles before he kisses my nose. "I love you so much. I love Aarabelle, and I'm going to love this baby just as much."

Right there. Those words solidify everything. He not only included Aara, he said her first. Once again, he proves why he has my heart. He didn't choose to love his own child any more or any differently. Liam is the man who will be a father to both my children, because to him, Aara is his as well.

"I want you to be happy, but I need to be honest," I say and we sit. "I had a huge scare. You know some of what I went through to have Aarabelle, and the fact that I've carried this long is promising. I cramped pretty bad the other day and have been trying to stay off my feet . . ."

Liam cuts me off. "You're not going with me then."

"Stop. I got the clear from the doctor to go."

"Natalie, you and the baby come first. I want you with

me, more than you know, but I'm not going to argue."

"You're not going to boss me around either," I snap.

Liam smiles at my small outburst. "I'm not?"

"No, you're not." I cross my arms.

He cups my face and his smirk only irritates me. "I'm so in love with you."

Well, that doesn't make me hate him. "You're confusing me."

"I'm loving you. And loving that my super sperm knocked you up."

I roll my eyes and fight my smile. "You've been home five minutes and I've already cried, yelled, gotten mad, and smiled. You're something else."

"I'm yours," he replies.

"And I'm yours."

"Yeah, sweetheart. You sure are. Okay, so tell me what the doctor said," he requests.

I go over all the rules, how far along I am, and more about the scare. His emotions play across his face like a movie. The one thing that remains clear is how happy he is and how much love he has for me. I've never seen a man look at me like he does. Liam sees through me and even with every flaw showing, he only loves me more. What we share is rare and precious, just like the child we've made.

He hoists the bag on his back with a grin. "Got it," Liam puffs up. He stands with sheer determination across his face. Then, he bows down and lifts me into his arms.

"What are you doing?" I ask practically yelling.

"You said to stay off your feet. So, you're staying off your feet." He somehow manages to shrug while holding me.

"Liam!" I laugh but wrap my arms around his neck. "I could get used to this, but you know if we make it through this, I'll just get bigger."

"I'll make sure I keep hitting the gym," he smiles.

He walks with me to the car and frowns when he sees I brought my car.

"Oh, stop it. I hate driving your car."

"When is our flight?" he asks opening the door.

"We should head to the airport now. I tried to space it in case you were late, but I think we should get there sooner than later," I explain getting in my seat and he nods. "Why?"

"I wanted to see Aara if we had time."

I don't think he could be any more perfect. My heart swells, and I lean up as he fusses over me and grab his face. He looks at me with wonder and then I pull him close. Our lips touch and his hand threads in my hair. I'm whole again. No matter what happens from here, we'll save each other. If I lose this baby, if his mother passes, if the world around us collapses, we'll make it.

My mouth opens and Liam's tongue clashes with mine. He licks and pushes me back into my seat. I let him take the lead as I hold his lips against mine. I want to kiss him forever, but we have to go. I push him back, but when his blue eyes hone in on me, I pull him to me again.

Liam smiles against my mouth and gives me a small peck. "You're so cute when you want me."

"I've missed your smart ass," I laugh and he kisses me once more before closing the door.

We head to the airport and the sweet mood of reunion morphs into the fear of what we're heading to. During the drive, I explain to Liam the information I have and he calls his father while we wait for the plane to board. Liam slips into his mask but keeps his hands on me in some way. His hands never leave my skin other than when he has no choice.

Early in the flight to Cincinnati, Liam and I talk briefly about what he's missed with Aaron and Aarabelle.

"Are you going to tell me why no one could get in

touch with you?" I ask. It's been driving me insane, but I wasn't sure whether to bring it up.

"It was a clusterfuck." He looks away.

"Is that all I get?" I ask softly. There's a line between significant other and SEAL. He and I have to establish it and this is one of those defining moments. It's not a matter of trust and I know this. It's a matter of protection.

Aaron wouldn't tell me much other than it was no day at the beach. I knew that was his way of saying the discussion was over. Only once did he ever go in depth about a mission, and it was when they lost their three friends. He came home and lost it. I held him in my arms as he sobbed. That funeral was the most horrific day. All three caskets draped in our nation's colors. The tears flowed relentlessly through the entire ceremony.

"I wish I could tell you, but it's a lot. There wasn't one fucking thing that went right. Not one. It was as if there was someone sabotaging every move we made." He runs his hands down his face. "I swear, Lee, I work with some really smart guys, but they were all dumb that day."

I nod and hope he'll go on.

"They forgot batteries, rounds, a clip, I mean either that or someone was swiping shit before we left. But then we'd get it straight and all set and then something would break. We got to this one area to do some intel and none of our radios would work. I couldn't communicate with anyone. The guys were pinned down in one area of the village, and I stayed hidden until Quinn made visual. I figured the coast was clear, but it wasn't. As soon as we figured out we were being trailed, we split off again. The radio wasn't working, and I couldn't risk using the sat phone."

Liam grips my hand and looks away. His head rests against the seat as I wait.

"We're lucky. It was straight luck that we were able to get out of that one, but we had to double back a different route to make sure nothing led us back to the rest of the team. There were hostiles watching our every move. I wasn't able to get the intel we needed because of what a mess everything was. As soon as we got to a safer place, I got the message, and we high-tailed it home."

"I was so worried."

"I can imagine. But you'd have never known if this wasn't happening."

I let out a deep sigh and look down at our joined hands. "That doesn't comfort me either. I know you're at risk, but I'm pregnant again. I don't want to raise two babies as a single mom."

Liam lifts our hands then kisses the top of my hand. "I can't promise you anything in regards to this, Lee. You know that. I know it sucks worrying about me when I'm gone, but I can only promise that I love you and I'm doing everything I can."

He's right and I know that I have to be strong. I don't doubt our love. I know what we have is special but it's also fragile. We live in a world where they are trained to think they're invincible. They take chances everyday people don't take.

"You mean so much to me," I explain.

"Relax, I'm here now. We've got a long few days ahead of us."

I lay my head against his shoulder and inhale his scent. The sandalwood and cologne takes me back to where it all started. The way he held me and calmed me. I allow that feeling to wash over me again.

He doesn't say anything, but I know it's because his mind is lost on his mother. He lifts the seat divider and tucks me against his chest. My hand rests on his heart, and he keeps his on my belly. The exhaustion and overload of emotions takes over and we both fall asleep.

"Hey," Liam's voice breaks through my sleep-induced fog. "Come on, sweetheart."

He nudges me a little and I get up. "I haven't slept that good in a long time." I smile, and he looks at my stomach.

He puts his bags down and grabs my hips. I watch in awe as his head lowers and he kisses my belly. "Hi." Tears well in my eyes. "I'm going to be your Daddy."

A woman behind Liam stands with her hand over her chest. My fingers touch his dark brown hair and gently move of their own accord. He amazes me with the amount of care and tenderness he has. He's killed people, interrogated terrorists, climbed mountains, and who knows what, but with me . . . he's different.

Liam's head lifts and he kisses me, grabs the bags, and smiles.

"Why do you have to be so perfect?"

"Because I was made for you."

"There you go again." I smile and shake my head.

"You like me this way."

"I guess so," I shrug my shoulders and start to turn, but Liam grabs my hand. "What's wrong?"

"I don't know that I can say goodbye to her," he admits. "I didn't even see her before I left. I mean, what kind of piece of shit doesn't say goodbye to his own mom before deployment?"

The guilt rises because instead of Liam going home to see his family, we went away.

"I'll be with you the entire time," I try to reassure him. This will be hard on him and his father. I know what loss feels like, and I can only hope I give them a tiny amount of comfort.

We grab a cab then head toward the hospital. Liam is filled with nervous energy as his leg bounces and he keeps grabbing his neck. I've been there and I'm relying on my own memories to help get him through this. I remember the things I hated, but then in my situation, I also didn't know it was coming. I was distraught, but I try to imagine how it would be to know this is happening. To watch someone you love die must be worse.

Liam calls his father and he instructs us where to go.

"Liam," his father says in a half cry as he sees him.

"Dad." He takes him into his arms and both men begin to lose it.

"I can't lose her, son. I don't know a world without her." He cries on his shoulder and tears stream down my cheek. His father looks up and steps back. "You must be Natalie."

I nod and walk to him. "I am. I'm so sorry we are meeting this way." I go to shake his hand, but he embraces me immediately.

"I've heard so much about you and your daughter." He lets me go and Liam smiles.

Liam pulls me to his side then kisses my temple. He murmurs, "Go sit. It's been a lot of time on your feet."

I nod in agreement. I head over to a chair while the two men talk. He fills Liam in on more details, and Liam's head falls into his hands. They both cry with each other as they mourn the fact that she will never recover. She's on full life support and Aidan has been keeping her alive so Liam could say goodbye.

Liam heads over to me and squats down, taking my hand in his and rubbing his calloused thumb across the delicate skin. "I have to go in there," A tear falls. "I need you with me. I need to introduce you to her and tell her about our baby."

The sorrow in his eyes mirrors mine. I don't say anything, but I stand. He tugs me against his side and holds my hip. We walk slowly and I wrap my arms around his torso. I hold him while he holds me. I know he's hurting. You can feel it coming off of him. The smell of bleach and despair filters through the air.

He stops and glimpses at me as the mask I know all too well slips into place. He's shutting himself off to try to ease the pain. But I'm also aware that it doesn't stop it. You may think it does. You only hope to cloak yourself in the delusions of being fine. The pain though doesn't care. It penetrates through the open fibers, seeps through your soul, and eats at you if you let it. I won't let it consume him though. I'll fight for him to come to the light just as he did for me.

CHAPTER TWENTY-FIVE

LIAM

I'M SUPPOSED TO be a man. A man's man, the ones who can do anything. I'm a goddamn Navy SEAL. I've been to war and seen some awful shit. I've battled through things most men can only imagine. Yet here I stand like a little bitch hesitating to open that door.

This is the woman who fucking raised me. She gave me everything. Taught me how to treat a woman, slapped me around when I did it wrong. I never really thought about what it would be like to lose a parent. They're still young and I'm not ready to lose her.

"Liam," Natalie encourages. Her thin arms stay wrapped around me as if she's holding me together. And right now—she is. I look down at her and wait for some sort of courage to arrive. But it's there in her eyes. Her strength and love are there in her face. Even with all the crap that's come between us, she's been strong.

I nod and open the door. She lies there with tubes and monitors everywhere. The steady beeping tells me that she's alive, but only thanks to the machines. A white sheet is draped over her, keeping her warm, but everything around me is ice cold.

I step toward her slowly. Her chest rises and falls, but there's no life there. All I can pray for is that she doesn't feel any pain.

"Hi, Mom," I say as I reach her bedside. "I got here as soon as I could. It's a long story, but you know how it goes." I try to stay strong, but this is my mother. The woman who apparently did diapers and didn't rip the tabs. She's the one who wiped my knee and made me a cape when I needed to be Superman. Shannon Dempsey is the strongest woman in the world. She had kids, buried one, raised another, and I never saw her break down and lose it. I swear she could run laps around the SEALs and put us all to shame.

I failed her. I wasn't here to protect her.

"Please wake up, Mom. I don't know that there's any chance, but I'm begging you, please, if you can . . . do it now. I'm sorry . . . for so many things. I don't know how to say goodbye to you like this." I need to take a second, because I'm going to lose it.

Natalie rubs her fingers down my arm, and I close my eyes. "Hi, Mrs. Dempsey. We met once, but I'm Natalie."

The woman of my dreams stands here talking to my mother while I try to keep it together. She gives me the out so I don't feel so weak.

"I remember you loved to bake. I wish I had the chance to learn from you since I literally am the worst." Natalie smiles and releases my hand. Before I can grab it back, she grips my mother's. "Thank you for giving Liam life. Thank you for raising him to be the man he is. I'll be eternally grateful to you for the joy he's brought into my life." Natalie looks over at me with tears streaming down her face. "He loves me more than I deserve. He loves my daughter and he's given me more than he'll ever understand." She turns back, and I wipe my eyes. "I can only hope to raise my children to be like the man you've raised. He really is the best man I've ever known, and I attribute that to you, so thank you."

She leans down and kisses my mother's cheek. A

woman she's only met once. Then she whispers in her ear and squeezes her hand once more.

That's my undoing.

I fall to my knees and they hit the cold tile. My head falls on the side of the bed and I grip my mother's leg. "Haven't we lost enough? Hasn't my family suffered enough?" I mutter aloud.

We grew up with strict Irish-Catholic parents. Mom stayed home, but I think she worked harder than my father. He got to go to work and come home after Mom had the entire house cleaned and food on the table. Dad is a lawyer and worked his ass off to put me and Krissy in private school. He showed me that hard work was for the family, and when you want something, you don't slack off. You push harder and make your own destiny. So why can't I work to make her better?

"Talk to her, Liam," Natalie encourages while I keep my head bowed. I can't let her see me like this. "Tell her what you want to let her know. She loves you." Her soft voice calms me and I try to hold it, but it's all too fucking much. Everything crashes around me and I remember my sister. I remember her telling me the same thing. She would always tell me that Mom loved me, so I could tell her the truth.

"I'm so sorry, Mom! I'm so fucking sorry! I haven't seen you in a long time and I didn't say goodbye to you." I break apart as Natalie's hand rubs my back. "I lied to you and I didn't tell you all the things that you should've heard. I didn't tell you about how much I wished it were me and not Krissy. I didn't tell you about how much you mean to me. I should've always told you the truth. Like how I really did put gum in Krissy's hair on Easter. Or how I broke your rules about sneaking girls in the house. I took your car that day and then told you it was Krissy. I'm sorry I lied! I failed you."

"Shhh." Natalie runs her fingers through my hair as

I sob, crying at my mother's bedside. "It's okay, trust me, she's not upset or mad. She loves you, Liam. And she knew it was you, you didn't lie. She knows."

I pull back and look at her as we both cry for the pain that surrounds us. There's been so much we've dealt with, but I need Natalie by my side. I only wish my mom could've seen how special she is. That she could've held our children and they would know her love. She would've doted on them, baked cookies, spoiled them until they never wanted to come home to us. She would've been the best grandmother our children ever knew.

"Mom, I want you to meet Lee officially. I told you how I felt a few months ago and you said to follow my heart. She's my heart." I look at Natalie with her glossy eyes and then I stand. I walk and pull a chair over and point to it.

She shakes her head and sits.

"Anyway, I wanted you to be the first to know we're having a baby." Natalie grips my hand. God, I love this woman. "We're going to have a kid, and I'm going to marry her. She doesn't know that yet, but I am. I'm going to love her and be the man you told me to be. I'll give her the world because she deserves it. I'll make you proud."

I hear Natalie sniff and she lets her tears fall. I get down on one knee in front of her. I didn't plan this, I don't have a ring, but I have my heart and she already owns it.

"Natalie Gilcher, I love you more than anyone could love another. My world only makes sense since you've come into it. I want to marry you, love you, adore you, give you children and anything else you want. I'll provide for you and never take you for granted. I know what life is like without you, and I only want to live in a world with you by my side. When I'm gone, my heart will remain with you. Will you allow me the honor to love you from now until the end of time?"

chapter twenty-six

natalie

MY HEART RATE is through the roof and the tears won't stop long enough to see him clearly. I never in a million years expected him to propose now. I mean, we haven't been together that long, and while I know that he's the one for me in every way, I can't think.

"Liam," I say and he wipes the tears from my eyes. "Are you sure?"

I don't want him to do this out of some sense of obligation because we're having a baby. There's not a doubt that I love him and want to be his wife, but I know in grief you can do things impulsively. I want to marry him when he's sure that this is what he's ready for.

"I've never been more sure of anything. I love you, Natalie. I love you more than I can ever tell you. I want to hold you, wipe your tears, kiss you, console you, watch you smile, make love to you every day and every night. I know I don't have a ring—"

"Yes," I say before he can say another word. "Yes, I want to be your wife. I don't need a ring . . . I just need you."

Liam stands and takes me into his arms. He kisses

me with tears spilling between the two of us. He holds my face and looks at his mother who rests peacefully. "She said yes, Mom."

Liam's dad enters a few seconds later and walks to the end of the bed. "Dad, I'd like to tell you that Natalie and I are getting married and she's having our baby. I told Mom as well."

His father smiles and his lip quivers. He looks at his wife and my chest aches. You can see how badly he wants to share this moment. I extract myself from Liam's arms and walk to his father. He opens his arms and I embrace him.

"I'm so happy, but so sad at the same time," he murmurs. "She would've loved you."

I nod understanding exactly what he means. When I held Aarabelle for the first time when we thought Aaron was dead, I wasn't sure if smiling was okay. I remember feeling the utter despair of being without him in that moment but also elation that she was here. His happiness is clouded by his agony. The thing about grief is it comes in many forms and there's no right or wrong way.

"I'm sure I would've loved her as well. But her memory will be cherished. I promise our child will know the woman she was and how much she would've loved them." I vow this and I will live up to that. She was clearly loved and a wonderful woman.

We spend the next few hours in Shannon's room talking to her and telling her stories about Liam and Aarabelle. Aidan smiles and laughs when I tell him about Liam's diaper issues. He tells me stories about Liam as a kid and how he was always into some kind of trouble.

"The worst was when he got into sticking things up his nose," he chuckles and Liam groans.

"Really?"

"Oh, yeah . . . anything he could find. Shannon always wondered when he sneezed what might come out.

He was always talking my Kristine into doing something too. She would get stuck and Liam would pretend he knew nothing." Aidan gets lost in his memories. "I remember one time coming home from work and Shannon was baking a cake for a neighbor. She loved to do things for the other women on the block. She was always helping someone and bringing them food . . . anyway, she was busy, and Liam and Kristine were supposed to stay in the yard. Liam told Krissy that Shannon said it was okay for her to go to their friend's house. I came home and asked her where Kristine was and she panicked. Liam of course claimed Krissy said she didn't care that she wasn't allowed to go . . ."

I look at Liam, who for the first time since we arrived has a little life in his eyes. He smiles and shakes his head. "I think you exaggerate that, Dad. I was a good boy."

He gives one throaty cough-laugh. "I think you're mistaken, son. You were always doing something to get your sister in trouble."

"And she always believed me."

"She loved you," he murmurs. "Now I'll lose both my girls." Aidan looks at his wife and sighs.

"I know the pain you're feeling. It won't ever go away. But one day it won't hurt so bad." I take his hand in mine. "It won't be so hard to breathe. It won't feel like the world is crushing you. One day that will come and it just gets a little easier each day." I give him the small amount of hope I have. "I know right now that seems like a lie, but I've walked in your shoes."

"Thank you, Natalie. My son is very lucky." His other hand covers mine. "I had a great love with Shannon. I always prayed my children would find something like I was blessed to have. I only wish she could see that Liam has."

"I wish she could too," I reply.

"THIS IS HOME." Liam extends his hand forward, and I walk through the door. After spending a few more hours at the hospital, Aidan demanded I get some rest and care for the baby he already loves.

We offered to stay in a hotel, but he would hear nothing of it, and since he refuses to leave her side so there's no point in us giving him space. The house is just as I imagined based on what Liam described. It's an old, brick house with cute, white awnings. The front door is old oak and inside is immaculate. Everything is clean and homey. This is the home you want to spend Sunday dinners at.

"It's exactly like I pictured."

"What does that mean?" he grins.

"Just it's a home. I grew up on a farm in Arkansas, so I'm sure you have this idea of what it looks like. I always pictured you living on a quaint street with green lawns and plastic on the couches." I laugh and then Liam lifts me into his arms. "Put me down."

"Off your feet. I'll show you around."

"I can walk, Liam."

He leans closer and presses his lips against me. "Let me take care of you. I need to hold you."

I understand his need to care for something. When your world is falling apart, sometimes you need something to hold on to. He needs to feel grounded and in control of one aspect of his life.

"You make it really hard to say no."

"I'm counting on that."

I lightly slap his chest and he begins the tour. We find our way through the house. I admire how beautiful her taste is. She's classic with a touch of modern. The kitchen was recently redone, and you can tell that's the heart of the home. Everything is labeled and in its place. It's exactly the type of home where you'd expect Martha Stewart to come out at any moment.

Liam climbs the stairs laughing about how he's having flashbacks of basic training carrying a log. He gets another slap for that.

"This is my room." He opens the door, and I refrain from busting out laughing. It's covered in old posters and photos.

"Wow, this is something else," I say as he still refuses to put me down.

"Zip it."

"Is this Yasmine Bleeth? Like from Baywatch?" I can't stop the hysterical giggles that follow.

"She was hot," he defends and puts me on my feet.

"Will I find old Playboys under your mattress?" I mock him and lift the side up. Before I can get it high enough to see, his hands come around the front of me.

"I'd rather look at my fiancée."

"Liam," I chide. "We're at your parents' house."

"They already told you I don't follow rules well. Besides," his gruff voice drops as his mouth glides across my ear. "You're already pregnant. I think they know."

His tongue runs the rim of my ear and I shiver. "I've missed you," I say as my hand reaches up and wraps around his neck. I hold him against me as I feel his erection press against my ass.

"I need you, Lee. I need you so fucking bad. Are we allowed?"

I nod as his hand comes around my front and presses gently against my stomach. He slowly moves his fingers up and groans as he takes my breast in his hand. "So much better . . ." I trail off as he touches me.

Liam spins me and then lifts my shirt off. He stares at me as his eyes worship me. I decide to take the lead on this. I reach behind me and remove my bra. My breasts fall heavy as his pupils dilate.

I unbutton my jeans and slide them down. He licks his lips as I hook my fingers into my black lace underwear. I begin to slide them lower but decide I need to toy with him a little. I step closer, and his eyes close and his head falls back as I cup his dick. "I think you're overdressed, my future husband."

"Say it again."

"Overdressed." I know this isn't what he wants, but I want to control his mind. I want all that he thinks about is us, even if just for a few minutes.

Liam's thumb presses on my chin and lifts my head. "Not that, sweetheart."

"My," I bring his other hand to my lips and place a kiss on his palm, "Future," another kiss but this time on his thumb, "Husband," the final kiss is on his ring finger where we will be bonded.

He moans and holds my face between his hands. A moment later, his mouth is on mine. Liam controls the kiss. Our mouths stay connected as he devours me. His control is barely hanging on by a thread. Any moment it will fray and he'll obliterate me. I push my tongue against his as we both savor each other. It's been so long. Too long since he's touched me. I pull at him and we're flush against each other. My body burns for him and moisture pools in my core.

Liam removes his hands slowly and his touch becomes a caress. The passion is still present, but it's as if he's found himself again. "Get on the bed," he commands.

As he walks to the door to close it, I sprawl out and wait for him. His eyes burn with an intensity I've never seen. Our gazes stay locked as he stalks me, and I yearn for him. Once he reaches the edge of the bed, I'm nearly panting. "What are you going to do with me now that I'm here?"

Liam unbuttons his pants and removes them along with his underwear. His cock juts out and my eyes flutter. "I'm going to show you just how attentive your future husband will be."

He kneels at the end of the bed and pulls my underwear down. "After I watched you touch yourself, all I could do was replay it in my mind each night. To see you come apart just from the sound of my voice . . . was fucking heaven. So now, I'm going to see how many times I can replay it live."

I rest on my elbows with a grin. "I'm thinking you should put your money where your mouth is . . ."

"How about my mouth goes here?" he leans down and licks my center. My head falls back and he does it again. "Or maybe here?" Liam says as his tongue circles my clit.

"Oh," I moan in sheer bliss.

"Hmm, maybe you'd like me to do this?" he questions as his tongue presses against my entrance. I quake beneath him as he continues to set a pattern. Sweat forms and I start to climb. Between the hormones, and the fact that it's Liam, I can't hold off long.

"Liam," I croak out his name as I start to head toward the precipice.

He inserts a finger then begins to suck on my clit and I fall over it. I sink into the bed as he keeps going. Liam extracts every morsel of my orgasm possible. His tongue doesn't leave my body as he trails up to my stomach. He stays there for a few moments as I come down.

"I'm going to love watching you grow with my child. There will never be anything sexier than knowing you're holding a life we created." I open my eyes as his lips turn up. "We're okay to do this?"

"Yes, I promise we're okay." I press my fingers against the scruff on his face. The feel of it is like home to me.

He hovers over me not putting any weight on me,

and I fight the urge to laugh. "Liam, we can make love."

"What if I hurt the baby?"

"Hurt the baby how?"

"I mean, what if I poke it in the head?"

I begin to laugh hysterically and have to cover my mouth. "You're ridiculous."

"I'm serious! I'm well-endowed, you know . . . it could happen."

"Okay, I love you, so I'm going to pretend you're kidding."

"I'm not!"

Oh, for the love of God. He really has no clue.

"You're not going to poke the baby. First of all, the baby isn't anywhere near my canal. But secondly, it's not possible. We're fine. You and your giant penis will not cause any harm to the baby."

"Yeah, well, if it comes out dented, I'm telling the kid it's your fault."

I giggle while rolling my eyes. After we both stop laughing, I turn serious. "Deal. Now, make love to me. I need you."

He tilts closer and kisses me slowly and carefully. I feel him press inside of me and I sigh into his mouth. Everything feels more intense. Each stroke and thrust is ripping me apart in the best way.

"Fuck. You feel so incredible." Liam keeps his weight off of me but isn't gentle as he plunges deeper and deeper. But it's not far enough. I want to feel him everywhere.

"Let me get on top." I push him back and he turns us easily.

I close my eyes and sink down on his length. Liam's voice rasps as he tries to form words, but nothing is coherent. "Lee, fuck. God. You."

His hands hold my hips as he guides me to his pace. I feel the orgasm start to take shape again. It grows stronger with each brush of my clit and the feel of his cock inside me.

"I can't," I say aloud as the smell of sex and sweat fills the room.

"You can. Give me everything."

I close my eyes and Liam reaches between us and presses his thumb against my clit. I can't hold back. I come with such intensity I swear I black out. Liam grunts a few times and follows me over.

I lie against his chest listening to his heartbeat. After a few minutes of coming down from our incredible high, I go and clean myself. When I come back into his room, he's on his back staring at the ceiling.

He turns on his side as I climb in bed with him. "Hi," he says sounding forlorn.

"Hi."

"I think tomorrow is when they'll take her off the life support."

Liam wraps his arm around me and rubs my back. "I wish I had some magic words to make this easy. There's nothing that will ease this but time. And I'll be by your side every step. You'll never be alone." He kisses my forehead and I nestle into his chest. "I thought I lost you."

"It's going to take a lot more than some idiots to keep me from coming home to you."

I look up and he pushes my hair back. "It's a fear I'm always going to struggle with."

"And I'll try to ease it, but no matter what, I'll fight 'till the end."

"That's all we can do."

"Well, and love each other," Liam says, trying to lighten the mood.

"Good thing we've got that down."

"How about I make sure one more time?"

I smile and push him onto his back. "By all means . . . we should be sure."

"I THINK IT'S time. She wouldn't want this," Aidan says to the doctor. Liam and I stand on one side of her bed, waiting for what's to come.

"Okay, Mr. Dempsey. I'll give you each some time to say your goodbyes, and then we'll be back to start the process." He looks at all of us and no one speaks.

Aidan looks at his wife and then Liam. "I'll give you time first. I need a few minutes before I do this."

Liam looks lost. He gazes back and forth at his parents and my chest squeezes. Our fingers tangle and he stares at me. I'm not sure what to do, but I know that just holding his hand could help.

After a few moments, Liam lets go and heads to his mother's side.

"I can remember as a kid people talking about their moms and how they hated them. Do you know there was never a time I felt that way? I never hated you because there was never a reason for it. You were the mother people wish for. Yeah, you called me to the carpet, but I deserved it." Liam's voice is reverent as he speaks of her. "I don't think I ever told you how much you meant to me. I wish I had more time with you, Mom. I never thought you wouldn't be around. You'll never hold our baby or just be there to tell me to stop being stupid. What's Dad going to do? We're not a family without you."

Liam takes a break then walks toward the window. He discreetly tries to remove the tears that are falling. This wrecks me, watching him handle his grief. The pain that he feels I want to carry for him. Be the rock he needs and heal him like he did for me.

I walk over to him and place my hand on his back.

"I can't say goodbye to her. I can't tell her it's okay to die," he says defiantly.

"You love her and she loved you. You don't have to say goodbye."

"She's going to die the minute the machines stop."

"And she'll be surrounded by the two men in her life that she loves."

"My father is going to die alongside her, Lee. He's been with her since they were fifteen."

Their love story mimicked part of my own, but I won't say that. I want to point out that he'll be okay just as I was, but I don't. There will be a part of his father that won't ever recover. A young love that stands the test of time isn't something he'll ever find again. He might not ever love again, but he'll survive.

"Then you be the son you are. You remind him why he has to carry on. You give him the strength he'll need . . . just like you did for me. There's no one I know that's as strong as you."

"She was." Liam looks over at his mother again and heads toward her. He takes her delicate hand in his and kisses the top of it. "I'm going to miss you. I hope you find Kristine in heaven and tell her I loved her. Tell her how she'd be an aunt to two little girls. Hold her in your arms and know that you'll be in my heart. I was blessed to have you as a mother." Liam puts her hand down and leans in. He gently presses his lips to the top of her head and then let's out a deep sob.

I rush to his side and pull him into my arms. He holds me close and takes a few deep breaths.

"I'm here," is all I can say to him. There are no words that will comfort him, and I'm not stupid enough to try. I offer him my love and my heart.

Aidan walks in a few moments later and looks at his wife. "I've said my goodbyes to you, Shannon. And we will meet again, my love." He stands tall and almost ready. The Dempsey men stare at each other for a second before he speaks again. "Will you pray with me?"

We all gather around her bed and Liam's father grabs my hand. I take Liam's and they each grab Shannon's. Linked together, we stand, and Aidan begins to speak. "Today, I'll say goodbye to the only woman I've ever loved. We've lived a good life together. Had two children and learned that life isn't always fair. It isn't fair that Shannon will be taken from us so soon. It isn't fair that she'll never see the life that will come." His words are shaky as emotion begins to take him. "But I trust that you'll hold my love in your hands. You'll take her pain away and reunite her with part of her heart that was lost. I pray you'll keep her protected until I can make it to her. I'll be there soon, my angel."

Aidan releases my hand, but Liam won't drop my other.

My stomach starts to clench and my hand automatically flies to it. Liam reacts instantly and sits me in the chair. "Please, stay off your feet."

"It was just a small cramp," I try to reassure him. It wasn't even nearly as bad as the last time. I called Dr. Contreras yesterday and she explained the cramping would be normal and try to take it easy.

The doctor enters and explains what's to come. We gather around as the doctors and nurses start the process. Liam sits in the chair with me in his lap. Aidan holds Shannon's hand and refuses to let go. They work around him and he nods as they turn off the final machine. Thankfully, they turn the sound off on the heart monitor. Aidan tilts down and whispers in her ear with tears floating in his eyes. He speaks continuously until her heart stops beating.

He kisses her lips, lays her hand down on the bed, and walks out of the room.

I stand and Liam follows his father. I look out the window and see him pull him into his arms and keep his father from sinking to the ground.

chapter twenty-seven

WE SPENT A week in Ohio after she passed. Her will stated her wishes and she demanded no funeral. She wanted to be cremated and her ashes be spread in her homeland. Aidan booked a flight for Ireland, and Liam and I returned home. He's been quiet but seems okay. Aaron is coming over tonight and asked if they could talk. Mason and Liam had a call today and they're going to allow him to stay behind from the deployment since a few new guys checked in. Instead of sending him to finish out the month, he'll train and get everyone settled here.

Part of me thinks it was a favor, but all I can be is grateful.

"Okay, Aara, I've got ten bucks that says you can go on the potty." He sits on the floor and plays with her while I rest on the couch.

The flights were a lot for me, and even though I did my best to take it easy, I want to be more careful now that we can be.

"You know she's too young to be bought and you're about to have a whole heap of diapers in your life."

"But if we can get rid of one of them with diapers that's a win," he scoffs and goes back to Aarabelle. "Okay, princess, how does this work? Do you just tell me? Do we stick you on it?"

"Oh, Jesus." I lean up, and he pins me with his eyes.

"Don't make me tie you to the couch."

"You don't scare me."

He crawls toward me with a gleam in his eyes. "Oh?" His moves are lithe and catlike. Liam's mouth is a thin line as he approaches. "I think you like testing me."

"I think you like to be tested."

He reaches the couch and he scoops me into his arms. Quickly he places me on the floor and hovers over me. "No more tests. I think we've passed them all anyway."

I smile and thread my fingers in his hair. "I'd say we have."

Aarabelle stands and lies on top of Liam's back. "Dada, up?"

He does a push up with her hanging on his back and kisses me when he comes down. She giggles and I hold her sides so she doesn't fall. Liam goes slow and lingers when he reaches my lips.

"I think you're enjoying this," I giggle in between kisses.

"I'll enjoy it more when you're my wife."

I struggle with how fast we're moving. I want to marry him, give him a life, be his everything, but I also don't want to hurt Aaron terribly. Aaron's a good father and he's trying to be a good friend. The one thing I think both of these men need is their friendship back. Liam saved Aaron's life, and in a way, Aaron's death gave Liam something. It's messy and ugly, but my marriage wasn't what it appeared.

Aaron and I have worked to find a way to get along for Aarabelle, and Liam will be her stepfather. She'll live with us, and I want Aaron to be a part of Aara's life.

"Liam," I sigh and he stops. Aarabelle climbs into his lap when he sits. She's so attached to him. "I'm not trying to put anything off, but I don't think we need to rush."

He looks away and resignation paints his face. "I'm marrying you before you have this baby. I want to bring our child into the world with two loving and married parents. I'm not asking for anything big. All I want is you, me, and Aarabelle on the beach."

"This baby will have two loving parents whether we're married or not."

"This is going to sound really bad, but I don't ask you for much. I didn't push you to choose me because I knew you would. I don't get upset about your ex-husband hanging around the house because he's Aarabelle's father and he was my friend. I've sacrificed and lost a lot. Now, though . . . now, you are mine." Aara moves off his lap and he moves toward me. "I want this because life is short. I want this because if I have to leave again, I need to know you're set. I need this because *I* need it."

My mind spins in circles on how to respond. Before I can answer, a knock comes.

"We'll revisit this . . ." Liam says and he gets up to grab the door.

I look over and Aaron is standing there. Neither of them speaks and you can cut the tension with a knife.

Aaron steps a little closer and extends his hand. "I'm sorry about your mom."

Liam grips his hand. "I appreciate it."

"Glad to hear you're okay too. I know everyone was worried."

While this is the most awkward thing I've ever experienced, it gives me optimism. They're talking—civilly. Aarabelle peeks from behind the couch and begins to giggle.

"Hi, pumpkin!" Aaron exclaims and she runs full speed.

"It was a mess . . ." Liam begins but hesitates.

Aaron raises Aara up and kisses her, then turns to Liam. "The mission?"

I breathe a heavy sigh of relief and fight the smile that's building. Maybe we'll all get through this sooner than we thought.

Liam starts to tell Aaron about some of the stuff that went wrong on the mission and why they went dark. A lot of it either goes over my head, or I just don't want to know. These two have been friends for a long time and to see their friendship end was hard. I know that there was a lot of hurt between us all, but I think Aaron and I have come to a point where we also know our marriage was over before he died. Neither of us were ready to face facts.

"Athair," Aarabelle says, which is pronounced "*ah her.*" It means "father" in Gaelic. We decided to start pushing that more and more over the last few weeks. We want her to have something special to call Liam, but allow Aaron to be her Daddy.

"I'm here. I'm here." Liam gives her one of his hands as she gives him a toy.

We spend about an hour just playing with Aara. We talk about work and some of the things the doctors have told Aaron. His PTSD symptoms are gradually getting better and he's starting to feel like the person he was before the deployment where they lost half their friends.

"Do you think we could step out and talk for a minute?" Liam says and my eyes snap up.

"Sure," Aaron replies reluctantly.

Liam walks over and grabs my hand. "Trust me. This has to happen."

"Please," I beg.

"I'll be right back."

They step out of the room, heading out onto the deck. Fear grips me, and my chest tightens. I press my ear to the door but can't hear anything. Minutes pass, feeling hopeful they're getting along since I don't hear anything breaking.

"What the heck are they talking about, Aarabelle?" I ask rhetorically and lie down before I get myself worked up.

She climbs on the couch with me, I nestle her into my chest. I love the moments I get her like this. Usually if Liam or Aaron are around, she's climbing on them, but when it's me and her, she's my snuggle bunny.

"Pretty soon Mommy is going to be so big you're going to have to lie with me on the bed. You're going to be a big sister," I say animatedly. Her smile lights up her face, and although she doesn't know what I'm talking about, my excitement grows. "You'll get to be spoiled even more, because if I know your uncles, they'll overcompensate."

More minutes go by, and finally Liam walks in without Aaron.

Great.

"What happened?" I ask.

"We needed to talk, Lee. Man to man. He needed to know from me."

I turn my head and try to hold my anger in. "You should've talked to me."

"Natalie," he tries to capture my attention. "Look at me."

I let out a shaky breath and then turn to him.

"I did what I would want him to do. I told him the truth. The more we lie, the worse this will be. I know him. I know you're afraid to hurt him any more. And believe me, I don't want to watch him suffer either. He was my fucking friend. He's going to be a part of our lives forever." Liam looks at Aara. "He's her father. Aaron has a place in our family, and that's the reality we face. So I went to him as his friend and told him I asked you to marry me."

My throat feels like it's closing in. All of this is so overwhelming. My future husband is telling my former husband that he plans to marry me. I've decided that I'm the only one in the world who has to deal with this shit.

"He isn't happy, but he respects it. He said he knew it was coming and we talked. Will he be at our wedding? No. Will he be happy about it? I sure as fuck wouldn't be. But he knows and he won't be blindsided when it happens. We're both grown men and I won't lie, and I sure as hell am not going to hide. This is our life and we have to find a way to live it."

"I know. It's just a lot. A baby, a marriage, you just lost your mom. I just want us to be sure. I want to build a solid marriage, not one that you or I feel like is because of something else."

It's not me who I worry about . . . it's him. He asked me to marry me as his mother was dying. I'm pregnant with a very high-risk pregnancy. And that is on the heels of him having major complications on a very dangerous deployment.

"I know this . . . you and I have been through hell. We've come out stronger, in love, together, and a family. I want to marry you and know that when I'm gone, you'll have the military backing. I'd wait twenty years if it took you that long to be ready to marry me, but that's not what you're saying. You keep saying it's me. It's not me, Lee. If you don't want to get married because you need more time . . . just tell me. But don't turn this on me, sweetheart. I'd pack the car and go today."

"It's not me I worry about. But if you mean it, then let's do it."

Liam lifts me into his lap then pulls my face to his. We kiss, and I feel the joy coming from his body. It's as if I just gave him the best gift. Only it's him who is giving me more than I can express. I really don't know how I could've gotten so lucky.

We head into the kitchen and I start to fuss about how there's nothing to eat. I swear I never had any cravings with Aarabelle, but this one, all I want is chicken and cashews. I could eat it every meal and be happy. Of course, I don't, but I try to convince Liam to order out. Aara sits in her highchair eating her tiny pieces of chicken nuggets while I groan and moan about Liam not getting his pregnant fiancée what she wants.

"I have something for you."

"You do? Is it an eggroll?"

"Oh, I got your eggroll, sweetheart. I think you'll like this better."

"Doubtful," I huff playfully.

Aarabelle and I make faces at each other while Liam taps his foot. "Are you done being a brat?"

"You did not just call me a brat!" My eyes widen, and I drop the fork.

"I did . . . now, I'm trying to be romantic, and you're killing the mood."

"Romance in the kitchen? I'm excited now." I sit up, pretending to be fully engaged. I'm tired, hungry, and feel nauseated all at the same time.

"Brat," he repeats as he gets down on one knee again. "Now do I have your attention?" Liam's smile is soft and his eyes are full of love.

I nod as he extracts a black box and then places it on my knee unopened.

"Aarabelle, I'm going to ask you if this is okay . . ." She looks at him while he grins. "Eat, cry, whine, poop, stare off or at me, or smile if you want me to marry your mommy."

I laugh and she looks at me.

"Sold!" Liam exclaims. "Natalie and Aarabelle . . . I want to be a part of your lives forever. I want to care for you, love you, and be here for you." He grabs her hand and I cover my mouth with my hand. "I'll be your Dad even though I'm not your father. You already own me and I'll do anything for you."

A tear falls as he addresses the one thing in this world

that would've stopped me from being with him.

Liam's eyes shift and he touches my knee. "This was my mother's ring."

With shaky hands, I touch the box and open it slowly. Nestled in the velvet is the most beautiful antique ring. It's white gold with pave diamonds on the band and around the center stone. The large diamond is round and protected by the other diamonds. It's absolutely beautiful.

"Liam," I look up as another tear falls, "It's . . ."

"My father said he thinks she would want you to wear it. She would've loved you and he hopes we have as much love as they shared." He takes it out and slides it on my left ring finger.

"I think we'll have more," I press my lips against his. He holds my cheeks and kisses me with so much fierceness it nearly knocks me off the chair. Aarabelle starts to yell for him and bangs on the table.

"I love you too, princess." He kisses the top of her head and I melt.

He's going to make me very happy and I'm going to cherish every second I have with him.

chapter twenty-eight

"ARE YOU READY to see the baby?" Dr. Contreras asks as she puts the cold gel on my stomach. Liam stands next to me holding my hand.

"Yes," I nod and look up at him. His eyes are focused on the machine. It's finally time for my ultrasound and we're going to see our baby. We had to push back a few weeks with all the craziness, but I'm beyond ready.

"And we're doing the gender reveal later, so you don't want to know, correct?"

Liam groans then shifts his attention to me. "They don't have to know we know. We can pretend we don't know at this stupid party. Look, I even have a great shocked face." I glance over and he gives his best impression.

Such a dork.

I ignore him, "No, we don't want to know."

"You suck."

"You're being a baby. The party is in two weeks."

"Stupid. I'm the father. I should know before some damn baker."

"Zip it."

She laughs and puts the wand on my stomach. I swear I don't remember being so big with Aarabelle this early. I'm either retaining a lot of water or my body figures it's already done this so might as well return to form.

The room fills with the wooshing sound of the baby's heartbeat. Liam's eyes widen, and his jaw drops as it echoes around us.

"What the hell is that?"

Dr. Contreras smiles. "That's your baby's heart. Nice and strong."

"Our baby has a heart," he says sounding clearly surprised.

I giggle, "I know."

"I didn't mean that literally."

I twist my fingers with his and listen with a full heart. It's a miracle we're standing here hearing our baby or that any of this is happening.

"See that there," the doctor says pointing. "That's the baby's heart. You can see everything looks good there."

She continues to show us small glimpses of our peanut. Each time she points a new piece out, Liam claims he sees a penis, which she obviously won't confirm. She goes through all the organs then hands us a few photos.

"I'll let you get dressed and then I'll be back to go over everything," she explains.

"Is there anything to be concerned about?"

"I just want to look at the timeline and set a plan." Her voice is reassuring, but something has me on edge.

Liam kisses the top of my head, and hands me a towel to clean off.

"I have a bad feeling," I relay my fears to him.

"Everything looks fine, Lee. I know you're worried, but from what I saw, the kid's got all the parts."

"Says the man who thought he would dent him or her with his giant penis."

"Can't help the equipment that was bestowed upon me."

I stare, waiting until he looks over so he can see my face. He's smiles then sits next to me.

"All joking aside, if there's something wrong, we'll

handle it. But you've had a rough go at getting pregnant and staying pregnant . . . so, this is good. We're at twenty-three weeks now. I'm handling everything I can so you can stay off your feet. Let's just wait before we freak out."

My head falls on his shoulder, and he wraps his arm around me. There are times in my life I feel so weak. As if all anyone does is reassure me that things will be fine. It's just this baby . . . this life inside of me . . . is my chance. It's my chance to prove I wasn't broken or marred, but that I was meant to be a mother.

We sit here quietly and Dr. Contreras knocks and enters. "Okay, everything looked good. The baby's heart and all of the organs are great. I've sent the gender off to the cake people, so yes, we were able to get a clear picture of that." She smiles and then looks at the chart. "Only issue I have is your weight. You need to eat a little more. So far, you're not gaining much and you said you weren't having morning sickness. Are you eating healthy?"

"I have a kid who has no idea how to sit for two seconds so that could be why."

She nods. "I want you to make sure you're taking in enough calories for you and the baby."

"She'll eat." Liam offers his promise.

"I'll be more mindful."

Dr. Contreras smiles and shakes my hand. "Good. I'll see you in a few weeks."

She turns to Liam and he returns the gesture. "She'll eat . . . no worries."

"Thanks, caveman. Go put your club away before you hit yourself on the head," I say grabbing my coat.

The doctor laughs while leaving the room. Liam and I head to the car, I look closer at the sonogram to see if I can figure out if it's a boy or girl. It's going to kill me to wait until the gender reveal. Reanell and her stupid party. I was against it from the beginning, but somehow she tricked Liam into thinking this would be a fun idea.

Aidan returns from Ireland next week and is coming into Dulles, so he asked if he could come for a visit and meet Aarabelle. We figured we could spend the week with him and then find out the sex of the baby.

I groan, "I can't tell if I see a penis." I huff and throw myself back on the seat.

"Careful with the pushing on the seat please."

"You're kidding me?"

"Sweetheart, Robin has been good to us."

"Robin can't fit two kids in the back." I call this to his attention and the shock ripples across his face.

"That's not even funny if you're telling me what I think you're telling me."

I turn slightly so I can watch this. "You and Robin are going to need to come to some kind of understanding. You're going to need a new woman."

"Robin is mine and I am hers."

"I thought I was yours," I raise my brow.

"But . . . you . . . but . . ." Liam splutters and grips the wheel. I wouldn't ask him to sell his car, but this is almost too fun.

"It's just not practical." I shrug and turn my head so he can't see my smile.

"What if we have an every other weekend deal?"

I swear I've never seen a man so attached to a piece of metal before, but this is Liam. The man who fed my child cake and tied her diaper on with rope. He's the guy who will wax his car by hand for two hours to ensure the paint stays pristine. I really hope we have a girl, because if it's a boy, he'll be teaching him this same craziness.

"I'll think about it."

"I'll make it worth your while." Liam's voice is full of promise.

I giggle and sink into the seat. I'm happy. Deliriously happy. I have the most amazing man, a beautiful little girl, and another baby on the way. Aaron is alive, and we both have a way to find peace. He and Liam have been speaking in very small doses, but it feels like things are how they were meant to be.

"YOU LOOK BEAUTIFUL," Jackson says as he kisses my cheek.

"Thanks, I'm getting huge." I feel like I keep saying the same thing. I swear, I'm going to wind up giving birth to a damn toddler.

It's finally gender reveal day. I've had to fight the urge to call the bakery pretending I'm Reanell and need the color of the cake. It's been killing me not knowing. I've debated killing her for talking me into this. She claims I owe her since Mason is deployed and she has no other means of fun.

"Nonsense." Jackson steps inside before I see Catherine behind him.

"Cat!" I scream and embrace her. "You didn't say you were coming."

"I wouldn't miss it. I had to come to New York for a meeting, so I planned it so I could be here."

"How's wedding planning?"

"Going . . . we're not in a rush. What about you? Jackson said you and Liam . . ."

I show her the ring and she gasps. "Wow, that's breathtaking."

"It was his mother's ring."

"It's beautiful. Any guesses on the baby?" She smiles as her shoulders scrunch up.

"I think it's a girl. Liam swears it's a girl too."

We've argued for two weeks about the sex. Before I can explain, I feel a hand on my lower back.

"It's a girl," Liam's husky voice says from behind me.

"I really think you should change to thinking it's a

boy," I say for the tenth time today.

"Not a chance, sweetheart. If you want someone to be wrong, it's going to be you." Liam's hand snakes down and squeezes my butt.

I slap him and scoff, "He's impossible."

"Wait," Catherine says confused. "You want him to think opposite?"

"Yes, that way he's wrong, and I can gloat." Makes perfect sense to me.

"I thought Jackson and I were competitive." Catherine laughs as someone else knocks on the door.

"Excuse me," I say and walk to see who's is here.

"Now," Reanell says as soon as the door opens. She has the cake in her hand, and I have to remember I need to keep it together. "Before you do something stupid like tackle me . . ." She waits until I look at her eyes. "You will behave, or I'll never watch your kids, and when Liam pisses you off, I'll tell him things to fuel his argument."

"Some friend you are."

"God, you're a peach when you're pregnant," she laughs and eyes me as she moves past me.

"Good enough to eat," Liam says hushed against my ear.

"Change your choice!" I yell and rush after him. I wrap my arms around his back and he sighs.

When we're like this, nothing can hurt me. He blankets the fears that threaten to smother me. With him there is peace.

Liam turns then his arms cross against my back. He holds me as his blue eyes prick with wonder. "You are trouble." He slants down and kisses me. "Good thing I like trouble." Another kiss to my lips.

"Let's go cut our cake . . ." I try to lure him.

"Have you been cramping at all?" Liam asks seriously.

I've had a few sparingly, but nothing like the last

time. I've been taking it easy and trying to stay off my feet. Of course, Aarabelle doesn't fully get that, so Paige has been brought on as a full-time nanny for a work-from-home mom. She helps with so much more than I could expect, and she's very attached to Aara.

"No, Dad. I've been good. I promise I'll be careful."

"There's my wife!" Mark comes in with his booming voice. "How's our sparkly baby coming along?"

"You're so dumb." I laugh and hit his arm.

"Hands off my woman, Twilight," Liam warns with a hint of playfulness in his voice.

"Or what?"

"I'll kick your ass."

"Bring it. I'm twice your age and twice your size." He winks at me and taunts Liam. "When the doctors told us the great news, we were thrilled... then we realized we'd have to tell you."

"Oh, for the love of God." I push Mark, and they both burst out laughing.

"Did you see her face?" Mark says between guffaws.

"Dude, we had her good."

"Assholes," I mutter and walk away.

Quinn arrives late as usual, and we all grab seats and catch up. This is more like a barbeque than anything else. Aarabelle is, of course, on Liam's lap most of the day and occasionally she and Jackson play a little. Knowing how Jackson also lost a child breaks my heart. His daughter or son would've been almost four I think. He will really be such an amazing dad one day.

Aidan and I spend a good amount of time talking. He's already head over heels in love with Aarabelle. She delivers him toys as she shares her half-eaten cookies. He never blinks an eye, just takes a bite and asks if he can have her call him *Seanathair,* which means "grandfather" in Gaelic.

Of course, this will take a long time to teach her, but

it means a lot to him. It also will help cause less confusion for the new baby as well. It gives the men the same name for both children.

"Okay, I'm going to eat the damn cake myself if we don't get to it now," Liam says and claps his hands.

Everyone laughs as Reanell glares at him. "One call and I'll have your ass back on a plane," she toys with him.

"That is, of course, if Commander's wife says it's okay to cut the cake."

We all laugh at Liam's quick rephrasing, and Rea smiles.

"Let's go find out what the bun in the oven is."

We head over to the table where there are two small egg shaped cakes. Both white, and once we cut them open, we'll know.

"Okay, the way this works is only one of you cuts the cake and the other announces the sex," Rea explains.

"Why are there two?" I ask.

"Maybe there are two babies," she jokes. Or at least she better be joking.

"Not even funny."

Rea smiles, "I got two because the one wouldn't feed this herd. Let's be real here, Mark could eat that cake on his own."

Mark scoffs, "I'm not the one named Muffin Top. Let us not forget who's the fat kid with the cake here."

"Funny," Jackson replies, and we all bust out laughing.

"Liam, why don't you cut the egg, and Lee can let us know what it is!" She bounces with excitement.

Liam's eyes focus on the cake as he grabs the knife. He places it down, my eyes look to him in confusion before hands grip my face, and he presses his lips to mine. You can hear the group laugh and make teasing noises, but all I focus on is him.

He pulls back and stares for a beat. "I love you and

right now . . . I'm just happy."

"Me too. You make me this way."

We both smile at each other and Liam starts to look around the room. "Aara?" he calls out.

Within seconds, she's running across the room toward us.

"There you are. Wanna see if you're going to have a sister or brother?" She starts to reach for the cake. "Or better let's have some cake."

Liam inclines, and I think he's going for the knife instead he sticks Aarabelle's hand in the cake.

"Liam!" I start to complain, but then when her hand comes out, we both just look at each other and smile.

chapter twenty-nine

"A BOY?" LIAM and I both start laughing. Which only increases as Aarabelle presses her now blue hand on Liam's face.

"Well," his eyes shine bright. "We were both wrong."

"It's going to be a boy!" I yell out as everyone claps.

Aarabelle goes back for more of the cake, which is now everywhere. Liam's face is covered in frosting and cake. He dips his finger down while I warn him with my eyes.

"Don't do it."

"But we should match."

"Liam Dempsey, you do it, and so help you God . . ."

"You wouldn't want to make me blue."

"Something else is going to be blue."

Liam leans forward and lifts Aara between us and she gets me straight on the nose. Her hands glide down my face as she smears it everywhere. We all laugh, and I can't help but feel as if the sun is shining down upon us.

We clean up and everyone comes over to talk to us. Liam reaches around and grabs my hand. Sometimes out of nowhere he'll do this. It's as if he needs to ground himself and I'm that for him. I love that through our touch he can feel like home.

I head into the kitchen and start to put away some of the dirty dishes. I look out the window at the ocean and smile. Arms come around my stomach, and I settle back against him. He holds me against his chest, and I rest my head on his shoulder.

"I just talked to Quinn," Liam grumbles softly.

"I'm sorry," I joke.

"He gave me the keys to the house in Corolla. I can call a priest and we can go next weekend. What do you say?"

I put the plate down and shut the water off. Liam moves back so I can turn and face him. Immediately his arms find their way around me again. I wrap mine around his neck and look into the eyes of the man I love. "This weekend?"

"I don't need anything but you and Aarabelle. Quinn said he'd stand in for me and I'm sure Reanell will. Jackson and Catherine are here . . . it's your call, sweetheart."

If it were any other man, I don't know that I could so soon. If it were any other SEAL, I wouldn't be able to. But this is Liam. While we didn't find each other in the most conventional way, we found each other when we needed to. He's truly my other half.

"Looks like you're about to get hitched, Dreamboat."

"I'm going to make you the happiest woman in the world."

My fingers glide across to the scruff that's trimmed again. His strong jawline and dark brown hair scratch against my skin. "You made me fall in love with you and then you gave me a child. You loved me even when I was a mess. I think you've fulfilled that promise."

Liam's lifts me gently and lowers himself. Our lips meet and I sigh. His tongue enters my mouth and pushes against mine slowly. Each slide against each other makes my body warm. I feel his fingers glide down my back as he cups my ass. Using the counter behind me he raises me up so I'm sitting. My legs naturally wrap around his waist and he continues to plunge into my mouth.

My fingers grip his hair, holding him against me, but he's just as urgent. Even though there's a house full of people, I can't push him away. I hold him close and I mold to him.

"Seriously, get a room," Reanell enters the kitchen.

I wipe my mouth and the tingle and swelling of my lips is torture. I want more.

"So," I say nonchalantly. "I'm getting married next weekend. Would you like to be my matron of honor?"

"Only if you don't call it matron. Makes me feel old."

"You are old."

"Whatever. You're pregnant."

"You're quick. So . . . will you?" I ask trying not to laugh.

Reanell rushes over and pushes Liam out of the way. She wraps her arms around me and rocks back and forth. "I would love to. You know I can't say no to you."

Mark walks in carrying a bunch of trash. "So the party is in here?"

Liam looks over with the biggest smile and I give him one right back. "Next weekend," Liam says. "We're getting married."

"You can't," Mark says deadpan.

"Why the hell not?" I ask.

"Because you're my wife and that's my baby. This is some Jerry Springer shit up in here."

Liam pushes his chest. "The wedding will be in Corolla, fuckstick." He laughs and walks out of the kitchen.

Mark heads over. "I'm happy for you, Lee. I don't know if I'll make it and I hope you understand. It's not choosing . . . it's just that if it were me . . ." he trails off and it clicks that he's talking about Aaron. "I wouldn't want to be alone."

"I don't want him to be either."

I've made peace with Aaron. Healing came despite great despair. Life may have thrown me around, but it's shown me that sometimes love can come in places we never thought to look.

"I'll let you know, but even if I'm not there, I want you to know I'm happy. I think you and Aaron made the right choice." Mark sits at the table and I join him.

"You know, all those years we were trying to make things work, there were times I wished he would leave. He was unhappy. I was unhappy, but I thought if we could just have a baby, it would make things okay. I really believed it would heal us."

Mark grabs my hand. "I think the mission we lost Brian, Devon, and Fernando altered all of our lives. Jackson was never the same, and I think Aaron carried more shit than we knew. All of us lost our friends that day and we lived. There's a level of guilt you carry through that. I dealt with mine and made peace with it. But I don't know that those two did. Aaron had you to focus on, and when a man can't do something he was made to do . . ." he trails off.

"Aaron didn't fail me, Mark. He wasn't the issue with getting pregnant, but he used that to be selfish. That's why I couldn't go backward."

"Just know that you're my friend too, and I'm not choosing sides. I didn't want you to be upset."

I stand and place my hand on Mark's. "I understand. Thank you for being a good friend. Aarabelle is lucky to have you and Jackson too."

"Well, I'm a fantastic godfather."

"The best."

We laugh and hug before he walks out. I stand here for a second and take in the fact that in a week, I'll be Mrs. Dempsey.

"SWEETHEART, I'M NOT going to tell you again," Liam

warns as he waits downstairs.

We came to Corolla the day after the party. It's been great being away just us and his father before everyone else arrives. Aidan has been enjoying the time with Liam and he's officially smitten with Aara. He offered to watch her so we could go to dinner just us tonight.

Jackson, Catherine, Reanell, Mark, and Quinn are coming tomorrow morning. Rea is bringing the cake and the reason Mark is now attending is Aaron went home to visit his mother. So instead of just attending, he got ordained. He decided that he couldn't miss it and he only felt it was fair to be the one to marry us. Liam thought it was brilliant—me, not so much.

"You know, it's not so easy when your stomach doesn't agree with zippers!" I yell down the stairs. One week and I can't zipper this damn dress. "Liam," I whine a little. "Please come zip me."

I hear him talking to himself about girls and how it's going to be great to have a little man to round out this group. "Sure, darling." The sarcasm drips from his tongue.

"You did this to me."

"Last I checked, you had to be present in order for me to have done this."

"Whatever. It's your fault."

"I have a feeling I'll be hearing that a lot."

I snort, "Yup."

"I didn't piss in your Cheerios, so be nice. And don't forget, tomorrow you'll legally be mine to do what I want with."

"Happy wife, happy life, buddy. Don't fuck it up," I joke and he laughs.

He zips the dress and his hands slide down my arms. His fingers touch the ring and he rubs the diamond. "She'll be here in a way tomorrow. My mom . . . she'll see us."

"She's always here with you." I turn in his arms and place my hand on his heart. "No matter how much you miss her, she lives here. Her memories can't ever be taken, and tomorrow you'll feel her presence."

"Yeah," he pauses and rubs his hands up and down my bare arms. It's laughable the dress I have on. Thanks to whoever made Lycra, because without the give there would be no way of squeezing in. "Do I seriously have to sleep in the other room?" Liam groans again.

His biggest issue is that he doesn't want to sleep apart. Let alone sleep in the same room as his father who snores so loud he's woken us twice.

"Yes."

"How about you sleep with Aarabelle, and I'll sleep in her room?"

"In the crib?"

He's out of his mind.

"I don't think we have bad luck coming our way. I'm pretty sure we've already surpassed it." Liam gives me his sly smile. His blue eyes gleam as he tries all of his moves.

"It's tradition."

"There's nothing traditional about us."

I laugh and lean in to kiss him. Our lips touch and his hands thread in my long hair. He tangles his fingers around my curls and holds my head to his. His tongue glides across the seam of my lips and I grant him access. The second our tongues touch, passion erupts between us. The slow, dull flame becomes an inferno and all I want to do is strip him down and let him take me.

My hands slide across his taut chest and I groan into his mouth as I feel each ripple of his skin. The heat burns through his shirt as he licks the inside of my mouth. I need to breathe, but I would sacrifice oxygen to keep kissing him. Liam reminds me of the good in the world just by being near me.

He pushes me against the bed and lays me down. "Liam," I say his name as a request. I'm not sure whether it's to keep going or to stop. I want him, but his father and Aarabelle are downstairs.

"I'll be quick," he whispers before his mouth meets mine again. He's careful with his weight not to push against my swollen belly.

Our tongues clash and his hands make their way up my dress. With one hand, he removes my underwear. I reach for the button of his pants and we hurriedly undress each other. There's no elegance or grace. Once I slide his pants off, I wrap my fingers around his dick. His head falls against my shoulder as I pump him slowly.

I push his shoulder and he falls onto his back. I smile as my hair creates a veil not allowing him to see my intention. Moving down his hard body with my tongue, he lets out a low groan.

In one quick movement, I take him fully into my mouth. My lips wrap around his dick and my tongue glides down the vein. "Fucking shit, Lee."

The way his voice cracks at the end makes me want to drive him to the brink like he's done to me so many times. I continue to go up and down, twisting my tongue around the tip.

"Natalie, now." Liam's voice is insistent, but I keep going. "Lee, I'm not going to last, sweetheart."

I go down one last time before leaning up. Within seconds, he pushes me onto my back and hovers over me. "Now that's a wedding present." He gives his signature smile and I don't know whether to laugh or slap him.

When he enters me, there's nothing funny about it. I'm home.

Complete.

Whole.

And I'm his.

Liam sets a slow pace, but neither of us is going to

last long. He reaches his hand between us and circles my clit. I climb higher as our eyes stay locked. All the emotion, love, desire, is on display. There's no shield we can't break through. No secrets between us right here. We give ourselves to one another in body and in our souls. Tomorrow, he will give me his name and I will give him my hand.

I crash over the edge and my orgasm rocks me.

Liam follows behind me silently as we lie panting on the bed.

"Who needs a bachelor party? I much prefer your way of sending me off into married life," Liam laughs and my hand slaps his chest.

"Are you ready?" I ask even though I already know.

Liam shifts onto his side and his face is next to mine. "I've never been more ready for anything. Not BUDs, not a mission, or anything that I live for. You, you are what I've been waiting for my whole life. I never knew it. I didn't expect it. But we've found it and whether we were making it official or not, you would always be meant for me."

"I love you."

"I love you. I mean it, Lee. Even if you had chosen someone else . . . there would never be anyone that would come close to you. Believe me. You'll never have to worry about me straying or running from you."

I turn slightly and press my hand against his chest. "I know. You don't have to worry either. I've never loved anyone like I've loved you."

chapter thirty

"ARABELLE'S DRESS IS hanging in the closet. I need to finish my makeup. Where the hell is my curling iron?" I rush around the room frantic as Reanell, Catherine, and Ashton sit on the bed trying not to laugh.

Catherine stands and walks over. "Sit. I'll do your hair. Just relax," she soothes and I listen.

Well, not about the relaxing part.

We spend the next hour getting ready and before I put my dress on, there's a knock at the door.

Ashton answers, and I hear her and Quinn talking, but soon she closes the door and hands me a small box.

"This is for you," she smiles and places it in my hands.

I open the lid and there sits another small box.

Then another.

And another.

Until I finally reach the final box. I open it while everyone looks over my shoulder. Inside sits a pair of diamond stud earrings.

"Oh my God," I gasp. Each one has to be a carat. They're gorgeous. I immediately put them in my ears and can't stop touching them.

Another knock on the door.

Catherine rushes over and sure enough, Jackson is on the other side. She walks over with a card and places it in my hands. "At least we didn't do makeup." She kisses my cheek and they all sit.

With shaky hands, I open the card. Before reading, I look at Aarabelle, Reanelle, Catherine, and Ashton curled in close to celebrate today. I really am blessed.

> *My sweetheart,*
>
> *When our worlds altered, I found myself unsure. The days of not knowing whether I should walk away or find a way to make you see how I felt were agony. I struggled, but then it became easy. The world became ours and we found true, undiluted love. I can now change a diaper. I know about the aftermath of cake for meals. But mostly, I know about love. Years from now when our children are grown, we'll be able to tell them how we came to be. They'll know nothing in this world comes easy, but if it's right, you fight for it. I'll fight everything and everyone in this world for you and our family. I give you my word—I'll never forsake you. Now, come get your ass down that aisle and marry me.*
>
> *I love you,*
> *Liam*

I laugh as tears stream down my face. Only he can make me do both at the same time.

"Mama cry," Aara says as she squirms off Rea's lap and comes over.

"It's okay, baby. Athair is just making Mommy

happy."

"Athair!" She looks around for Liam.

"Soon. Do you want your pretty dress?" I ask her as I lift her into my arms.

"Lee," Rea comes over and takes Aarabelle. "Please no heavy lifting. You've been on your feet a lot and you'll be sitting very little all day."

I nod and absently rub my stomach.

We get Aarabelle dressed and unzip my gown from its bag. It's a simple, white dress with large, white beads down the entire back to the train. It has a deep U cut that drapes almost to my butt. It's classic and has a lot of room for my belly.

Reanell fixes my dress and double-checks my hair. She stands me in front of the mirror and Aarabelle stands in front of me. "Wow," I say aloud. "You look so pretty, peanut," I say, trying to keep my mind off the fact that I'm standing in a wedding dress.

In the mirror is a blonde with bright, blue eyes and red lips. Her hair is curled and hangs down her back with a little over the side. In her eyes, you can see how happy she is. I realize as I see myself through someone else's eyes how right this is. I follow the tulip shaped dress, and even with my bump, it's perfect.

"Ready?" Reanell asks in a hushed tone.

I glance at Aara and then to her reflection. "I am."

"Okay, let's go. Your man is waiting."

"Rea." I grab her arm. She stops and looks at me with wide eyes. "I need to make sure I tell you how much I love you and how much you mean to me."

Her smile spreads and I fight back the emotions overwhelming me. "I know our lives met by chance, but you're family to me. No matter where the Navy takes us, you'll always be in my heart."

Catherine peeks her head in, "I hate to interrupt, but it's time. Mark is taking this minister thing a little too far, by the way. Just to warn you." She laughs and dips her head back out.

"Okay, Aara," I put my hand out. Her small hand wraps around my fingers and we head out the door.

This morning was a little misty out, but the sun is shining through now. We walk down the beach, and Aara and I stand and wait. I wish I had my parents here, but they said they couldn't make it back so soon after their last visit. My father hasn't been feeling so well and the travel is hard. Plus, we sprung it on them quickly. Still, I wish my daddy were here to give me away.

"I'm going to head down, and whenever you and Aara are ready . . ." Rea smiles and kisses my cheek.

I squat as best as I can by my daughter and hold her hands in mine. "Oh, Aara. So much has happened in your short, little life, but love has never been missing. Liam will love you, and your daddy will too. You'll have twice the amount that most little girls have. I love you."

She plays with the flower on her dress and I smile. Aara looks up and I pucker for a kiss. She leans in and then I pull her close.

"You look beautiful, darling." I gasp and turn my head only to see my father standing there in his suit.

"Daddy!" I call out and he helps me stand. "You came!" I wrap my arms around him and want to cry.

He laughs in his rich voice that I'd know anywhere. "I wouldn't miss this for the world. Liam called after we spoke and bought us plane tickets. He was very adamant and was willing to come down and drive us if he had to," he laughs again and pulls me back. "Quite a guy you got there."

"He really is special."

"So are you," he taps my nose. "And so are you! Hello, my gorgeous princess." My father lifts Aara and holds her in one arm. He loops his arm and I circle my hand through. "Let's go and see that man of yours."

"Okay." My voice shakes, but I'm not nervous. It's quite the opposite. I'm eager and ready. I want to see him. I want to say our vows and start our life together.

We begin the walk and I keep my eyes down so I don't trip. When I look up, I can hardly breathe. Liam stands with Quinn and Jackson behind him. Reanell and Catherine on my side and Mark stands in between. There's an archway with white tulle and red flowers all around. A few chairs sit on the side for my parents and Aidan. But it's the look on Liam's face that fills me.

His smile is bright and tears fall from his eyes. I walk toward him and he moves forward. My father chuckles as Liam seems to stop himself.

When we reach him, the sun shines from behind him, and his blue eyes pierce through me. "Hi," I say and wipe a tear from my eyes.

"Hi," he says and using the pad of his thumb wipes the other.

Aarabelle wiggles from my father's arms. "Mama!" she yells and Liam crouches down with his arms open. She rushes to him and he scoops her up.

"No one forgot you," he laughs and holds her on his side.

I press my one hand on his chest and another on Aarabelle's back. Right here the world is right.

"Dearly, beloved," Mark begins, and I look at him for the first time.

"You're kidding me," I say laughing. "You got a robe?"

"I'm a man of the cloth, my child. Now, simmer down and let my mercy and love come down upon this marriage."

"Idiot," I hear Jackson mutter under his breath.

"We are gathered here today to witness Sparkles and Dreamboat create a new world."

Liam and I both burst out laughing and then Jackson moves forward and slaps Mark on the back of the head.

This is the perfect wedding. Surrounded by our friends who are family, in a setting where we really fell in love, solidifying our union.

"Anyway," Mark straightens himself. "We are here to see two people I care about deeply get married. Liam and Natalie asked for a traditional ceremony, but well, I don't think there's much traditional here. So let's do this how they are . . . perfect."

I look at Mark and his eyes soften. We smile and Aarabelle starts to tug on Liam's face. He's right . . . there's nothing traditional here.

"Natalie, did you want to say your vows or let me do them? I got his all worked out," Mark smirks.

"I'll say them, thanks." Liam puts Aarabelle down and she rushes over to Jackson. I swear this kid would never have to walk with the men in her life. I take Liam's hand in mine and our eyes lock. "I didn't write anything, so this may be rambly and not make sense." I take a deep breath and try to work through the jumble of words in my head. "We weren't supposed to be. It was never in my plans or a possibility. You came to me during a dark part in my life where I wasn't sure light even existed. I remember when I started to see you as more. More than a friend, and someone I wanted to be near, to touch, to hold, to comfort. You never pushed me because you knew me more than I knew myself. Somehow, you see it all and love me with everything. You and I may not have been supposed to be, but we're meant to be. My heart is yours, my love is yours, my days and all my nights are yours. I'll hold you up, stand by you, and give you everything I have." I take a deep breath and then the dam breaks. "I love you so much. I'll love you with all that I have."

Liam's thumbs rub against the tops of my hand and he smiles. "You're cute when you're rambly."

Mark clears his throat, "Liam, let's hear your vows. Better do better than that, my son."

Liam gives him a look and then looks back at me.

"Natalie, I wasn't looking for love when we found it. I was looking to help. But it was you who helped me. Your smile, your eyes, and your heart showed me what I was lacking. Each day I would find a reason to see you because you made my day worth waking up for. I learned how to change diapers," he pauses and we smile. "Get a kid dressed, but more than anything, how to be a man. Not a man who cares only for himself and his job, but a man who stands by a woman and steps up. You showed me what love is. We'll have hard times and we'll struggle, but I'll never leave your side. I'll stand and fight for you no matter what life throws at us. I'll love Aarabelle and our son the same. I'll protect you and them at any cost. There will never be a day you feel unloved by me. And if you ever should, you have permission to slap me." Liam smiles and I laugh.

My heart is full as he says his vows. And with Liam, I know his vows ring true.

Liam pulls at my hands, and I see the struggle to rein in his emotions is strong. "I give you my word, my name, and everything I have as your husband."

Liam turns his attention to Mark who looks like he's about to cry. He shakes his head, and I hear sniffles from behind me.

"Rings!" It finally clicks for Mark. "Okay. Quinn, please hand them over."

Quinn steps forward and claps Liam on the back.

"Thank you, my child."

I roll my eyes and giggle. He's so stupid. "You know you got your training online, right?"

"Yes, now hush and allow the grace of my ordination to come upon this union." He goes back to looking at his booklet.

"I swear . . ." Jackson mutters and I giggle.

Liam and I recite our promises and place the rings we

picked out on each other's hands. His is a solid, tungsten ring with Celtic knots all along the middle. It's modern but the knots bring in his heritage. They also symbolize the forging of our lives and family. Mine is an eternity diamond band. He fought tooth and nail about it and how he was determined to spend his money how he wanted.

I wait for someone to tell him to kiss the bride, but he takes a third ring in his hand that's on a fine, gold chain. "Aarabelle," he squats down as she sits in the sand. I clutch my throat and try to stop from sobbing. "I know I'm not your father, but I'll be a daddy to you. Here's a ring of my promise to you. I'll protect you and kiss your knee, plus I promise to never be one of those jerk stepparents, because I'll never see you as anything but my daughter." He clasps the necklace around her neck. There's no holding back. Tears fall relentlessly, and Reanell, Catherine, Ashton, and my mother are all weeping too. "Oh, and I'll give you cake for breakfast and ice cream for lunch."

Liam stands and looks at me. He tugs me flush against him. "Loving you is the greatest honor of my life. You gave me not only you, but two children to love."

My hand rests against his beating heart. "You'll never know how much I love you." I sniffle and he once again wipes my eyes.

"Can I kiss my wife now?" he looks at Mark.

"Make it a good one," Mark smirks. "By the power bestowed on me from the website of ordained dot com, I now pronounce you husband and wife."

Liam wraps his arms tighter around my waist and dips me back. "You heard the reverend."

His lips press against mine as he cradles me back. Our lips mold to one another as I kiss my husband. The man who I know I'll spend the rest of my life with because we are a perfect match. He pulls me back up and then lifts Aarabelle. He kisses her cheek and she wraps her arms around him.

"I love you," Liam tells us both.

"I yuv you," Aara replies.

I glance at my family and friends around me and joy explodes from within. I've never been this happy or more sure of where I am. Sometimes you have to wade through the bad to find the good. Life isn't easy, but with Liam by my side, I know I don't have to carry it all on my own. Our love will heal us and lift us up.

EPILOGUE

LIAM

"IT'S TIME." NATALIE shakes me and I go to swat at her. Which then is followed by a slap on my back.

"Lee," I groan. I'm exhausted. We had a bunch of dives and training things this week. I've gotten a total of maybe ten hours of sleep all week. "Not now."

"No, wake up! It's time. Like the baby is coming."

What?

That wakes me up. I sit forward and look over as she looks unimpressed. "Okay, I'm awake now."

"I already called Aaron. He's on his way to get Aarabelle. I'm going to get my bag," she explains slowly as if I'm the two-year-old. Although, at this moment I feel a little out of my element.

She's going to have our son.

The last few months, Natalie's had a few minor complications. Her fake contractions were pretty much nonstop. I became a little crazy over this and asked the doctor several times to make it stop. The biggest scare came a few weeks ago when she couldn't feel him move. We had to go to the hospital for another ultrasound, which was great, but Lee was a mess. She cried for hours and begged him to move. I never felt more helpless.

"Okay, come on. We need to get the bag, get in the car . . ." I start to tick them off and another contraction must've hit because she grabs my shoulder and squeezes. "Shit!" I scream as her nails dig in.

"Aaron better get here soon or you're going to be

delivering our son."

"The hell I am!" She's lost her mind.

"Liam, get out of bed."

Right.

Bag.

Car.

Hospital.

I can do this.

We have our bag and Aarabelle's by the hall closet. I grab them and put them by the front door. I rush back upstairs and grab Aarabelle from her crib. She's going to be a beast when I wake her. I swear she's the cutest kid in the world, but she has horns. They come out when you interrupt her sleep.

I gently lift her and pray she doesn't open her eyes. I somehow manage to keep her asleep and put her down on the couch. If she wakes up the next time, it's on Aaron.

I hear a knock and open the door.

"Hey, man."

"Hey," I sound like I just ran a marathon. "Aara's on the couch and that pink bag is hers."

Aaron laughs and then stops. "I'm not waking her," he says as it dawns on him he'll get her wrath.

"All on you, bro."

"Thanks," he smirks. It was strained for the first few weeks after the wedding between all of us, but then Aaron met Rebecca, and that seems to have eased some of the tension. They've been together these last few months and he seems really happy.

After that, he didn't look at Natalie and me as if we were hurting him all the time. He comes and gets Aarabelle regularly, and when he dropped her off last week while Natalie was out, we sat and had a beer.

It was odd but a step in the right direction.

"Liam!" Natalie yells out, and I take the stairs two at a time.

"I'm here."

"Did you forget to grab me? I'm kind of the key piece here." Her face scrunches and I rush over.

"Never. Plus, you're kinda scary right now."

"Uh huh."

We get down the stairs. Aaron has Aarabelle in his arms as she shoots daggers at him. I laugh to myself because at least it's not me.

Lee walks over to her and rubs her back. "Bye, my sweet girl. I'll see you soon." She kisses her and I see the tears welling in her eyes.

"Lee, you'll see her as soon as we have the baby."

"I know," she says as she kisses the top of her head.

"I'll bring her by when Liam calls," Aaron explains. It's weird that we can all be around each other so easily, but hey, I'll take it. I think for Aara's sake, we all try extra hard. And now that Becky's around, I don't have to watch him eye fuck my wife.

"Okay, car now before we don't make it . . ." I nudge Lee and she nods.

I grab the towel and rush out to the car. I try to be discreet and not let her see what I'm doing. There's not much chance she won't catch me, but you can't blame me for trying to protect the seats.

"Liam Dempsey!" she yells as she waddles behind me. She's such a cute, little penguin. "I'll cut you."

"Oh, I love when you talk sweet to me," I reply playfully.

"You left me back there. Your pregnant and having contractions wife . . ."

"No, I was preparing Robin so you'll be comfortable."

Her eyes narrow and she tilts her head. I'm screwed. I rush over and grab her arm and help her to the car. She sits down and I rush over to the other side. I can feel her hostility and I haven't even gotten inside.

"You're dead."

"I figured."

"Good . . . it'll make it less awkward when I kill you."

I grab her hand and kiss the top. Maybe I can soothe her by being swoony. "I love you so much, sweetheart. You're going to make me the happiest man in the world today."

"You're still dead."

Or not. She squeezes my hand with herculean strength and I try to pry it away, but she just grabs harder.

"I need my hand."

She doesn't say anything, but I can feel her eyes burning holes into the side of my face.

We arrive at the hospital and they bring her to the room. Once she's connected to a bunch of monitors, I start making calls. I call my command to let them know, and I'm granted immediate baby leave. I'm half tempted to tell them to forget it since I'm apparently now married to the devil. Her face turns some funky color and she hates me.

"Liam." Her voice is suddenly sweet, and I wonder what the hell is going on.

"Yes, sweetheart?"

"I want you to promise that whatever I say in the next few hours you will forget."

"I can do that."

"Okay, good. Because I hate you." Her face turns bright red and all her muscles tense as the contraction hits. I look at the monitor in amazement.

"Wow, that's a strong one!" I look at the lines going up and down.

"You're a fucking genius!" she says through gritted teeth.

I look at her and smile. Which probably isn't the smartest thing in the world, but she's kinda busy and I enjoy playing with fire.

"I'm going to pretend you don't want me to forget that."

The contraction passes and the nurse comes in before she can reply. I make note to buy her something pretty for saving my ass.

"You're almost nine centimeters. It's too late for an epidural. I'm going to get the doctor. You're going to have this baby very soon." I suddenly feel faint.

I rush over to Lee's side and grab her hand and kiss her forehead. "We're going to have our son soon. You're so perfect, sweetheart. So amazing and perfect."

"Liam," she says sounding exhausted. "I love you and I'm scared."

"Why?"

"What if something goes wrong?"

"I'm right here. I'll be by your side the whole time. You can do this," I try to reassure her, but she's been having dreams that there will be something wrong with the baby or the birth. I can't really argue her insanity because they're dreams and she threatens to kill me quite often.

I do like to drive her nuts. I'll give her that.

"I don't want anything to be wrong." Her lower lip trembles.

My hands hold her face and I press my forehead to hers. "If something is wrong, we'll handle it. Don't worry until there's something to worry about. I've got you."

I don't know how to help her and it kills me, but I know I have to keep it together.

She nods and sucks in a deep breath.

"Are we ready, Mrs. Dempsey?" A small thrill runs through me each time I hear someone call her that. It reminds me that this woman is mine now. That she chose me, and I somehow convinced her to marry me.

"If he's ready to come out, then I guess we are." I squeeze her hand and then she adds on. "With no drugs."

"Drugs are overrated." Her eyes flash with hostility,

and I put my hands up in mock surrender. "Of course, I don't know this . . ."

"Hate."

"You love me."

Natalie grunts and the doctor gives me a sympathetic look. Dr. Contreras checks her for what I don't know. I mean, is it like a turkey that the little plastic thing pops? This whole checking her thing baffles me.

"Okay, Natalie. I need you to give me a push."

She looks at me and they lift her legs. I don't comment because I know it'll end with me getting punched in the balls, so I just stay by her side. She groans and sweat breaks across her face, and I'm pretty sure my hand is now detached from my body. Where the hell does this hundred and twenty-five pound woman have this strength?

"Hand, hand, hand," I say as it starts to turn purple.

Fucking hell.

"My vagina is on fire as I push your giant kid out. Suck it up," Natalie says with a little too much happiness at my pain.

"Again," the doctor orders.

I don't even have a second before my fingers mash together as she squeezes them and pops a few out of joint. Well, not really, but it feels like it.

"The baby is crowning," the doctor says.

"Crowning?" I ask.

"Come see."

I head down as Natalie breathes and lays her head on the pillow. There are some things I can't unsee, and this is one. I'm not queasy by nature, but I never can look at her pussy again and not think of this image. A giant, bald, nasty looking thing is stretching her, and I'm pretty sure I'm going to hurl.

Instead of freaking her out, I head back to her side. I'll take the broken fingers before that shit.

"Is he coming?" Lee asks.

Still unable to form words, I nod and offer her my hand.

"Liam?"

How the hell do I explain how disturbed I am? I know I need to say something, so I just let it out. "Yup, it's coming all right."

"Just a few more pushes, Lee, and you're right there." The doctor saves my ass this time because I don't know what I would've said if I had to go further than that. "Another contraction is coming."

"Okay," Lee says and then she pushes again. Her whole body is tight as she lets out a long cry.

"Do you want to see him?" the doctor asks. Is she high?

"No. I'm good."

She smiles knowingly. "Okay. One more, Lee. One more push and he'll be out," Dr. Contreras tells her and I look at Lee once more.

This is the woman who's going to bring my son into the world. The woman who gave me a family I could only dream of. We were meant to be and now we'll have another child. A son who will bear my name. This perfect, gorgeous woman who I hope to knock up at least ten more times.

"I love you, Natalie."

She huffs and puts her hand on my face. "I love you."

"Push!" the doctor yells and sheer determination covers Natalie's face.

She does what she's told and then I hear the most remarkable sound ever.

My son's first cry.

I look down as the doctors and nurses start to clean him and then they place him on my wife's chest. I stare at him in wonder. My son. A boy. Natalie cries as she holds him and touches his hands, feet, and face.

She looks up at me with tears and a smile. "He's perfect."

"He came from you; of course he would be," I reply and press my lips to hers. Then I touch my son's fingers. He's here and has all his fingers and toes. He's got the most important part too.

The doctor comes over and cuts the cord after I refuse. No, thank you. They weigh him and clean him up as I watch over him. I don't think my eyes leave him for even a moment.

Once he's wrapped in a blanket, the nurse extends her hands and places him in my arms.

I look at Natalie and then back to him. Tears fill my eyes as I hold my son for the first time. My heart just grew twice the size as I look at him, half me, half Natalie. I walk over and sit next to Lee as her hand touches his arm.

"Hi, Shane. I'm your dad."

The End

books by
corinne michaels

the Belonging Duet

Beloved (Book One)
Beholden (Book Two)

the Consolation Duet

Consolation (Book One)
Conviction (Book Two)

coming soon

Finding Serenity
(A Contemporary Standalone Romance)

More to come from The Salvation Series

Defenseless (Mark & Charlie)
Indefinite (Ashton & Quinn)

acknowledgements

MY ATTEMPT TO keep this short and sweet should be interesting.

My readers: I can never fully explain what it means to me that you not only took a chance on me, but that some of you have stuck with me. I know I tend to keep leaving you with these crazy cliffhangers and you still love me. The support that you give me is astonishing and humbling. I love you so much!

My beta readers: I really am the luckiest person because of you. Jennifer, Melissa, Katie, Roxana, Linda, and Mandi . . . you make me laugh, keep me on my toes, and always striving to impress you. You are some picky bitches but I wouldn't know what to do without you.

My early readers: Melissa & Alison, you guys are the first to get a full glimpse and each time I bite my nails. Thank you for dealing with my neurosis and messages. I love you to the moon!

Laurelin Paige: Without you, my world would be a dull place. Your support, friendship, and wisdom are insurmountable. You make me a better person and writer. You deal with my insecurities and constant crying but still love me and for that I'm eternally grateful. (I hope you at least pricked a damn tear at this.)

Christy Peckham: No words can explain how much your friendship means. None can come close. You make me smile daily, put up with my hilarious messages ← admit it they're funny, and still stick around.

Melissa Saneholtz & SFab Team: The word publicist

doesn't seem fitting for what you do. You run my life pretty much and I couldn't imagine anyone else doing this with me. To the team . . . oh, how we laugh. I love you guys and can't thank you enough for all the support.

Stabby Birds: You guys are the best people I know. You're my sisters through and through. We laugh, cry, and bond together like nothing I've ever seen before. I love you!

My Fairy Godmothers: Laura, Lauren, and Christine . . . you are the true meaning of friendship. You were behind me each step of the way. Cheering me on, messaging me, and making me smile. I learned so much from you and love you three!

FYW: The writing world could only be so lucky to know people like you. Thank you for being who you are. #WednesdaysWeWearPink

Claire Contreras, Mia Asher, Whitney Gracia Williams, Rebecca Yarros, Mandi Beck, Kyla Linde, Kennedy Ryan, SL Scott, Lucia Franco, EK Blair, Kristy Bromberg, Pepper Winters, Elisabeth Grace, Livia Jamerlan, & Angie McKeon—thank you for making me smile, laugh, talking through one of my crazy ideas, and just being my friends. I'm truly blessed to have you in my life.

Jesey: I haven't been able to do this until now. Thank you. Because of something we dreamt of two years ago, look where we are. It's amazing to think the friendship we've had has somehow twisted our worlds to this place. I love you!

My Instagram girls: You make the absolute most beautiful things I've ever seen. EVER! I love you all so much! @tiffany.the.bibliophile , @smuttybooklover, @fixtion_fangirl, @dragonflyreads, @butthisbook, @macie.reads, @thereadingruth, @jengare, @demeriahh & so many more.

My editor: Lisa, you make editing fun and often

funny. Thank you for the support and friendship through this process.

My formatter: Christine, I learned page breaks! Seriously, you are first-class in this business. Your professionalism and attention to detail are above and beyond. You work tirelessly and it doesn't go unnoticed.

My cover designer: Sarah, thank you for making two of the most beautiful covers ever.

My photographer: Lauren, thank you for capturing everything this story entails.

My proofreader: Ashley, thank you for finding all the errors and making it shine.

Lisa from The Rock Stars of Romance: THANK YOU! Your support has meant everything to the success of this series. I can't begin to thank you enough. I love your face!

Reanell: Thank you for letting me use your name and I didn't even make you a villain!

Bloggers: I don't think you guys understand what you do for the book world. It's not a job you get paid for (well, not nearly what you deserve). It's something you love and you do because of that. Thank you from the bottom of my heart.

To my husband and children, I'm so lucky to have you. You probably bear the worst part of this process. I love you three more than anything in this world. Thank you for putting up with all that you do. I know I need to put the computer and phone down more because you deserve that. Thank you for being here and supporting me day after day. Thank you for letting me cry when my feelings are hurt. Smile when something amazing happens. But mostly thank you for loving me and believing in me.